AMBER SCOTT IS STARTING OVER

Ruth Saberton

ISIS
LARGE PRINT
Oxford

First published in Great Britain 2012
by
Orion Books Ltd.

Published in Large Print 2013 by ISIS Publishing Ltd.,
7 Centremead, Osney Mead, Oxford OX2 0ES
by arrangement with
Orion Books Ltd.
An Hachette UK Company

British Library Cataloguing in Publication Data
Saberton, Ruth.
    Amber Scott is starting over.
    1. Fowey (England) - - Fiction.
    2. Large type books.
    I. Title
    823.9'2–dc23

ISBN 978–0–7531–9108–8 (hb)
ISBN 978–0–7531–9109–5 (pb)

Printed and bound in Great Britain by
T. J. International Ltd., Padstow, Cornwall

To Christopher, Ann and Christian Browning. Thanks so much for letting me use "Writer's Corner" this summer. I couldn't have written this book without you.

Acknowledgements

My love and deepest appreciation go to:

My fantastic family and everyone else who has been there for me this year — I will always be grateful for your love and support.

Nicola, Colin and the Chadwick family for letting me loose on their Rayburn — the inspiration for Amber's Aga.

The one and only Ann Raynor — your fiery, fun and forthright nature is the inspiration for Ali. We all need strong friends when life gets tough.

My dear friend Lizzie Bartlett — thanks for all the late-night heart-to-hearts. All good counselling practice! You will be fantastic.

All my readers for your support, enthusiasm and the wonderful emails and letters you send. I love hearing from you and I'm over the moon you like my books. Thank you!

Michael and Vanessa at the Talland Bay Hotel — drinking coffee on the terrace this summer certainly inspired my writing, and Amber had to visit!

Eve White, the loveliest agent ever, who always supports me and whose amazing mushroom and pesto dish has to be tasted to be believed!

And finally, of course, everybody at Orion. Thank you so much for all the hard work that you do on my behalf. You make every step of each book journey an absolute pleasure.

CHAPTER
ONE

Just breathe! Relax! Don't stress, Amber, it's only a job interview. It's not as though you're about to be tortured! All you have to do is look smart, sound intelligent and manage to make it into the boardroom without laddering your tights. Just how hard can it be?

You can do this! You can!

Unfortunately the reflection that peers nervously back at me, floating in the bright glass of the reception window, doesn't look particularly convinced by this pep talk, and I don't blame her. It feels like a washing machine on spin cycle has taken up residence in my stomach, and my mouth has that horrible pre-vomit tinny tang. Looking smart and sounding intelligent is a tall order anyway on an ordinary, just-going-to-work morning, so how I ever thought I'd be able to pull it off for the biggest moment of my professional life is a total mystery.

Oh Lord. Maybe I should just go home now? Who am I trying to kid that I stand a chance of getting this job? What on earth was I thinking? I'm rubbish at job interviews. Just thinking about sitting across the table from an interrogation squad and trying to sound intelligent turns me into such a quivering jelly that you could serve me up with ice cream. Look at my hands! I'm shaking!

Hmm. Better not apply that third coat of killer red lippy. I don't want to look like an extra from *Twilight*, do I? Although I'm already so pale with nerves that I could be mistaken for the undead. Edward Cullen, eat your heart out.

For as long as I can remember, I've dreaded job interviews. I hate having to squeeze myself into my Karen Millen strait-jacket. Why do I always think I can diet into it? Surely by the grand old age of twenty-nine I should have resigned myself to the fact that my body is stubbornly stuck at a generous size twelve? Even if I never eat again, I'll never be an eight. I also loathe bullying my curly hair into what's meant to be a sleek chignon but instead bears more resemblance to a scruffy nest where a pair of starlings has taken up residence. Although the Vicky Pollard facelift effect is strangely flattering, it feels like every hair's being plucked from my scalp, and I can't help worrying that my watering eyes are turning me into a dead ringer for Alice Cooper. So not a good look for impressing the editor of one of the UK's most cutting-edge fashion magazines.

Maybe I can fix all this before it's too late?

I reach into my bag and delve around for my mirror, which is easier said than done since I own the world's first Tardis bag. I swear that when I left home this morning all I'd put in there were my mirror, my purse, my BlackBerry and my keys, but it now appears that by some strange magic, leaky biros and fluffy Tampax have moved in too. My fingers grapple with gooey sweets and screwed-up till receipts for what feels like aeons until the bag has enough and leaps from my lap to vomit its contents all over the floor.

"Bollocks!" I say, and then want to rip my tongue out, because this is hardly language suitable for Britain's smartest glossy. "I mean, oops!"

I glance towards the enormous chrome and glass desk just in case the receptionist is looking in my direction. She's incredibly slim, with make-up that's such a work of art that the Louvre is probably bidding for it. She's been looking down her perfect nose at me all morning too, which I suppose isn't surprising really, because the hallowed offices of *Senora* magazine are staffed by people who all look like they've been genetically modified in order to meet some unwritten company policy. While I've been waiting nervously outside the editor's office, a mind-boggling identikit army of tall, thin women clad in designer labels has tripped past, balancing like tightrope-walkers on their Jimmy Choos and Manolo Blahniks. Their lips are slick with gloss, their nails expensively French-manicured and they all have names like Araminta and butterscotch-smooth tans from skiing. Their thick manes of expensively streaked blonde hair make my crazy frizz look like a comedy wig.

Feeling as though I've been beamed down from another planet, I sit on my hands just in case someone spots my tatty nails and passes out in sheer disgust. In my favour I am blonde, but that's where the similarity ends. Unlike these ironing-board women, I'm short and

3

curvy, with boobs and hips, and even though I'm nearly thirty, I'm as yet a stranger to Botox. If these stunning girls are supermodel wannabes, then I guess I'm more like a scruffy reject from the Playboy Mansion. How did I ever imagine I'd fit in here? Maybe I should just sneak out now, before it's too late. After I've scooped up all the crap from my bag, obviously.

The receptionist is on the telephone now, her impossibly narrow back to me, so I seize my chance and fall on to my knees, cramming the detritus back into my bag and hoping the reclaimed oak floorboards don't ladder my stockings, because you can bet your life the one thing I *won't* have in my bag is an emergency pair of tights. When I applied for this job at *Senora* I should have paid more attention to the advice they churn out each month. Who knows, I could even get a flat stomach and better orgasms if the latest edition is to be believed.

OK, who am I trying to kid? The flat stomach's *never* going to happen while I have this serious carrot-cake addiction, and even one measly orgasm would be an improvement. Complaining about the quality seems the height of picky. Ed's always so busy with work that the nearest I get to sex these days is walking past Ann Summers on the way to the tube, which is very depressing. Actually, what's more depressing is the fact that I can't even be bothered to wander in and browse. I blame the Marks and Spencer food hall opposite. How can a girl possibly concentrate on vibrators and suspender belts when crème brûlées and bagels are calling out to her? It's a sad sign of the times that I get more pleasure from ripping the lid off a sticky toffee pudding than I do from ripping off my fiancé's clothes. Still, I suppose that's only to be expected after almost ten years together. All these glossy women's magazines might try and convince us that the rest of the world is at it non-stop, but I bet in reality most people just want to crash out after a hard day. Who seriously wants to grind, and wiggle and worry about sucking in their stomach when they could be curled up on the sofa watching Phil and Kirstie? All that passion malarkey might be good for selling Mills & Boon novels, but in real life I'm with Boy George and sticking to a nice cup of tea instead.

And maybe a biscuit or too . . .

Bag safely stuffed full again and compact retrieved, I flip open the mirror and sure enough, as suspected, I've mutated into a giant panda. Licking my finger, I attempt a repair job but end up smearing mascara all over my giant eye bags and on to my cheeks. And because this is Dior going-absolutely-nowhere-unless-removed-with-a-blowtorch mascara, there is no way on earth I can scrub it off.

Oh God, Oh God. I can't possibly go in like this. I look like a Victorian consumptive. This is *Senora* magazine, the font of all fashion knowledge. What on earth was I thinking? Maybe it's time to do a runner. If I get right down on my hands and knees, the receptionist will never know . . .

"Amber Scott?" the receptionist calls, just as I'm contemplating a commando roll out of the room. She peers at me like somebody's shoved a rotting haddock under her nose and only just manages not to recoil at the sight of my Kiss-style make-up. "They're ready for you in the boardroom."

For a moment there's a roaring in my ears and I feel horribly light-headed. I couldn't be more terrified if Alan Sugar was in there too, waiting to verbally maul me. Can I make a run for it? My funky platform boots will surely give me a speed advantage over the receptionist's trendy spike heels.

"Miss Scott?" barks the receptionist. "Now, if you please?"

Oh crap, she's out from behind her desk and blocking the exit. There's no way I can escape now, unless I rugby-tackle her to the ground. For a split second I seriously consider this, but although she's thin, her biceps are pure Madonna, and there's a steely look in her eye that suggests she's not to be messed with.

Shit, bugger and damn. It looks like I'm going to have to brave the boardroom.

Shoving the mirror back into my bag with fingers more frozen than Captain Birdseye's, I clamber to my feet. Oh God. Oh God. Oh God. Why did I ever think it was a good idea to put myself through this?

Because, Amber, says a small voice deep down inside, you *really, really* want this job, and actually you could be really good at it. Give it a shot. After all, what have you got to lose?

Er, my dignity? Pride? And self-respect? But hey-ho, goodbye to those. It looks as though I really am going to do this interview. There is simply no way out, except through the window, and since we're on the twelfth floor, I don't fancy my chances if I exit that way. I'm not suicidal.

Yet.

Swinging my bag on to my shoulder, I clomp across the wooden floor and through the door that leads to my certain doom. Inside is a horseshoe arrangement of fashionistas, all so waxed and plucked and Botoxed and fake-tanned that they're probably entirely new creations. Fixing a smile to my face, I check for my mental parachute and jump.

"Amber, please take a seat."

A woman seated smack in the centre of the horseshoe barks this order at me. Wow, she's a dead ringer for Skeletor, if he'd ever worn a blonde wig and drag. One tiny leg is crossed over a bony knee, which glows greeny-white through gossamer-sheer stockings, and her collarbones look so sharp, they could possibly be classed as lethal weapons. She's holding my portfolio in her veiny, hands and while I hover, wondering which empty chair I'm allowed to perch on, she flicks through my work in a bored fashion. Just looking at her sunken cheeks and razor-blade shoulders fills me with regret for the huge wodge of carrot cake I stuffed my face with earlier. I'm never going to fit in here, not when I'm all squidgy. This job is never going to be mine — it has size zero written all over it. I never stood a chance.

Instantly I feel so much better. If I never stood a chance then there's nothing to lose, is there?

"Sit," orders the woman, still flicking through my portfolio, and I obey. Of course I do, because she's none other than Evangeline St Anthony, the iconic sixties model and famous editor of *Senora* magazine. Forget the notoriously difficult Miranda Priestley of *The Devil Wears Prada* fame. In comparison to Evangeline, she's a pussy! The woman in front of me right now is infamous for deciding on a whim the length of skirts fashionable across the globe or the definitive colour of a season's wardrobe. She can make or break a designer with one word, and her insightful comment, *black is the new black*, was quoted and debated as though uttered by a Nobel prizewinner.

I am not worthy.

"Thank you for seeing me," I squeak, as I attempt to perch on the teeny-weeny seat. I just about manage to squeeze one buttock on it and arrange my features in what is hopefully an intelligent expression. I feel horribly like a specimen in a lab. Any second now they'll start prodding me.

"Welcome to *Senora* magazine, Amber. I'm sure you know who I am." Evangeline pauses so that I can nod reverentially. "This is my team, the team that, if you are successful, you'll join as artistic director."

She continues to introduce the rest of the horseshoe one by one, while I nod and smile until I feel dizzy and their names drip from my mind like butter from hot toast. Everyone is so immaculate, from the small Chinese woman with skin like honey to the beautiful gay man sizing me up from beneath his floppy fringe.

What *was* I thinking? I could *never* fit in here! Beneath my pink suit I start to sweat. Why did I pick pink? I must have been mad! Everyone here is dressed in black; they could moonlight as funeral directors and nobody would bat an eyelid. And *why* did I think it was a good idea to wear my favourite Camden knee boots, biker-style and with platform soles higher than Ben Nevis? They seemed like a really funky statement when I pulled them on earlier, but I probably look more like Minnie Mouse in a suit.

"This is an extremely impressive portfolio," Evangeline tells me. She may be smiling but it's hard to tell because there's so much Botox swimming round her face. "I especially like the work you've done at *Blush!* magazine. Your seniors there have credited you entirely with their fresh new look."

"Thanks," I say, and it's really weird, because when I think about my work my heart rate starts to slow, and rather than sounding like I've been gulping helium, my voice is actually calm and measured. "The readership increased by forty-eight per cent after the repackaging and rebranding I devised."

And suddenly I'm up and running. Questions are fired at me quicker than tennis balls on Centre Court, but rather than turning into a gibbering wreck, I become the Rafael Nadal of the interview world. I lob figures about and volley stunning examples of my expertise. I even serve an ace when I point out that I've been commissioned to redesign *Blush!*'s sister magazine, *Femme*, the direct rival to *Senora*.

But enough of the tennis analogy already!

I *love* my job. I absolutely *love* it. Does this make me a sad no-life muppet? I actually look forward to getting up in the morning, listening to Radio 4 while I eat my muesli (*Radio 4*? Eek! How did that happen? Why don't I know any of the music played on Radio 1 any more?) and then walking to the tube. I love buying a skinny latte and blueberry muffin and reading the *Metro* while the Piccadilly Line burrows under the traffic jams and crowded streets. I even enjoy shoehorning myself into the creaking lift at Covent Garden and stumbling out blinking into the daylight, because there's something about London that fills me with excitement. All that life and energy teeming from every building, the hordes of office workers, the rumbling buses, the buskers and the rush of warm tube-driven air! Everything about city life gives me a thrill. I am so with Dr Johnson! I adore being part of something so vital and so alive and I feel really lucky to have made it this far. How many other twenty-somethings dream of working for a glossy magazine? Loads. But I actually do. And I never take it for granted, because I know how lucky I am.

In all my wildest dreams I never expected to work for a magazine. My fiancé, Ed, spent most of our university days mocking my Mickey Mouse degree (Art History with English Lit, as opposed to his Law) and told the joke "What do you say to an arts graduate? Big Mac and fries!" so many times that he wore it out. After graduating, most of my friends gave in to their hideous student debts and before the ink was even dry on their degree certificates signed away their souls to teacher training. I thought about it, but the idea of doing daily battle with bolshie adolescents was about as appealing as pulling off my own head. So instead I moved to

London with Ed, who was doing articles with the top law firm Colville and West, and in between working on my own paintings and completing endless job applications I did temp work in offices. This was originally meant to be a stopgap, but because it was easy and left me time for painting, I ended up doing it for five years.

Then, one rainy November morning, I surfaced from Covent Garden tube, clutching my A to Z, and set off for the offices of *Blush!*, a struggling teen magazine where I had a week's work. In my rucksack was a tatty copy of the latest edition, annotated and smothered in yellow Post-its on which I'd scrawled all my ideas and suggestions.

It was so obvious why the magazine wasn't selling. The typeface was plain, the colours muted, the masthead hardly noticeable and the layout so weary it practically yawned. My teenage niece, Kerrie, had curled her lip like a small hoodied version of Mick Jagger when I'd told her about my latest job, because apparently only really sad people read *Blush!*. Intrigued, I'd done some digging on the internet and discovered that the ABC figures spoke for themselves. Speculation on numerous media websites suggested that the magazine was doomed to fold unless some major changes were made.

I'd sensed an opportunity and gone for it. Once settled at my desk, I'd discovered that the senior designer spent all her time in Harvey Nicks and that her deputy was a Sloane with a brain like Aero. Within minutes I'd booted up the dusty Macs, taught Liz, the lowly junior, how to use Photoshop and mocked up a new front cover that was all hot pinks and acid limes. Complete with a photo of Kerrie as a cover girl and some bold teasers, this new cover didn't so much grab your attention as jump off the screen and tap-dance in front of you. It looked, even if I said so myself, amazing. I knew I was on to something . . .

Anyway, for once my guardian angel was on the case, because at the very moment I was admiring my handiwork, the editor-in-chief, Ali Jones, happened to pass through the office and catch sight of my work.

"Fuck me backwards!" she'd screeched, stopping dead in her tracks so that two acolytes cannoned into her. "What the fucking fuck is that?" Back then I didn't know that Ali always swore like a navvy. Instead I'd thought I was in big trouble for interfering. My face turned crimson, and muttering apologies I frantically tried to minimise the screen, but because this was bloody Mac OS, I couldn't remember how and my design refused to budge, glowing in all its neon glory into the mid-morning gloom.

"It was her idea!" Liz squeaked in terror, running her hands through her frizzy red curls. "She thought of it all."

Ali had taken a deep breath. With her beaky nose and heavy-lidded eyes, she looked like a bird of prey poised to pounce. "I'll get rid of it," I offered hastily. "I was just wondering what the magazine would look like with a different cover. Sorry, I'll get back to work."

"Leave it!" barked Ali. She stood with her hands on her hips and breathed heavily through her nose. "It's

bright. It's funky. There's an unknown on the cover."
She looked at me for a moment, and then her mouth
curved into a smile. "It's bloody brilliant, that's what it
is. I don't know who the fuck you are, but you're
hired."

And that was that. I was Senior Designer, Liz was my
deputy and my predecessor was history. Given carte
blanche to make whatever changes I thought best, I
immediately hired Kerrie and her friends to do some
audience research, and within six months *Blush!* had
become the must-read magazine for teenage girls. It
had the best freebies, was always first with the newest
looks and every month the front cover and fashion
pages featured real-life models. No half-starved waifs
ever made their way on to the pages of *Blush!*. The
press loved the idea, *This Morning* raved about it,
teachers and parents approved, and everyone was
happy, especially the chief executive of LivMags, who
awarded us all fat pay increases and bought himself a
villa in the Caribbean.

I'd found my calling. And for the past four years I've
loved every minute. The *Blush!* offices are on the first
two floors of a converted Georgian town house just off
Floral Street and only a pumice stone's throw from The
Sanctuary. Normally I'd make excuses not to go
anywhere near gyms and health clubs, but there's
something so wonderful about the fluffy bathrobes and
warm, spicy atmosphere there that I often buy an
evening pass and loll by the koi pool with Ali and Liz,
or bubble like a new potato in the spa bath. How many
people have this on their doorstep? At lunchtimes I

stroll on to the piazza and watch the jugglers, or browse the stalls in the covered market before popping into a coffee shop for a latte. Heaven. Who could ask for more?

But recently I've been yearning for something different. Cool colours, teen fashions and boy bands are starting to pall. It's that Radio 4 thing again. I'll be fantasising about magazines with cookery pages and knitting patterns soon if I'm not careful!

"You need to get off your arse and get promoted," Ali was constantly telling me. "You're too comfortable here. You need a new challenge. *Senora* wants an art director. That job has your name on it, babe."

"Am I up to it?" I kept wondering. "*Senora* is right up there with *Marie Claire* and *Vogue*."

"You'll piss all over it," Ali snorted. "I don't want to lose you, but you're ready for bigger things. Bike your CV over to them and I'll write you the best bloody reference Evangeline St Stick Insect has ever seen."

So I applied for the job, and Ali was as good as her word and wrote me a reference so glowing I needed Raybans to read it, which is how I've ended up being interrogated by the editorial team of *Senora* and finding that I can answer their questions easily and have no problem making a presentation of my vision for their publication. Eventually I grind to a halt, the room swims back into focus and I discover that my interrogators are nodding and smiling.

"Do you have an interest in fashion?" asks Evangeline, steepling her fingers under her chin and sweeping her gaze over my suit. "Is it your passion?"

Actually, I find the world of size-zero fashion models repellent, but now is probably not the time to share this thought. I open my mouth to give my rehearsed answer, something along the lines of living for fashion and longing to channel this into a creative force for *Senora*, but I'm pipped at the post by a cropped-haired man sporting trendy NHS-style glasses and a tan so orange it could be seen from the moon. He's none other than Quentin Olsen, the magazine's fashion director, well known in the industry as Queen Quentin, and I brace myself for an acerbic and bitchy deconstruction of my outfit. It's as clear as the designer stubble on his chin that my knowledge of fashion is very definitely size zero.

Oh crap. I've tried my best, but I'm about to be revealed for the fraud that I so clearly am. What a shame. For a moment I almost thought I stood a chance.

"Look at the girl! Just *look* at her!" trills Quentin, leaning forward and jabbing a finger in my direction. "Do you *need* to even ask whether or not she *lives* for fashion?"

I'm a bit offended, actually. I don't think I look *that* bad. At *Blush!*, lots of the juniors are always asking where I buy my clothes.

Oh dear, maybe it's so they can avoid those shops?

"Just *look* at her eye make-up," Quentin is gasping. "So smoky. So sooty. So now!"

I goggle at him. Surely he means so smudged?

"And as for the suit!" He beams at me. "I just *adore* it. What a colour! How did you know?"

"Know what?" I ask. I'm confused for a split second, and then I realise that I'm dreaming. What a bummer. I'll wake up in a minute and have to go through this whole charade again. Great.

"That pink is the new black," says Evangeline sagely, while her minions nod and mentally scribble this down. "Quentin is absolutely right; you're quite obviously a young woman with her finger on the pulse of the fashion industry. That's exactly what we need in our art director, somebody innovative and cutting edge just like you."

I'm speechless. Are they all mental?

"So," Evangeline lowers my portfolio and twitches her frozen lips into her version of a smile, "there's no point wasting time. Amber, welcome to *Senora*. You're hired."

Now this is the point where the alarm should shrill, Ed should leap out of bed as though he's been wired to the mains while I surface to the strains of John Humphrys bullying politicians. But instead everyone's shaking my hand and congratulating me, Quentin's asking where I found my boots and the pretty Chinese girl is exclaiming over the colour of my suit. I pinch myself hard and only get a bruise for my trouble.

Flipping heck! It appears that I really *am* the new art director of *Senora* magazine.

I can hardly wait to call Ed and tell him. He'll be over the moon. We're not exactly on the breadline, the rareness of poor solicitors equating with that of dead donkeys, but the mortgage on our pretty mews house in Clapham is definitely taking its toll. I've become so adept at juggling figures and switching credit cards that I could probably get a slot with the street entertainers in the piazza. It's going to be really nice, I think as the HR manager discusses my amazing new salary, to be able to contribute a bit more to our finances. Maybe we can even start planning our wedding at last.

Not that I don't already contribute to our finances. Far from it, actually, but there never seems to be enough left over for me once Waitrose, the council tax, Barclaycard and all the bills have taken their share. And after the standing orders have gone out, I make church mice look like the Beckhams. Although Ed would be happy to shoulder most of the bills, and, I sometimes worry, *more* than happy if I gave up work altogether and chained myself to the kitchen sink, there's something about being totally reliant on a man, even one I love, that makes me nervous.

I suppose seeing your dad walk out on your mum has that effect on a girl.

"For God's sake," Ed often sighs, "we're engaged, aren't we? Do you think my mother has a problem with my dad supporting her?"

I have to bite my tongue hard to refrain from pointing out that his parents live in a 1950s time warp and that as far as Mrs White is concerned, feminism is something rather unpleasant that happened to other people. Such subversive ideologies have yet to reach her little corner of Surrey. If I hear any more concrete-heavy hints about weddings and babies, I'll probably throttle the woman with her Hermes scarf. I hardly think Evangeline St Anthony will be particularly impressed if I swan off on honeymoon swiftly followed by six months' maternity leave; besides, varicose veins and swollen ankles are so *not* the new black. Ed's mum will just have to wait.

Why, I wonder as I brandish my Oyster card at the ticket barrier, is it so difficult to have it all if you're a woman?

Down in the bowels of the tube, the strains of a busker picking out "Cavatina" drift by on a rush of warm air. I toss a coin into an open guitar case and pick up speed, almost falling down the final steps when I hear the whine of my train. Diving through the throng of disembarking passengers, I plummet into a carriage, squash myself against the doors and tuck my face neatly into a stranger's armpit. Oh the pleasures of London life! Along the tracks the tube rattles, lights flickering on and off and all of us passengers swaying drunkenly with the movement. Sardines in a tin probably have more room.

It isn't that I don't want to be married or have a baby. Of course I do, one day. But this new job's going to be so exciting, and I can hardly wait to start. Ali's right; it really is the perfect opportunity for me to make my mark in the world of magazine journalism. Who knows, maybe one day it'll be me sitting in Evangeline's seat, interviewing trembling minions. I'll lean forward and utter wisely that black is the new pink, and I'll make everyone wear smudgy black mascara. Even the men! Well, OK then, maybe not the men; with the possible exception of Johnny Depp, I've yet to see a man who looks good in make-up.

18

Hmm, maybe I could stipulate that all male employees dress like Captain Jack Sparrow?

Deep in this pleasant daydream, where dashing young men with long dark gypsy curls and tight breeches hang on my every word, I begin to feel a bit disloyal, because Ed is sandy-haired and about as unlike Johnny Depp as it's possible to be. Very cute in his own way, obviously, but in a clean-cut public-schoolboy un-piratey manner, which I'm sure is much more use in day-to-day life. Who could imagine Captain Jack Sparrow in a suit and carrying a briefcase? Swashbuckling is all well and good, but I can't imagine it would pay a Clapham mortgage.

I tear myself away from these disloyal thoughts and glance across the carriage, catching sight of my reflection, flatteringly blurred by the double-glazed glass. Who would ever have thought that that small girl with the shocking pink suit and the unruly hair was actually the senior art director at Britain's top glossy magazine?

I can hardly believe it myself!

Ed's going to be so proud of what I've achieved. He'll be pleased for me even if it does set his plans back a year or two. We can afford a really great wedding now. Maybe we can even jet off to the Maldives and have a small romantic ceremony there.

Without his mother . . .

Once I get a mobile signal, I'll book us a table at the little Italian trattoria he loves and have them put the champagne on ice. Then we can discuss all the lovely ways that we can spend my big fat new salary.

We are going to celebrate in style!

CHAPTER
TWO

"The person you've called is not available. Please leave a message after the tone."

I flip my phone shut. Where on earth has Ed got to? I've dialled the Orange answerphone so many times I'm practically on first-name terms with the robotic-voiced woman. Honestly! My fiancé is more elusive than the Scarlet Pimpernel. He's never in the office when I call and his phone is always turned off. If I didn't know better, I'd start to think he's some kind of secret superhero.

This is *so* annoying! I'm dead excited about my new job and I'm going to explode unless I share the good news soon. I'm not telling him via the answering service, though. An announcement this big calls for champagne and flowers and being twirled round and round in his arms.

Hmm. In my dreams. Ed will do himself an injury if he tries such a thing at the minute. He's right, I really ought to go to the gym more often, especially now that I'm about to join the emaciated ranks of *Senora*, and I must give up those Starbucks panini and mountains of carrot cake I'm addicted to.

Anyway, I do go to the gym! Honestly! I go at least three times a week. The problem is that I never quite get around to using the equipment. Last Christmas, Ed bought me a year's pass to The Sanctuary, which is rather insulting when I think about it, so I started the year with the best of intentions. For about two weeks I pounded away on the treadmill, and swam so much that my hair started to go a funny colour, and I think I *may* have lost a pound or two. But then I got sidetracked by the treatments, and bubble tubs, and once I'd found the shop, I was lost. Good as Ed's intentions were, I don't think he anticipated my use of his present to be solely confined to guzzling organic food in the restaurant or lolling by the koi pool reading glossy magazines. Every now and again he prods my squidgy bits and makes sarcastic noises about demanding a refund.

Charming, eh? Anyway, no matter what Ed believes, I do think about getting fit, and everybody knows it's the thought that counts!

So now what? I'm desperate to share my amazing news and it's a real anticlimax to be standing in the street like a spare part when I should be quaffing champagne and feeling all smug. Maybe I need some retail therapy. That's a cure so effective it really ought to be on the NHS. It would probably save the economy billions.

Tucking my phone away, I hoist my bag on to my shoulder and meander along James Street. It's one of those perfect May afternoons when the sun remembers what it's actually for and the British people throw caution to the wind by taking off their jackets. Crowds of tourists throng the pavements, clapping and laughing at the human robot man or peering excitedly into Karen Millen. On the piazza there's a Mediterranean atmosphere as people sit at cafe tables, taking their time over a late lunch and enjoying the sun's warmth on their pale skin. A gaggle of French exchange students are sitting on the steps of the Opera House, munching on baguettes and scattering crumbs for the pigeons, and even the office workers seem to slow their frantic speed.

I need to book a restaurant for our celebratory dinner. Ed loves Trattoria Sorrentina, a small Italian restaurant tucked down a sweet little side road just off Henrietta Street. In the past we've enjoyed many romantic meals there, sipping thick, fruity red wine and savouring the most delicious pasta imaginable. Ed entertains clients there all the time apparently, but we haven't been together for ages, so it'll be a real treat to have some quality time together. Recently he's been too busy working late to want meals out, preferring to crash on the sofa with Marks and Spencer's finest, before falling asleep in front of the news. When I suggest an early night, he couldn't look more horrified if I'd proposed we just have a quick sprint up Ben Nevis before turning off the lights. He's working far too hard.

Well, stuff work! Tonight's going to be a night to remember. It's high time we took some time out for us. I'm sure that in the delicious garlicky atmosphere and romantic flickering candlelight I'll manage to switch the BlackBerry off and turn my fiancé on. I'll buy myself

22

some sexy new underwear and a bucketload of perfume. I may even throw all caution to the wind and get my hair done too. Then, feeling beautiful and confident, I'll show Ed exactly what he's been missing by spending his evenings with Huw Edwards.

See, I'm thinking like *Senora* magazine already!

I press the redial button but there's still no answer, only the voicemail woman again. I leave a message telling Ed I'm booking the restaurant, then I trek across the piazza and down Henrietta Street to make the reservation in person. Maybe I'll treat myself to a glass of white wine and a bowl of their yummy cheesy pasta. I reckon I've earned it.

I turn up a tiny side street and pause by a small shop that sells the most amazing lingerie. It's all pink satin, peach ribbons and frothing cream lace, exactly the sort of underwear I live in hope my boyfriend will buy me one day, the sort of underwear that screams *romance*, unlike my usual M&S specials, which are far more likely to elicit screams of horror. Who invented control pants anyway? Not somebody who ever had to wear them, I'm willing to bet. I've only been wearing mine since breakfast, and already it feels as though my kidneys are about to explode through my belly button. I'm probably doing myself a serious injury.

Catching sight of a particularly fetching pink and peach floral set, I imagine how it must feel to unwrap something so pretty, fingers rustling through layers of tissue paper and skimming across silk and lace. Sadly, imagining is about as close as I'm likely to get to this scenario, because it's not very likely it'll ever occur to

Ed to buy me lingerie. He just isn't that kind of guy. For my last birthday he proudly presented me with a state-of-the-art food processor, which he very soon ended up wearing on his head.

Not his finest hour.

Seriously, a food processor? What a totally sexless present. Is this really how my fiancé sees me? And if so, what on earth am I going to do about it?

I gaze at the pretty bras and French knickers like a Dickensian pauper staring at buns, and feel rather sorry for myself. Still, I suppose this is what happens after years of being together. The mystery is totally and utterly gone. If I ever had any to begin with, that is. Once a guy's seen you wax your upper lip and dye your roots, it's pretty hard to uphold the illusion that you're naturally a goddess. I'd defy even Derren Brown to manage such a feat.

"Life's a bitch and then you marry a pig," Ali had declared the day after Food Processorgate, laughing her throaty laugh and lighting a cigarette. "All men are wankers. Haven't you sussed that out by now?"

Unfortunately I hadn't. Live in hope has always been my motto.

"And die in despair," Ali snorted when I voiced this sentiment. "A food processor? Jesus!"

Liz had looked up from her Mac, her face pale and serious beneath the big pink bow perched on her crimson curls.

"I think you're lucky to have a fiancé who remembers your birthday," she'd said tartly.

24

Peering into the shop window, I concede that maybe Liz has a point, but I'd much prefer Ed saw me as some irresistibly sexy creature he can't keep his hands off rather than an extension of the cooker. I once tried doing that slurpy, sexy thing that Nigella has going on, but Ed just looked worried and asked if I'd washed my hands before dunking them in the pasta sauce. All my suggestive finger-sucking and gasping was totally lost on him, and I felt a right prat cooking dinner in a little black dress and killer heels. When I tossed my flowing locks and nearly set them alight on the gas, I knew it was time to give up and retreat back into my tracksuit bottoms. There's a good reason why Domino's and the Chinese are on speed dial. As Liz says, maybe I should just be grateful for what I have.

It's weird, but although Liz is one of my closest colleagues, I sometimes feel that I don't know her particularly well. Ali and I know everything about each other. We have one of those no-holds-barred friendships where nothing is a secret, but Liz plays her cards close to her chest. Unlike Ali, who enjoys nothing more than describing her latest sexual encounter, right down to the most excruciating and intimate details, Liz never breathes a word about her personal life. Sometimes she'll take a phone call and her cheeks will go all rosy and her eyes will sparkle like the Swarovski factory, then she'll pop out and buy a new outfit. Her dress sense is eccentric, to say the least, all lacy fingerless gloves, sweeping vintage skirts and big bows that she perches on the top of her tight curls, but she always looks eye-catching. She also texts non-stop on her mobile but never breathes a word regarding who, and sometimes she leaves the office early, her pale face all made up and sporting a new bow, but she never tells us where she's going or who she's going with. The secrecy drives Ali nuts.

"It's so fucking frustrating!" she wailed the last time Liz drifted out of the office in a new floor-length skirt and with a dreamy expression in her eyes. "I tell her everything and what do I get in return? Abso-fucking-lutely nothing. And after I've told her about David too."

David, the latest in a long line of disastrous men, might be a high-powered captain of industry by day, but apparently he likes to yell "And he scores!" at the moment of orgasm and keeps a glass of water by the bed to wash his willy in after the deed is done. Like I said, too much information. Now every time he pops in to *Blush!* I can barely look him in the eye and am possessed by a Tourette's-like compulsion to yell "Goal!" very loudly. I'm actually quite glad Liz keeps her private life private.

"Maybe she's gay?" Ali wondered, eyes saucer-wide at this sudden thought. "Christ, that's it! She's a secret lesbian!"

"Stop it," I said firmly, knowing that Ali was about to get well and truly carried away. She'd be picturing Liz in a civil partnership before you could say "dungarees and clompy shoes". "Maybe she just wants a bit of privacy. Just because you've got a bigger gob than Zippy when it comes to discussing your sex life, it doesn't mean we all feel the same. Some of us want romance."

26

"Romance?" echoed Ali, incredulously. "What the fuck's the point of that?"

Now I know this isn't very twenty-first century or feminist of me, but I'm an absolute sucker for romance, or would be if I actually got any. From the second I watched Disney's *Cinderella* I was hooked. As a teenager I devoured countless pastel-covered *Sweet Dreams* novels and dreamed of being the love interest of the football captain/school hunk/Arabian prince, even though my own dates fell way short of such lofty ideals. Since then I've progressed to bigger and better things, but the underlying sentiment is the same. From Jilly Cooper to Sophie Kinsella, I've read them all, and quite frankly a Class A drug habit would probably be cheaper. The shelves of my bookcase are groaning under the weight of all the pink-jacketed novels I've collected over the years. Sometimes when Ed's working late, the cat's being antisocial and I'm feeling lonely, I'll fish out my trusty old Jane Austen videos and ta-da! I'm Marianne Dashwood being rescued in the thunderstorm by the gorgeous Willoughby, or witty Lizzy Bennet dazzling the most eligible bachelor in Britain; am anyone in fact apart from Amber Scott, the boring sofa queen who spends most evenings watching the telly and waiting for her fiancé to come home.

That's the same Amber Scott, by the way, whose fiancé bought her a Moulinex for her twenty-ninth birthday.

Thank God for romantic fiction.

"Most girls like romance," I said, pointing to my Mac screen, which was emblazoned with the next issue's feature, "Twenty ways to tell if he really fancies you!" "We like flowers and candlelit meals and all that stuff you sneer at. We dream about finding a man who turns our insides to ice cream."

"Ice cream!" scoffed Ali. "Who gives a toss about their insides turning to ice cream as long as he's got an enormous knob!"

This comment rather killed the conversation, but I can't help smiling as I remember it. Ali wouldn't wait for a man to buy her some lingerie. She'd march right on into the shop, flash her gold AmEx and buy the lot. I suppose I could do that too, but somehow it isn't quite the same as Ed coming home and presenting me with a beautiful gift-wrapped box.

Face facts, it'll probably be a slow cooker for my next birthday, which although handy for making stew will be utterly hopeless in terms of uplift and support. I suppose if I want lovely underwear I'd be better off buying it myself rather than waiting for my fiancé to be inspired. Sad but true.

Almost before I know it, I'm pushing open the shop door, the bell is tinkling and an assistant appears from nowhere just like the shopkeeper in *Mr Benn*. Then I'm in a plush crimson cubicle, stripped down to my hideous fraying bra and control knickers while an impossibly glamorous assistant lassos my boobs with a tape measure and tuts disgustedly at the state of my underwear. At this point I have a bit of a weird out-of - body experience, lace, chiffon and silk fly right, left and centre, and a pair of fluffy pink high-heeled mules appear, along with a feather boa. This is followed by a heart-in-the-mouth moment when my credit card says hello to the machine, and then I stumble out of the door and back into the bright sunshine, blinking like a mole. A mole who's several hundred quid poorer and clutching three pink carrier bags bulging with designer knickers.

What was I thinking? Thank goodness Ed and I have separate bank accounts. Promotion or not, he'll freak out if he sees how much I've just spent on underwear.

To be fair, I'm starting to freak out a bit myself, especially when I glance at the Visa slip and clock just how many noughts there are on the end of the amount. That's ridiculous. I could buy everything in Primark for less!

For a moment I dither outside, toying with the idea of going in and returning the lot. I'm sure I could come up with a valid reason for the last twenty minutes of total insanity. Maybe this is some kind of delayed reaction to the shock of being grilled alive by Evangeline and her cronies. There's probably some kind of medical name for it, *Spendus aftershockus* or something, which will totally explain why I've just blown the best part of a month's salary on underwear. Gok Wan must come across it all the time.

I'm just on the brink of darting back inside and pleading temporary insanity when I remember the food processor and my resolve hardens. If I add up all the lingerie Ed *hasn't* bought me over the past ten years, I would probably be justified in cracking open the joint savings account and spending the same again. I'm saving money here!

Much cheered by this flash of economic genius, I set off for Trattoria Sorrentina, swinging my pink bags and feeling smug. Soon I'm deep in a lovely fantasy where Ed and I arrive home after our romantic meal, drunk with success and champagne, and he slowly starts to peel off my clothes to reveal the sexy wisps of silk beneath. He's so overcome with passion that he scoops me into his arms and carries me to the bedroom (with no sarky comments about needing a crane) and makes mad, passionate love to me. And at no point in the proceedings does he check his emails/switch on *Newsnight*/ prod my fat bits. Perfect.

This pleasant fantasy carries me merrily down the street and almost to Leicester Square before I realise I must have walked right past the restaurant. Turning round, I retrace my steps towards Covent Garden, but the really weird thing is that I still can't find the place. I trek up and down at least twice more, and with every footstep I feel more perplexed. Restaurants don't just vanish overnight, do they? But no matter how hard I look and how many times I check I've got the address right, I just can't find it. Where there was once a dark and cosy Italian, all dripping red waxy candles and basil-scented air, there now seems to be an exclusive-looking boutique, the kind where they only have about five garments, all of which are so exorbitantly expensive that mere mortals like me hardly dare to cross the threshold.

Feeling confused, I push open the door and instantly a desiccated-looking blonde with a paper-cut mouth and razor-sharp elbows is blocking my path. She daren't let the likes of me near her garments.

"Can I help you, madam?"

This is the same place, I know it is. Although the old and tatty scenes of Sorrento have vanished and the racks of clothes have replaced racks of lamb, I recognise the sloping ceilings and the rickety staircase.

"I'm sorry," I say. "I was looking for a restaurant. Luigi's place? Trattoria Sorrentina?"

Although this woman clearly never eats, she nods straight away. "You'd be surprised how many people still come in looking for Luigi even though we've been here six months now."

I must be going crazy. I'm sure Ed told me he was entertaining some clients here last week. In fact I know he did, because it was a Saturday night and I was really annoyed, until I realised I could watch telly in my pyjamas and eat the rest of the Ben and Jerry's without being moaned at for not going to the gym. Bliss.

"Six months?" I echo.

She nods again, and wow! Her hair doesn't even move. That must be some hairspray. "Luigi retired in the autumn. He and Luisa went back to Sorrento, I believe. He has a lot of very disappointed customers."

More confused than disappointed, I wander back outside, really wishing Luigi were here, because I certainly could do with a drink now. I'm clearly going mad. I mean, I know this morning's interview was tough, but I didn't realise quite how tough. It must have really pushed me over the edge.

I'm absolutely sure Ed said he was here last weekend. I was even a bit put out because it's been so long since we went out together. I tried to wangle myself an invite as his fiancée, but he was adamant that due to the current economic climate (a convenient excuse for being stingy, if you ask me), partners weren't included. He'd got a bit narky with me actually, and I'd been quite glad to see the back of him for a few hours.

By the time I reach the Lamb and Flag for a restorative glass of wine, I'm pretty convinced I must have got my wires crossed last weekend. After all, there's no way Ed would have told me he was going to a restaurant that no longer exists. It wouldn't make any sense at all. Like he says, I'm always lost in a day-dream or too busy sketching to listen carefully. I probably just misheard him, that's all. I've left a message with his secretary asking him to meet me in the wine bar just down the road from his office. We can have a nice celebratory drink together and decide where to eat before going home to relax and maybe explore my new lingerie. After I've lost the receipts, obviously.

I can hardly wait. This has been a *seriously* stressful day, and it's still only lunchtime.

CHAPTER
THREE

"So what's all this urgency about then?" asks Ed, smiling at me over his Guinness. "I've had three missed calls and two totally incoherent answerphone messages. Whatever it is you need to tell me, it must be pretty important. My PA tells me that you've been harassing her all afternoon."

"I was hardly harassing her!" I say indignantly. "I just wasn't convinced she was actually passing my messages on."

Ed raises his eyebrows and pulls a frustrated face. "Eliza MacAllen is one of the most effective personal assistants on the surface of the planet. I think you can trust her to let me know you've called."

Aren't men naïve? Scary Eliza, with her gore-hued talons and cat's-bum mouth, has the mother of all crushes on Ed and guards him with a ferocity that would put a Rottweiler to shame. I've lost count of the times I've called the office and she's told me he's out, only for Ed to be totally bemused by this when we catch up later. OK, I do admit that *maybe* eight calls is slightly excessive, but this promotion is big news! I can hardly wait to tell him.

Still, I don't want to get into a row about Eliza right now, not when I've got a big bag of sexy underwear to play with and some seriously good news to break. Lately Ed doesn't seem to need many excuses to slip into a bad mood. He's so ridiculously stressed at work that if I so much as breathe the wrong way he's likely to flip. Keeping him calm is a full-time job.

Ed plonks his glass on the table and dashes his hand across his mouth to wipe away the foamy moustache. "Anyway, what's so urgent that you needed to harass poor Eliza all afternoon?"

A smile the size of a watermelon slice spreads across my face. OMG! I really am the new art director of *Senora* magazine. How fan-flipping-tastic is that! OK, here it comes, good-news time!

"I've got something really important to tell you," I begin.

Ed's face drains of colour. "You're not pregnant, are you?"

Er. Hello? The last time I heard, you actually have to *have* sex to get pregnant. So unless the angel of the Lord is about to come down and break some pretty major news, I think my fiancé can rest assured on this one.

I roll my eyes. "Don't be silly, of course not. No, don't panic, it's nothing like that. It's work stuff."

Ed couldn't look more relieved if I'd announced the economic recovery was imminent.

"Right, work stuff. Well go on then. What's so exciting you can't wait to tell me? Have the Jonas Brothers been on a bender in Amsterdam? Or maybe skinny jeans are out at long last? No! Hang on, I know! Is there a must-have lime-green nail varnish giveaway on next month's issue?"

I'm a realistic kind of a woman. I know that when you've been in a relationship for a long time there are bound to be things that seriously annoy you about your partner. That's all part and parcel of real and adult life, isn't it? I may spend far too much time dreaming about Mr Darcy (the Colin Firth version, of course), but I bet once Lizzy Bennet moved into Pemberley she pretty soon got fed up with having to pick up his socks or being told that she didn't pack the shopping away properly and bruised all the fruit. Romance only goes so far, right, before reality kicks in. And one of the things that really, really annoys me about Ed is the fact that he has never taken my job seriously. So I don't split the atom on a daily basis, but there are legions of teenage girls out there who get a lot of help and advice from *Blush!*. And the feature we did on teen sexual health won several awards.

So there!

In matters of love, there are times when you just have to grit your teeth, and this is one of them. No point spoiling my nice news by having a row.

"Exciting as the lime-green giveaway is, I think I can come up with something even better than that," I say, excitement fizzing up in me like Berocca. "Do you remember I was talking about a promotion?"

Ed's eyes light up like a Christmas tree. "Strange you should bring that up, babe. That was exactly what I wanted to talk to you about."

"Really?" I'm taken aback. And there was I thinking that for weeks he's hardly listened to a word I've said. Whenever I mention the world of magazines, his eyes glaze over and like a Pavlovian response his index finger raises the volume of News 24. Being drowned out by Bill Turnbull doesn't tend to do a lot for a girl's ego.

Ed nods and takes another sip of his pint. "There's been so much stuff going on lately that we've hardly had time to talk."

It's true. Between CNN and Bloomberg I can scarcely get a word in. Still, I let this pass. He's been busy, I've been busy, and the telly's been extremely busy. Such is the real world. Sadly.

"We've both been working hard," I say, so diplomatically it's a wonder the Foreign Office doesn't sign me on the spot.

"Too busy. Ridiculously busy, and it shouldn't be that way," agrees Ed. He reaches out across the table and takes my left hand in his, his fingers searching for my engagement ring, which he turns thoughtfully. "But it doesn't have to be that way, Amber."

Er, actually it does. Working hard is what happens when you're paying a mortgage in London, running a BMW and your fiancé has a penchant for fillet steak and white Burgundy. Add to this my new and most alarming lingerie habit, and there you have it — an equation that only balances if we both work hard. But now I am about to break some news that will really put a smile on his face.

"That's exactly it!" I say excitedly, thinking about my amazing new salary. "It really doesn't!"

Ed squeezes my hand. "You feel the same way, I knew it! Babes, things are about to really change for us. We can drop out of the rat race for good, because I've got something to tell you."

I stare at him. Call me nuts, but I actually quite enjoy the rat race, especially today, when I feel that I am the Olympic champion of the rat-racing world. Ed's grasp on my hand tightens and his eyes are bright with excitement. Oh God, I really hope this isn't going to be some crazy male "I'm nearly thirty and need to change my life" crisis conversation. If he's decided it's time to throw caution to the wind and go trekking round the Andes, I think I'm going to cry.

"I've got a partnership in a law firm!" Ed says, and for an awful moment I think he's going to leap up on to the swanky zebra-print sofa and do the whole crazy jumping thing like a demented and pinstriped Tom Cruise. "Can you believe it, Ambs? All the hard work has paid off! I'm a partner!"

"That's fantastic!" I cry, a bit faint with relief if truth be told. "You totally deserve it!"

He does too. I know I might moan a bit, or maybe a lot, about the long hours and the endless watching of rolling news, but Ed has worked ridiculously hard lately to prove himself, and I know just how much becoming a partner means to him. He's been dreaming of this ever since he graduated.

Ed beams at me. "I told you I'd get there in the end! Now we're really going places."

My eyes are like saucers. "I can't believe it! Who's decided to leave? Was it old Mr Colville? Surely not! You always said he'd rather die than retire."

All of a sudden Ed looks so sheepish that all he needs is a fleece and a shepherd to complete the look.

"The partnership isn't at Colville and West."

"You've bought into another firm?"

"Sure have. A family friend approached me a few months back because he was looking to retire and needed someone to take over the business. It seemed like the perfect opportunity, and like you said, Derek Colville will only leave in a coffin. My dad lent me most of the money I needed, I dipped into my savings for the rest, and now you're looking at the junior partner at Renwick and Thompson."

"Renwick and Thompson?" I know I have a terrible habit of tuning out anything legal, but even so, this is a totally unfamiliar name. "Do I know them?"

Ed finds his empty crisp packet totally absorbing. "I wouldn't have thought so. They're in Cornwall."

"Cornwall?" I rack my brains, easier said than done after a stressful day, giving Barclaycard a pounding and necking two glasses of pink wine. "Cornwall Street? Where's that?"

"Not Cornwall Street," says Ed patiently, as though addressing a particularly stupid child. "Cornwall the place. It's in the south-west of England."

"I know where Cornwall is!"

"So don't ask foolish questions," says Ed. "And please lower your voice. We're in public."

I take a deep breath and count to five. Shouting and shrieking never works with Ed. He just ignores me and sulks. I lower my voice by a few decibels.

"Ed, what I'd like to know is why you've gone and bought into a legal partnership in Cornwall. And more than that, why you've done it without even thinking it might be a good idea to mention it to me first!"

He scowls. "I'm telling you now, aren't I?"

"Now it's all done and dusted! Talk about a fait accompli! Whatever happened to discussing things and making joint decisions? What about what *I* think? And where *I* want to live? Or doesn't that even come into it?"

"No wonder I didn't say anything. I knew you'd be like this," says my fiancé, looking pained.

"What? Annoyed? Confused? Pretty bloody pissed off?" I know I'm ranting now and that my volume is on a par with a 747 taking off, but I really don't care. Ed's lucky he's not wearing what's left of my pink wine.

"Unsupportive. Not interested. Difficult."

"Difficult! I'm difficult?" I know I'm sounding like Lady Bracknell here, but I'm beyond caring by now. Call me picky, but I happen to find it rather shocking that my fiancé has just decided to up sticks and move to Cornwall without so much as a by-your-leave.

"I'm doing this for us," Ed says self-righteously, visibly puffing himself up with every word. "This is for our future, Amber. Think of the quality of life we'll be able to have in the West Country. We can buy a bigger house, more for our money, and the children can spend their summers on the beach."

My mouth is literally swinging open. "What children? Ten minutes ago you nearly passed out because you thought I might be about to tell you I was pregnant!"

He swats my words away with a flick of his wrist. "Well obviously we'll have children eventually. That goes without saying. And if we're living in Cornwall, you'll be able to afford to give up work to look after them."

I glance about the pub for Dr Who, because this is the only explanation I can find for our sudden trip back to the 1950s, but unfortunately for me, there's no sign of a Tardis or a friendly Dalek I can borrow to exterminate my insane fiancé.

"I happen to like my job," I say through gritted teeth. "I. Enjoy. It. Actually, I more than enjoy it; I love it and I happen to be pretty bloody good at it too!"

Ed raises his eyes to heaven. "You know I want to be a partner in a law firm. It's what I've always wanted."

"In London! Not Cornwall! When did we ever discuss living in Cornwall?" My heart is doing the weirdest kick-boxing moves beneath my ribcage and I feel like a cardiac-arrest character from *Holby City*. "I never said anything about wanting to live in Cornwall! What on earth am I supposed to do there? It's probably escaped your notice, but it's hardly the centre of the magazine industry."

"Relax, Ambs, I'll be earning enough for us both. You can take some time out. You always said you wanted to be able to focus on your painting." Steepling his fingers beneath his chin, Ed fixes me with a beady look.

40

"Unless you don't want to come with me? Is that it? Don't you want to be with me any more? Is your career more important?"

Oh goody, here it is again — the old emotional blackmail trick. Don't you just love it when suddenly you're the one in the wrong? Why is it that in spite of everything he's just sprung on me, I feel a twinge of guilt?

"Of course I want to be with you, but what about *my* job?"

"That's what I've just said." Now he's got that *she never bloody listens* look on his face again. It's most unfair. I do listen, I really do. The problem is that nobody ever seems to be paying attention to a word I say. "We don't need your job to stay afloat now I'm a partner. My salary will more than cover the mortgage on a new place."

"My job isn't just about the money. I enjoy it, Ed!" As I speak, I thump my fist on the sticky table. Guinness sloshes on to the stained surface and Ed sighs wearily.

"I know you do, but at the end of the day you're only writing about boy bands and snogging. It's hardly finding a cure for cancer, is it?"

Now's the perfect time to drop my own little bombshell. "Actually, you're not the only one with a promotion. I got that job at *Senora* magazine! That was what I was dying to tell you all afternoon."

If I was expecting a round of applause or even a *well done* I'd be totally disappointed, because my fiancé supplies neither. Instead, he is far too busy mopping his drink up with a torn beer mat. Ed hates mess, and it's a bone of contention between us that I make loads. Honestly. I am a dirt magnet. I only have to be in the vicinity of grot and gunge and instantly I'm smothered. At all the posh Law Society dinners we have to attend, I live in fear that I'll splatter my frock with gravy or splosh red wine all down myself. I'm practically mainlining Rescue Remedy before we've even climbed out of the taxi.

"*Senora* is Britain's biggest-selling women's glossy," I point out when he doesn't respond. "It's got a monthly circulation of over six hundred thousand."

Mop. Mop. Mop.

"FYI, that's very good," I add, "just in case I'm not making it clear enough. In fact, it's better than good — it's bloody amazing! And you are looking at the newly appointed art director!"

Ed looks up from his cleaning. The beer mat is sodden and he isn't quite sure what to do with it. In the good old days of smoking, he could have plopped it in an ashtray, but now he has to place it in a soggy splat on the table and I know just how much this will bug him — almost as much as I am starting to think I sometimes do.

"That's great news, babes, well done," he says dutifully.

Well bloody done? After the interview hell I've just put myself through?

"This is the break I've been waiting for," I explain. "It's the job of a lifetime."

"Amber, I don't want to be disparaging, but at the end of the day, won't you just be churning out the same old crap but for middle-aged women rather than teenagers? Just how long can you write about diets and the importance of the clitoris?"

My eyes widen. So he *does* remember what a clitoris is.

"Besides," Ed ploughs on, "it's hardly vital, is it?"

"Some people might think the clitoris is very vital," I mutter.

"Don't be facetious. You know what I mean."

Indeed I do. For the past few years I've regularly been reminded that Ed's job is the "real" one in our household. While I design funky double-page spreads and features on cyber-bullying, he's drafting wills, settling acrimonious divorces and generally being Very Important Indeed. If Ed doesn't remind me of this, in a rather subtle manner, then his mother is more than happy to spell it out. It doesn't matter that I've spent years building up my reputation in the world of magazine publishing and making a major contribution to the huge success of Britain's biggest teen glossy. What I do is pink and glittery and feminine, and therefore frivolous.

Ed is lucky the Guinness is already spilled or he'd be wearing it as a hat. How dare he assume that I'll just step away from my career and my life without so much as a by-your-leave? Just because I'm the woman? Er, hello? The last time I looked, it was actually 2011.

"What about my promotion?" I ask.

"It's brilliant news, but it's hardly the same as becoming a partner in a legal practice. Let's face it, at the end of the day, your job is our second income."

"So I'm less valid because I earn less?"

He massages his temples with his forefingers. "I'm not saying that. What I am saying is that our future and our finances depend on my salary. You'll take a career break at some stage and you may even decide that you don't want to go back once we have a family. At the end of the day we've got to be realistic, and the fact of the matter is that I'm the main breadwinner."

I goggle at him. Breadwinner? Who still uses words like that? Where's Germaine Greer when you need her?

I'm not saying my fiancé is a sexist pig — he isn't, and most of the' time he's the sweetest guy in the world — but sometimes the results of his traditional upper-middle-class Surrey upbringing are very hard to stomach. I know too that he's been really super-stressed the last few months; whenever I gently suggest that he's working too hard and needs to maybe take some time out from the ridiculous hours he puts in at the office, he flies off the handle. Oh Lord. Maybe a slower pace of life in Cornwall is exactly what he needs.

"This is our future I'm working towards," he says. "I thought we wanted the same things. Since when did your career become more important than that?"

I have a horrible feeling I know where this conversation will be ending up. I'm going to give in, of course I am. I always do. Being a sap seems to be my default setting. It drives Ali mental. On the other hand, I love Ed. We've been together since uni, so of course I do, and I want to make him happy. There's nothing wrong with that. Being happy should be what life's all about.

Annoying that I always feel so miserable, then.

"I love my job," I say.

Ed reaches across the table and takes my hand. "This is a fresh start for us, babes, somewhere beautiful and new. Isn't it time we moved away from the city?"

"I like the city," I mutter.

"It's fun, sure, and I've enjoyed every minute of being in the mix of it, but there comes a time when you feel enough's enough," says my fiancé, who has clearly never heard of Dr Johnson. "This is the next adventure. A new phase in our lives."

Call me dull, but I was quite enjoying the old phase.

"Just think of the fun we'll have house-hunting. We can get so much more for our money," Ed says excitedly, morphing into Sarah Beeny before my very eyes. "We'll have some land, too. You can even keep chickens!"

Now I know he's flipped. Since when have I wanted chickens? The nearest I ever get to anything poultryfied is a chicken Caesar wrap from M&S.

"And a dog, too," Ed adds, mistaking my gobsmacked silence for delight. "And a horse."

"Whoa!" I hold my hands up. "Slow down! Since when have you wanted an entire petting zoo?"

"Not for me! It's for you. You love animals."

He's right. I do, and I've wanted a dog for years. In fact I'm starting to think there's something wrong with me. While my contemporaries are cooing over newborn babies and dragging their reluctant partners past Mothercare, I'm going gooey-eyed over puppies and sneakily reading the free ads to circle the ones I'd like to buy. There was even a very dangerous moment when I went to look at a litter of Labradors. Only the fact that you'd struggle to swing a gerbil in our house stopped me from bringing one home.

Oh, and maybe that Ed once remarked that *Marley & Me* was the worst film he'd ever seen . . .

"It could be fun," Ed says, sensing that I'm weakening and tightening his grip on my hands. "A change of scene is exactly what we need!"

"We could always have dinner in a new restaurant, or really break out and visit a different branch of Starbucks if it's a change of scene you're after," I suggest. "Moving to Cornwall is slightly excessive."

"I think it would do us good." He reaches forward and brushes a curl back from my cheek. It's been so long since he touched me this tenderly that I'm a little unnerved. Heck, he might want sex in a minute and I'm not sure I remember how to do it. "I know I've been neglecting you lately and we both work crazy hours. It's no good for us. This way we can have a whole new life and actually spend some quality time together."

Quality time? Since when did my fiancé speak like Oprah?

"You must admit things have been a bit stale," he says. "We need to be together more, to slow down and remember what life's about, don't you think?"

46

Stale doesn't really come close. But I can hardly expect us to be swinging off the chandeliers after all these years. I've just assumed that this is what happens in a long-term relationship. It's a bit depressing to be seen in terms of food processors and ironing boards, but this happens to all couples, right?

"So a new start is just what we need." Ed seals the argument by leaning across the table and brushing my lips with his. "I'm doing this for us. Everything I do is always for us, you know that, don't you?"

I nod. He does work long hours and I guess it is all for our future. I just never imagined that my life would end up quite like this. Somewhere along the line the fun guy I met at uni morphed into a stressed and snappy solicitor with a penchant for heavy wine and silly status-symbol cars. Maybe once he's out of the rat race and the stresses have been removed, he'll revert to the person I fell in love with. The guy who kidnapped the Dean for rag week and who splashed half of his grant to celebrate my twenty-first with a weekend in a luxury hotel. The generous, funny, chilled Ed has to still be there, buried beneath the pinstripes. All I need to do is find a way to excavate him and we'll be back to normal — better than normal. We'll be happier than we've ever been.

My text alert beeps. It's Ali, wanting to know all about my interview and offering to buy me disgusting amounts of celebratory champagne. I slide my hand from beneath Ed's and switch my BlackBerry off.

I already know that I won't be celebrating my new job.

Just as I also know, with a sinking heart, that I won't be accepting it.

Looks like I'm off to keep chickens in Cornwall.

CHAPTER
FOUR

"Mum! What a . . . what a lovely surprise!"

Although it's only nine o'clock on a Saturday morning, a time when normal non-rowing and loved-up couples might be lazing in bed or making love, my mother is standing on my doorstep. Behind her is a tatty trolley bulging with the New Age kit she sells on her market stall, and behind that an even tattier-looking youth complete with pimples, facial piercings and ratty dreads.

Oh joy. She's brought her boyfriend, Rain, with her. My cup runneth over. Some people's mothers have mid-life crises and take up snowboarding. Others go on cruises with Tango-tanned gigolos called Raoul. But not my mother. She just happened to go to Glastonbury with the WI and came back a New Age traveller. You couldn't make it up.

"Don't lie to me, Amber, it's bad for your energies," Mum says tartly, barging past me and whacking me in the shins with her trolley. "Hurry up, Rain. You're letting out the chi."

I feel like following the chi, quite frankly. Maybe it would take me down the road and round the corner to the local greasy spoon, where I could order builder's tea and a lardy bloater fry-up. That's how I wanted to start my weekend. Now I'll have to listen to Mum witter on about her chakras for an hour while Rain hogs the TV. It's just as well Ed had a breakfast meeting and stomped out over an hour ago. The last time he came home and found Rain shedding yak wool all over his beloved Eames leather recliner, he went mental. And let's face it, there was enough going mental last night to last a lifetime. We "discussed" Ed's promotion into the small hours and still there's no hint of a compromise. The bottom line is that if I love him, I'll sacrifice my career and follow him to Cornwall. Even pulling out my beautiful new lingerie failed to persuade him to consider my point of view.

Maybe I should ask for a refund? If all that lace and silk can't get his attention, then short of standing on the roof and threatening to jump, I can't think what would.

"You look tired, Amber. You need to take some echinacea," observes my mother as she parks her trolley in the hall and her twenty-year-old lover in the sitting room. Seconds later, the dulcet tones of Jeremy Clarkson fill the house. Actually, I'm not sure a pacifist and environmentally friendly hippie ought to be watching *Top Gear*, but I decide to keep this thought to myself. The last thing I need right now is another argument, and for a pacifist, my mother certainly enjoys a good debate.

"I didn't sleep that well," I say, which is an understatement.

"Too much red meat." Mum pulls off her hat and shakes out her mane of thick silver-streaked hair. "Your body's far too busy trying to digest it to sleep, that's the problem. No wonder you can't nod off. You should try being a vegan."

"Hmm," I say, hoping that she takes this as agreement. The point is that I could have lived on carrots for a year and still not have slept last night. Never mind trying to digest meat, I was far too busy trying to digest Ed's news and think up a way of turning down the promotion that wouldn't mean I was finished in the world of magazines. Not many people say no to Evangeline St Anthony and live to tell the tale. Once Ed had fallen into a Guinness-heavy slumber, I'd stared at the ceiling and tried as hard as I could to figure out a solution. Round and round in circles I'd gone until I felt quite giddy and my head was pounding with some awful techno beat. Seven hours and two Nurofen later, I'm still no clearer.

I'd better think of something soon, or we'll be packed and on the A303 before you can say "pasty".

"Eating meat is going to upset your chakras terribly," my mother continues, propelling me into my own kitchen and seating me at the George Nelson table. All trendy cutting-edge metal and glinting glass, it glances off my retinas and stabs at the remnants of my headache. I guess that Ed will be gagging to swap it for a huge refectory-style affair when we move.

When we move? I mean *if* we move.

"Darling? Are you listening to me?" A finger prods my ribs. "You're miles away."

She's not wrong. I was about 240 miles away and crossing the Tamar Bridge while screaming "Noooooo!" very loudly.

"Sorry, Mum." I drag myself back into the kitchen and am so relieved to see my glossy white units and granite worktops that I feel like weeping. "You were saying about meat and chakras?"

"As you eat the meat, your body absorbs all the fear and terror that the poor animals suffered in their last earthly moments. The negativity is then transferred to every cell in your body because in the way of the universe we are all as one," explains my cheerful mother, filling the kettle and wrinkling her nose as she peruses the tea caddy. "Where are the herbal tea bags, darling?"

"We don't have any." I place my head in my hands. Here we go.

"Don't have any? Amber Scott, do you have any idea what is in tea?"

Now, call me stupid if you like, but I've always assumed that the main ingredient of tea is, in fact, tea. I am, of course, totally wrong. Apparently it's full of stuff that will kill me instantly. I'd probably be safer shooting up heroin.

"Tannin to prohibit the secretion of juices in the digestive system, caffeine to unbalance your kidneys, cyanide, strychnine . . ." My mother checks off each toxin on her fingers. "I'm sure there was another one. Now, what on earth was it?"

"Cyanogen!" pipes up Rain from the sitting room.

"Thanks, darling!" trills my mother. "See, sweetie! That's why you need to stock up on some herbal tea. You'll sleep better too."

I place my head on the table, narrowly missing the lethal amethyst that she's plopped down to ward off any negative vibes. Pretty ironic really, since this whole house is brimming with them since yesterday. That poor crystal must have its work cut out.

"Luckily I've brought some of my own special tea bags," Mum says proudly. "Rain and I make them ourselves out of muslin and dandelions."

I am so drawing the line at this. It's one thing for a girl to be told that her entire life is about to be turned upside down but another entirely to be denied her cup of PG Tips. And I am *not* drinking anything that Mum and Rain offer me. Ed claims he's still not recovered from the mushroom risotto they dished up last time we visited the ashram, and judging by his recent behaviour, he may have a point. This moving to Cornwall madness is my mother's fault!

"I'll have normal tea, thanks," I say in my best I-will-not-be-messed-with voice.

"Darling, I'm not sure that's wise." Mum looks worried. "Red meat and tea? Maybe I should get my pendulum and see if I can realign you."

Until a few years ago, Mum's idea of heaven was cooking a big roast and drinking gallons of tea with her WI friends, so I still find this personality change rather alarming. Throw in a few crystals, a nose ring and a deck of tarot cards and it's very unnerving. No wonder Dad decided to take off in the yacht and leave her to it.

I often feel like doing the same, and I'm a girl who gets seasick in the bath.

"Up to you," Mum sniffs. "It's your body. But believe me, Amber, your aura does not look good today. It has an air of heaviness about it."

The way I'm feeling, my aura probably has the density and hue of reinforced concrete. While Mum busies herself with the tea (hers and Rain's has a nasty, suspicious yellow tint to it that makes me even more delighted I'm swigging PG's finest toxins), I check my mobile for messages, my heart sinking when I see two missed calls from Ali. She'll be wondering why on earth I'm not shouting about my triumph from just about every rooftop, and the thought of how let down she'll be if I don't take the job makes my heart plop into my Uggs.

"Tea up," calls Mum, and Rain comes shuffling into the kitchen. His eyes are glazed, which could be down to the dandelion tea but more likely a side effect of being glued to *Top Gear*. Ed wore a similar expression last week when they test-drove the new Ferrari FF.

"That was so cool," Rain says, plonking himself down at the table and wrapping his hands around my Emma Bridgewater mug. "They had a race between a Capri, a milk float and a Lada."

My mother scowls. "It's a deplorable waste of precious fossil fuels. Gaia is being raped on a daily basis just so that mankind can travel faster. It's wrong, Rain. You know better than that."

Rain looks suitably chastised and I feel a bit sorry for him. He's only twenty and he comes from Chigwell. He

54

ought to be hooning around in a souped-up Fiesta or getting plastered with his mates, not trying to save the planet with a fifty-something madwoman aka my mum.

To change the subject, and to avoid her trying to ram a crystal up my nose, I crack open some chocolate digestives, feeling pretty safe that no baby lambs or little calves died to make these. Soon Mum and Rain are munching happily and telling me all about just how well their tarot stall at Camden Market is doing, or would be doing if they ever turned up to man it.

"Don't be such a slave to the system," Mum says, when I point out that to run a stall you actually need to be there. "Anyway, I was on my way to Camden. It's not my fault that we never made it. It's yours."

"My fault?" I guess this figures. It seems I'm to blame for most things lately so why not this as well? The global downturn is probably my fault too.

"Great Running Wolf was most insistent I came straight to you this morning," my mother says. As she speaks, she gesticulates with her mug and wee-coloured water sloshes all over the reclaimed wooden floor. I fight the urge to fetch a cloth and mop it up, because Ed goes nuts if that floor gets so much as a speck on it. "Great Running Wolf must be listened to, mustn't he, Rain?"

Rain is nodding like the Churchill insurance dog, while I resist the impulse to scream. Great Running Wolf is my mother's spirit guide, and he has to be the most opinionated Sioux chief in the history of the Native American people. It amazes me how someone who (allegedly) lived hundreds of years ago can have a

55

view on everything from phone hacking to Katie Price, but apparently he can, and he tells my mother everything. I've asked for the EuroMillions numbers countless times but apparently that isn't ethical, which is just typical and Great Running Wolf's being a big meanie in my opinion. It wouldn't hurt him just to give me a few measly lottery numbers.

Dear Lord! Listen to me! I just said that like he really exists!

"Right," I respond wearily. "And what did he have to say this time?"

"Don't mock the spirits," Mum warns, peering at me from over the top of her glasses.

"As if I'd do that." Resigning myself to the fact that I am about to be subjected to some lengthy ramblings that make about as much sense as an episode of *Lost*, I reach for the biscuit tin and fish out some chocolate digestives. Judging from past experience, I'm going to need my strength.

My mother is not convinced. "Sometimes I think you're a disbeliever, Amber, but luckily for you the spirits don't hold grudges. They'll speak openly regardless of what's in your heart."

I chomp on a biscuit and Rain, who's so skinny he looks like he hasn't eaten for a month, snatches another fistful, while Mum closes her eyes, inhales slowly and then exhales even more slowly. This could take some time. Often Great Running Wolf proves to be a bit elusive.

"Ooooo!" says my mother, swaying like I normally do after a few too many pink wines. "Yes! I hear you."

If it wasn't nine fifteen in the morning, I'd be tempted to splosh some pink wine in a glass right now. Oh, sod it, the sun's over the yardarm somewhere, surely? While Mum moans and holds a conversation with thin air, I take a trip to the fridge and pour myself a generous mugful. Just in case you're wondering, I use a mug because if Ed comes home unexpectedly, I can do without a lecture on my drinking habits. He lives in fear of me becoming a booze-swilling journo who'll show him up at his law functions. Chance would be a fine thing. After several glasses I'm normally flat out, not living it up.

Mug in hand, I rejoin my mother, who's staring in the direction of the cooker with a rapt expression. Either there really is a Red Indian spirit guide perched on the hob or that wasn't dandelion leaves they filled their organic tea bags with.

"Great Running Wolf has a message for you, Amber Scott!"

"Great," I say, plopping myself back down at the table. "I can hardly wait."

"He says . . . he says . . ." Her brow pleats and her eyes snap open. "This doesn't make any sense to me, but he's telling me you should move west. At once."

It's unfortunate that just as my mother tells me this, I take a great big swig of rosé, which shoots out of my nose as I nearly choke with shock. What!

"Go west, he says. Go west. Over the bridge and to the water."

For a split second I teeter on the brink of insanity, before I realise she must have been chatting to Ed. He's probably let slip news of the move. There's no way Mum has really been told this by her imaginary friend. Of course not. It's a classic con trick.

"Your soulmate is there and waiting for you," she continues. "And there's the colour green too. A deep, smooth moss green. I see it everywhere! It'll lead you to him."

"Cool!" says Rain.

"Bollocks," says I. "I'm already with my soulmate, remember? I happen to be engaged to him. Ed? Remember him? About five foot ten with sandy hair and blue eyes?"

"Don't use that tone of voice with me, young lady," says Mum. "I'm only the messenger; don't shoot me. I'm just telling you what they pass on."

"Well they're talking nonsense. Honestly, Mum, I really wonder about you sometimes. No wonder Dad ran away to sea."

My mother assumes a pained expression. "Chris and I were never twin souls. We were destined to part. Great Running Wolf was right about that too; he told me that your father would venture somewhere blue."

"For God's sake, Mum! That could have been IKEA!"

She tuts. "Well mock all you like, but the spirits are never wrong. You'll be moving west, darling, it is all decreed. We cannot argue with our destiny, can we, Rain?"

"No, Laetitia," says Rain.

"I keep dreaming the colour green too, so it must mean something," she continues.

Since all Mum does these days is swing crystals and save the planet, this is hardly surprising. It's like Stalin being amazed about dreaming in red.

Wondering what bad fairy was excluded from my christening to land me with such a lunatic for a parent, I swig back the rest of my wine and make some vague noises about having to attend an urgent meeting. Well, my need to meet with a Starbucks is pretty urgent. And as for my appointment with a big lump of carrot cake — that's well overdue.

"You work too hard," Mum says, as I bundle her out of the front door. "You should relax more, sweetheart, take time to smell the daisies and listen to the quiet voice inside."

Right. Like that will pay the bills.

"Yeah, chill, Ambs," agrees Rain, a boy so chilled that he's possibly made of permafrost. "Be a bit more like Tish and me."

Only the fact that I am desperate for caffeine prevents me from throttling Rain with his own tasselled sun-and-moon scarf. Oh, and the knowledge that another display of temper from me will only result in yet another meat-and-chakras rant from my mother.

"The move to the west is coming. Ignore the spirits at your peril," says my cheerful mother as I bundle her out the door. Dear Lord, it's like hanging out with a character from *Julius Caesar*. I'm surprised she hasn't told me to beware the Ides of March.

As I shut the door on them, I wish for the millionth time that Dad had never suggested Mum went to Glastonbury. Isn't it weird that life can change forever in less time than a heartbeat? If only she was nagging me about setting a wedding date or producing a grandchild. It'd be annoying but at least it would be *normal*. I miss Dad too. It must be almost a year since I last saw him, and he looked rather lost without Mum, as though an appendage had dropped off and he wasn't quite sure how to handle life without it.

"It's great, Ambs, I have freedom," he'd said when I'd enquired how he was coping with his new and unexpected single life. We'd arranged to meet at a marina in Southampton, and I'd been taken aback by just how thin my father was. And had his hair always been quite that white? As we chatted over moules-frites I'd slowly come to realise that my father's aimless route around the Solent was worryingly metaphorical.

"Freedom to do what, exactly?" I'd asked. Call me closed-minded, but I could hardly imagine my dad living it up in the Playboy mansion or developing a drug habit. Before he split up with Mum, his idea of kicking back and being wild was checking out a new National Trust property.

"I can eat what I like, and after living on tofu and chickpeas, that's a blessed relief for any man," he'd said, stacking his mussel shells into some Turner prizewinning design. "Tish's bean casserole played havoc with my insides. I think it rotted the drains, too."

My own stomach clenched in sympathy. I remembered it well. Years in therapy wouldn't touch the horrors of Mum's bean casserole.

"And I can go where I want, whenever I want and with whoever I want," he'd added, only needing a defiant *so there* to completely protest too much. As it turned out, he was only cruising Southampton Water, maybe circling the Isle of Wight once or twice, and hanging out in Hamble — it was hardly the life of an international playboy. When I asked him exactly who the *whoever* might be, all I got was a vague mumble. A quick tour of his yacht and nose round his bleak cabin soon convinced me that Dad was living a solitary existence. The dusty surfaces, empty Vesta packets and general air of neglect told me all I needed to know. My dad was alone and lonely.

And there was nothing I could do about it.

So as I slam the door behind my insane mother, I think I can be forgiven for being a little less than tolerant of her weird and not so wonderful ways. They just spell *selfish* in my book.

"And you can sod off too," I say to the empty space above the hob, just on the off chance that Great Running Wolf is still there, perched in my Le Creuset wok.

Seriously, my parents take the biscuit, they really do. Twenty-seven years of marriage, and then wallop! It's over, just like that. It really knocks your faith in the happy-ever-after. Did Cinderella and Prince Charming part company when she started fancying her Pilates instructor? Or did the Beast trade Beauty in for a newer model when she started to go a bit saggy and grey? Did any of the great lovers from literature discover crystals and tarot and totally lose the plot?

At least Ed and I have made it this far. We may have our ups and downs but we're still a couple and we're working at it, which is what everyone says you have to do, isn't it? If you work at your relationship, everything will be fine in the end. Work and compromise. Doesn't sound like a whole heap of fun, but I'm beginning to think that's the reality of life. It's only in books that relationships are always wonderful and every day feels like it's been dusted with glitter. That's not the real world. Of course it isn't. Nobody really lives like that. Romantic novelists just make it up.

Somebody ought to sue bloody Mills & Boon. That's several generations of women sold down the river. Maybe it's time I stepped away from the pink books. If I really love Ed, then I guess I'll move to Cornwall for his sake. And not because my mum's imaginary friend thinks it's a good idea.

Coffee time, I think! It's only ten past ten, but already my nerves are jangling like crazy. Families. Aren't they great? Why couldn't I be an orphan like Harry Potter? Although even Voldemort would run away from my lot.

I fetch my massive (fake) Chloé Paddington and try to ignore the sad little voice telling me that if I took the job at *Senora* I could afford the real thing. Come on, Amber! What's a bag compared to the love of your life?

Although it has to be said, it would be a very nice bag . . .

Just as I'm having pangs of bag guilt and staging a massive hunt for my door keys, which seem to move about the house with a life of their own and, in spite of Ed's frustrated insistence that I always leave them in the same place, can never be found, the landline rings.

I ignore it — tracking down the pesky keys is a job that can take a while — but when the strident tones of my sister Emma begin to shriek at the answerphone, I have to abandon my task.

"I knew you were in!" booms Emma, as though she's shouting at me from her Wiltshire rectory rather than tapping into BT magic. Tribes in the Amazon are probably covering their ears. "Why do you always ignore the phone? It's bloody annoying! I'm starting to think you're screening your calls."

"I was looking for my keys," I pant. "Sorry."

I can't see my sister, but even so I know she's rolling her eyes. "Why don't you —"

"Always put them in the same place? I know, I know, I know. I do try."

"Hmm." Emma doesn't sound convinced. She knows me far too well, and after a childhood spent helping me search for lost stuff and complaining loudly about the mess in my half of our shared bedroom, she's given up hope that I will ever be neat and methodical. "Well anyway, you're here now. What's happening?"

I flick the switch on the kettle. When Emma calls, it's normally a lengthy chat, and I can't wait that long for my caffeine hit. I am a desperate woman.

"Mum just popped round with Rain. They've got a tarot stall at Camden now."

Emma snorts like one of her ponies. "Heaven help us all. No wonder you're in a state. What a start to the weekend, being saddled with those two. I feel I've got off lightly just dropping the kids off."

Emma and her husband, long-suffering Jeff, have four children each with the IQ of an evil Bond genius, and are devoted parents who spend every spare minute ferrying them from violin to Mandarin to pony club. Their average weekend requires the sort of detailed planning last seen for Prince William's wedding, and I'm exhausted just contemplating it. But compared to an hour with Mum, these activities are a walk in the park.

"She was off on a meat rant today," I say as I shovel Nescafé into a mug. "Great Running Wolf came along too, just to really add to the joy."

"Thank God Jeff bought a house in the country," says Emma with feeling. "I swear to God that one of these days I'll hit her over the head with a dream-catcher. What is the woman on?"

"Dandelion tea, allegedly." Suddenly, moving to pasty land doesn't seem *quite* so dreadful. Two hundred miles between Mystic Mum and me can only be a good thing. Sloshing hot water and milk into my mug, I pad into the sitting room and curl up on the sofa. "You may not be the only one who's made a break for freedom."

"I knew something was up!" There's a clatter at the end of the line. "Sorry! Dropped the phone. I don't have much excitement in my life, so I have to live vicariously! What's going on? Are you up the duff?"

"Jesus! Not you as well!" What is it with everyone lately? Is it because the dreaded 3-0 is looming? "No, nothing like that. It's Ed, he's only gone and got himself a partnership in Cornwall." And in between sips of my drink, I pour out the entire saga to my big sister. The promotion, the underwear, Ed's weird behaviour, the lack of consideration for what I want. Out it all comes in a big word-vomit. When I'm finished I feel shattered, ten stone lighter and oddly relieved. It's like confession. No wonder people are Catholics.

"Do you think he's having an affair?" says my sister, who wasn't in the queue when tact was being handed out. She was probably dropping one of the evil geniuses at tae kwon do.

I can't help but laugh out loud at this suggestion. "Hardly! He's not the type."

"He has a dick; believe me, that makes him the type," says Emma darkly.

"He's too busy working to have an affair. The office hours are punishing, that's why he's so keen to go to Cornwall. He wants an easier life."

"Or he wants to get away and escape a bunny boiler."

"Em, you really should work for a women's magazine," I chortle. "You could write a feature called 'Five Signs That He's Cheating on You'."

"One: he's always out. Two: he doesn't want sex. Three: he's always pissed off with you for no reason. Four: he visits restaurants that are closed. Five: he switches off his phone at odd times." My sister pauses. "Shall I go on? I think we could easily get to ten."

"Please don't." I feel a bit queasy. This is all surmise and circumstantial evidence, but even so, it's making a pretty alarming list. And a great feature. I wish I'd never told her about the restaurant confusion too because she's seized on this with great relish. To Emma

65

it's not my mistake but proof positive that Ed leads a double life that could put Clark Kent's to shame.

"Look," I say patiently, "this is Ed we're talking about. He's a creature of habit, remember? In a previous life I think he was possibly a sloth. This is a man who loathes change so much he won't even let me move the furniture or order him a different curry. He's not the sort to want to change a woman in a hurry."

"Oh believe me, they are all the sort," says Emma.

I ought to explain, just for the record, that twelve years ago, when incidentally they were on a relationship break, the saintly Jeff experienced some kind of mini brainstorm and slept with a colleague. Emma has never recovered and likes to use this as a stick to regularly beat her husband with. She's also so bitter you could stick her in your G and T and call her a lemon.

"Well Ed isn't," I say firmly. I am so nipping this line of enquiry in the bud, or she'll be hiring a private detective before you can say Poirot. Even worse, she might slip into bored housewife mode and decide to trail him herself as a new pastime. It would certainly be cheaper than horses or redecorating.

"If you say so. In which case, he just wants a new life in the country, lots of chubby babies and a Labrador. So what's your problem?"

"My problem is that I've just got a massive promotion and I'm not quite ready to bury myself alive."

"Hey! Watch it, that's my life you're dissing!"

"Dissing? Are you hanging out with Harry's teenage buddies again, Mrs Robinson?"

"I can't help but pick up the teen slang when he's home from school," huffs my sister. "Anyway, all that aside, Amber, I can't see your problem. You tell me that you love and trust Ed, you want to marry him presumably, and you can't wait to escape from Mum: so move to Cornwall. It's perfect! It is!" she insists when I don't reply. "You have no idea what you're missing. Life in the country is bliss!"

I don't share her enthusiasm. No Starbucks. A million miles to drive whenever you want a decent shop, and loads of yokels chewing straw and going ooh-ah. Not really my idea of bliss. And the last I heard, there's no tube in Cornwall. That's not much help to me given that Ed goes crackers if I so much as look at his beloved BMW. I'll have to give in, buy a horse, grow a huge bottom and wear a headscarf.

Oh God. Oh God. Oh God.

"Breathe!" says Emma. "It's fine, Ambs. The south-west is pretty civilised these days, or so I hear. Even Jamie Oliver and Richard and Judy go there."

I feel rather underwhelmed to hear this. Jamie's food-Nazism gives me the most rebellious urge to guzzle turkey twizzlers, and I'm sure I only got a 2:2 because I wasted far too much time at uni watching *This Morning*.

"Where's the firm based?"

"Do you know what, I have absolutely no idea. Somewhere near Fowey, I think."

"Fowey's lovely! There's a beach and a river and everything," says Emma. "Rock would have been better, obviously, but the south coast is on the up according to Jeff. You should get a lot for your money there. Make sure you're near a beach, won't you? The children love the beach, and there's nothing more tiresome than having to drive to the sea. We could share a little boat; maybe the children could sail!"

My sister is a force of nature when she gets an idea into her head. She's already moved her brood into my house for the summer and is living the *Swallows and Amazons* lifestyle. As she chatters away excitedly about picnics and smugglers and me having lots of children because my biological clock is tick-tocking away, I hear the clanging of a prison door.

Because of course she's right. Ed is offering me the perfect life. Everything a woman could possibly want is being handed to me on a silver platter. I ought to be jumping for joy, binning my stilettos and heading off for a trolley dash in the Joules store.

So why aren't I more excited?

What on earth is wrong with me?

CHAPTER
FIVE

Saturday-night telly is so addictive! If something ever happened to Simon Cowell it would be a national disaster, we'd all have to talk to one another or play charades or something. No wonder I don't have a social life when there's a choice between talented dancing dogs and testicle eating celebrities to entertain me at the weekend!

I'm lounging on the sofa with the Sky remote in my hand, something that doesn't happen that often, because it's normally welded to my fiancé's fingers. In fact, I'm so unfamiliar with the ways of the Digibox that I've already crashed the system once, erased three episodes of *CSI: Miami* and recorded *Britain's Got Talent* by mistake. At one point I almost channel-hopped to CNN just in case the TV was missing it, but then I got distracted by the Hoff raving about a man who can play the recorder with his nose, and boom! I was lost. Sucked into the twilight world of talentless people and greedy media moguls.

Well, it beats meting up with Ali and making excuses about why I'm not dancing with excitement regarding this new job, I suppose. She's sussed that something isn't right and has now left five messages on my

69

voicemail, each more arsey than the last, ending with a final call to the landline to the effect of "Fucking answer the fucking phone, you fucker!"

I'm ignoring it. Such ripe Anglo-Saxon before the watershed just isn't for my delicate ears.

I'm having an evening in on my own, for a change. So far me, myself and I are very happy drinking pink wine and working my way through a Domino's extra-large Pepperoni Passion. I've given up worrying about my expanding waist since a) my fiancé doesn't seem to notice what I look like and b) everyone thinks I'm pregnant anyway so I may as well just go up a few sizes and let them speculate. Anyway, once I'm buried in the country, nobody will care what I look like. I'll live in wellies and baggy jeans and probably use my lovely underwear as cleaning rags. I may as well start as I mean to go on.

Ed's got some work thing on; apparently he's entertaining clients again and as usual the budget doesn't stretch to partners. Hence my pizza-guzzling marathon. While he's out, I've also waxed my upper lip, plucked my eyebrows and touched up my roots, all things that should only be done when alone, according to *Senora*. I didn't realise this until I read "The Ten Things that Turn him Off" while researching my new job, and it's blooming bad luck that I'd performed every single one in the presence of my unfortunate partner. When it comes to mystery, it's pretty safe to say that there isn't much left in our relationship. But then we've been together for a long time. If Ed ever thought I was naturally beautiful, I think I've probably disabused him of that particular misconception. Anyway, all the effort I used to put in when I first met him to look groomed and glittery and gorgeous was pretty knackering. I defy any one human to keep that up for long.

Face pack slapped on, pizza congealing nicely and the Hoff muted, I boot up my laptop to indulge in a spot of media stacking. I peruse Facebook, stalking a few exes and checking up on the mean girls from school just to reassure myself that they really do now resemble Jeremy Kyle's audience, before getting bored and messing about with Google. It's always satisfying to type in your own name and see page upon page pop up, and even all these years into the job I feel excited to be reminded of the things I've achieved at *Blush!*. I'd love the chance to do the same, better even, at *Senora*. But in spite of what the magazines and feminists tell us, it really does seem that women can't have it all. There's always a choice to be made. Personal life versus professional life. Something has to give. Why this isn't the same for guys I really can't work out; it's got to be something to do with fundamental biology.

Or they really are much more selfish than us.

Pondering this abstract train of thought, I type "Fowey" into the search engine and within seconds the screen is teeming with images and information. Idly scrolling through the entries I surf countless photos of picture-book-perfect cobbled streets and crumpled cottages, smug seagulls perched jauntily on harbour walls and primary-coloured fishing boats bobbing in the swell. It's very pretty and for a brief moment I indulge in a fantasy where I walk along the quay in my Dubarry boots and cream cable sweater to buy fish straight off the boats, before I remember that the only fish I can bear is the breadcrumbed finger variety. From here it's only one small mouse click to Rightmove but one giant leap for Amber-kind. If I start looking at cute cottages with Agas and beams, or higgledy-piggledy farmhouses with outbuildings and paddocks, I'll be lost.

I have to keep strong. I cannot let my head rule my heart. What would Lizzy Bennet do?

Oh sod it. She'd move to Pemberley and live it up. I'm off to Rightmove.

Never mind the road to hell being paved with good intentions. It's a truth universally acknowledged that the route to living in Cornwall is paved with pretty properties. Within seconds I'm hooked, tapping in my budget and preferred location and mentally redecorating each house I view. When Ed comes home, I'm so engrossed (and busy renovating a sixteenth-century fisherman's cottage) that I practically shoot into orbit.

"God, you're jumpy. What are you looking at? Smut?" he asks, peering over my shoulder.

I snap the laptop shut. House porn is worse than real porn. If he thinks I'm trawling Rightmove then he'll suss I'm interested and I'll be fighting bin wars with seagulls by breakfast. There's only one thing guaranteed to make him step away from my browsing history . . .

"I was looking at wedding dresses!" I say brightly, my face pack cracking and powdering the lid of my Mac with green dust. "I've seen some amazing designs. Want to look?"

"Not now, babe, I'm knackered." Ed retreats into the kitchen and moments later I hear the hiss of a ring pull as he cracks open a beer. Wandering back into the sitting room, Foster's in hand, he collapses into an armchair. "Looks like you've had a busy evening."

I don't reply. I've been busy trying to convince myself I want to live in Fowey. My fingers are practically falling off, I've been tapping away so hard on my Mac.

"Go and look in the hallway." Ed loosens his tie. "There's a surprise for you."

"Really?" I'm taken aback. Ed isn't the kind of guy to do surprises, unless you count announcing that we're moving to Cornwall, which I'd say is more accurately categorised as a shock.

"Really." For once the Sky remote isn't glued to his hand, and he's smiling at me, a real smile rather than an exhausted grimace. Abandoning my laptop, I brush pizza crumbs from my trackie bottoms and venture into the hall. I'm not desperately excited — Food Processorgate has taught me never to expect too much — so when I see a massive bouquet of exquisite flowers that practically take up the entire hallway, I'm gobsmacked. Creamy lilies freckled with pink and dusted with yolk-yellow pollen jostle for pole position with plump roses and Sweet Williams, all woven together with raffia and silky peach ribbon.

"Do you like them?" Ed says over my shoulder. His arms snake around me and he pulls me close against his chest, brushing his lips against the nape of my neck.

I'm taken aback, both by this romantic gesture and by the affection. I wish I didn't have the green gloop on my face. Who knows, he may have even kissed me properly and, if I was really lucky, we could have gone up to bed. Stranger things have happened.

"Are these for me?" I ask. Better clarify, just to be on the safe side. It would be awful to get all excited and think they were for me and then discover that he's bought them for scary Eliza.

"Of course they're for you." His arms pull me closer and — oh my God! Is that a remote control in his pocket or is he pleased to see me? "I'm sorry I've neglected you lately, babe. I know I've been a crap partner. I've just had a lot on my mind. Do you forgive me?"

His lips stray along my neck to the spot just above my collarbone. Oh Lord, that's my sensitive place and Ed knows it too. Never mind flowers and apologies; I can hardly think straight when it feels like someone's put Alka-Seltzer in my knickers.

"Of course I do," I say, or rather I think I say. It could be gibberish for all I know.

"I'm so sorry I sprung the whole partnership thing on you," he murmurs, breath warm against my ear. "I should have told you from the start, but I wanted it to be a surprise."

"It was certainly that," I agree.

"So can I make it up to you?"

The lips are straying lower now and his left hand sneaks under my ancient Little Miss Sunshine T-shirt and rests against my ribcage. I breathe in hard. All the nights alone watching *Sex and the City* and eating junk food haven't exactly given me the body of a goddess — unless it's Mrs Buddha. Note to self: use that Sanctuary pass soon.

"I think I can probably come up with a way you can apologise," I say.

"I can think of one too," agrees Ed, and just as my libido is dusting itself down and hunting out its Jimmy Choos, he steps away from me and strides back into the sitting room. Flinging himself on to the sofa, he proceeds to open my Mac and boots it up, while tapping the seat next to him as an indication for me to join him.

What is he up to? I hope he doesn't want me to watch a dodgy film or something. I can't say that will do it for me at all. Call me boring, but actually all I need to get me going is some good old-fashioned romance.

"Look at this, babes," says Ed as I curl up next to him. I brace myself and look at the screen and am relieved to see a website for a stunning hotel. For a few moments I watch as images of lush gardens, sunny terraces and lawns sloping down to an azure sea scroll by like scenes from a beautiful dream. Deep zebra-striped sofas piled with plump cushions frame a large fireplace, gauzy curtains drift dreamily at windows facing out to sea, and a stately old house clad in ivy and wisteria drowses in golden sunlight while contented couples take tea on the lawn.

All it needs is for Hugh Grant to waltz by and there you have it: the perfect setting for the latest Richard Curtis film.

"What do you think?" he asks, once we've been through the slide show for the third time. "Do you like it?"

"It's beautiful," I say.

"It is, isn't it? And guess where it is?"

Now, I don't have to be Stephen Hawking to work out where this is going.

"Look, Ed, I know it's Cornwall, and you're totally right, it's beautiful there and everything, but —"

He places his finger over my lips. Green powder drifts on to the designer sofa and he tries not to wince.

"I know I've been a bit heavy handed about the whole move thing and I'm sorry. Of course it's about what you want too. It's a huge decision and I want you to be as up for this as I am."

I close my eyes wearily. I think we can safely say that won't be the case.

"Which is why I've decided it's only fair that you get to have an informed opinion. So I've booked us a long weekend in Cornwall, staying at the Talland Bay Hotel!" he announces proudly. "We need time together, and where better to go and kick back than one of the most beautiful places in the south-west? We can have a good look around the area, maybe scout out some properties and I'll introduce you to some of the partners at the firm. What do you say?"

What do *I* say? Do I get a say at all?

"Come on, Amber. At least give it a chance. You can't turn something down that you haven't even considered."

Here we go. I'm going to give in, aren't I, because yet again I feel guilty. There's Ed arranging something lovely and mean old Amber being an ingrate. He's right, the hotel does look idyllic and it would be fantastic to spend some time away together. It's been ages since we did that. I'd have to be mad to turn it down.

The trouble is that I know once we're away he'll work on me non-stop until I'm so giddy from his arguments that I'll be moving to Fowey before I know it. Nobody can argue as well as Ed. It's the lawyer in him.

"Don't you want to go away with me?"

Aargh! There it is, the guilt card. I feel bad because of course I want to go away for a romantic weekend; I'd just prefer it if there wasn't an agenda.

"You know I do," I say.

"You still fancy me, then?"

What a question. I'm sure I do. I mean, of course I do! The thing is, we've been together ages, so being close to him is hardly going to make me feel as though I'm plugged into the mains, is it? And catching the scent of him doesn't make my senses reel and my pulse start to gallop. I'm not sure if it ever did, to be honest. Anyway, I don't suppose anybody ever really feels like that in real life. Writers just make it up for books. I'm nearly thirty and we've been together for years. I expect even Angelina gets a bit worn out with Brad. Of course I still fancy my fiancé. We just never have time to show it any more. If we do spend time together, I'm sure everything will be just fine.

To prove my point, I lean in for a kiss, but Ed recoils as though faced with an anaconda.

"You're covered in stuff!"

"My face pack!"

Shit! How long have I had this stuff on? Ten minutes is optimum cooking time, according to the package. It's supposed to be drawing out the impurities and toxins from my skin, which I've never really understood, because if I can't see them, is it really a problem that such things are lurking beneath the surface? Anyway, it was a freebie in the office so I was happy to test-drive it for the beauty editor, but leaving it on for over three times the recommended time probably wasn't a good idea.

This could work two ways. I'll either have beautiful glowing skin or a face that looks like the surface of Mars.

"I'll scrub it off!" I gasp.

"Don't take too long," says Ed, glancing suggestively down at the trouser-pocket remote control.

I scoot to the bathroom and scrub the face pack away. Luckily my skin is pink and glowing rather than baboon-bum red. OK, Amber, you're still a babe. Put Cornwall out of your mind and think of the flowers. Time to show your fiancé that you still care.

While the telly chatters away downstairs, I busy myself rubbing in body lotion, carefully filling in the chips in my toenail varnish and spritzing myself with Miss Dior. Then I unpeel the tissue paper from my new lingerie and truss myself up in the black and pink set. If I don't breathe for a few hours I should just about look OK. I twist and turn in front of the dressing table mirror, trying to figure out just how bad my cellulite really is and wondering whether I ought to nip back to the bathroom to slap on some Fake Bake. Then I remind myself that this is Ed I'm about to seduce, not some new flame who has no idea that I bite my nails and have a less than flat stomach. Ed knows all my flaws and still loves me.

And anyway, what man ever turned down a woman in black underwear and suspenders just because she had a little bit of cellulite?

I fluff up my hair, slick some gloss on my lips and totter down the stairs in my new fluffy mules. In the lamplight and without my contact lenses in, even I think I look pretty hot. Ed is in for a treat. Stand by for action!

I pause in the doorway of the sitting room and let my new silky robe slip from my shoulders. I saw that in a movie once and I've always wanted to try it.

But Ed doesn't stir. In the background CNN chatters away to itself, interrupted only by a low rumbling snore.

"Ed?" I step forward, and sure enough he's fast asleep, the remote control in one hand and the laptop balanced precariously on his knees. "Ed!" I prod him in the chest. "Babes? Wake up!"

But all I get in answer is another snore. Bitter experience tells me that I could prod him and holler until dawn but I may as well not bother. Once Ed's asleep, that's it. He makes Rip Van Winkle look like an insomniac.

I'm dressed up in my best seduction gear and my boyfriend is dead to the world. Such things do not bolster a girl's ego. This is *not* what's supposed to happen.

I perch on the arm of the sofa — easier said than done in a basque — and scoop up my Mac. As the computer purrs back into life, the screen lights up with a shot of the boutique hotel, a bedroom this time, all wrought-iron fairy-tale bedstead, piles of white pillows and soft plush carpets. The perfect boudoir setting for seducing even the most stressed and exhausted of fiancés. Maybe my new lingerie needs a little trip away.

I bookmark the page, pull a throw over Ed and trudge back upstairs on my own.

Suddenly a trip to Cornwall doesn't seem like such a bad thing after all . . .

CHAPTER
SIX

"Are you out of your fucking mind? Nobody in the history of magazine journalism has ever turned down a job working for Evangeline St Anthony! God only knows how she'll react!" Ali stares at me in total disbelief. Her gooseberry-green eyes are wide with shock and even her trendy Mohican cut looks outraged. I'm really not surprised. I'm pretty shocked myself.

"She was very nice, actually. She even offered to add another ten K to my salary package as an incentive."

"Fuck me. She must really want you on the team! I hope you accepted?" Ali fixes me with a Paddington Bear stare. "Please tell me all this moving to the arse-end of nowhere bollocks is just a really hard-core negotiation strategy and you haven't actually lost the plot?"

I minimise Rightmove on my Mac and drag myself away from cottages in Fowey and back into the office.

"This isn't an episode of *The Apprentice*, Ali, this is my life. Ed has the chance of a partnership in Cornwall and there's a whole new future waiting for us if we just take the plunge. It's really exciting!"

"Who are you and what have you done with my friend?" Ali mutters.

I ignore her. To be honest, if you'd told me a week ago that I'd land my dream job only to turn it down and move to a small seaside town, I'd have thought I was bonkers too. But that was before I actually visited Cornwall and enjoyed what has to be the most idyllic weekend of my life.

After two days spent wandering hand in hand through winding streets, eating seafood in harbourside restaurants and curling up in a bedroom straight out of one of my favourite pink books, I'm a convert to life west of the Tamar. Add to this the long-awaited and most welcome end of my sexual famine, salt-heavy air that knocked me out at bedtime and awakening each morning to the call of gulls circling above the glittering blue sea, it didn't take much more persuasion from Ed to get me to appreciate the positive aspects of relocating. As we walked along Polperro quay, munching on pasties after nipping into the pub for a half of potent scrumpy, the thought of returning to my daily tube hell was not a happy one. But there's more to my change of heart than salt-sharp air and romance. The artist in me was jumping for joy, because every corner I turned had a view that exceeded the one before, and the pure quality of the light made my breath catch in my throat. Suddenly my fingers itched to hold a paintbrush.

Never mind my sexual famine (which was bad enough, and hardly good for a girl's ego!); my creative famine has been a hundred times worse. Nobody has yet come up with the artistic equivalent of Ann Summers, and every day that passes without a chance to experiment with oils or a quick charcoal drawing in my sketchpad is a day that leaves me more frustrated. Working at *Blush!* has given me some creative outlet, but it's limited and governed by seasonal shades and generic conventions and is no match for setting off with a box of watercolours and just painting whatever captures the heart. Still, money has to be earned, and much as I love painting, I have no desire to starve in a garret, so work has had to take priority and my own stuff has been set aside for the odd weekend trip or week off from the office. I'd almost forgotten that strange tug of the heartstrings, the desperate urgency, need even, to take up a paintbrush and capture an image on creamy cartridge paper. In fact I'd even started to worry that I'd lost the ability to paint.

Until I visited Cornwall at the weekend . . .

From practically the moment our BMW crossed the Tamar Bridge, something stirred deep within me, waking up slowly and stretching and yawning as it came back to life. Whether it was the sparkling water, the way the canopied trees rose above the shady lanes like a cathedral ceiling to dapple the road with light that danced between leaves in incalculable hues of green, or just the lemon-sharp light everything was bathed in, I can't say, but it was as though something was switched on inside me. Almost unconsciously I fished a pencil from my bag and started sketching the glittering river and dancing boats on to the inside cover of an old road map (Ed has an innate and very male distrust of satnavs), and by the time we crunched up the gravel drive of our hotel, I was running out of space. I'd no idea just how much I'd missed my drawing or how scared I'd been that I'd lost my talent for ever. We ate our dinner outside on a terrace overlooking the bay, and I could hardly tear myself away from sketching to eat my mussels or sip the champagne that Ed had splashed out on. The next day we visited Fowey and I dived into an art shop to buy a sketchbook and some watercolours, and in between browsing estate agents and visiting Ed's new office, I painted like a girl demented.

The muse was back and it seemed that she lived in Cornwall. My heady sense of joy was only heightened when that evening Ed finally remembered that bed isn't just a place where you go to sleep. By the time we left on the Sunday evening I was tired and satisfied in every way a person can be, and when he put the big move question to me again, it was a no-brainer.

What on earth was I burning myself out in London for when I could be painting in Cornwall? How had I allowed myself to let my career distract me from my painting?

I loved my fiancé and wanted to make him happy. That was the main reason to move west. I wanted us to be together. Of course I did. There's more to life than promotions and status symbols. And if being with Ed in Fowey made us as happy in the long term as it did in one weekend, then what was there to lose? I didn't think I'd seen him so relaxed for ages. The little furrow between his brows eased away and even his BlackBerry was switched off, bar one or two urgent calls he had to make to the office. Honestly, who do his firm think they are, ringing him at the weekend? It's totally unfair. I was almost ready to call Eliza and tell her that her boss needed some down time, but Ed was adamant that the calls were urgent so I resisted. But I was annoyed on my fiancé's behalf. Moving to Cornwall and a slower pace of life could only be a good thing.

So, buoyed up with positivity and visions of our happy new life, I went to work early on Monday morning, phoned *Senora* to decline the job offer and then wrote my resignation letter to Ali.

Who has flipped.

"Try to be happy for me," I say. "It's a new chapter."

"New chapter? It's another novel altogether! Fuck me."

"Gordon Ramsay wants the F word back," I say idly. "Come on, Al, look at this from my point of view. I can be free to paint all day."

Ali shakes her head. "Paint what exactly? Yourself into a corner?"

I ignore this. "Ed and I have been together a long time."

She grimaces. "Being together a long time doesn't mean you have to stay with him."

Since Ali changes men more often than I change pants, I'm not going to take relationship advice from her, thanks all the same. Besides, the fact that Ed and I have been together for a long time is a very good reason to make things work. We've both invested so much time and emotion in our relationship and have years of shared memories to draw upon. Then there are all the little things we know about one another, like him always cleaning his teeth under a warm tap and my irrational phobia of buttons. We have shorthand for situations — a gesture or a raised eyebrow can speak volumes — and then there's the thorny issue of joint finances and property. These things are the reality of grown-up relationships, aren't they? Red-hot sex can only continue for so long.

Sadly.

"I want to stay with him," I tell her. "I love him."

Ali rolls her eyes. "Whatever you say, hon, whatever you say."

I do say. OK, so Ed has his moments, quite a few of them recently if truth be told, but I do love him. We may seem like an odd match to a lot of people, but generally we rub along comfortably.

"Comfortably!" Ali screeches when I put this opinion forward. "You need some serious therapy, girlfriend. You're about to change your entire life for a man you are just rubbing along *comfortably* with? FYI, he should be melting your knickers!"

The nearest I ever come to melting knickers is getting carried away when I'm ironing, but I'm not going to bore Ali with such domestic and mundane matters. She doesn't strike me as the kind of woman who gets excited over a new variety of Vaporesse aroma. Instead I just shrug and pretend to be engrossed in the next month's cover proofs while Ali mutters and huffs and puffs and fiddles with her cigarettes. I know she's desperate for a fag now, and unless she gets her fix she'll spontaneously combust, leaving her leopard-skin Louboutins smoking beside my desk.

"And you're fucking half an hour late!" she barks when Liz eventually arrives, her auburn curls all springy from the damp morning. Her latest hair offering, a big silk lily, droops sadly, and judging by the sodden look of it, the hem of her skirt has soaked up most of the rain from the piazza. She looks like Marie Lloyd left out in a monsoon. I often wonder how Liz copes on the tube. Dressing like an Edwardian theatre star must seriously hamper her movement around the capital.

"What's got into you?" Liz asks mildly, drifting to her desk in a cloud of very peculiar scent, possible Eau de Mothballs from her latest vintage outfit. Booting up her Mac and peeling off her lacy gloves she says to me, "How was your weekend, Amber?"

Lord, news travels fast in this office. I can't remember telling Liz I was going away. The bush telegraph works so effectively I sometimes wonder why I ever bother paying Orange so much money.

"It was lovely, thanks," I say.

"It was more than fucking *lovely*," snarls Ali. "Amber's only decided to move to Cornwall with that tosser fiancé of hers."

I don't take this personally. Ali thinks that all men are tossers and says that until proven wrong she'll continue to hold this point of view, which I guess is fair enough seeing as most of the guys she meets *are* tossers.

But Liz drains of colour beneath her layer of pale foundation and her hand flies to her small red mouth.

"What!" she gasps. "You can't! You can't move away!"

I'm touched that she looks so upset. We've worked together for a long time, and although we haven't been close — especially since her mystery life really took off — it's nice that she wants me to stay.

"Oh, I think you'll find she can," says Ali, tapping a Benson's out of the packet and rolling it longingly between her fingers. "Ed has a new job in Fowey and he wants Amber to go with him. Selfish fucker. Just when she'd got the job at *Senora* too."

"Ed's got a new job?" Liz couldn't look more taken aback if Ali had told her that he was off to lead the first manned expedition to Mars.

I nod. "He's going to be a partner at a legal practice in Fowey."

Liz stares at me. "Since when?"

"What does it matter since when?" Ali barks. "Who gives a shit about Ed? He's just spent the weekend bonking Amber's brains out in some luxury hotel so that she'll go with him."

"I still have some brains left after all the bonking," I say mildly. "I think I can probably decide what I do and don't want to do. And I want to go with him. That's my decision."

"So there you go." Shaking her head, Ali turns to Liz in despair. "Amber and Ed are off to the land of Rick Stein. Never to be seen again."

But Liz has leapt up from her desk and is scuttling out of the office. "I don't feel too well," she gasps. "Excuse me."

Ali and I watch her go, weaving between the desks as she dashes to the loo. At one point the toe of her clompy boot catches a chair and she nearly goes flying, but she's so busy rummaging through her bag for her mobile that she hardly notices.

"That girl is odd," Ali says.

"It is a bit of an overreaction," I agree. As Liz turns and passes the tinted-glass office window, she's speaking frantically into her mobile and her chin is tucked so far into her chest that her nose is almost flush with her breastbone. Every fibre of her slender frame shrieks of agitation.

"I didn't know you and Liz were that close," Ali continues thoughtfully.

"We're not." I'm puzzled. I mean, I like Liz well enough and we've been colleagues for years now, but I wouldn't say we were close. She's not the kind of woman who invites female confidences or who has natural warmth that draws you in. She once mentioned that she didn't like dogs, finding them too needy, and her small pointy nose wrinkled disdainfully when I offered to lend her some of my chick-lit books — apparently she only reads proper literature! These two comments alone suggested to me that we were never destined to be BFFs, so her distress now is kind of odd.

To my mind, Liz's mask of perfectly applied Elizabeth Tudor-style pale make-up is a metaphor for her masked personality. We may work closely on a day-to-day basis, and on one occasion I invited her back to our place for dinner, but that's about as far as our friendship goes. In fact I seem to recall that the dinner party was a total disaster, chiefly because she and Ed seemed to hate each other on sight. They've met a few times since and can hardly bear to speak to one another, which is one of the main reasons I haven't really gone out of my way to include her in any other gatherings. The last thing I need after a hard week at work is Ed in (even more of) a bad mood.

Ali's brow crinkles thoughtfully. "Then it's back to my lesbian theory. Maybe she's secretly in love with you."

I swat my friend on the arm. "I hardly think so. I know this may seem rather dull, but perhaps she's worried about the team dynamic breaking up and her job security. Especially in the current climate, with magazines closing left, right and centre. What's to stop the company merging the art department with the creatives?"

"The fact that *Blush!* pisses all over everyone else's sales figures?"

"There is that." I shake my head. "Maybe she's just having a bad day."

"God only knows, but I will be if I don't have a fucking fag soon," says Ali. "Listen, Ambs, I don't want to try to tell you what to do or anything, but —"

"You'll have a try anyway?"

She laughs and holds up her hands. "OK! Guilty as charged! All I'm trying to say is don't rush into anything without really thinking it through. I know you love Ed and want to support him, but what about the things that are important to you? I know you're mad

90

keen to go off and paint pictures, bake bread and pop out sprogs —"

"Whoa! Whoa!" I say. "Who mentioned sprogs?"

"They're normally next on the list," she warns me. "And that's all cool if it's what you want, but make sure that you're not being railroaded into something you're not one hundred per cent certain about. Besides," she adds, as she picks up her jacket and heads to the door en route to her urgent meeting with Benson and Hedges, "Liz isn't the only one who'll be gutted you're going."

I'm stunned. Ali never, ever shows she cares, let alone says it. Her staple response to any touch-feely stuff is normally something along the lines of *bollocks to emotional fuckwittery*, so for her to actually say she'll miss me is unprecedented. While the staff of *Blush!* carry on around me, I gaze at the screen saver on my Mac as though hypnotised by the zooming stars. My throat feels all tight and funny and my eyes are prickling with the threat of tears, because I don't know if I'll ever find friends or colleagues like these again. What if my gut instinct was right all along? What if I really should stay in London, focus on my career and refuse to go? But then what about Ed? What would happen to us if I decided not to support him in the biggest move of his life? Would we ever be able to overcome it?

I place my head in my hands. The answer is as clear as the whirling stars on my screen: if I refuse to go then I am effectively calling time on our relationship. I'm ending it just as clearly as I would if I found someone else or simply decided we were over. Best-case scenario is that maybe we could see each other at weekends and holidays, but how long could you realistically keep up a 500-mile round commute before one of you decided it was too much? Something has to give, and unless I want it to be my relationship with Ed, I know what I have to do.

So he isn't perfect? Sometimes he's dead grumpy and yes, he watches far too much rolling news, but he's still my Ed, the shy middle-class nineteen-year-old who nearly died of terror when I took him hunt-sabbing and who won my heart when he nursed me through a really nasty encounter with homebrew. He might be older and greyer and not laugh so much as he used to, but I bet he can still recite all of Austin Powers with the sound on mute. He's still him and I guess the point is that I think we still have a pretty good chance of making it. I don't want to sacrifice my personal life for my professional one. I don't want to wake up in twenty years' time loaded and successful and single . . . and full of regrets. I don't want to end up like my parents.

Welcome to your thirties, Amber!

I feel like bashing my head against my Mac. I bet there isn't a man on the planet who's ever had to make this choice. Why can't I be like Ed and have it all? Why do women always have to compromise? Because I know that's exactly what I'm doing. Compromising. Yes, Cornwall's stunning, yes, I'll have a lovely house, and yes, I know I'll be able to paint to my heart's content, but the flip side of this is that I'll be leaving behind my friends, my career and my home. It's a big gamble, and the question I have to ask myself is whether or not Ed's worth it.

The fact that I'm asking this question at all fills me with unease, so I wiggle the mouse to wake my computer and maximise Rightmove. Seconds later I'm back in Fowey browsing property and burying any doubts underneath images of converted barns and ancient cottages. I need to be a bit more positive, that's all. This move is going to be amazing, the start of a whole new and wonderful life. I won't let Ali's cynicism or Liz's upset sway me. I'm nearly thirty and it's time for a change.

I think it's time to start over.

CHAPTER
SEVEN

"For God's sake, Amber! I said left! You've just turned right!"

Ed couldn't be more exasperated with me if he tried. So far today I've gone the wrong way down a one-way street, nearly wedged us tightly in a lane of Lilliputian proportions and then, just to really make Ed's day, scratched the brand-new Range Rover Sport when I pulled in far too close to a dry-stone wall. Now my usual left/right confusion has kicked in, and if I take my hands off the steering wheel one more time in order to see which one makes an L shape, I think he'll beat me to death with the map. Shaky with nerves, I grind the gears and watch him wince as I try to execute a three-point turn.

"I'm sorry," I gasp, desperately trying to use my mirrors to judge the distance between the rear bumper and a very solid-looking metal gate while the parking sensor beeps like crazy and puts me off even more. Why we need a car the size of a small bus totally evades me. We're moving to the country, not transporting a football team, for heaven's sake.

94

"Christ!" Ed buries his face in his hands as the bonnet misses a bank by several millimetres. "Stop the car right now. I'll drive."

"You will not," I say, craning my neck and trying again. In my experience, if you sit in the passenger seat, you soon forget how to drive, both literally and metaphorically. "If we're living here, I need to get used to driving on narrow lanes."

"Not in sixty grand's worth of brand-new car you don't! Jesus! Watch the bonnet! I'll buy you a banger for pootling round in."

Banger? Pootling around? We haven't even moved to Cornwall yet and already my fiancé is condemning me to life in a battered Nissan Micra. I feel most offended. In my natural environment, aka the M25, I am a shit-hot driver, up there with Schumacher and Hamilton. Show me four lanes of traffic and a bit of road rage and I'll show you a happy woman. It's all this faffing about for sheep and having to reverse miles for grumpy farmers on decrepit tractors that does my head in.

"This is your fault for refusing to use the satnav," I point out as I finally manage to manoeuvre the monster-sized new car so that we're facing the right way.

"If you can't tell left from right, I fail to see what difference that would make." Ed folds his arms and glowers at me.

"I could have looked at the picture on the screen and figured it out." It's very distracting driving such a mammoth car. I keep finding myself gazing over the hedges and wondering which colours I'd use to paint the ever-changing sea, which probably isn't a good idea when you need to keep your eyes on the road. Every time I get a weeny bit near to the hedges, Ed pulls his knees in dramatically and takes a sharp breath. I glance down at the cockpit-style dashboard in the vain hope that Land Rover might have added an ejector-seat function, but no such luck. It looks like I'm stuck with my irritable back-seat driver.

"Aren't the views lovely?" I trill, Joyce Grenfell style, as we bowl along the road that hugs the clifftops. Sometimes I find myself having to talk Ed out of a bad mood a bit like you would a toddler, and believe me, it's blooming hard work. No one ever bothers to talk *me* out of a bad mood — not that I'm ever given the opportunity to get into one. I sometimes feel that I'm far too low-maintenance and therefore undervalued as a result. Ali told me how she once had bad period pains that could only be cured by her then man toddling off to buy her a Mulberry bag. I was dead impressed, because Ed can barely be arsed to leave the sofa to fetch me a Nurofen, and made a mental note to become far more demanding. Maybe in my next life I'll come back as a glamorous stick-insect type who calls the shots rather than a small wimp with squidgy bits.

By way of reply Ed just grunts at me, so I ignore him and do my best not to notice the stunning coastal scenes and focus on the road, which I find tends to help when I'm driving. I do wish he wasn't in such a bad mood. We're house-hunting today and it should be a nice thing to do, searching together for our forever home, but all he can do is be sarky and picky.

When he isn't glued to his iPhone, that is.

"I can't live here, there's no bloody signal," he huffs, slamming his mobile on to the dashboard in disgust.

"Probably the wrong network, that's all. You can find out which one covers this area," I say soothingly. "Anyway, it's Saturday afternoon, who do you need to be in touch with now?"

"The office, of course." Ed runs an impatient hand through his thinning sandy hair and it stands up in clumps, making him look like a peed-off Easter chick. "Not that it's any of your business."

Charming, eh? I'm only his fiancée. But this is Ed in a stress for you. Everyone else has to suffer. Just because he hasn't liked any of the four houses we've already viewed, he's going to have a strop. Personally, I liked them all, especially the cottage on the cliffside in Polperro, but Ed thought it was too small and not nearly imposing enough for someone who's a partner in a law firm, so off we go again to visit property number five.

Or rather we will if I ever manage to get us there.

We cruise along in silence for a while. Green hedges blur past, blushed with campion and freckled with primroses. Every now and again a sliver of sea glistens on the horizon and I find myself consumed by a childlike urge to race to the beach, kick off my shoes and tear down to the water. Coming from London, I don't think I'll ever get over the novelty of having the beach on my doorstep. Maybe once Ed's less stressed he and I can spend some time exploring all the little coves. We could even take up sailing. That would be fun!

Apart from the small problem that I get seasick in the bath . . .

"Do I keep going?" I ask a few minutes later when the road decides to peter out and become little more than a set of tyre tracks with a mound of grass dividing them. I'd switch to four-wheel drive if I had a clue how.

Ed consults the estate agent's details. "This seems to be it. Polmerryn is the village off to the left — that's the side I'm sitting — and Polmerryn Manor is that big house you can see across the valley to your side."

I slow the car and follow his pointing finger. Sure enough a massive medieval-looking stone house dominates the hillside opposite us, overlooking patchwork fields stitched together with emerald hedges which tumble down to the sea.

"Wish that was for sale," says Ed.

"So you can buy it with your EuroMillions win?" I ask glibly, but when his expression darkens I know I've put my size four in it yet again.

"I can achieve that kind of wealth one day," he snaps, snatching up his phone and scowling at its empty screen. "Some people believe in me even if you don't."

"I do believe in you," I protest, but Ed ignores me. I crane my neck to try and see the map — Hawkstone House is where we're headed — and I'm so busy doing this that I nearly take out the lone walker who is pressed into the hedge at the side of the road. He leaps back and I miss his feet by inches, which is bad enough, but what's worse is that I also zoom straight through a puddle and shower him with filthy water. Before I can even register what has happened and stop to apologise, we've passed him, and the last thing I see is his face glowering at me in the rear-view mirror as he shakes the remnants of his impromptu shower from his hair.

Oh my God. He is absolutely gorgeous. Think Mr Darcy emerging from the lake, only muddier and sexier, and there you have it. Just my luck to nearly squash him and then drench him.

Oh, and to be engaged and off the market . . .

"Amber, you are a fucking liability!" snarls Ed.

"Shall I stop and go back to apologise?" I'm mortified. I don't even live here and already I'm upsetting the locals. Blooming emmets, as they say in these parts.

"Don't you dare, we're late as it is!" Sensing that I'm about to stop, Ed leans over and yanks at the wheel. "It's only some farmer. I'm sure he's used to a bit of mud."

"That wasn't a bit, Ed, that was a lot," I protest, but Ed isn't having it and in spite of my better judgement I cave in. Sometimes I really hate my tendency to settle for an easy life, but Ed can't bear being late and I really don't want to risk him getting even crosser, even if every cell in my body is telling me to turn back and offer the poor man a rub-down with the tartan car blanket. I need to get some therapy, I think. It can't be normal to be this much of a sap.

"Left! Now!" Ed barks, grabbing the wheel and turning it. By the skin of my teeth, and no thanks to his back-seat driving, I manage to guide the Range Rover through a pair of granite pillars and along a weed-strewn driveway that sweeps in a graceful semicircle before a large white house slumbering in the afternoon sunshine. A large slate propped up against a lichen-smothered stone mushroom reads *Hawkstone House*, and as I kill the engine I breathe a sigh of relief to have made it this far.

M25, you will never know just how much I miss you.

"Mr White?" As we clamber out of the car — it's so high up for short-arse me that I feel like writing to Land Rover and demanding they incorporate some kind of parachute device into future models — a rotund man with a florid face and a Super Mario Brothers moustache comes scuttling over. "I'm Bob Bishop, the estate agent. Of Bishop's Property."

Bad mood instantly banished, Ed is soon pumping Bishop's hand and making small talk. Housing market. Property slump. Interest rates, yada yada. Nobody's very interested in insignificant old me, so as they do the male bonding ritual I raise my face to the sun's warm kiss and look around me. Wow! This place is huge! Way too big for just the two of us. It must have at least five bedrooms, and what on earth are all these out-buildings for? There's no way we need half of this space. I think longingly of the little cottage in Polperro, with its low beams, cosy ceiling and harbourside view just crying out to be painted. I'd feel cosy and safe there, but this rambling sixteenth-century farmhouse terrifies me. There's no way I can live in a house this big.

As my heart sinks into my new Joules wellies, I glance across at my fiancé, but just one look at Ed's face tells me he feels exactly the opposite. All traces of bad temper have been smoothed away and now he's smiling broadly from ear to ear. While Bob Bishop drones on about investment property, holiday letting potential and the importance of purchasing the six acres of land that come with the property, I feel my stomach lurch. What on earth will I do with six acres? I can scarcely handle my window boxes!

"Money's not a problem, we've made a sizeable return on our London investment," Ed boasts as we troop into a lofty flagstoned hall and pause to admire the vast inglenook. I feel myself bristling. That investment, as he so bluntly puts it, just happens to be my *home*. I've poured love and care into every waxed floorboard and agonised over the exact shade of Farrow and Ball paint for each room. Then there are the hours I spent trawling around markets to find the perfect lamp or rug and the excitement that comes with seeing a room take shape in reality to match the vision you've had. Our house isn't an investment to me. It's something I've loved. I've hated showing potential viewers around; it feels like I'm selling a friend. Nonsense I know, but I can't help the way I feel.

I trail after Ed and the estate agent as they tour Hawkstone House. After a while I start to lose count of how many rooms we've tramped through. Boot room, utility room, enormous kitchen, even more enormous sitting room, snug, study, five big bedrooms. Dear Lord, we don't have enough furniture to fill half of this place. I'm pretty certain you could fit the entire floorplan of our London house into the kitchen and still have room left over. What on earth is Ed thinking?

"And this door leads from the dining room back into the kitchen," Bob Bishop says as proudly as though he personally built the house. "Which makes entertaining even easier."

Ed is nodding as though we entertain on a weekly basis, rather than merely brewing suspicious-looking tea for Mum and Rain or unpacking a Chinese whenever Ali and her plus-one turn up. I glance around the dining room, complete with refectory table, eight gothic-looking chairs and dark crimson walls, and feel as though I'm descending very fast in a lift. Who on earth am I supposed to be entertaining? And with what, exactly? The last time I looked, Marks and Spencer weren't big on ready-meals for Agas.

"It's perfect!" Ed says excitedly, striding back into the kitchen and gazing out into the garden. His face, which earlier was longer than a James Cameron movie, is now wreathed in smiles. "This is exactly what we've been looking for, isn't it, Amber?"

Oh. My. God. Can it really be true that my fiancé, the man I have loved and lived with since university, really knows so little about me? Does he actually think that I aspire to huge houses, expensive cars and a life entertaining his partners and clients? Has he ever listened to a word I've said?

I open my mouth to say that actually, no, this house is the antithesis of what I was hoping for, but it seems that Ed is now possessed of amazing ventriloquism skills, because suddenly I can hear his voice rather than my own.

"We love it, Bob. What can I say? This ticks all the boxes."

"I knew it would." Bishop beams so broadly that I almost reach for my shades. "Now, the owners are keen to sell and there is some room for negotiation on the price, so I'm pretty sure we can come to a deal."

"We're cash buyers," Ed boasts. "Our London place sold very fast."

"Wait a second," I pipe up. "Shouldn't we talk about this a bit? Like maybe discuss it?"

My fiancé looks at me, an all-too-familiar expression of annoyance settling across his face. He looks at me like this when I make a mess in the kitchen or lose the car keys. But this is buying a house, our future home! I think I should have some kind of say.

"What's to talk about? This is exactly what we want!"

Hang about! Who's this *we*, exactly? Time to put in my twopenn'orth, I think, or I'll be living here before you can say "overruled".

"It's a massive house," I venture. "Do we really need so many rooms? And what about the location? You'd have an hour's commute to work. It's miles from Fowey." And in the middle of nowhere, I add silently. I know we're here for a new and quieter life, but I'd rather hoped to be in the town or at the very least a village. I want to get to know people and make friends, not rattle around on my own all day long. I glance out of the kitchen window and across the valley. There's not a house in sight, only the big medieval pile I spotted earlier on from the car. The neighbours there probably make the Addams Family look normal. What will I do here alone all day? I'll go nuts and start talking to the wall like Shirley Valentine. Although judging by the amount of conversation I've had with Ed today, the wall may well be a chattier and less moody option . . .

"Everyone commutes miles in these parts, my love," says Bob Bishop jovially, but his cheerful tone doesn't fool me. I can see the steely glint in his eye. There's no way he's about to let a nice fat dollop of commission fall by the wayside.

"A quiet drive through country lanes is nothing compared to being crammed on the tube," agrees Ed. "I'd enjoy the journey to work, and anyway, Amber, it's not as though it's an issue for you. You'll be working from home. One of the outhouses could easily be converted into a studio for you. How about that? Your very own studio. Just like you've always wanted."

Talk about bribery and corruption. Sorry, Ed, but it ain't gonna work.

"It's a bit isolated here," I say tactfully. "I think I'd rather be in Fowey."

"Nonsense!" Bob Bishop roars, clapping me on the back with a meaty paw and nearly knocking me into the enormous sink. "The place is crawling with emmets in the summer and bloody dead in the winter. Here, Polmerryn's only a mile or so away and the shop and post office are open all year round. And the pub, of course!"

I feel my temper start to fizz. "I want neighbours, not a pub!"

He gives me another huge false smile. His teeth are the exact hue of old piano keys and it's all I can do not to recoil. "Polmerryn Manor is just across the valley, see that big old house there? You'd be neighbours with the Verney family. They've lived here since the thirteenth century, I believe, and are very well respected. There's only Lord Verney and his elderly mother there now, but I'm sure they'd be excellent company."

I glance across the valley to the ancient house, mullioned windows glittering in the sunshine like a million prying eyes, and try to imagine myself hanging out with a decrepit tweedy gent and his even more decrepit mother.

Nope. I'm not feeling it.

"They sound perfect! Just the kind of neighbours we want." Ed smiles at me, probably already picturing himself in plus fours and a Barbour, dragging a hapless Labrador towards his Defender. "That's great then, isn't it, Ambs? We'll really enjoy getting to know them. And the seclusion is excellent. Just what we need after life in the city."

I stare at my fiancé in disbelief. This is like *Invasion of the Body Snatchers*. Am I really talking to the man who gets twitchy if he's more than three minutes away from Costa or Waitrose?

"What about all the land, though? There's far too much for us, isn't there?" I know I'm clutching at straws now, but I can see the way this is going, and believe me, if you thought you were about to be marooned in a green wilderness with just a post office and a few pints of cider to relieve the boredom, then you'd be clutching at straws too.

"Land's only going to increase in value; they don't make it any more! Ha ha!" says bloody Bob Bishop.

"We'll get a ride-on lawnmower to keep the grass down," adds Ed. "You'd enjoy driving that, Amber, you couldn't do too much damage. And maybe you could have a horse."

"I get hay fever and I don't ride," I say through gritted teeth.

"How about we lease it out, then?" Ed says thoughtfully. "Or maybe you could grow vegetables."

I feel like bashing my brains out on the butler's sink. Did I turn into Charlie Dimmock and not notice? Grow vegetables? What for? Everyone knows vegetables come washed and prepped from Waitrose!

"Listen, I'll leave you folks to talk," says Bob Bishop, who can see that I'm about to explode. "You've got my number, Ed, so give us a call if you want to make an offer." He pauses, a well-timed pause designed to plant fear into the mind of a far too obviously keen buyer, aka my fiancé. "Just don't take too long, will you? Properties like this don't come on to the market very often. There's been a lot of interest and I've got another two viewings lined up."

He bids us farewell, and minutes later the throaty roar of his Jag can be heard zooming up the road. Then there's absolute quiet and all is still. Dust motes dance and spin in the shard of buttery sunshine streaming through the window and warming the worn stone floor.

My heart's skittering in time with their every movement, because I know what's coming next.

Ed shuts the door and crosses the kitchen. Then he wraps his arms round me and pulls me tightly against his chest.

"This is it, Ambs," he breathes into the top of my head. "This is our house. This is where we're going to start our new life together, I just know it."

I gulp. How has it come to this, that we are suddenly poles apart? This house, big and beautiful though it is, feels far too grown-up for me. I want somewhere smaller and cosier, somewhere I can make mine and where I can curl up to sketch or read a book. This house fits another life — the life that my fiancé wants to lead.

The problem is, now that it's all happening, I'm not entirely convinced it's a life I am ready for.

CHAPTER
EIGHT

"So, even though we all think she's out of her fucking mind to go and she's leaving us in the lurch, please raise your glasses and join me in wishing Amber the very best of luck in Cornwall." Ali brandishes her champagne flute at me as though she'd like to beat me round the head with it, and actually that's probably not too far from the truth. "To Amber!"

"To Amber!" chorus my friends and colleagues, holding up their own glasses. In the dim light of the Covent Garden Cocktail Club the flutes glitter like diamonds, although that could just be from the tears swimming in my eyes. I'm digging my nails into my hand so as to distract myself from crying with a hefty dose of pain, but this strategy isn't really working, because every now and again a big fat tear plops down my cheek and splashes on to the floor.

"Where's Ed?" asks Ali, sloshing more champagne into my glass. "He might at least have made your leaving party. Seeing as it's all his fault you've got to go."

"He sent a text saying he's delayed at work," I explain. "He'll be here as soon as he can."

She shakes her spiky head. "Not fucking good enough. In fact, piss-poor. You need all the support you can get today. Look at the state of you."

Attending my own leaving party has to be one of the most difficult things I've ever had to do. Keeping myself together while I say goodbye to everyone is easier said than done, and although I am excited about starting my new life in the country, I know I'm going to miss the old one horribly. I've spent most of my days with this bunch of people, closeted together for hours to perfect a front cover or find the sharpest angle to pitch an article. They've shared the highs when we've won awards and broken circulation records, as well as the lows of missing out on landing a new advertising account or losing a much-valued colleague to a rival publication. Unlike Ed, these guys appreciate that there's a lot more to creating a successful magazine than glittery covers and giveaways, and I'll miss them and the daily challenges more than I can ever say.

Still, I don't think I've scrubbed up too badly. My new Miu Miu trousers and funky green gypsy top look great teamed with my best red platforms.

"I look OK, don't I?" I ask, trying to catch my reflection in the glossy surface of the bar.

"I mean your emotional state!" Ali rolls her eyes. "You always look great, you dozy cow! If I had your boobs I'd walk around in a bikini even in the winter!"

I slosh her on the arm. "I'll miss you, Ali."

"Don't be bloody soft," she says, but her eyes are very bright and she looks away. "Anyway, I'll be down

109

to see you at some stage. I need to have a look at this mansion you've bought."

I laugh. "Hawkstone House is hardly a mansion, Al! It's just an old Cornish farmhouse. There's nothing glam about it, I promise. There's no infinity pool or gym, and the only means of cooking seems to be on a wood-fuelled Aga."

"It's hardly the waterside cottage you were dreaming of," Ali says, rather sharply.

OK, she's right. I didn't want Hawkstone House particularly. I had set my heart on a small cottage somewhere by the sea, a place I could fill with colour and big splashy pictures and where I could wake up to the sound of the gulls in the morning, but Ed had his heart set on the place and I didn't have the stomach for a fight.

After Bob Bishop had driven off, we'd looked around the house again and Ed's enthusiasm had been quite sweet. It was so long since I'd seen him get excited about anything that I didn't have the heart to be negative, and besides, maybe he was right. This house was a good investment; we could do up some of the outbuildings as holiday homes, and owning land meant that I could have some animals. As he'd talked animatedly I'd allowed myself to be drawn into his rose-tinted dreams and put aside the images of icy-cold mornings, long dark nights and sitting on my own twiddling my thumbs while Ed was at work. I had to think positive. Once I had the attic done up as a studio, I'd be far too busy with my painting to spare a minute thinking about London life. Everything was going to be great. Of course it was.

As for my emotional state, it does tend to veer between excitement and total panic, which I'm sure is absolutely normal for anyone in the midst of making enormous and life-changing decisions. I wouldn't be human if I didn't feel some trepidation.

"It's fine," I insist, draining my champagne glass and looking around for the next one. If in doubt, find alcohol has always been my motto. "I'm looking forward to moving in. And by the time you come and visit, the house will be perfect. You'll love it in the countryside."

Ali looks doubtful. "I fucking hate the countryside. Not a decent espresso in sight and too much mud for my liking, but because I love you, I'll make the sacrifice." A waiter passes with a tray of drinks and she takes two more, passing one to me while raising hers. "A new life in the country! Christ! Glad it's not me!"

We clink glasses and I can't help laughing. Yep, try as I might, I can't see Ali grappling with the temperamental Aga, and the pitted drive that leads to Hawkstone House would play havoc with the suspension of her Lotus. Even the new Range Rover is starting to complain.

"Speech! Speech!" demands somebody, and almost instantly there are stamping feet and clapping hands. I look at Ali in alarm. I hate public speaking at the best of times, and this hardly qualifies as such by any stretch of the imagination. My nose is tingly with tears and Gavin Henson must have trundled past and parked a rugby ball in my throat. There's no way I can possibly speak.

"Go on," hisses Ali, placing her hand in the small of my back. "Say something!"

I look around for Ed, but there's still no sign of him. He must be really held up at the office. It's actually a good thing he's leaving, because his firm work him far too hard and make totally unreasonable demands. No wonder he's been so tetchy; all the late nights and early-morning meetings are bound to have caught up with him. Hopefully once we're in Cornwall the slower pace of life will chill him out a bit.

With legs that feel like boiled string and a racing heart, I allow Ali to propel me to the front of the bar while my colleagues clap and cheer loudly. The party is in full swing and I don't blame them for making the most of it. Any excuse for a couple of hours off and a few free drinks! As I thank them and tell them how much I will miss them, I look at all the familiar faces and myriad memories gallop through my mind's eye. This is my team, a team that Ali and I have helped to build over the past few years, and we've really pulled together to create a successful magazine. I know them all so well. As I speak, I mention each person by name, from the office junior to Ali, recalling anecdotes and thanking each one for all their hard work. There's only one gap, and that's Liz, who was too upset to stay and say goodbye.

"I'm so sorry," she said, wiping her eyes with her sleeve after hugging me. "I'm just no use at farewells."

I hugged her back. Beneath today's purple velvet dress she felt rail thin, and I was alarmed. For the past few weeks Liz has looked increasingly strained and unhappy, texting like crazy on her mobile phone and repeatedly checking the screen for replies even though the text alert hasn't sounded. She even took a few days off sick, which was very unusual, and on her return stared miserably at her Mac and was, in Ali's succinct words, "worse than fucking useless". She was obviously having a tough time. Maybe the mystery lover wasn't playing ball.

"It's only Cornwall," I pointed out, touched by her obvious sadness. "You can come and visit me. I don't know what's going on with you — and I'm not going to pry — but you look like you could do with a break."

Liz looked down at the toes of her scuffed pink DMs. "It's complicated."

From the way her teeth worried at her small bottom lip, I could see that she wasn't exaggerating.

"And I'll miss working with you," she added. "We've come a long way since you first started at *Blush!*."

"Look on the bright side — now I've finally left, you've got the promotion you deserve," I said. "And it's high time too. You're so creative, Liz. I know you'll do an amazing job."

Liz looked awkward. Some people just can't bear to be praised, I guess. Soon after this she slipped away, and since then I've been thrown head first into the craziness of my leaving do. It's a shame she didn't feel she could stay, but everyone handles emotions differently. Ali gets even brasher, Ed works twice as

113

hard, and as for me — well, I just get pissed. I may as well make the most of the free-flowing champagne while I can — I can't imagine there'll be too much of that swilling around Polmerryn. I'll probably have to develop a cider habit, which I suppose is something to look forward to!

"Well done," Ali says once my ordeal is over. Handing me yet another glass of champagne, she adds, "Now brace yourself, I have a leaving present for you."

"Not another one! You've already done quite enough!" Seriously, this is getting embarrassing. I've been presented with easels, watercolours, tokens for art shops and from Ali the most exquisite Roy Connelly oil painting, that I'd admired for ages.

"Don't panic, this one is purely selfish," grins Ali. "On the altruistic side, it keeps your hand in in the world of journalism, gives you an excuse to nip up to London and earns you a few pennies as well."

"Right," I say slowly. "All sounding great so far, if slightly enigmatic. What exactly do I have to do, and more importantly, what's in it for you?"

"You have an excuse to come up to town and see me if you need to escape from the sticks, and it also wins me a few Brownie points with Mike Elton, which could come in very handy."

My eyebrows shoot into my fringe. Mike Elton is the notoriously spiky owner of the Liv Group, the multinational media conglomerate that owns *Blush!*, *Ladz!* and Britain's top tabloid, the *Dagger*. "What could I possibly do to win you Brownie points with him? You do know that phone hacking is illegal, don't you?"

She laughs. "Don't look so worried, Lois Lane! I'm not about to send you off on some investigative mission. With your sense of direction that would be a disaster. No, it's actually very simple. The women's section of the Sunday magazine needs a columnist, someone to give Liz Jones at the *Mail* a run for her money. I pitched your new life in pasty land to him the other day, and he loved it."

I stare at her. "I'm not a writer, Ali. I'm a creative."

"Come on, Amber! How hard can it be to knock out a thousand words a week about life in the country, recession-style? It's a piece of piss." Her eyes narrow. "Besides, I've promised Mike. I can't let him down."

I can imagine exactly what she's promised Mike and where their negotiations took place. "I'm not sure I'll have a lot to say."

"Then make it up!" says Ali, as though I'm stupid. "Christ, you don't think columnists tell the truth, do you?"

Call me naïve, but this is *exactly* what I've always thought.

"The pitch is '*Good Life* meets *Desperate Housewives* meets *Countryfile*'," Ali continues, swiping another glass of champagne as the waiter passes by while I shake my head in disbelief. "Throw in some recession chic, a bit about your bonkers New Age mum and some hunky farmers, and we're in business. You'll piss all over the *Mail*."

"And give me one good reason why I should do this — apart from keeping you in Mike Elton's good books," I say. "Although I am wondering why you want to be there quite so badly."

Ali takes a sip of her drink, then leans forward and whispers, "Let's just say you're not the only one who's moving on, babes. There's going to be a new editor of the *Sunday Dagger* women's section, and guess who that's going to be?"

My eyes widen. Since the *News of the World*'s demise, the *Sunday Dagger* is Britain's biggest Sunday paper, and the women's supplement has a circulation of millions. The format is desperately in need of a refresh, though, and who better to do it than Ali. She'll be brilliant.

"That's fantastic! Go, you!" I throw my arms around Ali and hug her tightly.

"It is, isn't it?" she beams. "God, I nearly exploded keeping that one quiet. Tell you what, though, if you weren't sodding off to the arse-end of nowhere, I'd poach you from *Senora* in a heartbeat. Wouldn't we make a dream team?"

For a second I'm almost floored with regret. The idea of working with Ali to revamp a women's supplement is so tempting that I'm almost surprised a snake doesn't mosey on by and offer me a bite of a Granny Smith. Then I remember that I'm going to have an amazing new life painting in Cornwall and spending quality time with Ed. Nowhere in that equation does working for the *Dagger* figure. I'm moving on to a new and, I'm sure, very happy stage of my life.

116

"Tempted?" asks Mephistopheles, aka my best friend.

I nod. "Of course I am, it would be amazing. If we weren't moving away, I'd turn *Senora* down in a heartbeat to come and work for you."

"Then do the next best thing: be my new columnist," says Ali swiftly. "At least that way we'll still be working together and you'll be helping me out. Come on, Amber! What do you say? You're not going to let me down when I need you most, are you? My entire career rests on finding a good columnist with something original to say!"

God, but Ali's good! Like a panther, she's spotted my weak point and leapt straight in for the kill. No wonder Mike Elton wants her on the team.

"I don't know," I say, shaking my head. "I'm not sure Ed would like the idea of me writing about our private lives."

"So change your names!" says Ali airily. "Liz Jones does. We may all know who her rock star is, but she never names him directly. And no disrespect to your Ed, but he's hardly Jon Bon Jovi, is he?"

"I'm not sure," I say hesitantly. "It isn't really my kind of thing."

"Well, maybe the salary will change your mind." Ali grins and then mentions the kind of money that I usually need oxygen to contemplate because it has a minus at the front and is called my overdraft.

I goggle at her. "Really?"

She laughs. "Yes, really! That's how much Mike and I want you on board. I warn you, though, I'm a hard taskmaster. I want illustrations too, a watercolour each week to illustrate the piece. Bright and funky; none of that washed-out shit."

I refrain from pointing out that *washed-out shit* is exactly in essence what watercolours are, because this is a commission! A real commission! Somebody actually wants to pay me for my paintings!

Bloody hell!

"Well?" Ali stares at me hard. "What do you say?"

I say that I'd have to be mad not to accept. This kind of money isn't to be sniffed at. If I'm honest, I had been really worried about my finances. I have some savings, but renovating the new house is swiftly gobbling them up, and transforming the dusty attic into a studio won't come cheap. If I can earn money writing and illustrating a column, it'll mean that I'm not totally reliant on Ed, which makes me feel much easier about everything. I know he's happy to support us both, wants to do it even, but giving up my financial independence is something that goes against the grain.

Ali holds out her hand. There's a steely glint in her eye, and as we shake on the deal, I can't help but feel a little shiver of trepidation.

I've just agreed to sell my private life to the nation without so much as running it by my fiancé, the fiancé who enjoys discretion and privacy just as much as Jordan craves celebrity and paps. On the other hand, it does allow me to keep a foothold in the world of journalism, just in case . . .

In case what? I ask myself sharply. That really isn't the way to approach my life. But as Ali sloshes more champagne into my glass and outlines the format of my column, I only feel excited. I'm a columnist for Britain's biggest Sunday paper! My career in journalism isn't over after all.

Time for another glass of champagne!

CHAPTER
NINE

"Bloody traffic!" Ed thumps the steering wheel in a fit of irritation, as though the poor Range Rover is to blame for the solid lines of cars snaking past Stonehenge and coiling over the rolling patchwork of Salisbury Plain. Windscreens wink and metallic paintwork glitters with migraine-inducing intensity in the sunshine. It seems that everyone and their granny is headed west for the weekend.

"Maybe we should stop off and have a break," I suggest gently. The traffic is crawling at a similar pace to the Space Shuttle on route to the launch pad, and at this rate we won't reach Cornwall until at least the August bank holiday. A tantalising mile or so ahead, a Little Chef sign beams a plump welcome, and I think longingly of peeling my legs away from the cream leather seats and moving about before DVT sets in. Some food might be in order too. When we left London I felt too choked to eat a thing, but three hours on, my stomach's starting to grumble.

Ed, however, is scowling. "We haven't got time for a break. The removal vans set off hours ago and I was hoping we'd be able to catch them up. I want us to arrive at the same time they do, Amber. I don't trust them to unpack properly."

I bite back a sigh. We've spent hours boxing up all of our belongings and labelling them, hours of my life I'll never get back, that's for certain. If the removal men can't figure out the location of *kitchen* or *sitting room* then there's no hope for anyone. Besides, it's not as though we have a huge amount of furniture. Our tiny mews house could fit four times over into the new one, and Ed and I will literally be rattling around.

Moving day has finally dawned. This morning I wandered around my empty house and bid each room a silent farewell. Already the place was feeling unfamiliar, with its bright patches on the walls where pictures used to be and the new dust falling silently through the air. Then I locked my lime-green front door for the last time, posted the keys through the letter box and squared my shoulders. That was one stage of my old life finished and with a line drawn firmly under it. Now a new stage and a new life were about to begin. It was exciting and something to celebrate.

Or at least I hoped it was.

Three hours on, I'm starting to wonder. The traffic heading west makes the M25 look free-flowing, and every degree that the car's thermometer rises is matched by Ed's rising temper.

"Do you want me to drive?" I offer, intending to help, but this idea only incenses him further and his brow pleats into a scowl.

"Do you seriously think I really want another dent in this car, Amber?"

Honestly, can't some people hold grudges? It was only a tiny dent. And that telegraph pole was in a really stupid place. I don't see why he's so upset about one teensy-weensy dent in what is actually a very big car. We're living in the country now. Surely a battered and mud-smothered four-by-four is obligatory? Ours is too neat and shiny by far — we'll stick out like a sore thumb.

Better I don't say any of this, though. I may be feeling low, but I'm not suicidal yet. Besides, an exploding fiancé would not be a pretty sight for all these tourists.

So on we crawl for another twenty minutes, along with most people in Wiltshire, before Ed finally loses patience and bullies the satnav into finding an alternative route. Quite to where I'm not sure, but he seems happy enough to listen to at least one woman in the car, and soon we're bowling along shady green lanes at the kind of speed Lewis Hamilton usually enjoys, while I cling to the hand strap and pray I'll live to see thirty. If it looks to me as though we're heading in completely the wrong direction I keep my opinion to myself. I can't face a falling-out on the first day of our new life.

We drive in silence for another hour, both deep in thought. Ed fiddles with the state-of-the-art navigation system, which is so complicated-looking that I half expect Captain Kirk to pop up from the back seat and demand we put the car into warp factor eight, while I look out of the window and watch the patchwork eiderdown fields roll past. In my head I'm already putting together my first piece of copy for Ali and picturing the images I can paint to accompany it. I'm not short of ideas either: the mist-shrouded teeth of Stonehenge ringed by slow-moving visitors moving in awe like some latter-day mystic ritual; the picnicking couples eating warm ham sandwiches in lay-bys only metres away from rumbling juggernaut wheels. I'd be making notes in my new pink Pukka Pad except that Ed will start asking what I'm up to. I haven't plucked up the courage to tell him yet, and I have a sneaking suspicion that a busy drive to Cornwall isn't the best time to break the news that I'm about to sell our personal life to the papers.

I'm not worried about telling him, in case you're wondering. Of course not! I know he'll be really pleased that I'm still working and bringing in extra funds. Hawkstone House won't come cheap to do up, and as they say in the advert, *every little helps*. It's just that I'm not going to be writing about generic and random things this time, am I? It's one thing to be telling readers how to cure cellulite, and quite another to be laying my own soul bare to the women of Great Britain. Ali was quite specific that the last thing she's looking for is another sickly-sweet Kirstie Allsopp/Sarah Beeny fest. No, her readers want the nuts and bolts of the reality of exchanging my city life for the joys of rural bliss, the twist on this being a kind of *Sex and the City* approach to country life.

Sex and the Country? Hmm, that could work . . .

"Think Carrie Bradshaw meets Belle de Jour," was Ali's alarming parting advice over drinks in the Punch

123

and Judy, just off the Covent Garden piazza. "They must all be at it like rabbits in Cornwall, surely? Christ knows, there's fuck all else to do."

I sincerely doubted this was the case. So far the only evidence of anything approaching sexual activity in south-east Cornwall was passing the vet on his way to AI some cattle. If Ali thought my new neighbours were at it like a West Country version of a Jackie Collins novel, then she was in for a huge disappointment.

"There must be millions of hot guys there," she continued, running her finger around the rim of her glass in a rather worrying manner. "I've read about all those lonely farmers desperate for wives, and what about all the young bronzed surfers? And some of those fishermen off *Extreme Trawling* looked pretty hot. Christ! You're one lucky cow. You'll be able to come just looking out of the window!"

I nearly snorted pink wine out of my nostrils at this. Apart from the fact that the nearest farmer to us has to be at least eighty and a stranger to teeth, hair and washing, the only view out of my window is of fields. There's possibly more chance of spotting human life on Mars. And as for surf — well, the closest I'm likely to come to that in Polmerryn is loading the washing machine. Unlike Carrie Bradshaw and friends, I'm not exactly going to be surrounded by sexy male talent. And even if I was, I'm with Ed.

I'm engaged to Ed.

I love Ed.

"So window-shop, for Christ's sake!" Ali said impatiently when I voiced these (unwelcome) obstacles

124

to my writing a racy diary for her. "Seriously, Amber, you're engaged, not dead from the groin down. Surely you can still appreciate a hot guy?"

To be honest, I was so exhausted from trekking up and down the M4 and M5 for the past six weekends, lugging bags round IKEA and packing up my entire worldly goods that Brad Pitt could have wandered past starkers and not warranted a second glance. In fact I'd probably be more inclined to ask him for a hand carrying my boxes. That would be a far more useful skill to me these days.

In spite of what Ali says, I actually think this attitude is quite normal for someone of my age. The passion and excitement only happens when you're really young; people who are nearly thirty are over all that stuff, aren't they? And passion kind of dies out after a while anyway in my experience, with the exception of Ali, of course, who seems to get more wild sex than the rest of us put together. But then she's single and can spend hours worrying about her toenails and her G-spot while the rest of us are cleaning, picking up socks and trawling Asda for bargains. Real life isn't all passion and excitement, is it? Nobody could function otherwise. That's why women buy romantic fiction.

"You're very quiet," Ed remarks eventually, while I'm still musing on these salient points. "Is everything OK?" His hand slides from the gear stick to my knee, which he squeezes in the same manner he'd knead his stress ball. "I know this move has been a huge deal for you, Ambs, and I do appreciate what you're doing by supporting me. I know a new start is exactly what we need."

I cover his hand with mine and knit our fingers together. I know his hand so well, and there's comfort and safety in the familiarity of it. My history, our history, is in those hands. This is why I'm prepared to start over.

"I'm fine," I say.

And I am fine, or rather I will be. It's just that every mile that takes me further away from the familiarity of my home, my friends and my work makes my heart sink a little more. I'm going to miss my old life so much, but there's no point trying to explain this to Ed, because he simply doesn't get it. As far as he's concerned, it's onwards and upwards to bigger and better things, and he's mystified — and rather irritated — by my sadness. As he chats on about how wonderful things will be, I nod and make all the right noises, but my insides are churning. I have a sense of unease that I really can't explain, because it doesn't make sense. Perhaps I just need to relax.

By the time we rejoin the A303 at Yeovil, my mind is buzzing from all Ed's ideas. Wet rooms, hot tubs, holiday lets and smallholdings gallop through my mind's eye like Black Beauty on speed, and I can hardly think straight. While he talks with increasing enthusiasm, I gaze out of the window at the passing landscape and marvel at all the different shades of green. It's awesome. I could never, ever hope to match nature's palette even if I painted for a thousand years. The further west we travel, the deeper red the earth becomes, while the hills swell gently into the distance, fields rippling with wheat like an inland sea.

The traffic is still heinous and we crawl behind caravans and laden family wagons all making their pilgrimage to the sea. While Ed tuts and mutters under his breath, I lean my head against the cool glass. The sky is bruised with purple and a sickly lemony light trickles between swollen clouds. Soon rain starts to spit, and moments later it is pouring down in a deluge, the drops hammering against the bonnet and bouncing off the tarmac like machine-gun fire.

The Range Rover's automatic wipers go crazy, and somebody ahead swerves into the back of another car. Moments later the traffic is at a standstill again and the wail of a siren can be heard in the distance. Cornwall has never seemed so far away. I think it would have been quicker to visit the moon.

"Bloody great," says Ed, running a stressed hand across his face. "Fan-fucking-tastic."

But I'm not listening. Instead my eyes are drawn to the side of the road, where straggling bushes reach down to coil green fingers into the sodden ground. Beneath the foliage something has moved. I know it has! My eyes narrow and I wipe the mist from the window with my fingers to get a closer view. Is that a pile of rags, maybe? Or a sodden old coat that someone's abandoned? Or is it . . .

It looks like a dog! A large dog with wrinkly suede-soft fur and the biggest, saddest eyes in the world has just shot into the foliage and is cowering under the bushes as the relentless rain hammers down. Why is a dog outside in the pouring rain, and all alone?

Without thinking, I fling open the door and dash outside into the downpour. Within seconds my hair is plastered to my face and I'm wet through to my knickers, but I hardly notice because I'm so busy peering into the hedge.

"Here, boy!" I call, trying to push leaves away and lever myself into the undergrowth. "Good boy!"

"Amber!" yells Ed. "You're soaking! You'll mark the seats! Get out of the rain right now!"

Ignoring him, I shove branches out of the way, not caring that I'm scratching my arms and snagging my new Olivier Strelli tights. Seconds later, two big brown eyes are gazing back at me and a loud bark makes me jump and almost skewer myself on a branch. When my heart rate returns to a less cardiac-arrest level, I see that shivering among the leaves, coat curling like noodles in the damp, is a huge dog that is whining pitifully and looking pathetically grateful to see me.

"Hey there," I say softly, crouching down and reaching out my hand so that he can get my scent. "What are you doing out in the rain all by yourself?"

The dog cocks its head to one side and regards me thoughtfully. He's probably thinking what a stupid question to ask when it's blatantly obvious he's sheltering. A pink tongues lolls from his mouth and he whines again before raising his paw to me. Aw, bless! He wants to shake hands!

"Hello, you," I say, taking his paw. "I'm Amber."

The dog regards me thoughtfully. He's so wet and cold that even his big black nose looks like it's shivering. Gently I reach forward and touch the top of his head, which is bony and chilled beneath my fingertips. He looks like some kind of mastiff to me, but in the gloom of the undergrowth it's hard to tell. There's no sign of any collar, and the side of the road is devoid of people, so it's clear that nobody's trying to look for him. Why would such a lovely dog be abandoned? I know that with the recession lots of people can't afford their pets any more, and a big chap like this must cost a fortune to feed, but even so, how could you just abandon him? It makes me savage.

"How could anyone leave you here?" I say, and the dog looks up at me with such sad, melting-chocolate-button eyes that my heart goes into free-fall. He's so adorable!

"Amber!" I hear Ed holler. "What the bloody hell are you doing in there? Are you ill?"

Touched as I am by my fiancé's concern for my health, I do notice that he doesn't actually venture out of the warm, dry Range Rover to check on me. Willoughby rescuing Marianne Dashwood this ain't! Well, you know what they say. A dog is for life. A man isn't.

"Come on," I say to the dog. "I'm not leaving you in the rain. Let's get you out of here."

The dog licks my hand and barks. Curling my hands into his damp coat, I encourage him out of the hedge and on to the soggy grass verge. Once out of the green gloom I can see that he is indeed a bullmastiff, albeit a

129

very wet and very thin one. Without a second thought, I fling open the rear passenger door of the Range Rover, and without being asked twice, my new canine friend leaps in, barking joyfully and shaking himself dry all over the pristine cream leather seats.

Oops.

"What the hell!" bellows Ed, as he's showered in muddy dog-scented droplets. "Amber! Get that mutt out of my car! Get it off the seats this minute!"

I dive in after the dog and slam the car door shut with a bang, trying not to see how my fiancé winces at such a blatant display of vehicle abuse. Grabbing the tartan car blanket — good to finally find a use for it — I attempt to grab the dog and rub him down, but he's far too busy trying to leap into the boot and investigate the Marks and Spencer's carriers.

"For Christ's sake!" Ed explodes, as the dog unearths a cold chicken and tucks in with gusto. "That's our bloody supper! Get it out!"

"Ed, he's starving! The poor thing's been hiding in the undergrowth and he's totally soaked," I point out as I attempt to dry the dog, which is easier said than done when you're practically upside down over a car seat and contorting yourself into the kind of positions that yoga gurus take lifetimes to perfect. This is possibly the most interesting action my body's seen for years. "We can't leave him out there on his own."

"We bloody can," says Ed. "It's probably got fleas. And look at the mess it's made of the interior. For fuck's sake, Amber. This is only weeks off the forecourt. I'll have to get it valeted when we get to Cornwall."

Good luck with that in Polmerryn! I think most of the vehicles I've seen there are held together with muddy water and dog hair. It's possibly some specialised local building material. Still, I make agreeing noises and offer to clean the car myself, polish the seats with my best silk underwear if it really makes him happy. As I towel-dry the dog, Ed simultaneously attempts to crawl along in the traffic and mop the dashboard with a tissue. Thank God we're stuck in the world's slowest traffic jam. Ed is to multitasking what I am to nuclear physics, and we'd be a splat on the A303 quicker than you can say "distracted".

"If that dog has stained the leather, it's going to cost a fortune to get the marks off," Ed moans, mopping ever more frantically, his forehead crinkling like something from a McCoy's packet. Honestly, what a fuss. Since when did my fiancé become such an old woman about his car?

"It's a four-by-four," I say. "It should have a dog and a bit of mud in it. Chillax, Ed. We live in the country now, remember?"

"It's a four-by-four that cost me over sixty grand," Ed hisses. "It is not a car to fill with your manky strays, Amber. I'll pull over in a minute and you can kick it out. I'm sure somebody's looking for it."

I fling my arms around the dog's neck. "I'm not throwing him out on to the road! How heartless are you?"

"If you really must have a dog, I'll buy you a Labrador once we've settled in."

I pause in my drying and the dog stops chewing on a smoked salmon and cream cheese bagel for a second. We both stare at Ed and it's hard to say who has the more pleading expression on their face.

"You'd seriously kick this poor dog out into the rain?"

I'm horrified at Ed. Even Adolf Hitler liked dogs. Lord, it's a bad day when a girl's fiancé makes Hitler look like a kind and caring alternative.

"Of course not," Ed says wearily, although the expression on his face says the exact opposite. "But you must admit it smells."

He has a point. Eau de Vanilla Tree has been very swiftly replaced by Eau de Pongy Hound. A pongy hound that's eaten all the chicken, the smoked salmon and now the quiche Lorraine too. Oops. Maybe we'll be getting a takeaway for dinner. If they have takeaways in Polmerryn, that is.

"I'll give him a bath when we get to the house," I say, hastily shoving the chewed-up quiche box under the back seat. "Then I'll call the vet. He looks like a bullmastiff to me; he's bound to be microchipped."

"He looks more like Ken Barlow to me, with that hangdog expression," Ed observes drily.

"Ken," I say thoughtfully, and the dog looks at me and thumps his tail. "Do you know what? It suits him. Are you coming to Cornwall with us, Ken?"

"Woof!" says Ken happily, and I know it's ridiculous but my heart lifts. Suddenly it feels as though I have an ally.

Ed plucks a wet wipe out of the glovebox and continues his mopping.

"It can come with us, but once we get to Cornwall you are sorting this out and that mutt goes to the RSPCA or something. Agreed?"

"Agreed!" I say, crossing my fingers behind my back and winking at Ken. I already know that if I can't trace his owner then I'm keeping him. Some things are just meant to be, aren't they? I scratch the top of his velvety head and the dog rolls his eyes adoringly. Hey. I'm adored! That feels good.

The drool dripping from his jowls and on to the cream carpet isn't quite so good, but I'm sure it's nothing that the Vax can't deal with.

Luckily, before Ed notices the drool puddle or has time to whack any more conditions on to Ken coming to Polmerryn with us, the traffic decides to clear and we're off again at long last.

And suddenly, for the first time since we left London, I feel excited about reaching my new home.

CHAPTER
TEN

"Where the bloody hell are the removal men?"

Ed pulls up in front of Hawkstone House and yanks the handbrake up so hard that he almost wrenches it from the car. I wince. He's been in a vile mood all the way from Yeovil, thanks to a lethal and temper-boiling combination of hideous traffic, ruined upholstery and Ken vomiting Marks and Spencer's finest all over the back seat. To finally arrive at the house only to discover that none of our furniture has turned up is like lighting a touchpaper, and his ears have turned scarlet, a sure sign of his fury. I gulp. He's going to explode at any moment unless I can calm him down — which is easier said than done, seeing as I was the one who landed him with ten stone of vomiting canine, and then delayed us even further when Ken's pained expression and whining said very clearly that unless he vacated the car soon, vomit on the seats would be the least of our problems.

So when it comes to soothing my stressed fiancé, I am probably not particularly well qualified.

I glance at my watch. "It's only just gone five. They're probably still held up somewhere. Aren't there rules about how long people can drive lorries?"

134

Ed looks at me witheringly. "That's for long-haul lorry drivers crossing the Continent. Not removal men who are only going from London to Fowey."

OK. My mistake. Maybe I'll try and take his mind off things. I would offer a blowjob, but even that doesn't seem to work these days. I decide to try the next best thing.

"Why don't we go inside and make a cup of tea and see if they arrive in the next hour?" I say brightly. Tea never fails, right?

No. Wrong, actually.

"They've got our fucking kettle," snarls Ed. "I told you not to pack it in the kitchen box. It's not as though we can just nip off to Starbucks."

OK, that is a minor inconvenience, and it's a little too early to hit the pink wine, so I rack my brains for something soothing to say but draw a blank. Ed's dark moods are getting harder and harder to shift. I hope to God he cheers up now we've relocated. It's like living with a young Victor Meldrew.

While Ed huffs and puffs, I look out of the window and drink in the view. I could point out how beautiful the house looks in the afternoon sunshine, the old Cornish stone all warm as though it's been drizzled with golden syrup, the dog roses nodding sleepily in the garden while the sea sparkles in the small dip between the hills. I could say how peaceful it is here with only the drone of bees and the trembling bleat of a sheep breaking the silence, a million miles away from the wailing sirens and constant rumbling of traffic in London. I should offer to massage Ed's aching shoulders and stiff back. These are all things I *ought* to do, but the grim look on his face tells me that he won't take very kindly to any of them. Ed likes everything to go according to plan, and so far today absolutely nothing has. No wonder he's fuming.

"Woof!" says Ken, thumping his tail against the seat. Brown dog hair swirls into the air and Ed winces. The smells of damp dog, vomit and vanilla air freshener mingle in a very unpleasant way.

"Maybe they're lost?" I venture.

"They have satnav," Ed snaps. "I'll call them."

"Good idea," I say soothingly. "They can't be far away."

He grimaces. "They'd better not be, or I won't be paying them the extortionate amount they're demanding."

Ed lifts up the centre console and fishes out the latest love of his life, aka his iPhone. Honestly, if that phone was a woman, I'd have serious issues with it, because he spends a great deal more time polishing its screen and running his fingers over its sleek black case than he ever does running his hands over my less-than-sleek exterior. That flipping phone gets turned on far more often than me! Even right now, in the midst of his foul mood, I see him visibly relax as he slides his index finger over the touch screen to unlock it, and like the sun peeking out from behind a cloud there's a small smile playing around the corners of his mouth. Phew!

Unfortunately my relief is short-lived. Within seconds the tension is rocketing back into his every cell when he discovers that there's no signal. Even the poor iPhone's in the bad books and is slammed on to the dashboard.

"I'm going to drive somewhere I can get reception," Ed snarls. "In the meantime, why don't you hose that bloody dog down and air the house?"

I feel like clicking my heels and saying "*Ja, mein Führer!*" but because Ed is having a total sense-of-humour failure today and I've added to his stress levels by foisting a very big and very drooly dog on him, it's probably not a good idea. So I bite my tongue for the umpteenth time — wondering if this actually counts as self-harming — and hop out of the car with what's left of the M&S goodies. Ken bounds after me, barking and racing in circles round the courtyard, while Ed tears back along the drive with what's left of the gravel showering in his wake.

And suddenly I can breathe again. What a relief. Much as I love Ed, I have never met anyone who can fly into a black mood like he can, and not just fly there for a bit either, but stay put stewing for hours on end. The journey from London would have been more fun in the company of a Dementor, and I'm exhausted from being soothing and tactful. Pulling out the wine from the detritus of the M&S bag, I call Ken and head for the back door. I hope to God there's a corkscrew somewhere in the kitchen, because I really need a drink.

Or two.

"This is it," I tell the dog as I fish the big brass key out of my bag and unlock the door. "Home at last."

Ken thumps his tail and nudges his wet nose against my hand. I know it sounds crazy, but I'm really glad to have him here with me. Hawkstone House is beautiful, but large and echoey, and it doesn't feel anything like home. Quite the opposite actually — it's so grand and imposing that I feel like an impostor playing at being a grown-up. Maybe once it's full of my paintings and our things it will start to feel warmer and more familiar. I just need time to settle in, that's all.

Once inside, the kitchen seems twice as big, now that the vendors have taken all their belongings. They've left us the huge farmhouse table, now marooned in the middle of the slate-floor sea and looking very empty. Starting as I mean to go on, I dump my bags right in the middle before checking out the Aga. When I say *checking out*, what I actually mean is I sidle nervously up to it and lay my hand against its cream flank to see if it's on or not, because this is about as far as my Aga expertise goes. To be honest, the bloody thing terrifies the life out of a girl whose culinary skills just about stretch as far as programming a microwave. If it doesn't take four minutes to cook and have a *ping!* sound at the end of it, then I'm stuffed.

If the removal men really are lost, and with them my microwave, then we're in big trouble. We'll probably starve. Or have to eat Ken . . .

Ken luckily can't read my thoughts and has no reservations about making himself at home. With a huge grunt of delight he crumples down next to the Aga, leaning his bulk against the toasty metal and closing his eyes in bliss. If he could have climbed into the warming oven he would have done.

"That's your place then, is it?" I smile, patting his head and receiving an adoring stare in return that would surely melt the stoniest heart. Then I lift the lid from the hot plates and peer nervously beneath at the grimy cast iron. Hmm, I wonder what this does? Curious, I touch the tips of my fingers against it and leap backwards as my flesh sizzles.

Ouch! Shit! That's scalding! These things are dangerous! No wonder Nigella's always sucking her fingers! What the hell is wrong with a microwave?

Nursing my throbbing hand, I turn on one of the big brass taps above the butler's sink and stick it under the icy water. That's better.

So, Amber, Aga lesson number one. Hot surfaces cook stuff, including you. It's a lot fiercer than I imagined, but I think I'm starting to get the gist of how this works. If I can make it through till bedtime without first-degree burns I should be fine. Not sure how I'd cook a pizza in it, but surely to God there's a Domino's or a Pizza Hut somewhere fairly close?

Wrapping my hand in a wet tea towel and leaving Ken to slumber, I decide to explore my new kitchen, opening and shutting cupboards and even venturing into the cool undersea gloom of the pantry. Discovering an ancient jar of Nescafé is an added bonus, and feeling hopeful, I dig out an elderly saucepan from the back of a spidery cupboard and fill it with water.

"Now we're going to seriously road-test this baby!" I say to Ken as I wallop the saucepan on to the hotplate,

139

but he's far too busy dreaming lovely doggy dreams, nose twitching and legs kicking, to listen to me.

The water takes a while to boil, so as I wait, I unpack what remains of our groceries. Since the fridge has yet to arrive, I fill the sink with cold water and bob the wine bottle into it. Then I rinse a chipped mug that's lurking under the sink, make myself a coffee and curl up in the window seat that overlooks the garden, my garden now, I suppose. Maybe I can grow a few veggies and plant some flowers. Learn the difference between a broad bean and a runner bean and get excited about carrots rather than Jimmy Choos. Become the sort of woman who has earth under her toenails.

God help me, I'll be fancying Alan Titchmarsh and listening to *Gardeners' Question Time* before I know it. If this is what my new life in the country amounts to, Ali's column is going to be very dull indeed! Still, dull or not, there's a lot to be said for sipping coffee while basking in the late afternoon sunshine and gazing at the velvety green front lawn. Shadows pour themselves over the grass like dark wine, and bees almost too obese to fly work the lavender drowsily. Down in the V between hills like Jordan's boobs glitters a sliver of periwinkle sea, its brightness only matched by the molten gold of the shimmering corn fields. The leaded window framing all this and brushed by honeysuckle fingers would make a perfect picture to accompany my first column, even if it isn't quite what Ali has in mind. I think she'd prefer something from the *Kama Sutra* set in fields, or at a push on the beach or the deck of a boat, rather than Wordsworthian musings.

What on earth can I write about that will give her what she wants?

"Any ideas?" I ask Ken, but he ignores me and continues to doze contentedly by the Aga. He looks so peaceful and cute with his paws over his eyes that I fetch my shoulder bag, dig out a pencil and start to sketch him. Then I draw the view through the open side door and the cobwebby corner above the empty Welsh dresser where a fat black spider snoozes, before finally indulging myself and turning my attention to the glorious view across the garden.

Just as I'm planning the framing, angles and colour spectrum I'd like to use for this scene, my peace and quiet is rudely interrupted by Ken leaping up from his warm spot and hurling himself into the space beside me, barking so loudly that my eardrums throb. Coffee spills all down my white top, and the mug goes flying, shattering as it lands on the unforgiving ground. I practically orbit the moon, I jump so high. Years of Flotex have lulled me into a false sense of security. I truly thought that mugs bounced, unlike my sketches, which fly up into the air before fluttering down to earth and turning into a coffee-speckled splat.

"Thanks a million!" I say to Ken, who's frantically trying to heave his bulk over the stable door. "Get down! If you pull that off its hinges, Ed will kill you. And then beat me to death with your carcass."

But Ken ignores me, barking like crazy. He barks so much and so loudly that he sounds like an entire pack of dogs. I think there must be something wrong with my ears, because I'm convinced I hear another dog bark, then another, then another . . .

Wait a second. Unless my stray pal has super-canine ventriloquist powers, I don't think it's just him making this din.

What is going on? Where is all the noise coming from?

I'm just trying to figure out what's happening and unsuccessfully attempting to tug ten stone of very determined bullmastiff away from the door when the garden fills with dogs. Where only a moment ago there was a sweep of overgrown grass, now there's a swirling mass of white and tan bodies, wagging tails and lolling pink tongues. There's a cacophony of barking, egged on by Ken, who is growing ever more determined to join the canine intruders, and the garden seems to move and sway as the canine massive bound about. With one enormous twist of his powerful haunches, Ken leaps the stable door and hurtles joyfully into their midst, while I'm catapulted backwards like the farmer's wife in *The Enormous Turnip* at the kind of speed more usually experienced by fighter pilots. Then my backside slams against the hard stone floor, closely followed by my head. Ouch! For a second I don't so much see stars as the entire Milky Way.

Right, that's it. I am *never* rescuing another dog as long as I live! Slowly sitting up, my unburned hand probing the back of my skull, which is now sporting a lump the size of a cream egg, I watch ten dogs marauding across the garden.

Hang about! These aren't just any old dogs out for afternoon walkies, are they? I don't know much about country stuff, but these look like hounds. The kind of hounds that usually appear in *Country Life* with buxom girls called Clarissa and Emily.

My chin is nearly on the flagstones. What on earth is going on? Why is there a pack of hounds wandering around my garden? They're not supposed to be here; I never signed up for animal cruelty when I agreed to move to Cornwall. Hounds hunt stuff like . . . like . . . foxes! They chase them for miles until the poor little things are exhausted, before ripping them to pieces while bloodthirsty posh people drink brandy out of hip flasks and make rah-rah noises. It's totally barbaric and the reason why I spent lots of my student Saturdays out sabbing.

I can't stand hunting.

Or shooting.

Or anything that seeks to hurt animals. It makes my blood boil!

Staggering to my feet, I lurch to the door and gasp when I see how many hounds have rocked up. It's like a canine *Skins* party on my lawn!

"Duchess! Viper! Archer!" calls a firm voice, and instantly the churning mass springs to attention, tails almost at ninety degrees to their quivering bodies. Moments later a tall, muscular man dressed in a moss-green sweater and battered jeans strides on to the lawn as though he owns it. Instantly the dogs flock to his side in total obedience, apart from Ken, who bounds about like Tigger on speed.

143

"Get down!" hollers the stranger in such a masterful way that even I duck down behind my stable door, my heart rattling against my ribcage. Then, remembering that this is actually *my* home and that *he's* the one who's trespassing, I stand up again and see, to my total amazement, Ken flop on to the ground and roll over on to his back, vast belly raised for a pat and legs waggling in the air.

Wow! Talk about control! For a split second I'm lost in awe at the man's effect on the dogs, before I remember that he's a bloodthirsty hunting type who has the bare-faced cheek to let his hounds wander all over my land. Just who the hell does he think he is? If he imagines for a second that he can bring his horrible fox-munching mutts through here, then he's in for a shock!

"Hey! What do you think you're doing bringing those hounds into my garden?" I shout as I tear outside. "How dare you hunt poor innocent foxes here?"

The man is crouched down now talking to the hounds, his fingers smoothing their silky ears.

"I'm not hunting, I'm working the young entry," he says, without even looking up at me. "Besides, have you ever seen a chicken coop after a fox has visited? You may not find them quite so poor and innocent then."

There aren't many chicken coops in London so I haven't got a clue what he's on about, and to be quite frank I don't care either.

"This is private property! Anyway, I thought hunting was supposed to be illegal. It bloody well should be, because it's cruel and horrible and people like you should be hunted yourselves!"

The man gives the bony skull of one hound a pat before slowly straightening up and looking in my direction. Instantly I wish I'd stayed hidden, and not just because he's looking at me with thinly veiled irritation. No, if that was all, I'd be fine. The problem is that this dark and stomach-lurchingly attractive man is horribly familiar. And judging by the way he's looking at me through narrowed jade eyes, he's thinking exactly the same about me. I cross my burned fingers and pray that he won't be able to place me, because there's no mistaking those bright eyes or the long mane of dark gypsy curls framing that high-cheekboned face.

There's no doubt about it. The interloper in my garden is none other than the man I soaked in the lane the day Ed and I viewed Hawkstone House. Today he's a lot less soggy, but the firm set of his dark-stubbled jaw and his challenging expression as he looks at me are exactly the same.

Fate flicks a V sign at me yet again.

"It's you," he says slowly. "Puddle woman."

"Sorry about that," I say brightly.

"Not as sorry as I was," says the stranger. "It was a very cold five-mile walk home for me. Is that a driving style peculiar to London? Or do you soak everyone you meet?"

His green eyes glitter with challenge. Even though I'm the colour of a Babybel with a heady cocktail of embarrassment and fury at the fact that he's a barbaric trespasser, I can't help but be struck by the incredible hue of his irises; if I were to paint them, I'd say they were the exact clear green of Cornish rock pools in the sunshine. Not that I'm looking at his eyes too closely, though, because I'm very irritated by the lightly mocking note in his voice.

Criticising my skill behind the wheel is a guaranteed way to wind me up. I *hate* people taking the piss out of my driving, hate it, hate it, hate it! And it's so unfair. I only ever make mistakes when Ed's setting my nerves on edge or getting me to drive some ridiculously overpowered and overpriced new toy. When I had my little Fiesta back in the early noughties, I never so much as scratched the bumper. It may not have had ABS or power steering, but I could paint my nails and drive, that's how flipping skilled I am. Lewis Hamilton, watch me and weep in my own car, but put me in any of Ed's high-tech willy-mobiles and I go to pieces.

There's probably some law of physics to explain it.

Riled by a total (and trespassing) stranger commenting on my driving, I shove my curls behind my ears and raise my chin a fraction. What I'd really like to do is point a shotgun at him and say "Git off mah land!" but sadly this isn't an option because a) I don't own a gun and b) for some strange reason my mouth seems to have stopped working.

"I'll be on my way then," says the stranger while I struggle to find my vocal cords. "Dancer! Amble! Victory! Here!"

Calling the hounds, he spins around on his booted heel and strides away with the dogs leaping adoringly behind him.

What? He's about to wander off without so much as a by-your-leave? Where's the grovelling apology he owes me for traipsing his horrible fox-killing hounds across my garden?

"Hey!" I yell, finding my voice at last. "What about an apology for trespassing? And while you're here, how about one for murdering all those poor foxes too? Ripping them to pieces for your own enjoyment! It's disgusting! People like you make me sick!"

The man stops dead in his tracks, hounds cannoning into his legs. Uh-oh, Amber. You may have gone *slightly* too far. After all, you have no idea who this man is. He may look like Brad Pitt's better-looking brother, but for all you know he could be the local psycho. He might chop you up and feed you to his hounds just to pass the time on a Friday night. God knows, there's probably sod all else to do here for fun at the weekend.

Actually, he looks quite a bit like Heathcliff, and didn't Heathcliff kill people's pets and lock up young girls for a laugh? And dig up dead bodies too as I remember. I swallow nervously but my mouth seems to have turned into the Sahara. Oh God. I wish I'd stayed in London. I was safe there with the hoodies, gangs and drug-pushers. The countryside is bloody scary!

Slowly Heathcliff turns around and fixes me with such an icy jade-eyed gaze that I take a step backwards. Possibly my eyeballs have frostbite.

"Typical townie," he says coldly. "Moving here and thinking they own the place, blocking the roads with big cars they can't drive and foisting their ignorant assumptions on everybody else."

"I'm ignorant?" I shriek. "You're the one hunting innocent animals for fun and *I'm* ignorant?"

Blimey. I've only lived in Cornwall approximately two hours and already fishwife seems to be my default setting. Not that I care whether I'm screeching like a banshee because I'm up and running now, giving him the lowdown on cruel sports and telling him exactly what I think. Heathcliff can't get a word in edgeways because I scarcely come up for air, pausing only briefly to recall another fact or figure to lob at him like a verbal grenade. By the time I've finished this tirade he can be in no doubt that in my opinion he's worse than even Vlad the Impaler when it comes to cruelty. With a dash of Genghis Khan and Idi Amin thrown in for good measure.

"Finished?" asks the man when finally, breathless and looking even more like an Edam, I grind to a halt. His eyes have narrowed into angry slits, which glitter dangerously, not so much rock pools now as a stormy and dangerous ocean. "Have you completely finished assassinating my character? Or is there more?"

My breathing is ragged and my heart is racing. And I thought Ed was the one with the temper.

We glower at one another across the garden.

"Yes," I say, my hands on my hips. Great retort, Amber. Nice one. If Lord Coe were passing, he'd sign you on the spot for the Olympic verbal gymnastics squad.

"Good," Heathcliff says. "So now shut up and listen to me. I have three things to say to you. Number one, I'm not trespassing; there's a right of way across your

148

garden and has been for years. Number two, these hounds haven't seen a fox in their lives; we use them for drag hunting . . ." He pauses and stares at me, his eyes sweeping my body in such a way that I feel my face grow even hotter than it already is from hearing all this. "And number three . . ."

His eyes hold mine, and strangely they are no longer glacier cold but make me feel as though I've stepped into a blast furnace. Weird. Maybe it's the Aga burn taking its toll.

Heathcliff raises an eyebrow, looks as though he's about to speak, but instead just shakes his head. "No," he says slowly, "never mind that."

What? Don't you just hate it when people do that to you? I can't stand being left in suspense! I'm the girl who has to have the fortune cookie before the takeaway!

"Don't hold back on my account," I say with as much dignity as someone who's just made a total prat of herself can possibly manage. "Number three is what exactly?"

He shrugs, then his gaze strays to my chest before rising back to hold mine. Now, though, a mocking smile curves the corners of his mouth and there's a glitter of amusement dancing in his eyes. "Number three is I can see every inch of your red bra through your wet top. Must be some new London fashion we country bumpkins don't understand. Not that I'm complaining, but I just thought you ought to know."

And contented with firing this closing shot, Heathcliff strides out of my garden leaving me staring after him in mortification, my arms crossed — rather too late — over my chest.

Fan-flipping-tastic. Nice one, Amber.

I don't need a mirror to know that my face is every bit as red as my red plunge bra.

CHAPTER
ELEVEN

"So how's country life treating you, babes? Have you gone feral yet?" Ali's questions, fired at me from the comfort of her office, make me smile. Although she's more than two hundred miles away, I know she's jamming her mobile under her chin, tilting back her office chair to plonk her Louboutins on her desk and fiddling with her cigarettes while casting her eagle eye across the office. Ali lives life at one hundred miles an hour, and even though it's only mid-morning, she'll have already had a breakfast meeting, filed copy, torn a strip off somebody, planned the next issue and smoked her way through at least ten fags. I feel exhausted just thinking about it.

Exhausted and rather inadequate. So far today I have managed to get dressed and make some toast on the Aga, which believe me is easier said than done. I will probably smell of burned crust for the next six days and my ears are still ringing from the smoke alarm. Ken's been much busier. Already this morning he's chewed my favourite glittery sandals, bitten through the toaster cable — hence the Aga experiment — and emptied the bin all over the kitchen.

Not bad for only ten a.m.

"It's great," I tell Ali, as I attempt to scoop up detritus from the floor and scoop it into the Dalek-like Brabantia bin. God, I miss Flotex. Hoovering the kitchen was far easier than this constant sweeping lark. It's like the Forth Bridge without the height but with considerably more crumbs.

"Don't bullshit me," Ali says. "I want the truth."

I sit back on my haunches and sigh. "I've only been here for three days. I hardly know what it's like. All I seem to do is unpack boxes and scald myself."

"Scald yourself?" Ali sounds alarmed. "What's going on? Are you self-harming already? Come back, for fuck's sake!"

"Nothing like that. It's the Aga," I explain. "It's all we have to cook on since the removal men dropped the microwave."

I must admit this was a severe blow, not just to the unlucky Samsung combination oven, but also to me, because for some bizarre reason known only to himself, Ed seems to be under the impression that since moving to the sticks I've magically acquired domestic goddess skills that would make Nigella green with envy. He's wrong. Boobs aside, Nigella and I have as much in common as Tom and Jerry. Less, in fact, because at least Tom and Jerry share a cartoon. He'll be bitterly disappointed to realise that I didn't automatically understand the Aga from the second we crossed the Tamar. The fact that I have already melted a pot all over the inside and cremated the breakfast is testament to this.

Hey-ho. At least I'll lose some weight.

"An Aga? People really use those? But don't they take for ever?" asks Ali, who gets antsy if her broadband doesn't connect within a few seconds. Patience isn't one of her virtues, presumably because she couldn't be arsed to wait when it was being dished out.

"It's pretty fast for toast," I say, scooping the charred remains into the bin.

"Sod the toast," Ali shudders. "Whatever happened to smoked salmon and scrambled eggs?"

Whatever indeed? I glance out of the window at my six acres and wonder whether I should actually get some chickens. Then I look at Ken's huge drooling mouth and decide this might be a very bad idea. And anyway, the funky pink Eglu that would have looked so cute in a small London garden would look a bit daft stuck out in the middle of the field. Maybe I'll just pop to Waitrose instead. Although since Ed has taken the Range Rover to work, how will I get there? I've been here three days and I'm yet to see a bus or anything remotely resembling public transport, unless you count horses.

Then a very nasty thought occurs. Do they even have Waitrose in Cornwall?

Oh shit.

"You all right, babes?" Ali asks. "You're very quiet."

"I'm great! How's life in the office?" I say brightly, keen to change the subject and distract myself from the horror of life sans John Lewis. Ali knows me so well that in a moment she'll suss I'm feeling unsettled. Everything's new; I'm bound to feel a little odd. It's just going to take time to settle in and find some

153

friends, that's all. I know I live in the middle of nowhere, but there's bound to be people around somewhere, surely? I'm certain that in a couple of weeks I'll be fine and I'll know everyone and have so many people coming into the kitchen to drink tea, and hopefully give me Aga lessons, that I won't know what to do with myself.

The weekend was OK, because I was so busy unpacking and hiding indoors just in case Heathcliff came past again that time flew. Apart from one nasty moment when I thought Ken had swallowed the iPhone, and several bouts of Aga wrestling, I've been so flat out trying to make Hawkstone House resemble a home rather than the set of a period drama that I haven't had much time to think. But now it's Tuesday, Ed has set off to his new job and I'm rattling around the house wondering what on earth to do with all the acres of time suddenly on my hands. The Range Rover has gone to Fowey with Ed — not that I'm trusted anywhere near it since I lost the smart key yesterday — and I am stranded. Thank God for Ken, who, although more destructive than any weapons Saddam Hussein could have dreamed up, is at least somebody to chat to.

"Same old shit as always," Ali says cheerfully. "I've only got a week left myself, thank Christ, and then I'll really kick some arse at the *Dagger*! Talking of which, how's my column coming along? Lots of juice and testosterone for me?"

There's a thread of steel in her voice that I know only too well. It's the same steel that reduces office juniors and media magnates alike to jelly and ensures that deadlines are never missed. Ignore it at your peril.

"Oh fine, fine!" I say airily, crossing my fingers, toes and everything else crossable and ignoring the fact that the Word document on my Mac is as empty as Kerry Katona's bank account. The only thing even emptier is the testosterone count. And as for juice? Ken just knocked that over. "I'll file copy by Thursday, no problem."

"Cool," says Ali. "Listen, babe, I've got to shoot. Liz is off sick again and I'm flat out here. Quite frankly, some of this lot couldn't wipe their own arses. Get that copy to me as soon as you can, OK."

"OK," I agree, pulling a face at Ken and miming winding a noose around my neck. Ali rings off on the pretext of kicking office butt, although we both know she's actually hanging off the fire escape for a smoke, and I lean against the sink and gaze thoughtfully out at the heart-stopping view. I have to find something to write about. I need to be inspired. But how? And what on earth can I write about when the most exciting thing that's happened to me all morning is picking up rubbish?

"I need to do something," I tell Ken, who thumps his tail in agreement. "If I just sit here staring out of the window all day I'll go crazy."

What I need to do is treat being here as a job. Painting, writing and sorting out the house all need to be put into some kind of timetable that I make myself actually stick to, rather than expending more energy getting out of doing things than I would if I just made myself do them. It's all part of having a creative mind, or rather that's what I tell myself. It's a better self-view than accepting that, as Ed less charitably puts it, I'm disorganised and lazy.

Well, not today! The kitchen is clean. The floor swept and almost spotless. Although the Aga is gloating at me, the smell of burning has almost gone and every kitchen box has been unpacked. Time to go and explore the wider world, and since it's a weekday, with any luck Heathcliff will be at work so I won't bump into him. God, my face is the same temperature as the hotplate just thinking about our last encounter. I can't believe I said all that stuff to him! I was really rude. No wonder he was pissed off.

I also can't believe that while I was busily spouting invective, he had full view of my boobs. How totally and utterly mortifying is that?

At least I was wearing that red plunge bra. It would have been a gazillion times worse if I'd been sporting a greyed and fraying M&S special. Though why that actually matters I'm not entirely sure. It must be all the fresh air doing weird stuff to my hormones. Why do I care what such a rude man thinks of my lingerie?

Unsure where this train of thought is headed, or why I've even boarded it in the first place, I decide that it's time to take a walk into the village. Maybe there's a Tesco Metro and I can pick up some Aga-friendly bits and pieces for supper? I need to find a vet too and get Ken scanned for microchips just in case there's an owner out there longing to have back their tenstone house- and relationship-wrecking dog. Ed is still barely speaking to me after seeing the back of the Range Rover following Project Rescue Ken, and when he clocked the state of the kitchen this morning I thought he'd combust. For a moment I thought I saw smoke coming out of his ears before I realised that I'd set the toast alight. It was lucky he was starting work today, otherwise I think Ken would have been off to the pound, on a one-way ticket, do not pass Go, do not collect two hundred pounds. I'd be going as well, because make no mistake about it, I am seriously in the doghouse too.

"We need to impress your master," I tell Ken. "Because otherwise life is going to be very tricky indeed."

Ken stares up at me with such adoration that my heart melts. Just look at that face (but maybe ignore the drool); how could anyone resist? Ed will come round. How can he not? If I hide the teeth marks on his Kurt Geigers with a bit of polish and pretend that the new sofa always had muddy paw marks on it, then things will be fine. A trip to Battersea can surely be avoided if I am careful.

"Walkies?" I say to Ken, who instantly starts to pogo around the kitchen in excitement. One wag of his tail sends a coffee mug hurtling through the air; a second sends a plate in its wake. I bury my face in my hands. At this rate I'll need to write two columns a week just to pay for all the damage.

"I love you to bits," I tell Ken, as I make an improvised lead out of a bit of old washing line borrowed from the garden and lash it to the belt I've looped into a collar. "But my life would have been much easier if you'd been a Paris Hilton handbag dog! I could have popped you into my bag, but you need a wheelie bin."

"Woof!" says Ken happily, tugging at the washing line and practically skinning my palms in his haste to get outside. Grabbing my bag and the keys as I'm towed along, I manage to lock the door and hide the heavy key under a tub of geraniums before I'm dragged along the path and into the lane, where I dither for a moment, uncertain as to which way to go. I've only been here for three days and already I'm institutionalised! I've not ventured out of Hawkstone House alone, have I? And certainly not into the village. Ed and I drove to Plymouth on Saturday night for food, and did Padstow for lunch yesterday (he wasn't happy to discover you have to book well in advance for Rick Stein's and sulked all the way through his meal at a lovely pasta restaurant), but the local area is uncharted territory. For a moment I dither — me, the girl who rides the tube with her eyes shut — before deciding to head into Polmerryn.

I'm boldly going where no Amber has gone before!

"Come on," I say to Ken. "Time to see if the natives are friendly."

Turning left, we set off down the lane that winds slowly towards the sea. It's a lovely morning; a fried-egg sun sits in the sky, and birds sing their heads off from hedges foaming with cow parsley. The air is salt sharp and fresh, and a cheeky breeze teases my curls out of my hair clip and bounces them against my cheeks. I tilt

158

my face up to the sky and smile. The sun is warm, the countryside heart-stoppingly beautiful and I'm outside enjoying it rather than stuck in an office. As I walk, or rather run after Ken, down leafy lanes dappled with dancing leaf shade, I feel my heart rise like a hot-air balloon. It's all going to be fine. I know it. Maybe moving to Cornwall isn't a big mistake after all.

After a good twenty minutes of charging downhill, my arms nearly pulled out of their sockets by a very keen dog, I reach the village. I say village, but that may be an exaggeration; what I actually see is a cluster of crumpled cottages that look as though they've had one too many in the small pub and staggered a few feet before collapsing in a heap by the church. Calling this a village could lead to being sued under the Trade Descriptions Act.

Ken bounces along with me scuttling behind him. By now I'm really hot, and when I spot the village shop I'm almost weeping with relief at the thought of a cold drink. Then I see that it only opens three days a week and I feel like sobbing even more. I am so thirsty I'm tempted to elbow Ken out of the way and share the ice-cream container of dog water that he's selfishly enjoying.

"I'm afraid we lost our post office, so the village shop has all but closed down," says an apologetic voice over my shoulder. "Isn't it a shame? I blame Tony Blair. Him and that Gordon Brown, they should be ashamed."

At this moment in time I'm so annoyed the shop is shut that I could cheerfully drown both Blair and Brown in the dog bowl. Turning around, I'm greeted by the rather alarming sight of a woman in her sixties with livid red lipstick and hair the exact matching hue, topped with a large beret in a shade of cat-sick yellow so startling that I almost recoil.

"What a beautiful dog," continues beret lady with a beaming smile. "I just adore mastiffs, don't you? My father had several, swore they kept the poachers on their toes."

She bends down and makes a fuss of Ken, who in return raises a paw in greeting. Beret lady is in raptures at this.

"What a clever boy! Did Mummy teach you to do that?"

Now, I love Ken already but I must admit I take exception to being called his mummy. There's no way we look alike, and I've never drooled that much — not even when Ali and I went to see Take That.

"I didn't know he could do that," I say, and when I notice her look of confusion, I explain. "He was at the side of the A303 shivering under a hedge. I'm not sure whether he's been lost or abandoned, so until I can get a vet to scan him for microchips, I'm looking after him."

"Who could abandon such a handsome boy?" says yellow beret to Ken, who promptly rolls on to his back, shamelessly begging for his tummy to be tickled. To me she says, "We have a most marvellous vet here, Jinx Jackson. You must pop this little darling up to see him."

Since Ken weighs more than me — which is saying something, since I am more Dairy Milk than woman lately — popping him anywhere is easier said than done. Still, I like the sound of a vet called Jinx. That's very Jilly Cooper. Maybe he'll be fodder for *Sex and the Country*.

"Thanks, I'll make sure I do," I say. "I'm Amber Scott, by the way, and this is Ken. We've just moved into Hawkstone House."

"Ah! So you're the girl with the Range Rover! The one who splashes people!" The woman straightens up and smiles at me while I cringe. Fan-flipping-tastic. Heathcliff hasn't wasted any time telling tales. He's probably already started a hate campaign. There'll be dead animals through my letter box and airgun pellets lodged in the door before you can say "soggy".

"Yep," I say. "Afraid so."

She laughs. "Don't look so worried. Word travels fast in small villages. You're the most exciting thing to happen to us for a very long time." She extends a red and rather chapped hand in my direction. "I'm Virginia Verney. It's wonderful to meet you, Amber, and you too of course, Ken."

We shake hands in that very formal and slightly awkward British fashion. Virginia's vice-like grip makes my hand tingle.

"Now, the shop might be shut, but the pub's open," she observes, nodding her head in the direction of the Ship Inn several doors down. "How about we nip in and have a little drinkie?"

I'm very thirsty but rather alarmed by this idea. I've only lived here a few days; surely it's a little soon to become a rural alcoholic.

"Is it open?" I ask. "It's not even eleven yet."

Virginia laughs. "Don't worry about that. Terry Tipple's always open."

Taking my arm, she leads me along the lane, past a couple of chatting locals who wave and say hello, before turning into a sunny beer garden where hanging baskets brim with geraniums and tubs fizz with Busy Lizzies. Intrigued now by Terry Tipple, and so thirsty that my tongue is practically welded to the roof of my mouth, I follow her into the beer-scented gloom of the pub.

"Morning, Lady V!" booms a large man busily polishing glasses. Wow. I don't think I've ever seen hands so big. They're like hams.

"Morning, Terry!" Virginia trills, hauling herself up on to a bar stool and beaming at him. "Usual for me, please. This is Amber. She's just moved to Hawkstone House."

"Aah," says Terry, eyeing me thoughtfully as he cracks open a Pils and hands it across the bar. Intrigued, I watch as Virginia necks a mouthful and passes the bottle back for him to add a shot of Tia Maria. Dear God. What is this place where pensioners mix their drinks and get stuck into shots before noon? It makes Club 18–30 binge drinking in Magaluf look like a civilised cocktail party.

Terry regards me beadily. "You're the one with the big car, then?"

Great. Tarred for ever by my association with a monster Range Rover that I never even wanted and that makes me feel sick every time I attempt to drive it.

"Yes," I say wearily. "That'll be me."

"Don't tease her, Terry! Now, Amber, what do you want to drink?" Virginia asks, fishing a purse out of her vast William Morris print holdall. "G and T? Wine? Lager?"

Bloody hell. We don't even drink this hard or this early in the world of journalism.

"Er, just a Diet Coke for me."

"Diet Coke?" Virginia echoes, looking as horrified as though I'd ordered distilled baby's blood. "Oh darling, surely not? Have a proper drink. On me."

"We do a nice Moët," says Terry hopefully.

That Range Rover *totally* gives the wrong impression. I open my mouth to insist on Coke, but since even Ken is now slurping happily at a dog bowl full of stout, it seems almost rude of me. Figuring that when in Rome, I give in and order a glass of rosé.

Well, if Ken is on the lash, I may as well keep him company.

I clamber up on to a bar stool and accept a huge glass of wine, and with it my fate. More than two of these and I'll not even remember my name, never mind the way home. While Terry Tipple restocks the fridge and a scary emo-type barmaid takes his place, Virginia and I chat away about the village, and it isn't long before I realise that I'm getting pissed with the lady of the manor, albeit one who dresses like a refugee from Oxfam and whose bright red wig is starting to slip over one eye.

"Bloody thing," she says, taking it off after her second Pils and Tia Maria and running her fingers through a shock of white hair. "I was tidying up the third dressing-up room and I found it. Think it belonged to Mad Red Verney, who did something quite awful to one of George the Third's daughters. I quite fancied being a redhead for the day, but the damn thing just won't stay put." She shoves it under my nose. "Would you like it?"

The wig looks horribly like she's scalped Amy Childs, and I shrink away. I am drinking at half eleven in the morning, with a dog and a crazy aristocrat who has at least three dressing-up rooms. You couldn't make it up.

"I'm fine for hair, thanks," I say.

"Yes, you are," Virginia agrees. "Such beautiful golden curls too. You are lucky."

She wouldn't say that if she had to foot my Frizz-Ease bill. I think I've single-handedly paid for John Frieda's mansion.

"Thanks," I say, but Virginia isn't really paying attention, too busy listing on her stool now like a sailor taking part in the America's Cup and regarding me thoughtfully through rather bloodshot eyes.

"So, Amber. I know you were an art director for a magazine, and it sounds marvellous, but what are you planning to do with yourself now that you're living here?"

I decide not to mention the column. Just in case she thinks I might be using her for material.

OK. Let's be honest. Of course I am.

"I'm not sure," I reply. "My fiancé is working, so I thought I'd take some time out to sort the house and do some painting."

164

"You're an artist!" Virginia claps her hands in delight and rocks the bar stool so dangerously that Terry has to stride across on his giant redwood legs to steady her.

"Well, I paint," I say. "Mostly watercolours, but I'd like to try acrylics too. The light here is wonderful."

"Isn't it? You should see the views across Polmerryn Bay from the Manor! In fact you must come up and paint them!"

"That would be wonderful." I can see the manor house from Hawkstone. The tower room has had a light on every night. Even when I've had to get up in the small hours to tend to a howling Ken ('For fuck's sake, Amber, will you sort that mutt out? Some of us have got to work tomorrow'), the tiny window has been illuminated and I've been intrigued as to who my fellow insomniac is.

"In fact, I've just had a fantastic idea!" Virginia exclaims, her beret sliding over her nose.

"Careful," Terry warns me. "Her last fantastic idea involved growing cannabis and nearly got her locked away. His lordship went mental."

"Alex has no imagination," sighs Virginia. "And anyway, it worked in *Saving Grace*. She managed to save her house and," she fixes Terry with a steely glare, "nobody dobbed her in to her son."

"I was saving you from yourself," says Terry sternly. "That police helicopter was circling the village far too often for my liking. No one dared come to the lock-ins any more. It's enough of a struggle making ends meet since the smoking ban without you adding to it."

Virginia tuts. "Me, me, me. You try running a twelve-bedroomed stately home, young man. That doesn't heat itself or mend its own roof, you know. And don't even get me started on the death duties. It really was very inconsiderate of Archie to die when he did. It's all right for him, he's not the one having to sort the house out and open it up to the public."

"Who's Archie?" I ask, totally confused now.

"My husband," Virginia says, ripping into a packet of pork scratchings. "He always was an awkward bugger and never about when you needed him. Typical. Still, never mind him. To be honest, he did take up a lot of space, and he snored *terribly*. My biggest problem is getting the house ready in time for the summer visitors. Alex is simply useless when it comes to organising things, which is why you, Amber dear, must have been sent from heaven."

Er, excuse me? Did I miss something?

"Me? Why?"

"My dear, you simply have to come and work for us! Immediately! And I won't hear of any refusals," says Virginia with all the finesse of a bull rampaging through Emma Bridgewater's studio. "With your artistic skills you could dress the rooms, and I'm sure you could organise us all; you seem like a very together young woman. Besides, you can't rattle around that empty house all day, you'll go crazy. I would if I didn't have my Alex."

I am currently two thirds of the way through my second glass of pink wine, the floor is rolling like the sea and I am seeing two Virginia Verneys, and neither looks very sober. Besides, I think I am probably the antithesis of a together young woman.

"I'm not sure . . ." I begin, but Virginia isn't listening. She's far too busy digging a gore-red lipstick out of her bag and scrawling a telephone number on to a beer mat.

"Take this and give me a call," she says, shoving it into my fist. "It would be wonderful to have you about the place. Such a breath of fresh air! It would cheer poor Alex up so much too to have another young person about, especially after the hard time he's had."

I'm intrigued. "What happened?"

But suddenly Virginia isn't quite so keen to gossip. "It's all in the past; doesn't do to dwell on it. Alex hates that, and he'll go nuts if he thinks I've been talking out of turn. I blame Princess Diana for all this needing to talk about emotions. Dreadful, people will get cricks in their necks from navel-gazing. Stiff upper lip is best. That's what I always say."

"Jeremy Kyle would be out of a job if we all thought like that!" I laugh.

"Jeremy who?" Virginia looks confused. "Is he a politician?"

"Not exactly," I say. "It's kind of hard to explain. Tune into ITV at about half nine in the morning and all will become clear."

"I will," promises Virginia. "If you think hard about coming to give me a hand."

Maybe it's the pink wine, or maybe it's just because there's something I like about this eccentric woman, but I find myself agreeing. Then Virginia slithers from her bar stool and, kissing me on the cheek, says that she has to go. It's nearly two and her son will be worried.

"He should be worried," says Sam, the emo barmaid, gloomily as we watch Lady Verney stagger out of the door. "She's riding a bicycle! Along the cliff path."

I picture Alex Verney. In my mind he's a chinless wonder with thinning hair, wearing cords and one of those strange sweaters with leather elbow patches that posh people seem to always favour. Goodness only knows where they buy them; there must be a special road full of posh people's clothes shops, a bit like the street in Harry Potter where they get their magic wands.

Can't imagine I'd be much help cheering him up, though. I spin the beer mat in my fingers and frown. On the other hand, Virginia is a lot of fun, and giving her a hand could be a nicer way to fill my time than rattling around Hawkstone House on my own. And think of the views from the manor. Perhaps there's a sexy gardener too, who could be inspiration for my column . . .

Maybe I'll give her a call.

"What happened to her son?" I ask Sam once Virginia is out of earshot.

"Alex Verney?" The girl's heavily kohled eyes widen. "Nobody really knows, and he keeps himself to himself so we don't see much of him in the village. Mind you, he's the lord of the manor and the most eligible bachelor in Cornwall, so he probably has much better things to do than get pissed in here. Miserable git."

168

I swirl my drink thoughtfully. "Virginia hinted at a tragedy. What happened?" Come on, emo girl! You must love doom and tragedy! Spill!

"It's a bit of a mystery. There was a wife, Vanessa I think she was called, and she died."

"So he's a widower?" My eyes widen. My God, that is tragic.

She nods. "Nobody knows quite how she died, though. She went away with Alex and never came back. Or rather she never came back alive. People had all sorts of theories about what happened. Some say she tried to leave him and he killed her. Others say that she killed herself. All I know is that nobody from the big house ever talks about it, not even Virginia, and as you can see, she'll chat about pretty much anything."

Now I'm really intrigued. Alex Verney, tragic widower or modern-day Bluebeard? The lord of the manor with the dark past; it's kind of Lord Byron meets Edward Cullen. So what if in reality he looks more Millets than Mills & Boon? The readers of my column don't need to know that, do they? And by the time I'm finished writing, Lord Verney will be so well disguised he won't even recognise himself.

I glance down at the beer mat and know that my mind is made up. I am going to visit Polmerryn Manor. I may even take Virginia up on her offer of a job.

And not because I'm a little, teeny bit drunk.

It's all in the name of research!

CHAPTER
TWELVE

Goodness only knows how I'm going to make it home. Once I finish my third glass of pink wine, I stand up and call to Ken, only to discover that I don't have legs any more, only soggy string, and the bar is spinning around more than Kylie Minogue.

Oh bollocks. I'm pissed. How on earth has that happened?

Well, the usual way obviously. I drank two enormous glasses of wine with Virginia and then another with the emo barmaid, which is seriously huge amounts for a feeble lightweight like me. Normally I only have to wander down the liquor aisle in the supermarket to feel tipsy, so no wonder I feel wrecked now that I probably have pink wine for blood.

"Here, get this down you, maid," says Terry Tipple, plonking a ginormous pasty in front of me. "The missus baked it this morning. That'll put hairs on your chest."

I gaze at the pasty in alarm. Firstly, hairs on my chest are not top of my list of beauty must-haves, and secondly, the strong aroma of onion and pastry makes my stomach churn. I'm pissed by noon and eating pasties. Now I know I live in Cornwall. Oh sushi, I miss you more than I can say.

"Go on," Terry says, arms folded across his enormous stomach. "Don't be shy. It's good for you. I eat one a day."

Terry looks like Mr Greedy on a fat day. I gulp. I think that pasty probably contains my annual calorie allowance. Still, not wanting to offend him, I pick up my knife and fork, hack a chunk off and start to chew, and something amazing happens . . .

My taste buds have a party in my mouth.

Wedges of swede, hunks of steak so tender they melt on my tongue and delicious fried onions compete for my attention. Before I know it, I've wolfed the entire lot, much to the disgust of Ken, who's watching my gluttony and drooling with envy. Oh. My. God. This is an even better revelation than my first orgasm! Whoever knew a Cornish pasty could be so good?

"Ginsters have a lot to answer for," Terry says darkly when I voice this thought (minus the sexual references, obviously; I haven't known him that long after all). "My Morwenna, she makes the best pasties in south-east Cornwall. They cure anything."

The pasty certainly seems to have cured my state of total inebriation. Feeling mildly and pleasantly pissed now rather than roaringly drunk, I set off for home with Ken lolloping alongside. Actually, given the large bowl of stout he swigged, the dog is probably drunk too. In any case he's given up pulling and tugging on the lead and the walk home is very pleasant. As I trudge up the final steep bit of hill, feeling virtuous because I'm surely burning off all the calories, my thoughts wander to my column. Much as the mysterious Alex Verney fascinates me, I don't have anywhere like enough time to do some digging in order to uncover the bare bones of a story. So I have less than two days to find something else I can write about, something that will satisfy Ali and, more importantly, justify the money that has been paid into my bank account. This money has already been spent on the ride-on lawnmower that Ed insists he can't live without, so there's no way I can send it back if I fail to come up with the goods. Well I suppose I could, but a ride-on lawnmower wouldn't really be much use in the newsroom and Ali is more than capable of cutting folk down to size on her own.

So, in the immortal words of Lord Sugar, failure is not an option.

What can I write about? Something that will really grab my readers is an absolute must. They need to know all about my exciting new life, and as much fun as this morning has been, I don't really think that getting pissed with pensioners will cut it. No, I need to write about something exciting. If only I lived next door to a rock star or a famous actor!

I open the garden gate and stomp up the path as I attempt to dredge ideas from my brain. I must admit that every time I so much as glance into the garden I feel a tsunami of mortification as I recall my falling-out with Heathcliff. Honestly, I don't think I've ever met a man so infuriating and arrogant and attractive.

Hang on . . .

I think I may be on to something! What is it they always say? Write about what you know.

On a mission now, I storm into the kitchen like a paratrooper, kick off my sandals and tear upstairs to fetch my Mac. While it boots up, I make a cup of tea, with the kettle this time, while Ken collapses by the Aga, snoring so loudly that the windows rattle. I feel rather guilty, because when he wakes up he is going to have the mother of all hangovers. When I take him to see the exciting-sounding Jinx Jackson, I'll probably be done for canine abuse and put on some kind of bad pet-owners' register.

Right, Amber. Time to get to work!

I sit at the kitchen table, flex my fingers above the keyboard and begin to type. When I finally stop, my tea is cold, my hands are tingly and the sun has slipped below the trees, but best of all there's over a thousand words on my screen. I love it when writing takes me over like that! It's one of the best feelings in the world, like being transported to another place entirely.

Before my brain has time to catch up with my fingers, I've composed an email to Ali, attached the piece and — *zap!* — sent it whizzing through the ether without so much as even reading it through and leaving it to cook. Then I yawn. Goodness, all this writing is exhausting. How on earth does Carrie Bradshaw manage to file a column, look amazing *and* have lots of great sex? I may have written a thousand words, but my make-up has slithered off and my roots are showing. And as for great sex . . .

Maybe I won't dwell on that bit. One out of three isn't doing too badly, is it?

I lay my head on the table and close my eyes. I really am very, very tired. That walk to Polmerryn has taken it out of me. And drinking in the daytime is a bad idea. Perhaps I'll just have a power nap . . .

It's some power nap. When Ken's wet nose pushes against my face, I jolt awake, stiff, achy and disorientated. The light has bled from the sky and shadows pool across the kitchen floor. The tea has congealed in my mug and even the laptop has given up and powered down. Bloody hell! I've been asleep for over three hours!

Or should that be I've been passed out for over three hours?

Ken barks and my head thuds.

"I know you're hungry," I say, when I can un-Velcro my tongue from the roof of my mouth. "Give me a minute, boy."

I sit up and my brain swivels in my skull. For a hideous moment I think I'm going to be sick.

Dear Lord. I can't have a hangover at five p.m.! This is ridiculous.

Peeling myself off the table, I shuffle across the kitchen, a headache pounding behind my eyes and my stomach sloshing horribly. As I fork dog food into a bowl, I nearly vomit just from the stench and have to race to the sink, where I gulp water straight from the tap.

Just how drunk was I? Very, judging by the state of me. I glance in a teaspoon and wince at the

174

bleary-eyed, white-faced gorgon floating in it. Gross! I am sticking to mineral water from now on in. I am *never* touching alcohol again, and especially not when I'm anywhere near Virginia Verney. My liver is probably damaged beyond repair . . .

Oh God. Talking of being damaged beyond repair, what on earth did I write and send to Ali?

Did I write what I *think* I did?

Heart pounding and throbbing head forgotten, I race across to the laptop, fire it up and start to pray. Like drunken eBaying and Facebooking, writing columns while under the influence of pink wine is *never* going to end well. What was I thinking?

With a horrible sensation of dread, I scroll through my document, and with every word I read I feel sicker.

Welcome to the reality of life in the country.

Agas don't understand ready-meals, satnavs tell lies and Waitrose is just something that happens to other people. Binge drinking takes place in quaint thatched pubs and pensioners peddle cannabis to pay for fuel.

How did I get from London to here?

Well that's a long story. Maybe it was for love or maybe it was just because I needed a change. I'm a racing rat at heart, not a country mouse, and I feel more lost than Matthew Fox.

Either way it's been a long journey, and not just in terms of miles either.

The countryside is another world, they do things differently here, and all are perplexed when you take exception to their customs.

Like wandering on to other people's property, for example ...

Oh God, oh God, oh God. I can hardly bear to read on, but like watching a horror movie or picking at a spot, I cannot resist. Slowly, and feeling cold to the core with horror, I scan my piece.

Note to self: never, *ever* write when pissed.

What I have written, and not just written but sent to Ali to be published in the national press, is a total character assassination of Heathcliff. With one hand over my eyes, but just peeking through the gaps between my fingers, I read about how he swaggered on to my land with his drooling blood-thirsty dogs and all but demanded *droit de seigneur*. He's now a cross between Heathcliff and the Marquis de Sade, with just a little bit of Byron thrown in to sex up the mix. I must admit I do possess a very impressive imagination, although the haughty sculpted face and those smouldering green eyes are totally factual.

I bury my face in my hands and groan. There are two things that could happen now. The first is that Heathcliff will rock up and shoot me with his twelve-bore. The second is that an erotic fiction publisher will sign me on the spot. Eat your heart out, Candace Bushnell. *Sex and the Country* is go.

OK, don't panic. How likely is it that Heathcliff is going to read the women's section of the *Sunday Dagger*? And even if by some freakish chance he does, he'll never recognise himself, will he? Anyway, if I wear a hoody and skulk about in the dark, I'll probably never see him again.

So that's all right then.

On the other hand, what if he does read it?

Fuck. I am so dead.

With trembling hands, I fish my BlackBerry out of my bag, thanking God that I am on the only network that seems to work here, though even so I don't dare move from the draughty spot outside the larder that has the one feeble bar of signal available.

Once in position, I speed-dial Ali and pray that she hasn't swanned off to a glamorous party or taken the afternoon off to bonk Mike Elton's brains out.

"Amber!" bellows Ali, almost shattering my left eardrum. "Couldn't wait to hear what I thought of the piece, eh? Wait no longer, babe! I fucking love it! That was exactly what I wanted and you totally nailed it! Bloody well done."

My heart has plummeted so far that it's probably about to surface in Sydney Harbour.

"Actually, Ali, I was wondering if I could withdraw it."

"What?" Ali's shock is palpable even from this distance. "Are you fucking kidding? No way! It's amazing. I can't wait to see the illustrations. Our readers are going to adore this. A grumpy, sexy Mr Darcy right on your doorstep. They love all that shit."

"He's nothing like Mr Darcy," I say, offended on Jane Austen's behalf. "And he certainly isn't sexy. He's arrogant and rude and . . . and . . . horrible."

"Really?" Ali sounds amused. "So you wouldn't shag him, then?"

I nearly choke. "No I bloody well wouldn't. I'd rather die first."

"Right, if you say so."

"Yes, I do say so! He's truly, truly horrible."

"Well in that case you won't mind using him for your column, will you?" says Ali.

I'm silenced. She's good. She's very good. In fact she should just run the world. Nobody would dare mess with her.

"Anyway, you've disguised him a bit," she continues, prepared to humour me now she knows she's totally got me where she wants me. "And since he's so nasty, who gives a fuck what he thinks? In fact, wind him up some more. It's fantastic copy. I can hardly wait for the next instalment. So unless you've anything better to give us, then I'm running with it."

Totally defeated, I slither down the larder door and collapse in a heap on the chilly tiles. I'll probably get piles now, but since Heathcliff is going to murder me after Sunday, I'm not going to worry too much about that.

"There is the local lord of the manor," I say, and go on to tell her all about the tragic Alex Verney and his vanishing bride. Ali listens carefully but I can tell her thoughts are elsewhere.

"That's all very interesting, babes," she interrupts, "but it's not quite the tone I want. Find out the details by all means, but I want more about hunt man. He's hot."

"He really isn't," I say, but Ali isn't listening.

"Have you heard from Liz?" she's asking, the column a done deal as far as she's concerned.

"Liz? No, not a word," I say. To be honest, I was a bit hurt. After all the histrionics when I left, I had expected a text at the very least, but there's been nothing. I left a voicemail message a few days ago, but so far so silent. Still, that's Liz. She always did keep her cards close to her chest.

"So you had no idea she was about to resign?"

It's just as well I'm sitting down. "You have to be kidding me! Liz has resigned? Just when I've left and she's got the job she always wanted? That's crazy. It doesn't make sense."

"You're telling me it doesn't," Ali says grimly. "New editor, new artistic team; that isn't good news for *Blush!*. Thank God it's not my problem."

"You sound stressed. Come and stay here for a bit," I suggest, thinking how nice it would be to spend time with Ali and put the world to rights. She won't get annoyed with me because I can't work an Aga or because I've installed a very drooly stray in the house. Nor will she text to say that she's working late and won't be back until at least eleven p.m., as Ed did this morning. Ali will just be hilarious and good nicotine-scented company. Then I add, because I too can be cunning, "You can check out hunt man for yourself."

"Hmm, I'm seriously tempted," she says, "but I've got far too much on right now. I would say come to the city and see me, but you've only just moved, and besides, I need you there to get more column fodder."

We make plans to talk in a few days and Ali agrees to let me see the edited copy before it's published, then she rings off, leaving me sitting alone in the dark. I toy with the idea of putting on the lamps and watching telly in the sitting room, but the house feels cavernous and unfamiliar, so instead I rouse Ken, grab a handful of biscuits and a cup of tea and go upstairs. I'm still feeling delicate, so an early night with a book sounds like bliss.

Hmm. Not sure why I picked up *Wuthering Heights*, though. Probably not the wisest choice under the circumstances . . .

The main bedroom is huge and takes up the majority of the front of the first floor, and our furniture looks ridiculous, like something out of a doll's house. Even the king-sized bed that practically filled the bedroom in London is swamped by the acres of empty space. I click on the bedside lamp and buttery light soothes the dark corners, but even so I feel very small and very alone. I really miss Ed.

I pad across to the window and lean against the sill. Night has fallen now and the landscape outside is inky, spotted only by the solitary and intermittent beam of a lighthouse far out to sea. It's so quiet that I can almost hear my blood zooming through my veins. I can certainly hear Ken's heavy breathing he'd put any nuisance phone-caller to shame. Just as I'm about to pull the curtains, a light catches my eye high up in the turret window of Polmerryn Manor.

180

Interesting. This is the same light that's been shining every night since I moved in. Somebody spends a lot of time up there, that's for certain. But why? Who on earth would be up in the turret when they have the entire run of a mansion?

Maybe the mysterious Alex Verney has done a Rochester and locked his wife away.

I shiver at this thought. Rochester and Heathcliff both in the same village. Whoever would have thought it? I certainly don't like the thought of Heathcliff storming about with his pack of hounds and his glowering temper. This, combined with the column I have written, is not a happy thought and won't make for a good night's sleep. Maybe I'll forget *Wuthering Heights* after all. Something by Jackie Collins might be more appropriate if I'm to do Ali proud. I think about going downstairs to raid the bookcase, but there's something about the creaky floors and the dark stairwell that makes me reluctant to move from my cosy bedroom. Maybe I'll just have an early night and sleep off all the booze. Things will look better in the morning. They always do, don't they?

I hop into bed and Ken leaps up beside me. Ed will go mental if he sees him there, but do you know what? Am I bothered? I bury my face in his warm fur and feel slightly better, but even so, the thought of that attic room and the mysterious fate of Alex Verney's wife haunts me, and it's a very long time before I fall asleep.

CHAPTER
THIRTEEN

As things turn out, I don't have time to dwell on being lonely while Ed works non-stop. Nor do I have a second to stress over my certain doom once the column hits the news-stands, because on Thursday morning my sister calls to announce that she and my mother are coming to see me, en route to Glastonbury.

En route to Glastonbury? The last time I checked, Glastonbury and Cornwall were at least one hundred miles apart. Coming to be nosy is what she means. There's no point trying to put her off either. Once Emma makes her mind up, she makes mules look indecisive and flexible.

I glance around the kitchen in alarm. There's no way I'm in a state to receive visitors, even family members. Last night I admitted total defeat with the Aga and sent a very disgruntled Ed off to Fowey to pick up an Indian. I thought I'd secured the leftovers but somehow Ken managed to break out of the boot room — aka the prison where Ed insists he sleeps — and spent a very happy night noshing on chicken tikka masala and sag aloo, naans, poppadoms, cartons and all, before regurgitating the lot just about everywhere. When I came down to make Ed some breakfast, the kitchen resembled a Jackson Pollock painting.

"For Christ's sake!" groaned Ed, surveying the disaster zone. "That dog has to go, Amber! I mean it. I cannot live like this! Call the vet and see if it's microchipped. And if it isn't, then take it to the RSPCA. Please."

I'd not been overjoyed with this mess myself, but there was no way I was giving up Ken. No way at all. Ed had only been in his new job for two days but already I could see, in spite of all his promises to the contrary, that his old workaholic ways were creeping back. For the last two nights he hadn't been home before nine, and he was already making noises about working on Saturday morning. If it wasn't for Ken to chat to and take on long rambling walks through the Cornish countryside, I would be seriously cheesed off. This move was supposed to be about our new life together.

"And it will be," Ed promised, when I voiced this complaint late last night over the takeaway. "But I have to get established first and make my mark. You know that, Ambs."

I did know, but I was still disappointed. To me it felt as though I'd just swapped being on my own in London, where at least I had a job and lots of friends, for being alone in the middle of nowhere. I knew I ought to start painting, but somehow I just didn't seem to be able to motivate myself now that I had acres of time on my hands. Maybe once I felt more settled I'd

183

be able to get into it. And once I'd looked at turning the attic into a studio.

"Weren't you supposed to be taking that dog to the vet to get its microchip checked on Monday?" Ed added, as he stepped over a pool of lurid crimson vomit and backed away from the kitchen.

I nodded. To be honest, I'd been putting this off because I couldn't bear the thought of losing Ken, but I was hardly being fair. What if there was a heartbroken owner out there who loved him just as much as I did? Maybe he'd escaped from a car, or had been stolen. Just because he was left all alone at the side of the road didn't mean that he wasn't wanted.

"There's a local vet, apparently. I'll call him this morning," I promised.

Ed ran a hand across his face. "Please do, Amber. We can't live like this."

And off he stomped to have a shower, leaving me feeling relieved that he hadn't yet noticed the teeth marks in his new Mulberry briefcase. Or that one of his Kurt Geiger shoes was looking decidedly the worse for wear. If he sees any of this, Ken's days at Hawkstone House really will be numbered.

"Amber! Are you listening to me?" My sister's impatient tone whips me back into the present. At least now the kitchen is pretty much sorted, although even emptying half a can of Oust into the atmosphere can't quite dispel the unpleasant odour of mingled curry and dog vomit.

"Of course I am," I say, pulling a face at Ken. "But Em, surely Glastonbury isn't anywhere near Cornwall?"

"It's all in the West Country," says Emma breezily. "Chillax, sis. The kids are with Jeff's parents, so Mum and I are having a mini break. We're going down to Tintagel first, because Mum's decided that she's actually a reincarnation of the Lady of the Lake or something. We're going to do the whole Avalon experience so that she can reconnect."

I feel exhausted just listening to all this. Last month my mother was a reincarnation of an Egyptian queen. Just my luck to live in an Arthurian hotspot when she decides that this is her latest craze. I was pretty relaxed when I thought she was about to carry on up the Nile.

"Dozmary Pool's near you too; that's where Excalibur was returned to me," I hear my mother say. "I told Arthur not to throw it so high, but he never did listen. Oh look, darling! Isn't that an interesting standing stone?"

There's the sound of a horn blaring and a screech of tyres.

"Mum!" shrieks Emma. "Keep your eyes on the road!"

"Are you in the car?" I ask. Oh please God, no . . .

"Yes, it's Jeff's new car, and that bloody lunatic, our mother, is behind the wheel! Fuck! Mother! Will you look at the road! Jesus! Did you hit him?"

"If I did, it was only because he was in our way," I hear my mother say sulkily. "Stop fussing, Emma. It blocks my chi."

"Where are you?" I ask. Please, please say London, Wiltshire, the moon, anywhere but —

"Cornwall!" says Emma happily, while I thump my head against the kitchen table. "Ta-da! We started at four a.m. so we could surprise you. In fact we're just leaving Saltash now! We'll be with you any minute! How's that for a surprise?"

Surprise? Shock more like. I need a brandy. Or six. Can today get any worse?

Once my sister rings off, I tear around the house like a Tasmanian devil on speed, frantically trying to make the place look as though it has some kind of order. We're still living out of boxes, but at least the kitchen is almost habitable. With the bright morning sunlight streaming through the top half of the stable door, Ken slumbering by the Aga and the kettle whistling merrily from the hotplate, it's almost like a scene from *Country Living*.

Just as long as I hold my nose . . .

I'm contemplating wandering into the garden and yanking up some daisies to stuff into a vase when there's a scrunching of tyres on gravel and the roaring of some super-powered engine. Sticking my head over the half-door, I'm greeted by the sight of a navy blue Áston Martin tearing to a halt and spraying what's left of our thinning gravel into the flower beds.

I'm both stunned and appalled. Jeff must be doing really well to be driving one of these James Bond numbers, and my sister must be totally mental to let Mum anywhere near it. And where's Rain? In the boot?

The door opens, but instead of my mother's lumpy cheese-cloth-clad body, I'm faced with the far more enjoyable vision of a powerful male body uncoiling itself from the front seat. Long, muscular denim-clad legs are followed by a plaid-shirted torso, strong tanned arms and hands and a smiley face topped with a thick shock of white-blonde hair. The eyes I can't see yet because they're hidden' by Aviator mirrored shades, but they're crinkled at the edges and the large, generous mouth is smiling so widely that my own curves upwards in response. Goodness, his teeth are so perfect and white that I feel like dashing upstairs to fetch my own sunnies before I'm dazzled.

Note to self: buy some Pearl Drops ASAP.

Pinching myself just in case I've been overcome by vomit fumes and passed out, I'm delighted to discover that the man is still here and striding towards the house, the sun gleaming off his hair and burnishing golden skin lightly dusted with stubble. I feel like James Bond has arrived.

Ali was right. This column is so going to write itself!

"Hi!" says 007, striding towards me and pulling off his shades to reveal eyes as blue as the cloudless sky.

"Hi!" I squeak. Why oh why didn't I make more of an effort this morning? Tatty cut-off jeans, stinky Skechers and an old Cure T-shirt might be all very well for cleaning the kitchen but they're hardly fitting attire for a Bond girl. And why didn't I straighten my hair? It could have been in a flowing golden sheet rather than a tangled mess rammed up on my head with a bulldog clip. Ali would despair. I've not even been here a week and already my standards are down the bog.

Bollocks. I haven't put on my make-up either, or bothered with a decent bra. Where's Gok Wan when you need him?

"I'm Jinx Jackson," Bond says, taking my grubby mitt in his large, well-manicured one and folding it in a strong grip. "I'm the local vet. Lady Verney said you needed me."

Oh God, Lady Verney is so right! And I had no idea. Who put dynamite in my knickers? Hello, libido, old friend. I thought you'd curled up and died long ago.

"Amber Scott," I say, sounding as though I've been inhaling helium.

"Nice to meet you, Amber Scott," says Jinx Jackson, tucking his glasses into his top pocket and smiling down at me in such a practised way that if my brain was in gear I would be alarmed. "I'm going to have to have stern words with Virginia. She never mentioned how beautiful you are."

OK. This man is so cheesy he ought to work for Cathedral City. I am so not beautiful. I have lumpy bits, and dimply bits, and frizzy hair and am far too curvy and I know he's totally bullshitting me here, but, and this is the weirdest thing, *I don't care!*

"Thanks," I giggle. Giggle! I haven't giggled since about 1996. I think I'm blushing too. This country air is doing the weirdest things to my brain.

"So," says Jinx, his gaze sliding just below my collarbone before slowly rising again. Either he's a big fan of Robert Smith's work or he's checking me out. *Me!* "Are you called Amber because of your amazing eyes?"

188

Now my eyes are not amber. More a murky shade of hazel if we're honest, but this charm offensive is pretty intense. He could tell me the earth was flat and I'd probably agree.

"Are you called Jinx because you have accidents?" I counter.

Jinx laughs, a low, velvety sound that makes goose bumps ripple across my arms. Looking deep into my eyes he says, "Nothing I do is ever an accident, Amber. No, I got my name because I used to get up to lots of high jinks when I was younger. Can you imagine?"

Actually I can, but as a nearly-thirty-something engaged woman I probably oughtn't.

"Do you want to come in and have a coffee?" I say to change the subject, and then want to rip my tongue out. Isn't coffee a euphemism for sex?

If it is, though, Jinx hasn't noticed. He checks a chunky watch on his left wrist and nods. "Coffee sounds great. I've been on the go since half five. A difficult foaling over at Bodmin and then one of Lady Virginia's hens again. I'm gasping."

He follows me into the kitchen, and while I fill the kettle he makes a big fuss of Ken, who rolls over to have his tummy tickled. Some dogs get all the fun!

"What a lovely boy," says Jinx, while Ken writhes around in ecstasy. To me he says, "Lady V says you found him at the side of the road?"

"Just off the 303," I nod, so busy watching him caress the dog that my heaped teaspoons of coffee totally miss the mugs. Oops. Come on, Amber. Keep

189

focus here! "Why would somebody abandon such a gorgeous dog?"

Jinx shrugs his burly shoulders. "Times are tough and a big dog like him will cost a lot to feed. What have you been giving him?"

Probably best not to tell a vet that I've been feeding the dog curry and M&S goodies. Won't win me any Brownie points with Jinx — not that I want any, of course, but nor do I want to be labelled a bad dog-owner or have him take Ken away from me because I can't be trusted with his diet.

"This and that," I hedge.

Jinx's nose is wrinkling. "Do I suspect an upset tummy?"

So much for the Oust. I ought to demand a refund.

"Afraid so," I say.

"Big dogs like mastiffs can have sensitive digestion," Jinx explains, as I slosh hot water into the mugs. "Try feeding him chicken and rice. That's kinder on his tummy."

"Chicken and rice?" I echo. Didn't Ken just have exactly that, although maybe the rich, spicy sauces weren't the best choice.

He nods. "A big boy like that needs a lot of grub. A couple of chickens a day, and some dry food too. If you want to keep him, you'll need to bear in mind that he'll be expensive to feed."

Crumbs. I'd better give Lady V a call. I may need her job after all. Ed will go mental if I tell him he needs to keep Ken in organic corn-fed poultry.

Jinx reaches into his pocket and pulls out a small handheld scanner, the type I used to use on my shopping in the good old days of Waitrose. While I place the mugs on the table and decant some digestives on to a plate, he runs the scanner between Ken's shoulder blades and then over the rest of his body. Those large, strong hands are surprisingly gentle as they caress the dog's velvety fur, and I gulp. Look away, Amber. Think about arranging the biscuits.

"There's no microchip," says Jinx as I tip biscuits everywhere, and with an amazing burst of speed for such an idle dog, Ken leaps across the kitchen to hoover them up. "That means you have to decide what to do. I can make some enquiries as to whether anyone has reported him stolen or lost while he stays here with you, or I can take him to the RSPCA."

"There's no choice to make," I say firmly. "He stays."

Jinx gives me a crinkly smile, so sexy that my stomach flips, and the weirdest thing happens — I lose my desire to eat biscuits. Jinx needs to hang out with me more. I'll be a size zero by Christmas.

"I had a feeling you'd say that."

Ken looks at me with big sad eyes and my heart constricts. Of course I'll keep him. Ed will go mental, but he'll have to live with it. If I can give up my job and my life to move here for him, then the least he can do is let me keep Ken. And once I get his diet sorted, there'll be no more accidents.

I hope.

So I sit at the table with Jinx, who is super-professional and talks me through all the salient points about dog ownership. Now and again he makes a flirty comment and I turn the same colour as the leftover chicken tikka masala, but mostly he is very well behaved. Sadly. It was really nice to feel like a woman again. I think Ed just sees me as an extension of the Aga: a bit frayed around the edges and smelling of burned stuff and dog vomit. The annoyed note has crept back into his voice again too. I'm not sure what I can do to change that, apart from a total personality transplant, or maybe a very intense diet that will turn me into a supermodel.

OK, that will take more than a diet. More like a miracle.

Three coffees and a packet of Ginger Nuts later, we are still chatting away, Ken is snoozing with an adoring head on my knee and Jinx is well at home rustling up a doggy lunch of chicken breast and Uncle Ben's, courtesy of the Aga. I'm having such a lovely time talking to somebody intelligent, friendly and dog-loving that I totally lose track of time. All of a sudden there's the blast of a horn, followed by a hideous scraping sound of metal against gatepost. Moments later the dulcet tones of shrieking women are heard.

"You absolute idiot, Mother! I told you that was far too close!"

Jinx and I tear to the door. His face is white, probably at the thought of what might have happened to his beautiful car, and mine is possibly even whiter as I imagine what Ed will say if any serious damage has been done to our gates.

Fortunately for both of us, the only victim is a beautiful deep blue Mercedes. Deep blue that is apart from an ugly silver scrape along the right wing where it has become very intimate with my gatepost.

"Christ," breathes Jinx. "Who the hell is driving that?"

I have my hand over my eyes and peek through my fingers. "My mother. I didn't even know she *could* drive."

"She can't," says Jinx, wincing as in an attempt to park, my mother scrapes the wing again. "She looks like she's taking part in *Scrapheap Challenge*."

"Your problem is that you are far too attached to material goods," I hear my mother say to Emma as she kills the engine. "Stop making such a fuss. It's only a little bump."

"Little bump!" screeches Emma, sounding like Lady Bracknell. "You've taken half the wing out, you stupid old bag! Jeff will go mental."

"Jeff should learn to detach himself from his possessions," says my mother, very airily for someone who has just done thousands of pounds' worth of damage to a brand-new car. "Materialism is a cancer of the soul. That's why Rain and I don't own anything."

"Yes, you just trash other people's things instead!" my sister wails, but Mum isn't listening; she's drifting across my lawn exclaiming in rapture over the honeysuckle, her orange cheese-cloth kaftan swirling around her hairy legs.

"Hello, darling!" she calls to me. "What a lovely place! It has a beautiful energy. I'll dowse for you in a minute and tell you about the ley lines."

Jinx looks at me, stunned. "That's your *mother*?"

I sigh. "It's a long story. Believe me, I never realised what a strange effect the menopause can have on a woman."

Emma, puce with rage, stomps into the kitchen, barges past Jinx and me and collapses at the kitchen table with her head in her hands.

"I need a drink," she says.

"It's only half eleven," I point out.

My sister raises her head and looks at me with bloodshot eyes. "I have just driven for an hour with a lunatic who doesn't give a hoot for the Highway Code because it apparently exists only to enslave us all and to stunt her creativity as a driver. She then ignored the one-way system in Fowey, nearly drove us into the river and now she's wrecked my husband's pride and joy. I don't give a toss about the time, Amber! Just give me a bloody drink!"

Fair enough, and I do as I'm told. Minutes later, Emma is glugging back Merlot like it's Ribena. When Mum drifts into the kitchen, complete with dowsing crystal and chatting nineteen to the dozen to her spirit guide, I feel like joining her.

Jinx, probably fearing for his Aston, sidles to the door. "I'll pop by tomorrow with some diet sheets for Ken," he promises me, laying a land on my shoulder. "Maybe when you're less busy we can have a good chat about him. Perhaps even a drink?"

194

It's a sign of how stressed my bloody family get me that I'm not dancing around the kitchen with joy at this thought. Yes, Jinx is sex on a stick, he's funny and flirty and makes me forget that as far as my fiancé is concerned I'm about as attractive as Ugly Betty on a very ugly day, but now my insane family has descended, I am so wound up I'm almost screwing myself into the floor.

Once Jinx roars away, I slam the stable door shut and am greeted by the sight of my mother tucking into the dog rice while wagging her pendant around like a loon. Ken has taken one look at this insanity and hidden in the boot room, and I don't blame him at all. In fact it seems like a very good idea.

"Lovely house, darling," Mum says happily. "The energy flow is just right."

"Your energy flow isn't," mutters my sister darkly. "It just flowed my car right into a fucking gate."

"Language, Emma!" reproves my mother. "Swearing is a negativity magnet."

"See what I've had to put up with?" says my sister. "If she makes another comment like that, she'll be a fist magnet."

While they squabble and Emma texts her long-suffering husband, I make yet more coffee. Then I give them a tour of the house, introduce them to Ken and, to defuse another row, tell them about my new friends, Lady Virginia and Jinx.

"The hot vet!" Emma's eyes light up. "He's lush. Get in there, sis!"

I laugh and waggle my left hand under her nose. "I'm engaged to Ed, remember?"

My sister pulls a face. "And how is dear old Ed? Spending lots of time with you now that you're living the good life?"

"He's working really hard," I say defensively.

"Of course he is," says Mum kindly. "But it must be lonely for you, darling, being here while he's in the office. What are you up to?"

I shrug. "This and that. I'll do some painting soon, and maybe I'll find some part-time work. And of course I have Ken to look after."

Emma shoots me a look. "The dog? Sure that isn't a substitute baby?"

I lob a cushion at her. "No!"

"But you must be pretty lonely stuck out here on your own," Mum says, catching the cushion, plumping it up and putting it back on the sofa. "Maybe it's time you and Ed thought about starting a family. That would be nice for you."

"Mother! They're not even married yet!" exclaims my sister.

Mum pulls a face. "Darling, however did you become so bourgeois? It certainly isn't my influence. It must be your father's, he always was conservative. Amber doesn't have to be married to have children. Goodness, Emma, you sound like David Cameron."

Sometimes it's easy to be with your family. Nothing you say can shock them. So here goes.

"Don't you have to have sex to get pregnant?" I say idly.

Emma and Mum's bottom jaws swing on their hinges.

OK. Maybe I was wrong about that shocking your family thing.

"Are you telling me you don't have sex with Ed?" Emma asks, eyes like saucers. "Like, not at all?"

Me and my big gob. "Not never, exactly, just not very often. But that's normal when you've been together a while, isn't it? All that wears off after a bit, right?"

"Wrong," says Emma.

"Sex is the lifeblood of a relationship," my mother says sagely. "Rain and I try to have sex at least twice a week, unless we're doing tantric. Then it can take days."

"Ew!" Emma and I chorus.

Too much information already!

"Seriously, though, Ambs," Emma says to me when we're just about recovered from these gruesome thoughts. "Even Jeff and I manage to do the deed on a Saturday night. It's a bit of a pain fitting it in between *The X Factor* and having dinner, but it's important. Are you telling me you don't have sex at all?"

I am so regretting starting this conversation. "No! I'm not saying that!"

My sister regards me beadily. "So, when was the last time you and Ed slept together?"

Oh Lord. This is the million-pound question. I can't phone a friend because Ali is working, and the audience are staring at me, so it's fifty-fifty, which basically means hedging my bets.

"She can't remember!" My mother leans forward and grabs my hand. "Oh darling, a woman in her prime should be worshipped and adored. When Rain and I —"

"Shut up!" I clap my hands over my ears. Any more hints at my mother's rampant sex life will seriously send me over the edge. Apart from the fact that the thought makes me queasy, it's unfair in the extreme that a woman in her sixties is getting more action than me. "I can remember! It was when we went away for the weekend!"

Emma looks horrified. "But that was ages ago! It's nearly June now! What's the matter with him?"

He's tired? He's stressed? He's working? I don't know. I haven't given it that much thought.

"Has he got someone else?" my sister says. "Because if he has, I'll chop his bollocks off and make them into earrings."

"Of course he hasn't!" I shake my head at this ridiculous thought, and ignore the horrible little cold hand of doubt that squeezes my heart. "This is Ed we're talking about. Hardworking, rather dull Ed. He's not the kind to cheat."

"I've told you before, they're all the kind," says Emma bleakly. "Mark my words. If I were you, I'd get in first and shag that hunky vet. That's what happens in *The Archers*."

I roll my eyes. "This is Polmerryn, not Ambridge. Jinx just came to check the dog for microchips. Besides, I don't want to shag him, as you so nicely put it."

Now my sister rolls her eyes. "Then you're mental and there's no hope."

"I'm mental? I'm not the one listening to *The Archers*."

"Girls, girls! That's enough!" Mum intervenes, transporting us back to childhood squabbles that she always had to referee. "Great Running Wolf is getting quite upset by all this discord." She cups her hand to her ear and crinkles her forehead, as though listening hard.

"Oh Christ." Emma puts her head back in her hands. "Here we go again. He's worse than the bloody satnav. At least I can turn that off."

"Right, yes, good idea," Mum says to thin air. Turning to me, she adds, "Darling, my guides say that you and Ed need to rekindle your passion."

"No shit, Sherlock," I mutter, which my mother ignores.

"I have an old spell in my book of hours that's guaranteed to work wonders," she announces.

"Just get Viagra," says Emma, "or failing that some stockings."

Mum rounds on her. "The old ways work, my girl, so have some respect! Women have been casting spells for centuries to help their menfolk literally rise to the occasion."

Personally, I'm thinking that a month at Champneys, a trip to the hairdresser and a new wardrobe are what I need to help Ed rise to the occasion. He's pointed out my squidgy belly enough times to make it clear he finds that a turn-off. My biscuit and curry habit is getting in the way of my love life, I need to go cold turkey, and being locked in a health farm is probably the only way

I can do it. Still, Mum means well, so I try not to knock her offer back. Obviously I'll ignore everything she says. Of course I will. It's obligatory daughterly behaviour.

"I've tried this one myself, and believe me, it certainly ignites passion! You and Ed won't know yourselves." Fishing into her huge raffia sack, she pulls out a tatty notebook, which she flips through several times before locating the right page and tearing it out. Offering it to me with a flourish, she sits back and beams at me, clearly waiting for a reaction.

"Thanks." I scan the spell. Goodness, it looks like an A-level chemistry lesson. Boil this, sieve the other, strain something else. And as for the ingredients! Who on earth grows hyssop and myrtle? And it's a douche? She seriously expects me to shove green slime up my fanny? Like that's going to turn Ed on! And make sure he's the first man who sees me? How many other blokes are going to saunter past my bed while my girlie bits are covered in goo? Seriously?

Is it time to think about having my mother committed?

"Stop looking at me like that, Amber," she says sternly. "Don't knock it until you've tried it. What have you got to lose?"

She has a point. Now that I've thought about how long it actually is since Ed and I made love, I'm rather alarmed. What's even more alarming is the fact that I hadn't really noticed. Is this normal?

I tuck the spell into the back pocket of my jeans. Where I fully intend it to stay. But as we make lunch and chat, my fingers keep returning to it, and by the time Mum and Emma head off, I pretty much know it off by heart. I've even checked to see what herbs are growing in my own rather brambly garden. I think I may be more desperate than I thought. I don't intend to make the potion, but the idea is rather appealing and certainly cheaper than new underwear, which, let's face it, has never worked in the past. It won't hurt to find some hyssop just in case, either. It's not as though I have anything else to do, is it?

And if this means I can turn Ed on and eat bickies, then it can only be a good thing.

CHAPTER
FOURTEEN

Take three hearts of precious pink rose
That under stars and moonlight grows
Then three spoons of honey gold
Awakens loving thoughts of old
Lavender of palest blue
Awakens what I mean to you
Greenest mint to sharpen desire
When you touch me lights the fire
Nettles sharp are true love's bite
So you will hold me close at night
Three silver spoons of brandy wine
You shall be mine, you shall be mine.

I read the spell through for what has to be the hundredth time, and groan. I can't believe I'm seriously contemplating brewing up this crazy concoction and giving it a whirl, but I've unfolded the paper and looked at it so often now that the ingredients and the brewing process are etched on my brain. I've even trawled through the tangled flower beds at Hawkstone House with my *I-Spy Flowers* book in an attempt to try and figure out what I already have available. Luckily for me, the people who lived here before must have been very keen gardeners, because there's pretty much everything growing here, from pink roses tumbling over the dry-stone walls to rampant armies of nettles and feral straggly mint. All I'm missing is lavender and brandy wine, whatever that is.

"All I'm missing?" I say to Ken, who rolls his eyes at my insanity. "Am I seriously going to do this? Am I really so desperate that I'm actually listening to my mother's mumbo-jumbo?"

This is a slippery slope. If I'm not careful, I'll be chatting to Great Running Wolf before I know it, but the sad truth is that actually I am desperate. The conversation with Mum and Emma shook me, because I really hadn't noticed quite how badly our love life had deteriorated. Once my bonkers family had departed for Dozmary Pool, I raced up the stairs to my bedroom, stripped down to my underwear and examined myself critically in front of the full-length mirror. In the harsh light of day this was a brave move; still, although what I saw didn't exactly cheer me up, neither did I run from the room screaming. So I had a bit of cellulite and my stomach wasn't as flat as it could be. At least my boobs were pretty good for a girl who was nearly thirty. Elle Macpherson probably wasn't shaking in her skinny jeans, but I didn't think the sight of me would send small children screaming for their mummies. I spun about and craned my neck to examine myself from just about *every* angle, but I didn't think I looked too bad; nothing that a bit of Fake Bake and biscuit-tin avoidance couldn't cure. I just needed to chivvy Ed up a bit, that was all. Everything would be fine. We'd just become complacent.

So that evening I dug out my best lingerie and cooked — as best I could given the Aga handicap — a seafood pasta dish that I knew Ed loved. I even opened a nice bottle of wine and wore a scoop-neck top to show off the frilly edge of my bra. In short, I did all the things that *Senora* always advises its readers to do, and as far as I was concerned, I was on my way to Wembley when it came to a night of passion. Apart from installing a pole, or maybe in my case a girder, and doing a dance, there wasn't much more I could think of. As I lit the candles, I'd have bet my first pay cheque from the *Dagger* that I was home and dry.

It's just as well I'm not a betting woman. By the time Ed walked through the door at half past nine, the pasta was a congealed splat in the pan, the candles had sputtered to greasy stumps and I was finishing the bottle of wine and watching *Sex and the City* reruns, which, let's face it, was the closest I was going to get to sexual adventuring any time soon. Cue my fiancé pulling a face, switching on Bloomberg and sticking a pizza in the Aga before nodding off and leaving me to rescue a charred crust. I left him snoring on the sofa and went to bed with Ken, who, although lovely, wasn't the male I'd intended to watch me stripping off to my underwear. As I lay alone in the big bed, and looked across the valley to the solitary light at Polmerryn Manor, I reread my mother's spell and suddenly it didn't look quite so silly.

If my mother, my sixty-year-old mother who hasn't shaved her armpits since Gordon Brown was PM, can have amazing sex with a toy boy, then maybe, just maybe, there's something in this spell malarkey. After all, what do I have to lose, apart from my sanity, of

204

course, which at this point in time I'm starting to seriously question. I am an educated twenty-nine-year-old twenty-first-century woman and I'm boiling up nettles and chanting at the moon. What on earth am I playing at?

"I'm a twenty-nine-year-old woman whose fiancé thinks she's considerably less exciting than the rolling news," I say to Ken, who looks up at me with big brown eyes. "Desperate times call for desperate measures."

And these are certainly desperate measures. I'm standing in the kitchen surveying all the ingredients that I have gathered so far, which I have laid out with Ramsayesque precision on the table. On the positive side, I've hopefully toned up a bit by lifting my biggest Le Creuset from the pan cupboard without the help of a crane. On the negative, apart from probably needing some serious therapy, I have covered my arms in nettle stings in the process of gathering the required amount and now look like a plague victim. I have collected up sieves, old stockings to strain the concoction through and a giant wooden spoon that I found in the outhouse, and I am almost good to go. It's just a shame I don't have a cauldron. That would really complete the look.

So, apart from the lavender and the brandy wine, I have just about everything I need to brew this love potion. Sizzling sex life, here I come!

"The brandy wine is easy," I say to Ken as I slip on his lead. "We'll nip down to the Ship for that. And we're bound to see some lavender somewhere. I only need a few handfuls."

"Woof!" agrees Ken, thumping his tail excitedly, and before long we're strolling down into Polmerryn, enjoying the glorious summer day. Once in the pub, Terry Tipple decants me some brandy wine (which looks suspiciously like Courvoisier to me) and Virginia, propping up the bar as usual, suggests that I walk along to the manor house and help myself to some lavender.

"We have oodles of the stuff," she says. "Honestly, darling, take as much as you want. We have an entire lavender garden just begging to be enjoyed. If you go through the side gate off Summer Lane, you'll be in just the right spot."

Relieved and a little concerned that nobody has thought to ask me why I want brandy and lavender at half eleven in the morning, I set off towards Polmerryn Manor. In the warm sunshine the old medieval house slumbers amid lush green gardens like a sultana reclining on velvet pillows, and as I push open the creaky side gate I have the feeling that I've been whizzed back in time. I half expect Henry VIII to stroll past singing "Greensleeves" while strumming a lute, because I'm in a walled garden crammed brimful with the most wonderful herbs and flowers. I know that all I have in common with Charlie Dimmock are my boobs, but even I can recognise jasmine and rosemary and thyme. The air thrums with the drowsy buzzing of bees and the soft breeze carries with it the heady scents of summer flowers. Tying Ken to a peeling white bench, I wander along the rows of plants, trailing my hands through the leaves and flowers to release the most delicious perfumes and raising my face to feel the kiss of the sun. Pulling off my scrunchie, I shake back my curls from my face and slip my gypsy top from my shoulders. Assume romantic heroine position! All I need now is a trailing skirt, a wicker basket over my arm and Mr Darcy — in a wet shirt obviously — and I'd be right there in pink-book land!

Blissed out, I stroll through the herbs until eventually I find the lavender garden. Goodness, Virginia wasn't exaggerating. A smooth green grass pathway winds its way through dense lavender bushes, which fill the air with scent and rain small blue beads on to my feet as I brush past. What a tranquil spot, I think happily as I pull a clump away from a bush and place it into my shoulder bag. I could spend hours here painting and sketching. Maybe if I ask Virginia she'll let me. I could design some postcards that she could sell to her visitors, if she and her mysterious son ever get their butts in gear and open the place, that is.

My mind full of ideas, patterns and colours and my bag stuffed full of lavender, I meander back to the bench to collect Ken. Then I'll go home, make some lunch — a low-calorie one just to help Project Get Desirable on its way — and get stuck into Mum's spell. If you can't beat 'em, join 'em, eh?

But by the bench, where there should be ten stone of solid bullmastiff slumbering in the sunshine, there is just an empty space. The bench is lying on its side with the lead and collar still attached to the metal arm, but of Ken there is no sign, the only clue to his whereabouts being a flattened path leading through the ornamental flower beds that spread in hexagonal glory before the manor house.

Oh shit.

Where has Ken gone? And, more importantly, just how much damage can a big hungry dog do in a short space of time?

"Ken!" I holler, as I follow in his wake through the trampled flowers. "Ken! Where are you?"

Unsurprisingly, Ken fails to respond. Huffing and puffing like Thomas the Tank Engine on a very steep incline and with the Fat Controller on board, I run up the sloping lawn towards the house, and then, spotting a shattered flowerpot, veer around to the side. Gravel is scattered everywhere, a bay tree lists drunkenly on its side and the sound of excited barking can be heard from just around the corner.

Passing the back of the manor house, I follow a cobbled path that leads me into a stable yard. Several beautiful equine heads look at me with interest and a small Jack Russell bounds over, but I am oblivious, because all I can register is that Ken, my lovable cuddly Ken, is getting intimate with a very beautiful black Labrador. I didn't think he was that kind of dog! He's only just met her! He doesn't even know her name.

Have I rescued the Ashley Cole of the bullmastiff world? And hang about — it's *my* sex life the love potion is supposed to perk up, not my dog's. How unfair is that?

"Ken! Bad dog! Get off her!" I yell.

Oh God, what on earth do I do? I have no idea. I'm just dithering about whether to try and pull Ken off or

208

just run away and hide myself until the earth swallows me whole when none other than Heathcliff strides into the yard, gun over his shoulder and with a face blacker than Darth Vader's cloak.

"Is this your bloody dog?" he roars, looming over me and totally blocking out the sun.

"Not technically," I squeak, shrinking back. Oh God, he's furious. Those green eyes are like rage lasers and my irises feel scorched. "I rescued him."

Heathcliff makes a sound that's a cross between a snort and a laugh. "Yes, he looks badly in need of rescuing. Perhaps you shouldn't bother in future. Or stick to a dog you can control. Maybe a poodle."

I'm incensed. Do I look like the kind of girl who would buy a poodle? Then I catch a glimpse of my wild curls in the smeary glass of the tack room window and wince. Maybe he has a point.

Ken, job done, flops on to the cobblestones, tongue lolling. All he needs is a post-coital cigarette to complete the look.

"I'm so sorry," I say uselessly. "I didn't think he'd do that."

Heathcliff looks at me as though I'm totally stupid, which come to think of it is the way he looked at me the first time we met.

"He's entire, so what the hell did you think he'd do if he caught the scent of a bitch on heat?"

I stare at him.

"You did know your dog was entire?" says Heathcliff slowly.

I gulp. "What does *entire* mean?"

"That he's in full working order."

I stare at him blankly.

Healthcliff shakes his head. Dark curls flop across his face and he pushes them away impatiently with a strong tanned hand.

"That he still has balls. In other words, he hasn't been castrated. He can still mate. Does that explain it sufficiently for you?"

My hand flies to my mouth. Oh Lord. I *think* Jinx did mention something along these lines when he popped over the other day, but I was so busy checking out the vet himself, who is certainly entire, that I wasn't really paying full attention. See, this is why I have to make the love potion work. If I don't, I'm just a slave to my hormones. Who knows what could happen.

"Is that a problem?" I say, weakly. Heathcliff is carrying a gun, so I don't want to wind him up. If I do, I have a nasty feeling I'll go the same way as the two sad-looking bunnies he's dropped on the ground. Sad-looking and very dead bunnies. What a horrible man! Who on earth shoots Thumper for fun?

He raises his eyes to heaven. "It might have been nice if he'd bought her dinner first. Of *course* it matters! She's a pure-bred bitch! What is it with you? Do you enjoy causing destruction wherever you go? Of course I don't want any old mutt interfering with her bloodlines."

"Ken is not any old mutt!" I say, stung by this. "He's lovely! And I'm sure his breeding is just as good as your dog's, if not better. Anyway, it's not about breeding. They obviously really like each other."

Heathcliff is looking at me as though I'm mental. "Are you trying to tell me this is all fine because our dogs are in love?"

Er. Put like that, I must admit it sounds nuts.

"Because if you are," he continues, so icily that it's amazing a couple of glaciers don't glide past, "you're even more of a stupid townie than I thought you were. People like you shouldn't be allowed to have animals."

"*I* shouldn't be allowed to have animals?" I shriek, my blood boiling at this slur. "I'm not the one killing rabbits! I'd much rather be a stupid townie than a rabbit murderer! At least I like animals and don't kill them for fun. Come on, Ken, we're going!"

Grabbing the reluctant Ken by the scruff of his neck, I drag him out of the yard, so angry I'm amazed I don't combust. All the way to the gate I'm fuming, and I can feel Heathcliff's gaze burning into my shoulder blades so intensely that my bare skin is probably scorched. I don't need to turn around to know that his firm mouth will be set in a tight line and his strong arms folded across his chest. Assuming angry positions seems to be his default mode whenever I am nearby.

As I stomp up the hill to Hawkstone House, I am shaking with a horrible cocktail of rage and embarrassment. I know I should have had more control over Ken, and I know I should have listened more carefully to Jinx rather than becoming totally distracted by his sexy denim-blue-eyed smile, but even so, these things surely happen all the time in the country, don't they? It's nature's way. Heathcliff is just a miserable,

211

nasty piece of work. Never mind splashing him that day, I should have bloody well drowned him!

What a horrible, horrible man! How dare he call Ken a mutt and say I shouldn't have animals.

I'm glad now that I used him for my column. My only regret is that I was actually far too nice. I should have done a total hatchet job on him and really gone to town. Well, Heathcliff, just you wait until next Sunday! You and your gun and your dead animals and your stupid green jumper. Ali wanted *Sex and the Country* and now she's got it, even if the only ones having sex around here are the pets. The evil gamekeeper is about to become a national hate figure.

Once home, Ken, in true male fashion, falls into a deep slumber on the kitchen sofa while I decant my lavender and brandy on to the table. Thanks to Heathcliff, I'm far too razzed up to think about eating, so I get busy with my recipe and before long I'm bubbling pans and sieving soggy nettles like something out of *The Crucible*. The kitchen smells foul, I'm up to my elbows in green goo, two Le Creuset pans are totally cremated and even the Aga looks as though it's about to admit defeat. After three hours of intense labour, and wondering in what parallel universe did I ever think it was a good idea to listen to my mother — a woman who talks to invisible friends, for heaven's sake — I finally have a finished product.

I sniff the vat of shimmering bluey-green liquid and my nose wrinkles thoughtfully. Hmm, not bad. I hope I've followed the instructions to the letter. A drop or two of brandy *may* have just found its way into my mouth, but that was just quality control, and to be honest, I need to be a teeny bit pissed if I'm going to anoint myself with this goo, shove a load up my fanny and decorate my bits with rose petals. I may need to get Ed pissed too, otherwise he'll die of shock.

Hmm . . . getting Ed upstairs, into bed and into my knickers before he realises I'm doing an impression of a pot of pesto is probably easier said than done. Maybe I should have saved some of that brandy.

Never mind, I tell myself as I wash my hands and try to restore order to the kitchen, I'll figure all that out later. Hopefully if the spell does its stuff he'll be powerless to resist from the second he opens the front door. And at least thinking about my spell and the logistics of Operation Seduce Ed has taken my mind off horrible Heathcliff and his eyes, which are as dark green and as liquid bright as my potion. I feel as though that gaze has been seared on to my retinas and I don't like it one little bit. It's like he's cast an evil spell on me.

I'm just planning my next column, and thinking of some really sharp and cutting observations that I can make, when there's a sharp rat-tat-tat at the door and Virginia pokes her head through. Today she's *sans* wig and sporting a jaunty yellow bonnet complete with Easter chicks and matching yellow Hermes scarf.

"You have been busy!" she exclaims, marching up to the Aga and burying her nose in my last surviving pan. "That smells delicious, Amber! Nettle and lavender soup! Jolly well done!" and before I can warn her, she's plunged a finger into the potion and smacked her lips around it, licking them greedily. Oh God. Oh God. I have just fed the local lady of the manor goop that is supposed to go up my fanny! What if she drops dead right here? Will I be done for poisoning her?

"Delicious!" Virginia pronounces, beaming at me and helping herself to more. "Well done you!"

I hold my breath, waiting for her to clutch her throat and fall down at my feet writhing like something out of *Alien*, but nada. She seems absolutely fine.

Maybe I won't tell her quite what I'm intending to do with this gunk.

"Now, I can see you're very busy cooking," Virginia is saying, nodding at me approvingly, "so I won't keep you long, because I'm sure you've got a lot to do for the main course."

She isn't wrong. The main course is me, and I have a lot of shaving, eyelash tinting and moisturising to be getting on with before I serve myself up on a silver platter.

"Is that open? May I?" Spotting the cooking wine on the counter, she helps herself to a mug and pours a generous measure. "Ah, lovely. Now, what was it I was going to say?"

"No idea." I follow suit, and soon we're sitting at the table swigging Merlot and eating biscuits. None of this was on my diet plan, but hopefully if the spell is a success, my wobbly bits will be the last thing on Ed's mind. Several mugs of red wine later, they're the last thing on my mind too.

"I know what I came to say!" Virginia announces after giving me the gossip about everyone from the

214

psychic postman to Terry Tipple. "I managed to finally convince Alex that we need to open the manor house to the public and get a bit organised."

"Great," I say, dunking a biscuit into my wine. Mmm. Tastes interesting but tea works better. "So what's the plan?"

"That's entirely up to Alex," sighs his mother. "The boy is such a control freak. He won't agree to anything until he's met you formally and seen a portfolio of your work."

I'm slightly alarmed. "Virginia, I'm a magazine designer, not an interior decorator. I don't have a portfolio."

"If you can do one, you can do the other," Virginia says airily, dismissing my concerns with a flap of her aristocratic hand. "That Laurence Llewelyn chap has done terribly well."

"If you want zebra print and purple walls, maybe he's your man," I say, but Virginia shakes her head.

"We already have plenty of that, darling! I just want you to give Alex a few ideas about which rooms you think would look the best and how we could present them. Call it consultancy! I think you'd be brilliant. I love what you've done with this place."

"All right," I say. "Why not? It could be interesting."

Virginia claps her hands. "I so hoped you'd agree. And you'll love Alex. He's such fun! You and he will hit it off and be great friends, I just know it."

I laugh. "I'm always happy to make friends."

It can't hurt just to have a chat, can it? I must admit that the mysterious Alex of the vanishing wife intrigues me. And any money I earn can only help to sort the house out and keep Ed happy. Everybody wins. Perfect.

Eventually Virginia staggers down the garden and back towards the manor. Leaving the back door ajar, to air out the rather pungent scent of stewing nettles, and Ken still fast asleep, I then spend a happy few hours doing girlie stuff in the bathroom. By the time dusk falls, my toenails are coral pink, my legs so hairless they squeak and my mad curls have been bullied into a sheet of gold by the GHDs. A layer of shimmery moisturiser, a squirt of Mademoiselle and a slick of peachy lip gloss and ta-da! I'm good to go.

Or come, with any luck!

Starkers, I wander back into the hall and carry out the final part of my ritual. Lots of candles, gleaned from the meagre supply in the village shop, flicker across the kitchen and a trail of tea lights leads enticingly up the stairs towards the bedroom. Now all I have to do is dot my nipples and girlie bits with the goo and scatter rose petals across my body. I could be in *American Beauty*! This is fun. I'm starting to understand exactly what my mother sees in all this nonsense; in fact, in the soft candlelight I don't look too bad at all. My body is all peachy and curvy rather than sludgy and dimpled, and my hair is for once doing exactly what it's been told, thanks to the two cans of Elnett I've blasted it with. As long as I don't wander too near a candle I should be OK . . .

Now, should I put a touch more mascara on? Or maybe I should wrap up in a duvet until Ed arrives. It's very cold here. My nipples look positively indecent, but

216

maybe that's the point. Oh dear, I am useless at this seduction lark. Life is easier when we just eat pizza and fall asleep on the sofa.

I'm contemplating digging out the fan heater when there's a thud from the kitchen. Aha! That'll be the dulcet sound of a male boot kicking the bottom half of the back door open. Ed is home from a hard day's solicitoring, and much earlier than usual too! Well, here I am! Prepare to be seduced!

I fly along the hall and race into the kitchen.

"Hello, darling!" I trill, spinning around with hair and boobs flying as my eyes adjust to the candlelit gloom. "Surprised?"

There's a nervous throat-clearing.

"You could say so," replies a horribly familiar voice.

I stop mid-spin and nearly topple over. Hang about, that's a voice that only a few hours earlier was bellowing at me.

"This wasn't quite what I expected to find when I brought your dog back from his second attempt to molest my Lab," the voice continues, sounding amused now. "I presume this is also standard city behaviour?"

My blood turns to ice and I have a horrible sinking sensation. Please God, no. I will do anything at all, adopt orphans, be a nun, give what little money I earn to charity, anything at all if this isn't really happening. What on earth did I do wrong in my last life to deserve karma coming over and giving me a double whammy?

Whatever I did, it must have been very bad, for standing in my kitchen, holding Ken by a piece of rope and faced with the sight of my very naked rose-petal-covered self, is none other than Heathcliff.

And he isn't looking away.

CHAPTER
FIFTEEN

Mortified, I dive towards the sofa and cower behind it. Let me die now, God, please.

Please?

Great, I'm still here. Thanks a bundle, God!

"I'm so sorry, I had no idea you were so busy," says Heathcliff, looking stunned. "Can I get you anything?"

Some dignity? And a dash of pride? Saving that, a bathrobe.

"I thought you were someone else!" I splutter, my cheeks burning — all four of them. "Could you please grab me something to cover up with?"

"Right, yes," Heathcliff says, dragging his gaze away from me and to the flagstones. Grabbing a duvet cover from the top of the ironing basket, he lobs it in my direction and I wind it around my body, not giving a toss that it's Egyptian cotton and that the green goo will probably trash it. No, the most horrible man in Cornwall has just seen me stark naked, so I have more important things on my mind than ruining the bedlinen.

Oh God, I really hope he didn't see my cellulite. And does he think my stomach is fat?

"You can't just come bursting in to other people's houses!" I squeak.

"Oh, I don't know. It can be very *interesting*." He grins. "Besides, I wasn't bursting in, I was dragged in by your dog, who has somehow managed to find his way back to visit mine. Believe me, I find his intrusion equally inconvenient."

"Inconvenient!" I splutter. "You didn't even knock."

"And he didn't even buy Sadie a bone," drawls Heathcliff, still watching me as I attempt to cover my body and pick rose petals off my boobs at the same time, which is easier said than done. "Anyway, here's your dog back," he says to the floor now while I wrestle myself into an almost decent state, boob flashes aside. "You really need to keep a closer eye on him."

"I will, I will," I promise, clenching my arms down to keep the duvet cover up as I hobble out of hiding. "I'm really sorry, I hadn't noticed that he'd gone. I've been very busy."

Heathcliff's emerald gaze slides up from the flagstones, flickers down my body and then back up to my glowing face. My heart does the weirdest tap dance in my throat.

A ghost of a smile plays across his lips.

"So I see," he says.

"It's a beauty treatment," I stutter, not sure why I need to explain myself. "It's natural and organic."

His eyes stray to my chest and I tug the duvet cover a bit higher.

220

"Well, for what it's worth, I'd say it's working very well indeed. Just try and keep an eye on that dog of yours in between *beauty treatments*, will you?"

I gulp. "I'm so sorry. It won't happen again. I promise."

Heathcliff's eyebrows shoot into his dark hair. "Somehow, I don't believe that. And if it does, I am going to have to think of a penalty for bad behaviour."

His eyes hold mine and I feel a bit quivery. It must be something in the potion that's making my head spin, because I am suddenly starting to imagine all kinds of punishments. For one awful and insane moment I have a vision of myself winding my fingers into those thick ebony curls and pulling his head down towards —

Whoa! Stop right there! What is happening to me? Is the potion working backwards? I am so not having erotic thoughts about this man. No way.

"Anyway, I'll leave you to your *beauty treatments*," says Heathcliff slowly, making me wonder if he's just read my thoughts, a notion that makes me feel even more jelly-legged. "I would apologise for interrupting, but I'd be lying if I said I was sorry."

The git! He's actually laughing at me now; his eyes are crinkling at the corners and his mouth has curled into a smile. It suits him, a bit like the way the sunshine suits the sea once the storm has passed. As he bends down to pat Ken, he looks up at me with amusement, and for a split second I find myself smiling back before I remember that this is Heathcliff, bunny killer and trespasser.

And the man who has now not only seen my red underwear but also what I keep in it.

Can life get any worse than this?

"How dare you!" I say, with as much dignity as someone who's been parading about wearing nothing but rose petals can. "Go away and . . . and shoot some bunnies or something!"

He straightens up. "Yes, I'd better be getting on. As you say, the bunnies need dealing with. Besides, you should get dressed; you'll catch your death like that. Parts of you are clearly very chilly."

I follow his glance and discover that the duvet cover has slipped and it's obvious from certain parts of my body that I am indeed rather cold. With a shriek of horror I yank it up to my chin and flee into the hallway. The subsequent thump of the back door and following stomp of booted feet announce that Heathcliff has left the building. Possessed by a devouring and inexplicable curiosity, I tear up the stairs to the landing, clutching my duvet cover to my body, and watch him stride along the lane. The windows are a little smeary, but I swear to God he's grinning.

He's laughing at me. How totally and utterly humiliating. Oh Lord. Why do these things always happen to me?

I slide to the floor and bury my head in my hands. I've wrecked the best bedlinen, which will infuriate Ed, ruined all the hard work of making the spell and, worst of all, displayed my less than perfect body to the man who is fast becoming my nemesis. Can life possibly get

222

any worse? What will I do tomorrow? Halt the economic recovery? Start a nuclear war?

And he was laughing at me too! I feel like bashing my head against the wall with frustration. Heathcliff was totally mocking me. He saw me naked and he laughed. How totally and utterly soul-destroying. I mean, obviously I don't care what a horrible person like him thinks of me, but I really wish I'd bothered to diet and tone up. If I had a body like Elle McPherson I wouldn't be feeling this mortified, would I? And he wouldn't have laughed then. No way. God, life sucks sometimes.

I'm still sitting at the top of the stairs feeling alternately hot and cold with shame when there's the sound of tyres scrunching across gravel followed by the slam of the back door and Ken's crazed barking.

"Amber!" yells Ed. "Will you please tell this dog I live here too?"

Great. The one time I'd actually like him to stay out late, Ed is home at seven on the dot. Now instead of being greeted by a sex goddess and taken on a trip to heaven and back he'll see a straggle-haired wreck sporting green-smeared bedlinen. I look like I've been wrestling naked in a vat of mushy peas.

"Ken's only saying hello," I explain as, duvet cover clutched across my chest, I descend the stairs and shuffle into the kitchen. "He's pleased to see you."

Ed, his back to me, plonks his car keys on the table. "Well I am not pleased to see him. I thought you were taking him to the vet for rehoming."

I have no intention of taking Ken anywhere, but luckily this argument is very quickly defused when my fiancé finally turns around and sees me.

"Christ!" Ed steps back in alarm. "What the fuck has happened to you? Have you been gardening?"

"Yep. Naked gardening. It's all the rage in south-east Cornwall," I say flippantly. I let the duvet cover slide a bit to expose the swell of my breasts. Heathcliff was mesmerised, albeit with horror, so surely my fiancé will want a glimpse? Come on, spell! Do your stuff!

But Ed, it seems, is immune to both magic and my boobs. He runs a hand through his sandy hair and shakes his head.

"And what's going on with all these candles everywhere? Are you trying to raze the place to the ground?" he lectures, less interested in my cleavage than a potential fire hazard. It really has come to this. He'd probably fancy me more if I was wrapped in the fire blanket.

Right, desperate times call for desperate measures. There's nothing for it now but to spell this out. Stepping forward, I drop the duvet cover and display myself in all my rose-petalled glory. Unfortunately, though, the concoction has turned into a sludgy mess, which is sliding down my thighs and slithering between my toes. I look like I've been bathing in Swarfega.

"What the hell is wrong with you?" Ed asks in alarm, recoiling. "And what have you done to the duvet cover?" His eyes bulge when he clocks exactly what it is I have been wearing. "Amber, please tell me that isn't the Egyptian thousand-thread cotton one from Heal's?"

There comes a point in every woman's life when she realises that her sex appeal has well and truly exceeded its sell-by date, and this is my moment. Here I am standing before my fiancé naked and ready for action, and all he can think about is the state of the duvet cover. Admit defeat, Amber. Donate your sexual organs to charity and start to wear granny pants and slacks. Your love life is officially over.

"Yes, Ed," I say wearily. "It is."

He looks at me as though I'm insane. It's a look I'm seeing increasingly often.

"And what is all this green stuff? We'll never get the stains out. You'll have to buy some Vanish."

I decide to tell him the truth. I must admit that as I explain about the love spell, my mother's advice and how I'd hoped for an evening of passion, it sounds increasingly bonkers, even to my own ears, and the incredulous expression on my fiancé's face speaks volumes. What was I thinking to ever imagine that Ed would be up for rolling around in nettle slime? This is a man who practically bathes in hand gel. He's right. I am insane.

"So, how about it? Fancy a shag?" I finish lamely. "Joke!"

Ed gawps at me. "You seriously believe all that crap your mother comes up with?"

"No, of course not! But you must admit things haven't exactly been good between us. I wanted to see if I could help."

"I'm working, Amber! In case it's escaped your notice, I've been really busy starting a new job and

225

being a partner in a law firm. Forgive me if I don't feel like being on stud duty whenever the mood takes you."

"That's a horrible thing to say!" Tears prickle my eyes. "I'd never expect that of you. I miss being close and I just wanted things to be better between us."

"And they will be," Ed says, loosening his tie. "Just not when you're parading around naked and covered in slime. How you expected that to turn me on I'll never know. Anyway, we wouldn't have had time; we're going to the Marchants' for dinner tonight."

We are? I stare at him.

"You hadn't forgotten, had you?" says Ed.

I stare at him. I had forgotten, or rather totally blanked it out.

"Derek Marchant is the senior partner at the firm, Amber. I told you that he and Rosemary had invited us for kitchen sups to welcome us to Cornwall. They know all kinds of important people who could be very useful to me. He may invite me to join the Masons too." Ed appears pleased at this idea. "I'm really looking forward to tonight."

Oh Lord. Have we really grown so far apart that Ed would prefer to spend an evening toadying to local dignitaries than making love to me? I know it would have been slimy and squidgy and messy but it could also have been a lot of fun. Isn't that supposed to be the point? Whatever happened to desire and losing control and being spontaneous? Whatever happened to not being able to keep our hands off one another?

As I'm thinking this, I catch a glimpse of my reflection in the window and suddenly I don't feel all golden and curvy and sexy any more. Just lumpy and straggly-haired and sad. For a second I recall Heathcliff's expression when the duvet cover slipped, the dark glitter in those emerald eyes. I'd almost misread that look as one of desire, when of course he was probably laughing at me. This is what you get for reading too many romantic novels. It's like McDonald's for the brain. For some weird reason, thinking that Heathcliff was disgusted makes me feel even more desperate than Ed's rejection. Maybe I did mess the spell up after all. Perhaps it's worked backwards and repulses men. I always was a rubbish cook. Why did I think I could get a spell right?

"Go and have a shower," Ed says, pouring himself a drink. "And wear something smart, please. We're meant to be making a good impression."

I dump the duvet cover in the laundry basket, then dutifully shower, scrub off the potion and disguise my green-tinged limbs inside a flowing green and purple maxi dress. I dust on some glittery body powder to try and detract from the strange hue and leave my hair loose, figuring I may as well make the most of having straightened it. Then I trudge back downstairs only to discover Ed going mental because he can't find the smart key to the Range Rover.

"For fuck's sake! I left it on the table!" he snarls, lifting up candles and pots and pans and clattering them back down again. "I put it right here. You saw me do it. It can't have gone."

With a sinking heart I help him search. By the time we've finished, the kitchen looks as though it's been

227

burgled and Ed is doing a pretty good Vesuvius impression. As we tear about, Ken watches us indulgently and with a satisfied expression, which is fair enough seeing as he's had sex at least twice today. There's something about the way he's drooling and licking his lips, though, that is starting to worry me. It doesn't bode well; in fact didn't he last look like that when he stole the chicken from the boot of the car?

Surely he can't have . . .

He couldn't have . . .

It's impossible.

Isn't it?

"Um, Ed," I venture, "while I was in the shower, did you leave Ken in the kitchen?"

"Of course. You know I don't agree with having animals in the sitting room."

I do know. It pisses me off greatly. Since when did he become the dog-hair police?

"On his own?"

Ed looks at me, then slowly at Ken, who lifts a paw and whines before licking his lips again. The colour drains from Ed's face.

"He couldn't have eaten it," he whispers. "Amber, tell me that's not happened. Not my Range Rover proximity key. Please, anything but that."

"The keys were on the table, now they're not," I say slowly. "Nor are they anywhere else. The only person who can reach those keys apart from us is Ken."

Ed says, in a dangerously low voice, "If your dog has eaten the key to my Range Rover, I will personally make sure it's the last thing he ever eats."

228

"If he ate it, I know he didn't mean to. It would have been an accident."

Ed blanches but the tips of his ears turn pink, which is a very bad sign.

"Have you any idea how much it will cost to replace that key? The dealer will have to have the entire system reprogrammed. We're not talking about nipping down to the high street and getting a key cut. This is going to cost hundreds of pounds. That fucking dog is costing me a fortune."

I gulp. "I'll pay for it."

He rounds on me. "With what? Magic beans?"

I open my mouth to tell him about my column, but then shut it again hastily. I don't think this is the time to reveal that our private life has been sold to Mike Elton and the *Dagger* group. But Ed isn't listening anyway.

"How the fuck am I supposed to drive my car now? I'll be late for the dinner! What's that going to look like?" Ed slams his hand on to the table. "Shit."

We both stare out of the window at sixty grand's worth of new car. New and keyless car. Keyless car that we cannot drive.

Then I have a brainwave. "The smart key only has to be in the proximity of the car to start it. If Ken's in the car with us, then all we need to do is press the ignition start button." I am a genius. Mensa would be well jel, as they say in Essex.

"But that means that everywhere I go in the car I have to take that brute with me!" Ed couldn't look more horrified if I'd told him he was going to be handcuffed to Jeremy Kyle for the day.

"Only until the key comes out," I say. "If indeed it's there. We're probably maligning poor Ken."

Ed's eyes narrow. Ken and I shrink away. "You think?" he says quietly. "Well, let's see."

With a face like thunder, Ed locks the house while I haul a sheepish Ken away from the Aga and into the car, which fortunately is unlocked. Once Ken is safely sprawled across the back seat, I hop into the driver's side, press the ignition and *brrm brrm!* the car roars into life.

Oh bollocks. Thanks a million, Ken. Drive another nail into my coffin, why don't you?

Ed buries his face in his hands. "That bloody dog has to go, Amber. This is the last straw."

Thank goodness he doesn't know about today's exploits with the lovely Lab. Ken must have canine ADHD or something. Maybe Jinx can sort him out with some Ritalin.

"How can I drive the car now?" Ed looks close to tears.

"Don't worry," I say brightly. "We know where the keys are. We just have to keep Ken in the car while we drive for a bit, that's all."

"I have to take him to work?"

"Or I can drop you there." I stick the Range Rover into reverse and it bounces down the drive like the Andrex puppy. "Poor Ken, it isn't his fault. These things happen."

230

But Ed doesn't look convinced, and to be honest neither am I. It seems that these things have a habit of happening to me, and with a nastily frequent regularity.

"I am not going to be the one who waits for the key to appear, or retrieves it when it does," Ed says, crossing his arms and scowling at me. "It's your dog; you can do that."

I nod. Gee, ain't life fun? I glance in the rear-view mirror at Ken, sprawled across the white leather seats and looking so at home he's almost a part of the car — well, I guess in a way he is now. I can't believe how much trouble he's caused me. I wouldn't swap him, though.

As we drive towards Fowey I make small talk, to which Ed just replies with grunts before ignoring me totally and staring sulkily out of the window. So I give up and focus on the road, anything actually rather than the embarrassing flashbacks to my naked body smeared with nettle slime and the alarmed look on Heathcliff's face when I danced into the kitchen. I feel hot all over at the memory, and not in a good way either.

While we're on the Bodinnick Ferry my mobile rings and I see from the caller ID that it's Liz calling. This is unusual; we haven't spoken for a while, and certainly not since Ali told me she'd resigned so unexpectedly. Her behaviour is odd to say the least and I am gagging to find out what's really going on. Ali reckons that the mystery man is at the bottom of it all, so maybe I can do some digging. I'm just about to switch to hands free for a good natter when Ed, seeing who's ringing, presses the ignore-call button.

"Hey! I wanted to talk to Liz," I say, annoyed. "We haven't caught up for ages."

Ed shrugs. "She's no loss to you, Amber, the girl hung on to your coat tails for a long time. She's probably just after a reference or something."

I sigh. Ed has never liked Liz and vice versa. They used to go out of their way to ignore one another at *Blush!* dos, and if she ever came to the house he'd make sure he was off playing squash or out with his friends. I've never really understood it. I guess it's just a clash of personalities, because as far as I know they never fell out. Still, I think I've antagonised Ed enough today. I'll call Liz back once I have a quiet minute to myself.

And let's be honest, I seem to have enough of those now. Maybe it's time I took Lady V up on her job offer after all.

CHAPTER
SIXTEEN

"God, I really need a cigarette," whispers Jinx, his breath warm against my ear. "Fancy scooting outside for one?"

I haven't smoked since uni, but the stress of sitting through a stuffy dinner with a load of half-dead lawyers and their wives, having to explain why my skin has a strange green tinge and feeling a nervous wreck because Ken, the canine weapon of mass destruction, has been shut in the Marchants' cloakroom and is probably wrecking the place, is taking its toll. Suddenly I can't think of anything I would like more than a lovely hit of nicotine, and sneaking outside with the gorgeous Jinx has a certain appeal too. Glancing at Ed, who's deep in discussion with a group of braying men and their equally braying wives, I decide to chance resuming my addiction. Anything's better than staying here — I'll probably grow an Alice band!

"Having fun?" Jinx asks as, once on the balcony, he flips open his Zippo and lights two cigarettes. One of these he passes smoothly from his own lips to mine, a cheeky smile lifting the corner of his mouth as he does so. It's a practised move but a good one, and from the way his gaze flickers from my mouth and back to my eyes I know he's measuring the effect it has on me. Weirdly, it actually has very little. I'm still too annoyed by Heathcliff and his sardonic amusement at my naked antics to be able to think straight. That annoying man! He's ruining everything. I knew I'd buggered up that love spell. What if I've gone and wrecked what teeny-weeny bit of libido I have left? Here I am in a dark garden overlooking the churning sea and next to a gorgeous man who could double for Daniel Craig, and all I can think about is bloody Heathcliff.

Sometimes life really sucks.

"Amber?" Jinx says, nudging me gently. "Is everything OK?"

Mentally shaking myself and consigning all thoughts of this afternoon and Heathcliff to the spam box of my memory, I smile up at him.

"I'm having an interesting time," I say. "The company is certainly different."

Seriously, even if I hadn't painted myself green I would never have fitted in in a million years. Derek and his male cronies are puffed up and self-important and hardly let any of us without willies get a word in edgeways. I think for them feminism was just something that happened to other folk. I'm more than a little alarmed to see that Ed is trying as hard as possible to fit in with them.

Jinx laughs. "Thank God you're here tonight. When I saw that Rosemary had lined me up to sit with Caro Evans, I nearly died. Lovely girl and a cracking rider, but slap a saddle on her and she could double for one of her horses!"

I wag my finger at him. "Don't be nasty, she seems very nice."

"She is nice," Jinx agrees, "and I normally love riding horses, but you have to draw the line somewhere!"

I inhale thoughtfully on my cigarette. Caro is obviously very taken by Jinx, as are most of the ladies in the room regardless of their age and marital status. Jinx is very charming to them all, certainly knowing how to boost egos and smooth feathers, and it's been most amusing to watch him work the room. I can't help but be flattered that he's sought me out as real company once he's exhausted his charm offensive on the other women. When you've been mocked by one man and rejected by another, having the attention of somebody as gorgeous and in demand as Jinx is like balm to the wounded pride. I have no idea why he's seeking me out, but he's certainly good company. And, cheeky as it is, the free advice about retrieving the car key from Ken has been very helpful. Although what wasn't quite so helpful was the way Jinx laughed almost until he cried when I told him. Only fear of being sued stopped Ed from thumping him.

Mock Ed's Range Rover at your peril.

"So Rosemary Marchant was doing some matchmaking tonight?" I say. Apart from the long-faced Caro, there were several other single girls, all of whom had batted their eyelashes at Jinx so much that he'd probably felt like he was in a wind tunnel.

He laughs. "Welcome to Fowey! Matchmaking and Partner-swapping Central! She certainly was, but I'm afraid I'm a very poor second choice. Just before you and your partner arrived, she was having a cow because her star guest had pulled out at the last minute. Can you guess who it was?"

I rack my brains, but try as I might, I can't think of any celebrity hunks in south-east Cornwall.

"Alex Verney!" Jinx flicks his cigarette butt over the balustrade and fantails spark into the inky sea. "No wonder she was pissed off when he didn't make it."

"Virginia's son?"

He nods. "The very same. Now that Alex is back on the scene, with his title and his stately home, not one of the girls will look at a humble vet."

Jinx, with his striking good looks and sports car, is as far from a humble vet as I am from Claudia Schiffer, and I'm intrigued. Alex Verney must really be something special.

"So what's the story with him?" I ask as casually as I can, and Jinx groans.

"Oh God, not you as well? I must get myself a tragic past ASAP. You women really go for all that, don't you? And there was I thinking that being kind to animals and having a sports car was my key to finding love."

"I'm just a nosy journalist really," I say. "If there's a good story then I'm on it. And you," I add, as I stub out my cigarette and fix him with a stern look, "are not looking for love. You're looking for a fling."

He places his hand on his heart and opens his eyes wide. "Amber Scott, you're beautiful and clever and incredibly sexy. And you have a nice dog too. A fling with you would be wonderful. I think we could have a lot of fun."

236

Oh Lord. What is wrong with me? Here is sex-on-a-stick Jinx flirting like crazy and I feel as though my fanny's turned into a glacier. Maybe I really am over the hill. On the other hand, I've never been much good at flings. I wish I could be like Ali with her "fuck 'em and chuck 'em" mentality, but I have a horrible habit of falling in love and then getting my heart trampled into smithereens. So gorgeous as Jinx is, I'm relieved that my self-preservation instincts seem to have kicked in.

"Thanks for the offer," I say. "But FYI I am a happily engaged woman."

"Really?" He looks doubtful.

"Really," I say firmly. "Now tell me about Alex Verney. And I mean *all*."

"Story of my life," sighs Jinx. "All alone with a sexy, beautiful woman —"

I snort. "Hello? You are not about to seduce me. I think you can put the trowel down."

"Trowel?"

"For laying it on so thick with?"

Jinx laughs and shakes his blond head. "Fair dos," he says, putting his hands up. "I can see that you're not interested. Let's just be mates."

"Mates," I agree, with mingled relief and regret. Emma would throttle me if she knew I'd turned down the chance of some fun with this man. I just hope Great Running Wolf doesn't dob me in to Mum.

"So, Alex Verney. Money, title, good looks. You name it, he had it. Never mind being born with a silver spoon. He had the entire canteen of silver cutlery in his mouth."

Oh! This doesn't quite tie in with my image of Alex Verney as a chinless wonder.

"Anyway, when he married a model, none of us were particularly surprised," Jinx continues, leaning against the railings and peering into the water below where our host's powerboat bobs on the swell. "Vanessa was gorgeous. French, tall, slim, and with legs up to her armpits, and Alex seemed to adore her. They were the perfect couple, the Posh and Becks of Fowey, but we never really saw much of her. Alex is a pretty private kind of guy and he kept her to himself. Can't say I blame him. If I'd been married to Vanessa I'd probably never have got out of bed."

I think of Ed shrinking away from me. A cold hand squeezes my heart.

"Anyway, to cut a long story short, Alex and Vanessa were only married for two years. They went away on a holiday and she never came back."

I stare at him. "Never came back? What do you mean?"

"Exactly that," says Jinx. "Alex came back on his own. Apparently Vanessa had died."

"Died? How?"

He shrugs. "No idea. Alex never said. Like I told you, he's a secretive one. Some people say she left him and he couldn't bear the shame, others think he did away with her."

A shiver ripples across my flesh. "Killed her?"

238

"Or maybe she's still in the house but as his prisoner," Jinx whispers. "In any case, it's all a big mystery. Nobody really knows the truth, and unusually for Lady V, she isn't talking either."

I think of the solitary attic light that beams across Polmerryn Valley every night. Maybe Alex Verney really has done a Rochester and locked Vanessa in the attic. Is she pacing up and down night after night like a modern Bertha Mason? The hairs on my forearms ripple.

I'm just about to ask Jinx for more details when Ed joins us on the terrace. One look at the set of his shoulders tells me the kind of mood he's in.

"Can you get the dog?" he snaps. "We need to leave, I've got an early start tomorrow."

"The dog car key!" Jinx laughs.

Ed's fists clench. "How much do you charge to put dogs down and retrieve swallowed goods?"

"Ed!" I'm horrified, even though I know he's only joking. At least I hope he's only joking.

"Sorry, mate," says Jinx, slapping him on the shoulder. "You'll just have to wait until nature takes its course there." To me he says, "Nice chatting to you, Amber. Give us a bell if you have any dog- or key-related problems."

Once Jinx is out of earshot, Ed hisses, "What the hell are you playing at?"

I'm confused. "I'm not playing at anything. What are you talking about?"

"Out here all alone with the most notorious womaniser in Fowey. Everyone knows Jinx Jackson. If it moves he'll shag it. They'll all be talking about you now."

"Really?" I smile at him sweetly. Wow. Watch my street cred rocket. "What a shame I stood so still."

"I'm not joking, Amber," says Ed. "You're my fiancée and I have a reputation to protect here. If you're seen spending time with the likes of him, then people will start to talk."

I bristle at his tone. Since when did we become Victorians? He'll be sticking me in a corset and covering the table legs in bloomers at this rate. "Actually, Ed, Jinx is great company and I enjoyed talking to him. Please give me some credit. I'm twenty-nine. I think I can choose my own friends."

"He doesn't want to be your friend. He just wants to get in your knickers," Ed says nastily.

"Well, thank God somebody does," I shoot back.

For a moment we stand bristling at one another like two cats. Then Ed spins on his heel and stalks away, looking every inch the wounded party, while I stare after him in confusion. Er, what was all that about exactly? Am I mistaken, or does my fiancé not trust me in the company of another guy? Ed and I have always trusted one another implicitly. What on earth is going on here?

Something's changed, but quite what I'm not certain.

The journey back home is about as comfortable as sleeping on a bed of nails. Apart from the fact that Ken is still in disgrace, I too am in the metaphorical doghouse for talking to Jinx and for daring to suggest that women have a right to work when I overheard some deeply sexist and misogynist conversations at the dinner table. Apparently I am a disgrace as a corporate wife and Ed is very disappointed in me.

Once home, he barricades himself in the sitting room with a bottle of brandy and CNN while I pop Ken to bed and clear away the last of my candles and tea lights. As they plop sadly into the bin, I feel like all my hopes and dreams are plopping in there with them.

I can't bear living in this atmosphere. You couldn't cut it with a chainsaw, never mind a knife. Knowing that I won't be able to sleep if I don't put things right between us, I wander into the sitting room and perch on the arm of the sofa next to Ed, winding my arms about his neck and laying my head on his shoulder.

He flinches at my touch. "Excuse me, I can't see the screen."

I swallow back the lump in my throat. "Ed, what's going on?"

He cricks his neck to see the telly. "It's simple. Gaddafi's supporters just won't give in."

"Not in Tripoli!" I cry in despair. "With us?"

"Nothing," Ed says impatiently. "Can you be quiet, Amber? I don't know what your take on it is, but I happen to think the situation in Libya is rather important. Much more important than you flirting with the local stud."

"I wasn't flirting!" I say, hurt.

Christ on a bike. Thank goodness he has no idea that the local gamekeeper has seen me starkers and ogled my bra. He'd freak.

241

Ed continues to ignore me, so with a heavy heart, I leave him to the news and make my way upstairs alone. Once in bed, I turn off the lamp and gaze out into the pitch blackness towards Polmerryn Manor. As usual the attic light is on, burning a small solitary beam across the valley. Somebody is up there, looking out into the inky stillness, somebody maybe as lonely and as sad as me. Perhaps it's the mysterious heartbroken Alex Verney weeping into the night, or is it the tragic Vanessa pacing her attic prison?

Oh get a grip, Amber! Maybe it's just Virginia sorting out yet another dressing-up chest and picking out a hat?

But as I close my eyes, all I can see is a brooding Byronic figure, gazing out across the valley and straight into my bedroom. I shiver and burrow deeper under my covers. If Ali wanted a good story then this is it: supermodels, handsome aristocrats, mystery and murder. Whoever said that life in the countryside was dull?

Tomorrow I am going over to Polmerryn Manor to have a chat with Virginia and take her up on her job offer.

And if I meet the mysterious Alex Verney, so much the better!

CHAPTER
SEVENTEEN

Because I apparently dared to express forthright opinions over dinner and flirted outrageously with the local Casanova, Ed sulks right on into the weekend. On Friday night he works ridiculously late; on Saturday he barricades himself in the study under piles of paperwork and only comes out to raid the fridge or drive off with Ken to use his iPhone for urgent business calls. In between all this he sighs heavily and looks so pained that I'm forced to eat massive portions of humble pie and feel quite sick. By Sunday I have serious indigestion and it's with relief that I watch Ed drive off to Fowey. It's a strange day to go to the office, but he has always been a workaholic, and to be honest, it's such a relief to be left in peace that I don't complain or try to persuade him to spend some quality time with me. I'm sorry to see Ken go, but the Range Rover smart key has yet to reappear so Ed has no option but to take the dog to work. He's not happy about it, but what choice does he have? I just hope Ken behaves. I've seen what he's done to the sofa — now pushed against the wall so Ed won't spot the teeth marks — so the thought of what he could do to the soft cream leather of the car makes me feel quite faint.

Once the tail lights have turned the corner of the lane, I have a quick tidy-up of the kitchen, which entails binning a badly burned roasting tin (never try to bake in an Aga and then get distracted by the telly) and shoving everything else in the dishwasher. Chores out of the way, I decide to pop down to the village and pick up a copy of the *Sunday Dagger*. It's my first column today and I can't wait to see it in print, especially with my watercolour of a drenched and fist-shaking Heathcliff alongside a flatteringly slim image of myself. Ali has already called to say how delighted she is. Apparently there are emails and texts galore as readers' comments flood in.

"It's fucking great!" she said. "You're a genius, Amber Scott! You've created a national hate figure!"

Phone tucked under my chin, I paused mid-scrub of the roasting tray.

"Hate figure?"

"The public love a good villain," Ali laughed. "What sort of man hunts poor little foxes?"

I felt a little twinge of nervousness. "The hounds were for drag hunting, Ali. I thought I said that in my piece. He wasn't actually hunting."

"Oh that? I may have edited it out," said Ali airily. "It makes a much better story now. Go buy a copy and read it, you'll see." And with this comment she rang off, leaving me staring down into grey water that was swirling down the plughole in a way that was rather metaphorical of my life right now.

Oh crap. I know I'm pissed off with Heathcliff, but I didn't want to set out to make the British public hate him. Still, I'm pretty sure that I've disguised him so well that nobody will ever recognise him. Come on, Amber, don't be wet! This is exciting! Ali's pleased, the bank manager's pleased and Heathcliff will never know. A brute like him probably only reads the *Shooting Times* anyway. I am a little alarmed about how much I may have been edited, though. Ali has a nasty habit of fiddling with articles until she may as well have written them herself. It's the control freak in her and the reason she won't let her writers have copy approval.

There's nothing for it. I'm going to have to go out right now and buy the paper.

It's one of those days when the British weather just can't make its mind up. The sun is playing hide and seek with the clouds and a sharp wind ruffles my hair as I stomp down the hill. The sea, nestling in the hilly cleavage, is a deep green, which reminds me uncomfortably of the darker rings that circle Heathcliff's irises. The waves are flecked with lacy foam as white as his teeth. Not that I'm going to waste another second thinking about his eyes. Or his mouth. No way.

I stomp down the hill, the wind whipping my curls into a bird's nest, and before long I'm in Polmerryn. As I walk down the high street I have the strangest feeling that people are looking at me, and that as I pass they stop chatting. This of course is all in my mind; it has to be. Why on earth would everyone be staring at me? Heaven help me, I've only been living in rural isolation for a week. I can't be paranoid already, can I?

It's not my imagination. There's certainly something funny going on in the village shop this morning, because I don't think I've ever seen it so packed. As I push the door open, several locals have to move out of the way, and I can't even hear the bell tinkle above the buzz of chatter.

"Morning, Amber!" beams Terry Tipple, who is leaning against the counter with his nose buried in a magazine. "Great column!"

"Yes, great column!" agree two middle-aged women, nodding their headscarves in my direction. "You've certainly put him in his place!"

"I love the picture," chips in Sam the barmaid. "It looks just like him!"

I have that horrible sensation when it feels as though the floor is dissolving underneath your feet, as suddenly I realise that every local in the shop is either reading or in the process of buying a copy of the *Dagger*, and all are avidly discussing my column. This isn't a problem in itself, except that they all seem to know exactly who it is I've written about and find it highly amusing.

So much for doing a really good job of disguising his identity! I *knew* I spent too long over that illustration. No matter how hard I tried to make him look different, it was as though my paintbrush had a mind of its own and just kept reproducing the strong set of his jaw and that full angry mouth. Even the watercolours got in on the act and pooled out the exact hue of his eyes and the inky dark hair. I should have made him blond or something but I was proud of my work and just scanned it and emailed it without really thinking too hard.

Which I am starting to see was a *big* mistake.

If they all recognise Heathcliff, then it's only a matter of time before someone tells him or, worse still, he reads the piece for himself.

I've seen that gun and those poor bunnies and I've seen him lose his temper too, and that was just over Ken getting a little bit carried away. Who knows what he'll do when he reads this character assassination?

I am so dead. Thanks a million, Ali.

With a mouth that feels as though somebody's tipped most of Polmerryn beach into it, I manage to ask for a copy of the *Dagger*. Figuring that it's best to be out of the village, where I now seem to have become a celebrity, I head away from Polmerryn as fast as my short legs can carry me. The paper whips about in my hands, but once in the shelter of the high-banked lane, I turn as fast as I can to the supplement and flick through until ta-da! There it is, my column, in its full glossy glory.

Sex in the Sticks
The single girl's guide to country pursuits
by Amber Scott

What! With my mouth hanging open, I read my piece, which has been so spiced up by Ali that you could call it a vindaloo and serve it with pilau rice. Once I've finished, I feel like throwing myself into the nearest slurry pit. Never mind that Ed will go mental when he sees the "single girl" tag; Ali has now villained Heathcliff up so much that all he needs to complete the look is a moustache to twirl and a railway line to tie me to. He storms through the piece with his bloodthirsty hounds while I quake and try to hide a baby fox, in between describing his manly physique and adding a few pithy asides. It's a fun read, it's a sexy read and it's everything that Ali asked for, and I would read it myself and laugh except that this is going to land me in water so hot I'm getting-third degree burns just thinking about it.

I stuff the paper into my bag. I am going to have to have serious words with Ali if she wants me to keep writing for her. Not that I'm likely to be able to keep writing for her, since Heathcliff will throttle me as soon as he gets wind of this. I gulp and look over my shoulder just in case he's about to pop out from behind a hedge. Why do I get myself into these situations? I'm supposed to be having a quiet life in the country, not winding up the locals. I'll just have to lie low and keep out of his way. How hard can that be? Ed has the car and Ken is locked inside it, so no puddle splashing or canine romance can take place. If I just stay in the house, preferably below the level of the windows, he'll never find me.

Cheered by this plan, I meander along the lane. I could also dye my hair and do all my shopping in the next village along. That way there's no chance we'll meet. And next week I'll make certain that I write nothing at all about Heathcliff. I was toying with using the car keys incident, but maybe I'll write about Jinx instead. I'll ask him first, but something tells me he would love it.

Deep in thought about my next column — something along the lines of women with Münchausen Syndrome by Proxy using their pets so that they can see the hunky vet — I'm surprised to find myself outside the gates of Polmerryn Manor. Sunshine races across the lawns in dapples as clouds scud across the sky, and in the sickly lemon sunshine the old building is a deep brooding grey. I glance up at the turret window. Who is up there every night? Whoever it is, they don't sleep. Often when I wake up in the small hours the light is still on. Is it the mysterious Alex Verney?

Intrigued, I peer in through the gates, curling my fingers around the cold iron. It's such a beautiful house, and the views down to Polmerryn Bay are enough to make you breathless. Even on a grey day like this, the sea is constantly shifting and the light is never the same from one second to the next. Then there are the gardens filled with beautiful flowers and the secret shady lavender walk where every breath smells like heaven. This house deserves to be opened up and enjoyed rather than locked away behind walls and gates, slumbering like Sleeping Beauty and dreaming about the past. Virginia is right: it should be open to the public, and I'm going to take her up on her offer of work.

With my mind suddenly filled with colour schemes and images of four-poster beds draped with brocade and velvet, I'm pushing open the gate and crunching up the drive before I've even thought about it. A quick hop up a flight of lichen-smothered steps leads me to a vast front door, gnarled and weathered from centuries of wild Cornish rain and gales. I turn the heavy iron handle but the door refuses to budge no matter how hard I push. To my left there's a vast bell pull, and I'm just contemplating whether or not to tug it — the rope looks a bit frayed — when Virginia's head pops out from the window above.

"Amber! What a lovely surprise! But don't try and use the front door, I don't think it's been opened for at least five years. Alex and I just use the back. Pop round and let yourself in."

I do as I'm bid, very stealthily, just in case Heathcliff is skulking about with a few dead bunnies, but luckily there's no sign of him. He's probably busy setting mantraps and plucking pheasants or whatever else it is that gamekeepers do for fun.

"Come in, come in!" Virginia says to me as she opens the back door. "I've just put the kettle on. We'll have tea, or would you prefer something a little stronger?"

I laugh. "Tea's fine. I think I need to take a breather from the daytime drinking."

I follow Virginia along a cool flagstoned passageway. Light pools in from narrow windows high up in the wall, but the corridor is still very dark and I have the sensation that I'm almost underground.

"You are," explains Virginia when I venture this opinion. "This used to be the dungeons, I believe, back when this was a proper feudal manor. Alex could tell you more about it; he's done a lot of work on the history of the house. He spends hours researching it. He can talk about it for hours."

Alex sounds like a right barrel of laughs.

The kitchen is huge, like something out of a National Trust property, which I suppose it could be. The floor is tiled in black and white, there's a massive fireplace with a spit, two huge butler's sinks, and beneath a mullioned window the mother of all wood-fired ranges. An enormous refectory table stretches across the vast expanse of floor with an assortment of mismatched chairs clustered around it. I sit at one and look around me with great interest while Virginia busies herself making tea in an enormous chipped brown teapot. This room is amazing! With the exception of a fan heater, which is feebly puffing out some heat into the icy wastes, it doesn't look as though it's changed since the turn of the last century. Imagine this room all dressed up in the style of the Victorian age. It could look fantastic.

"Do you want a tour?" Virginia asks when I tell her this. She claps her hands excitedly. "Oh Amber, I knew that you would be perfect for this! You're such a creative girl and you have such vision!"

I laugh. If she'd read today's *Dagger*, she'd know just how creative I am. Still, since Lady V seems to be one of the few people in Polmerryn who *hasn't* read it, I keep quiet.

"I'd love a tour," I tell her.

Clutching mugs of treacle-dark tea, we set off along a maze of corridors that leads through a labyrinth of rooms, each more interesting than the last. We pass through a great hall where dusty suits of armour lurch drunkenly against the walls and the painted eyes of long-dead ancestors watch us as we pause beneath their portraits, before crossing into a dining room draped in crimson and with sconces lining the walls. After that there's the ballroom, the library, the billiards room, the chapel, and then we wander upstairs to the bedrooms. I'm absolutely speechless, because although everything is faded and dusty, the place is virtually untouched. It's a perfect time capsule, and the air of peace is like a balm to the mind. People will adore this house if it could be presented to them in a way that preserves the stillness and creates the impression that the Tudor family who live here have just nipped out for a moment. It's like a giant virtual-reality magazine, with rooms rather than pages and historical periods as themes. There's so much I could do.

"Do you like it?" Virginia asks me as we stand at the window of the great bedroom and gaze over the formal gardens. The sun is out at the minute and throws jewelled rays of light through the stained-glass coat of arms to dance on the oak floor.

My mind is bubbling with ideas. "I love it! There's so much you could do here."

She looks delighted, and the feathers on today's headgear — a green turban — bounce enthusiastically. "I knew you would! Oh Amber, what fun we'll have."

"We could create a family who lived here," I say excitedly. "I'm sure your son would help with some history, and we could dress each room for a person. Lady Elizabeth's bedroom, Lord Henry's bathroom, Mrs Mop's kitchen."

Virginia nods. "That's a wonderful idea!"

252

"And the gardens, too," I continue, growing more and more excited by the minute. "People would love to see the beautiful plants and flowers you have. It's like Heligan; you could market it as Polmerryn's version."

Virginia lights up like Oxford Street at Christmas time. "Oh yes! I adore the gardens, that's my own work."

"And you have to open up the lavender walk," I add, my eye drawn to the sea of swaying blue. "It's so peaceful."

Her face falls. "I'm not so sure about that. Alex planted the lavender garden for his wife and it's very special to him. I'm not sure how he'd feel about having strangers in it."

My ears prick up. "His wife?"

Virginia sighs. "Vanessa, such a lovely girl. He adored her, was absolutely devoted to her. She loved the scent of lavender so Alex had the garden created especially for her. I don't think he'd want anybody else to use it."

I swallow nervously, thinking of all the blooms I hacked off the other day.

"Maybe we could ask him? If Alex wants to open up the house, then I'm sure he'll be expecting visitors. Maybe he'll have some ideas. Or Vanessa?"

"Vanessa is dead," Virginia says sadly. "And I'd appreciate it, Amber, if you didn't mention her in front of my son when you meet him. He's very sensitive about the subject."

So I hear. "Of course not," I assure her.

"He's not been himself lately either. He cancelled a shoot, which is most unusual, especially since it raises good money for the estate," she continues, taking my arm and leading me through the long gallery and back into the kitchen. "He's been so irritable the last few days. This morning I thought he was going to smash something, he was in such a rage when he came back from the village."

"What was the matter?" I ask.

Virginia shrugs. "I have no idea. He's usually such an easy-going person, but just lately he's been storming around the place. He was most peculiar the other evening too." She fills the kettle, slams it on to the hotplate and then sinks into a chair, where she fixes me with a worried look. "He left in a dreadful rage, something about a stray dog that keeps interfering with Sadie, our prize Lab. She was Vanessa's dog, you see, and Alex is dreadfully precious about anything that used to belong to Vanessa. I haven't seen him so angry for a long time. Not since that day he had to walk home soaking wet."

All of a sudden the blood is rushing in my ears and I feel very, very peculiar. It's just as well I'm leaning against the table or I think my legs might have given way.

"So he jumped in the Defender and tore off up the road," continues Virginia, oblivious to the fact that the colour has drained from my face and I could probably pass for the undead. "When he came back he was really quiet, and although I kept asking him, he just wouldn't talk about what had happened." She sighs. "It must have been something terrible, because that was when he cancelled the shooting party. Why do you think he'd do that?"

My hands grip the tabletop so hard that I can see my knuckles glowing through the skin. I think I need to get out of here. Like now.

"I have no idea," I say faintly.

"Silly me, of course you don't, you haven't met him yet, have you?" smiles Virginia. "Well, now's your chance! Here he is!" Over my shoulder she says, "Alex darling, here you are! I've just been talking about you. This is the young lady who's going to help us sort out the house, the one I've been telling you about. This is Amber Scott."

"I know," says a voice that's horribly and gut-churningly familiar.

There's a loud whooshing of blood in my ears and for a hideous moment I think I'm going to pass out. Please God, please God, don't let it be him. With a growing sense of doom I turn around, very slowly.

My prayers go unanswered. A very angry pair of sea-green eyes meets mine and my pulse goes into ambulance-calling mode. Heathcliff is standing in the kitchen, and from the rigid set of his jaw he's none too impressed to see me.

"We've already met, haven't we, Amber?" says Heathcliff/Alex icily. "Although I must admit I recall our encounter quite differently."

I gulp. "I'm so sorry about the piece in the *Dagger*. I never meant to offend you."

His eyebrows shoot up into his thick curls. "Really? Then quite what did you intend to do?"

He stomps across the kitchen and crashes around with the kettle and a mug. Fridge doors slam, cups rattle and I shake in my pink wellies. Oh Christ, I hope he's looking through the drawers for a teaspoon and not a meat cleaver. I don't fancy being turned into Amber confetti, even if it's totally what I deserve.

"I was just trying to write about country life," I say apologetically.

Alex snorts. "Like you know so much about that."

"I'm trying to learn," I say. "And I know what *entire* means now."

Virginia's hand flies to her mouth. "It was your dog? Oh dear."

I hang my head. Oh dear indeed. "I'm afraid so. But he's under control now."

Alex laughs, or at least I think he does. It's a harsh noise and doesn't sound very joyful.

"At least one of you is," he says. Crash. Clatter. Thud. Goodness, I'm glad I'm not a teapot right now.

"I promise I won't write anything else about you," I say. "Ever."

Alex Verney rounds on me with such speed he probably gives himself whiplash.

"You'd better not. Or I will sue you and your dirty little rag to kingdom come. Have you got that into your empty blonde head, or do I have to spell it out?"

I swallow. No, I think I get the message loud and clear.

"Darling! Please!" Lady V looks distraught. "Whatever has happened, I'm sure it was just a misunderstanding. Please make up. You're going to be working together."

"We are not," Alex says firmly. To me he adds, "We are doing absolutely nothing together, let's get that clear. If my mother in her wisdom wants you working here then that's her prerogative, but don't expect me to get involved. You are to stay well out of my way. Got it?"

I'm so anxious to prove that I've indeed got it that I do a Churchill dog impression.

"And since I'm now technically your boss," Alex Verney continues, fixing me with a very hard green-eyed stare, "one foot out of line, one tiny mention in a newspaper, or if your dog so much as looks at mine, you're off the property. Understood?"

"Totally," I say. To be honest, I hardly dare breathe.

"And," he adds, his gaze holding mine, some emotion I can't quite define making his eyes glitter, "if I ever find you covered in green slime in this kitchen, I won't be accountable for my actions. Got it?"

I blush to the roots of my hair and nod frantically. How utterly, utterly mean of him to remind me that he's seen me totally naked and looking like a complete idiot! I decide right here and now that I hate Alex Verney. He's no gentleman; in fact I've never met such a horrible and totally humourless man. Right now he makes Ed look like a cheery soul, and that's saying something.

"Good, so we have an understanding then. I'll leave you both to it," he says, and mug in hand stalks out of the room without so much as a backwards glance.

I bury my face in my hands. How on earth have I managed to end up working for a man who hates the sight of me? I don't think I can bear the thought of living in the same county as Alex Verney, never mind actually having to be in close proximity to him. I feel quite faint and giddy at the thought.

I'm starting to wish I'd never left London.

CHAPTER
EIGHTEEN

"Don't look so horrified, darling, I'm your mother. I am allowed to visit you."

It's half past eight on Monday morning. In a fit of house-wifely zeal, I've hung the washing out in the sparkling June sunshine, waved Ed and Ken off to the office, and am just about to call Jinx for key-retrieving advice when a loud tooting horn and following thump on the door herald the arrival of my mother.

I can't believe it. I didn't see this much of her when she was only a few miles up the road. More proof, as if I needed it after the whole Alex Verney debacle, that I really should have stayed in London.

"Where's Emma?" I ask. There's no sign of either the scratched Mercedes or my sister, which doesn't bode well, since they were supposed to be travelling together on their quest for King Arthur. Instead, there's a beaten-up Bedford Rascal parked outside my house and a dreadlocked man sitting behind the wheel puffing contentedly on a roll-up.

"Emma?" Mum drifts into the kitchen in a cloud of patchouli oil and helps herself to my plate of toast and Marmite. "Oh darling, honestly! White bread is so bad for you. Mother Nature didn't intend your intestines to

259

have to deal with all this refined matter. Maybe you should try one of my colonics? Rain swears by them."

I'm really not in the mood to discuss the finer workings of Rain's bowels. Suddenly my toast and Marmite doesn't seem half as appealing. What a great diet aid my mother is. I could lose stones just thinking about all the disgusting so-called healthy things she does.

"Emma? About five six, dark hair? My sister? Your first-born?" I say, as my mother drifts about the kitchen, tutting over my bottle of Domestos and sighing at the presence of the dishwasher. "Where's she gone?"

My mother pulls a face. "She got into a terrible mood about the little bump to that car of hers. She's far too materialistic, that one."

"You did about two grand's worth of damage," I remind her, but there's no point really, because as usual Mum isn't listening to a word I'm saying. She's far too busy waving at her companion out of the window.

"That's my new friend Rahma," she tells me. "We met at Tintagel right by the castle. He's the reincarnation of Merlin. Isn't that a coincidence?"

Not really. I've not lived here long, but already I can see that my small part of the south-west has more than its fair share of eccentrics. I nod at Rahma, who waves back merrily before turning his attention to rolling his next cigarette. At least I *hope* it's just a cigarette . . .

"He won't come in," Mum says, clearly under the mistaken impression that I'm gagging to invite her NBF in for a cuppa. "He loves to be out in the elements, just like he did when he was Merlin. Rahma lives in a teepee. Isn't that wonderful? And he only washes in recycled rainwater."

Mum at a tangent is like a force of nature. I know that if I don't interrupt soon, the entire morning will drift by, and I really have to get going. I promised Virginia that we would make a start on the house today and brainstorm some ideas, and I really don't want to let her down. I know it's silly, but I also want to show Alex that I'm serious about helping and that there's more to me than just a clueless townie who loses dogs and writes invective for tabloids. When I went to bed last night, his brooding face and the strange expression in his eyes were seared on to my eyelids and it was hours before I could drop off. Even when I did, my sleep was uneasy and I woke several times with his angry words echoing through my dreams. I know it doesn't make any sense, and he's still a horrible bad-tempered man who shoots poor bunnies, but I really want to prove him wrong.

"Mum," I say again. "What are you doing here? Where's Emma? And who the hell is Rahma?"

"I do wish you wouldn't shout, Amber," sighs Mum. "It's very bad for your chi. If you'd only give me a moment to get a word in, I'd tell you." She reaches for the last piece of toast. "Emma got all stressed after my little bump in her car so she went home. Luckily I bumped into Rahma in Tintagel and he offered to put me up for a few days. He's dropping me at the station now so I can catch the train home. Don't panic, I'm not moving in!"

261

I breathe a sigh of relief. Don't get me wrong, I really love my mum, but for one hideous moment I thought she was about to descend on me. I shudder. The house would be fengshuied and mung-beaned before you could say "crystal".

"I only popped in to give you a housewarming present." My mother reaches into her pocket and pulls out a small phial. "And to ask a favour."

I'm always nervous of my mother's favours. The last one involved her and Rain moving in for three weeks while they were house-hunting. When I say house-hunting, I mean it in the loosest sense of the word. They drifted about my place drinking green tea, and now and again one of them would pop out to buy a copy of *Loot*, which would gather toast crumbs and coffee-cup rings until eventually Ed lost patience and binned it. He actually slept at the office during that time, as I remember . . .

"Mum, you can't stay," I say quickly. "We're still trying to sort the place out and I've just agreed to take on a job as well."

Mum looks insulted. "I do have my own home to go to, you know. And besides, Rain will be really missing me by now. I just wanted to drop off a couple of presents, that's all." She waves the small glass jar under my nose. "I picked this love potion up for you when I was in Boscastle."

I back away. The last time I took love-life advice from my mother was hardly a roaring success; even if he didn't hate me, I don't think I could ever look Alex Verney in the face again. No man who has never put my bins out or trudged round the supermarket with me should see my fat bits. Ever.

"Just put a few drops of this in Ed's tea," she tells me. "It's powerful stuff; I promise it'll solve all your problems."

Since the last love spell only *caused* me loads of problems, I think I can be excused for not jumping for joy at this promise. Besides, I have a horrible feeling that Ed and I have more issues than a love potion can cure. Like retrieving the Range Rover smart key, for a start. Still, because I'd like to get to Polmerryn Manor sometime this millennium, arguing the toss with a barking-mad menopausal woman probably isn't the way to go.

"Thanks." I take the phial and place it on the windowsill. "That's very kind."

"It isn't kind at all, Amber. I can't bear to see you neglected and unhappy. Any mother would do her best to help."

"I'm not neglected and unhappy!"

Mum gives me a beady look. "You've moved miles away from your friends and your job, you're rattling about in this big house, and Ed spends all his time working. When he comes home he should be spending every spare minute with you. Darling, you're young and gorgeous; he should be counting his blessings to have a goddess like you!"

Hmm. When Ed left this morning he didn't look like a man who was counting his blessings, more like somebody with the weight of the world on his shoulders actually. And as for being young and gorgeous — well, hardly. I'm wearing my ancient denim cut-offs teamed with a long-sleeved T-shirt and pink wellies, and my hair is a crazy mass of curls. If I'm a goddess, then it's Medusa.

"Thanks, Mum," I say. Parents have to think their kids are great. It's the law. But if I'm so amazing, surely Ed would spend more time with me. It's a simple equation.

"Two drops in his tea, and bingo!" Mum grins. "Try it!"

There's a hoot from the Bedford Rascal.

"I mustn't stand here all day chatting, I have a train to catch," she says. "So, darling, about that favour."

Why do I have a sinking feeling?

"Right," I say slowly. "What is it exactly?"

"You've got some land here, haven't you?"

She knows we do. She was very excited about our six acres and had big plans for yurts and eco-villages until Ed set her straight. Calling him a fascist capitalist may not have done much to cement mother- and son-in-law relations . . .

"A bit," I hedge.

"And it's empty?"

I nod. "Why?"

"I'll show you! Follow me!" she cries, grabbing my hand and pulling me after her into the courtyard. "Close your eyes."

I do as I'm told. To be honest, it's nice and dark and peaceful with them shut. And I can't see her either. As I stand there, I hear the van door slam and the creaking of the rear doors opening.

"Got her?" I hear my mother say to Rahma. At least I assume Rahma has joined her, because there's suddenly a very pungent aroma of unwashed body and tobacco.

"Open your eyes!" Mum orders and, like a fool, I obey. Honestly, you would think I'd know better, given that the woman is totally bonkers. "Surprise!"

Surprise? Shock more like.

I am looking at a goat.

"What," I say slowly, "is that?"

Mum looks at me as though I'm stupid.

"I'd have thought that was obvious, Amber. It's a goat."

"I know it's a goat," I say, through teeth clenched so hard that I'm amazed I don't break my own jaw. "I can see it's a goat. What I want to know is why it is in my garden."

"We rescued her. The poor darling was in a farmyard just off Bodmin Moor, all lonely and tethered and up to her little ankles in mud." My mother's eyes fill and she kisses the goat on the nose. "The farmer let us have her for twenty pounds. She's called Mabel."

I look at Mabel and Mabel looks at me. Neither of us is particularly impressed by what we see.

"Technically goats don't have ankles," chips in Rahma. "But you know what we mean. It's cruelty to animals to tie them up. We had to rescue her."

Wow. Rahma's a Brummie. No disrespect to Brummies, but this wasn't quite what I was expecting. It doesn't really go with the tie-dye and airy-fairy attitude.

"That's lovely of you." I step back from Mabel. Is it my imagination, or is she eyeing up my shorts rather hungrily? "But what are you going to do with a goat in London?"

"She's not coming to London, silly! We thought we'd leave her with you." Mum beams at me as though she's just given me a really exciting present. Look, Mum, I never got that Barbie Playhouse when I was eight. Don't think giving me a flea-bitten goat when I'm twenty-nine will make up for it.

"She can live in your field," adds Rahma. It's good of him to be telling me what I will be doing with his goat. "She won't be any trouble. Just bung her some food and she'll be fine. She's a very well-behaved animal. Ouch!"

Mabel has just head-butted him in the nuts. I am starting to warm to this animal. Rahma *is* very annoying.

"But I don't know the first thing about goats!" I point out. "I don't even know what she'll eat."

Mum flaps her hand airily. "Anything, according to the farmer. She'll be good company for you when Ed's working."

I have a crazy mental picture of Mabel and me snuggled up on the sofa watching telly. Has my life really come to this?

"But I know nothing about goats!" I repeat desperately.

"Google them," suggests Rahma. "Right, come on, Tish. Your train leaves in half an hour. Jog on."

266

Somehow I find that I'm holding Mabel's lead rope while Mum and Rahma clamber back into the Bedford.

"I don't want a goat!" I shout as the engine revs and the horn toots. "I can't look after it!"

"Don't be silly, darling," calls Mum, waving out of the window while Rahma reverses and knocks an ornamental stone mushroom flying. "Just pop her in your field and feed her. Goodness, if you think that's hard, what will you do when you have a baby?"

Die of shock. Unless immaculate conceptions are all the rage round here, there's no way I'm going to be a mother any time soon, or not while Ed and I are in a state of cold war anyway. He's going to freak when he sees the goat.

I open my mouth to protest, but Rahma has bullied the Bedford into gear and with a splutter of very unenvironmentally friendly fumes it lurches off down the drive.

"Don't worry, I'll be back to check on her very soon," shouts Mum as they turn out on to the lane. "Think of her as a moving-in present! Love you, darling."

"The feeling is not mutual," I mutter. I have a goat. Bloody great. Thanks a lot, Mum. Why couldn't she have bought me a mug or maybe a new duvet cover as a moving in-present?

"Because she's mad, that's why," I tell Mabel, who stares back at me with her weird unblinking eyes. "Right, what am I meant to do with you?"

But Mabel can't talk, and I am late meeting Virginia and have no time to mess about with the internet, so I tie the goat to the gate and go inside to find some suitable food. Muesli and carrots are about all I can think of, but when I return to feed her, Mabel has chewed through the rope and wandered over to the washing line, where she's chomping contentedly on Ed's Armani jeans.

The Armani jeans that Ed loves.

Fuck. I am so dead.

With a wail of horror, I drag Mabel, still munching merrily on designer denim, away by the collar and deposit her in the small field next to the house. It's got a thick hedge and lots of yummy grass, so she should be all right in there for a bit, surely?

"Bad goat. No wonder the farmer couldn't wait to be rid of you," I say sternly as I slam the gate shut and shoot the bolts across. That should keep her safe until I get a minute to call Jinx and ask for his help. Maybe he knows somebody who'd like a goat. Or perhaps he can zoom over in his Aston and have a look at her. This could be great column fodder! Just the thought of seeing Jinx's merry freckled face and sexy sleepy eyes really cheers me up. At least I have another excuse to call him.

Excuse? I mean reason.

I check the gate again just to make sure, then hide the remnants of Ed's jeans in the cupboard under the stairs (where the Hoover lives, so it's unlikely he'll go snooping in there) before grabbing my sketchbook, pencil and watercolours, which I stuff into my bag. Goodness, I'm really late.

Panicking that Virginia will have given up on me and gone to the Ship, I run as fast as I can along the lane and across the valley to the manor house. It's a sad fact of life that I'm not really designed to run. Firstly I'm dead unfit, and secondly my boobs bounce about like the Andrex puppy on a very lively day. Ouch, not good. Paula Radcliffe has nothing to fear.

I'm just pausing for breath at the bottom of the hill, doubled over and with an entire sewing machine's worth of stitches running a seam up my side, when a battered blue Defender pulls up alongside and a scowling face appears.

Fortune dumps on me again. It's none other than Alex bloody Verney. What have I done wrong now? Surely Ken can't have run all the way from Fowey to Polmerryn?

"Amber," says Alex curtly, inclining his dark head. He's unshaven today and his sharp-cheekboned face is dusted with jet-black stubble, giving him an even more dangerous air than normal. "What are you doing?"

I open my mouth to reply, but I'm so short of breath that I end up sounding like the bagpipes. It's either terror at seeing him again or I'm so unfit I can't even breathe.

"Are you all right?" Alex asks, looking alarmed.

"I'm fine," I croak. How can people run for fun? They must be nuts!

Alex leans across the car and opens the passenger door. "You look terrible. Get in."

Get in? Now, my mother might be barking mad these days, but one sensible thing she did tell me as a kid was never to get in the car with a strange man, and I don't think they come much stranger than Alex Verney. And anyway, isn't he supposed to have murdered his wife? I'd quite like to live to see thirty, thanks all the same.

"I'm fine," I insist. Or I try to, because even my vocal cords are too knackered to speak.

"You are not fine, you look like you're about to collapse," Alex observes, sounding amused. "Get in, for God's sake. I'm not having you write a column about how I left you to die in the road."

"If I die, I can't write it," I puff, leaning against the car as I struggle to breathe. I always knew exercise was bad for you. "So don't worry."

"Imagine the unfortunate scenario that you survive against all the odds and do write about it. I really don't think I can take the risk," Alex deadpans. "I'm already a fox-cub killer and terroriser of small scared city girls. If I actually left you to die in the road, I think the good people of Polmerryn and the UK at large would hate me even more. Now jump in, or do I have to get out and pick you up?"

The thought of Alex Verney's strong arms lifting me up makes me feel faint, although this could just be the lack of oxygen from the running. He's wearing a dark blue T-shirt and his tanned arms are muscled and corded with sinew. Wow. They are strong. Even so, I can't risk him finding out just how heavy I am. No way is he picking me up. Against my better judgement, I clamber into the car.

"I'm really sorry about my piece in the paper. I didn't mean to make everyone in Polmerryn hate you," I say as Alex reaches over and buckles my seat belt. I suck my stomach in so hard I think it practically sticks to my spine. Can't have him brushing against my squidgy bits. He may have seen them already, but I still have some pride left.

"Forget it. They all hated me anyway," shrugs Alex, as he pulls away. "I murdered my wife, didn't I? Surely you must have heard that?"

Those deep ocean-green eyes slide to mine. His face is expressionless and I gulp. He could be kidding or he could be serious, I have no idea.

I'm alone in a car with a self-confessed wife-killer, and it's only ten a.m. Nice going, Amber. What next? Lunch with Sweeney Todd?

"Er, maybe," I say.

Alex laughs. "Come on, I know what they say about me in the village. Somebody will have passed on the gossip and warned you to be careful."

"OK," I admit. "I have heard what they say."

"And do you believe it?" He focuses on the road now, his face turned away from me. His hand is clenched tightly on the steering wheel and a muscle ticks in his taut cheek.

Do I believe it? Actually, right now, I think I do. Where's that gun gone, anyway?

"Of course I don't believe it," I fib. How's he going to kill me? Strangulation? A bullet? Knife? All three?

He shakes his head. "You do. I can see it in your face. Right now you're wondering how I'm going to do away with you."

I always was useless at hiding my emotions. I'd be a rubbish poker player.

"Don't worry," Alex continues, shifting the car into third gear. "I've got a meeting with my accountant in a bit, so I'm far too busy to spare a morning strangling you and chopping you up. The blood is a pain to get off my clothes too. You're safe."

"Phew, that's a relief," I say.

He shoots me a sideways look. "Anyway, I can think of much better things to do with you than murder."

He can? Such as? For a split second I almost think he's making a cheeky reference to Green Slimegate, and I go all tingly at the thought of what I could do with Alex Verney.

"Yes," he says thoughtfully. "Like putting you to work in the house and keeping Ma occupied instead of in the pub. That's much more use. For now, anyway."

I feel oddly disappointed. I really must slip some of that potion into Ed's tea. My hormones are going crazy. For a minute there I almost hoped that Alex, with his hawk-like profile and glittering eyes, was saying something completely different.

"Your house is exactly where I was going," I tell him, patting my bag. "I've got my sketchpad in here to work on some ideas for dressing the rooms."

"Ah yes, you're an artist." Alex swings the Defender through the big wrought-iron gates and up the drive to

272

the house. "I was most impressed by your picture of me. It was very flattering."

"Artistic licence," I say quickly.

He laughs. "Of course. What else? That seems to be your speciality."

"That column was totally changed by my editor," I protest.

Alex shrugs. "Look, I won't say I wasn't annoyed, but people will always believe what they want to anyway. It isn't the end of the world. Believe me, far worse things have happened to me than that."

I want to ask him what has happened to him, but I daren't. I'm scared of what he might say or do. There's an aloof air about Alex that doesn't invite confidences, and I've seen him angry too often to want to risk provoking another outburst.

We stop at the back of the house. The engine idles and Alex pulls up the handbrake. Then he turns to me and sighs.

"Amber," he says slowly, "I'm sorry if we got off to a bad start."

"Me too," I say. "Although just for the record, I did want to stop and apologise that time I splashed you, but Ed — that's my fiancé — was in a real hurry and wouldn't let me stop."

Alex glances down at my left hand. "Of course. The solicitor."

"That's him. Then when I saw you with the hounds, I just assumed the worst. And then there was Ken running away to see Sadie and you got so angry. And then you came round and I was . . . I was . . ." I falter.

Quite what I was I'm not sure. Insane? Starkers? Hideously embarrassed?

"Wearing red underwear? Or are you referring to the time you were naked?" asks Alex. His wide mouth curves into a smile, and it's like the sun peeking out from behind a cloud, because it totally transforms his face. The green eyes crinkle and two deep dimples dance in his cheeks. It's like looking at a different man, and I'm so taken aback that for a brief moment I don't register what he has said. When I do, though, I wish I could roll out of the car, down the hill and into the sea with a splash.

I bury my face in my hands. "I was doing —"

"Beauty treatments?" He reaches forward and gently peels my hands back from my hot face. "Sorry, Amber, I'm only teasing you. How about we draw a line under the other stuff and start again?"

I'm not convinced that once a man has seen you naked you can ever draw a line under it and start again, but since Alex is in effect my boss and I'm so very relieved he isn't about to sue me for libel, I agree. Once he's driven off, though, I bang my forehead several times against the weathered granite wall and groan.

How totally and utterly embarrassing. Note to self: wear a polo neck at all times from now on, or failing that, a burka.

And stop thinking about Alex's crinkly-eyed smile and dimples.

Once I feel that I have sufficiently recovered what few wits I do possess, I join Virginia in the kitchen, where we spend a happy few hours brainstorming ideas for the first rooms she wants to open. We discuss the history of the house and all the colourful characters who have lived there over the centuries. After a gallon or so of tea and copious note-taking, I leave Virginia turning out yet another cupboard and wander upstairs to put some ideas together for how to dress Lady Elizabeth's bedroom. It needs to be romantic and sensual, a combination of Tudor period detail and Mills & Boon-style fantasy. Maybe I could bring the outside in? How about linking this room with the lavender walk by using the same colours? That could really work!

Excited and inspired, I curl up in the window seat with my sketchpad and gaze thoughtfully down at the lavender walk. I'm just on the brink of picking up my pencil to begin a design when I'm halted in my tracks. For once the beautiful garden isn't deserted. Eyes screwed up against the sun's glare off the sea, I press my face to the diamond-paned glass and stare downwards. It looks like . . . I think it's . . .

It is. It's Alex.

Alex Verney, angry and aloof Alex Verney, is walking through the lavender, one strong hand trailing in the fragrant blooms as he brushes past. He is the lord of the manor, so I suppose there's nothing surprising or even unusual about him enjoying his own grounds. In fact I remember now that Virginia told me he planted the lavender walk especially for his wife. Of course he walks there. Why ever not? It isn't seeing Alex in his own garden that takes me aback.

No, it's something far more than this. What makes my breath catch in my throat as I watch him walk slowly through the swaying blooms is the bleak look on his face.

It's an expression of total and utter despair.

CHAPTER
NINETEEN

They say that time flies when you are having fun. The same is also true when you're flat out with work, walking a very boisterous dog, caring for an escapologist goat and doing your best to avoid rows with a fiancé who, in spite of all his promises to the contrary, seems to be working even harder than ever. I've been so busy helping Virginia to set up the manor for her visitors and painting the breathtaking seascapes that I've hardly had time to be lonely as Ed continues to work his ridiculously long hours. Last week he even had to go away on business for several days, leaving me with only Ken and Mabel for company. Back in London I would have been glued to the sofa watching telly and working my way through the contents of Häagen-Dazs' distribution centre, but in Cornwall I just don't have time to veg out. If I'm not painting, then I'm writing my column (no more mention of Alex), walking Ken for miles or sorting out the manor house with Lady V. I've even started to make inroads on attacking the wilderness that surrounds Hawkstone House. I don't think I've ever been so busy.

I'm not sure how it's happened, but somewhere along the line, June has blossomed into a hot July. The narrow Cornish lanes fill with drivers whose reversing skills are even worse than mine, parking in Fowey becomes an aspiration rather than a reality and Polmerryn beach is speckled with colourful towels and stripy windbreaks. Everyone wants a slice of Cornish living and suddenly my phone rings non-stop with friends and family very keen to come and visit me. I put them off as much as I can, because I'm so wrapped up in my work at the manor house.

When I first met Virginia in the Ship, I must admit that I didn't take her offer of a job seriously, mainly because I saw myself as an artist and journalist as opposed to any kind of designer, but Polmerryn Manor has proved to be the most amazing canvas that I could ever have dreamed of being able to work on. Ideas seem to flow from me, and now, nearly eight weeks on, the rooms have taken shape and reflect themes and personalities just as vividly as the pages of *Blush!* and *Senora*. Every morning I wander along to the house with Ken, drink tea so strong it could rip up a stack of Yellow Pages, and then set to work. Using Virginia's knowledge, Alex's historical research and my own eye for design, we've managed to create a tour of the house and gardens that will transport any visitor back in time and to another world. By the end of the year, once the guide sheets with my illustrations are back from the printers, we should be ready to open the doors to our first batch of visitors. I don't think I've felt this excited since I got the job at *Senora*.

I've been seeing a lot of Jinx, who's become a good pal and the star of my column. We go to the pub together, and our weekly pilgrimage to the Saltash Waitrose has become a ritual. He's good fun and very easy on the eye and we never seem to stop laughing, which is a stark contrast to life at home, where Ed is increasingly monosyllabic. We did retrieve the Range Rover key, but Ed couldn't stomach the thought of where it had been, so ended up paying a fortune to replace it, an expense for which he berates me on an almost daily basis.

Although our relationship isn't in great shape at the moment, I live in hope that when Ed stops working so hard and is established within the firm, we might actually start to have some quality time. I see more of Jeremy Kyle than I do of my fiancé, which is worrying. Still, at least I have Jinx to cheer me up. Tales of his exploits, with both animals and humans, fill my column every Sunday, and they are as colourful as anything that Jilly Cooper could dream up. Every week there's another girl on Jinx's arm, or a bunny boiler stalking him, or he's being pursued by an irate husband, so hanging out with me buys him some good cover and keeps the adoring hordes at bay. And because I'm engaged and not a six-foot blonde stick insect, there's no way he could ever fancy me. It's perfect. I'm also relieved that Ed isn't at all bothered about the column either, in fact he seemed almost grateful for the money that it's bringing in. I'm surprised at this but I'm not complaining.

As for Alex Verney, things between us seem to have drifted into an unspoken truce. I don't see much of him, but when I do, he's nothing but polite. I had hoped that we'd become friends, but we hardly see each other. We do pass in the house but never really stop to talk. There are certainly no more veiled references to Green Slimegate, and I've kept my promise and haven't mentioned him once in my column. I just don't think he likes me very much and does his best to steer clear, which is fine. I clearly irritate him as much as a tight G-string, and it's rather a relief not to have to deal with his brooding presence. The man is so dark he'd make hanging out with Darth Vader look like light relief. Still, I often think of how sad he looked in the lavender garden, but if I try to bring the subject of Vanessa up with Virginia, she remains tight-lipped. Alex Verney is a closed book.

One Friday morning in late July, I'm woken up at the crack of dawn by the sunshine streaming through the crack in the curtains. Ed is away at some solicitors' conference, which is how I've been able to sneak Ken on to the bed, where's he's snored contentedly all night and lain across my feet like a tenstone hot-water bottle. Sharing a bed with my dog is actually a lot nicer than sharing a bed with my fiancé, I decide as I open the curtains and peer out at the valley already shimmering in the sunshine. At least Ken doesn't hog the duvet, and he's always over the moon to see me when he wakes up.

Hmm. It says it all when the only male who wakes up next to me with a smile on his face is the dog.

"Come on, boy! Time to get up!" I say to Ken, who raises his head and slowly peels open one large eye. "Auntie Ali's coming today! We need to get ready!"

I'm so excited that Ali has finally agreed to leave London for a few days and come down to Cornwall. For a woman who regularly flies to New York and Milan, she's very twitchy about a mere two-hundred-mile trip down the M5. I had to reassure her that Truro does have a Starbucks, M&S in Plymouth sell sushi and I won't force-feed her pasties before she finally bit the bullet and said she'd come. Thank goodness the weather is on side for once and bathing Polmerryn in warm honeyed rays. The corn fields are a sunny yellow, the sea purest blue and the pastures the kind of green that Robin Hood would covet, which makes a far more appealing picture than the damp mist and low cloud we seem to get here rather too often for my liking. I really want Ali to see my new home looking wonderful so that she won't berate me about giving up my career. Not that she can berate me. I seem to have a budding future as a newspaper columnist. "Sex in the Sticks", starring Jinx, has been a massive hit and Ali is delighted. Ditto the locals, because any that I do mention immediately become mini celebrities. Terry Tipple tells me his trade has gone up fifty per cent since I name-checked the Ship last weekend, and Annie from the shop regularly has visitors asking if Polmerryn is the village I write about. Sam the barmaid has even asked if I'll include her in the next one, and as for Jinx, well, he tells me that his list of patients has never been so long, and soon he'll be able to buy himself a Ferrari. Go me!

Maybe I should rename my column "The Only Way is Cornwall"?

The only cloud on my horizon is that Ed has decided we need to entertain, and has chosen tonight as the perfect time to throw a dinner party. When he says *we need to entertain*, what he actually means is that *I* need to up the ante and produce food and drink to wow his guests. These are mostly people he wants to impress, like his starchy old boss, members of the Rotary Club, and bizarrely even Virginia in her capacity as lady of the manor. I'm delighted she's on board, and I've managed to add some extra moral support by sticking Jinx and Ali on the list too.

It should be an interesting mix of folk, I think as I slip into my jeans. Wow. This outdoorsy lifestyle really agrees with me. I'm now back into my old size tens without even trying to diet. It must be all that stomping up and down hills with Ken and having to go everywhere on foot because Ed has the Range Rover most of the time and still resists buying a second car. In spite of living on biscuits and drinking far too much cider with Lady V when we have team meetings in the pub, I don't think I've ever felt better. Walking Ken in all weathers has put so much colour in my face that I hardly bother with make-up, and my twice-monthly hair appointments have certainly fallen by the wayside. Instead of being bullied straight and kept strictly at shoulder length, my hair is now a mass of springy curls and in danger of growing past my shoulder blades.

"Amber Scott," I say to the rosy-cheeked and freckled woman in my bedroom mirror, "you have gone feral!"

Dragging Ken off the bed — he's not allowed upstairs when Ed's about, and is so happy to be allowed on the bed that he'd stay there all day — I go downstairs, make coffee, collect a couple of custard creams and munch them thoughtfully on the doorstep outside the kitchen. I've got a lot on today, and as I eat, I run through my mental "to do" list.

Top priority is to find myself something to wear for tonight. Since I can't get to Plymouth very easily from here — the one bus we have a week probably left yesterday — Lady Virginia has very kindly offered to let me rummage through some of the clothes at the manor house. The last time we rummaged, when we were sorting out Lady Elizabeth's boudoir, I was gobsmacked to come across vintage Chanel, still wrapped in tissue paper and smelling of No. 5 and total sophistication.

"Oh yes, that was my mother-in-law's," Virginia said blithely, as I almost passed out with rapture. "She used to visit Paris every spring to kit herself out. Feel free to try it on. Or anything else of hers you like the look of."

She went on to show me an entire dressing room literally stuffed with vintage fifties fashion that would make the likes of Evangeline St Anthony weep. Having a rather retro Kelly Brook-style figure, I just know I can find something that will suit me for tonight. Who needs to trek to Plymouth? And as for food, Ali has promised that the boot of her red Lotus will be stuffed with Marks & Spencer's finest. Now that I've nearly got the hang of the Aga, and as long as I remember to remove the plastic trays and stick it all in the Le Creuset, I'm sure I'll be able to pass it off as home cooking. How hard can it be?

Biscuit breakfast over, I rinse my mug and decide to leave Ken in the boot room, because much as I adore him, his company isn't conducive to trying on clothes. I'm just on the brink of setting off for the manor house when I spot a white flash in the corner of the garden. Fan-flipping-tastic. Mabel's on the loose again. Honestly, that goat. No wonder the farmer was delighted to get rid of it. Ed is still searching for his Armani jeans, and I've lost count of everything else she's demolished. Brushing crumbs off my front, I set off for the flower bed and round her up for the umpteenth time.

"They should have called you Houdini," I say as I drag her by her pink collar back into the field. "Or failing that, Total Pain in the Bum."

Seriously, cute as she is to look at, Mabel is quickly becoming the bane of my life. Since the morning Mum kindly dumped her on me, barely a day has gone by without somebody calling to say that my goat has wandered into their garden/allotment/beer garden. Mabel, it soon becomes clear, was tied up in that farmyard for a very good reason, namely that she has escapologist skills David Blaine can only dream of. No fence, gate or hedge can hold her.

With Mabel safely back in the paddock for at least twenty minutes or so, I set off for Polmerryn Manor. It's a stunning walk. The hedges foam with cow parsley and are freckled with campions and buttercups. As I pass through green lanes, sunlight spills through the macramé of branches and dances upon the road. From the beach, the sounds of laughter and the shrieking of children drift on the soft breeze, and I'm almost sorry when I reach the house. It's really a day to be out in the sunshine, lazing on a beach or maybe at sea, racing across the waves in a boat, rather than in the cool interior of an ancient manor.

There's no answer when I knock on the back door, so I let myself in with the key that Virginia has given me and make my way up to the first floor. What was once a rabbit warren of claustrophobic passageways now makes perfect sense, and very soon I'm in the large suite towards the rear of the property where Virginia and I have been storing the clothes. We have something of a catalogue going on — it's a long-term plan of mine to maybe put together an exhibition of fashion and see if Ali wants to run a feature on it in the women's section of the *Dagger* — so I know exactly what I'm looking for and just where it's going to be. I only hope that I've lost enough weight to fit into it. Women in the fifties were still slender from the years of wartime rationing and probably didn't eat biscuits for breakfast. Still, it's amazing what being isolated from McDonald's can do for a girl's waistline and I live in hope.

I rummage through the rails, my fingers brushing past silks and satins, until I finally find what I'm looking for. Sliding the padded hanger from the rail, I slip the dress off and hold it against myself, and look critically in the mirror. Red velvet, deep and rich as claret, nestles against my skin and pools on to the floor, while the green splash of silken sash whispers over my

285

fingers. This off-the-shoulder evening dress, nipped in at the waist and falling in forgiving and graceful folds to the feet, is exactly what I'm looking for. Do I dare try it? The kind of Coco I'm usually acquainted with is drunk at bedtime rather than worn to dinner parties.

Oh sod it. Why not? The dress is only gathering dust here, and Virginia said it would be fine. Without any further delay, I shrug off my clothes and then my underwear too in an attempt to be as streamlined as possible. Then I'm stepping into the dress and twisting like a yoga guru to fasten the laces and tie the sash. Ouch! That really hurt. I haven't been in an interesting position like this for a very long time, sadly, but the pain is worth it because the dress fits! Even with the laces undone I can see that it really, really fits!

Amazed, I twirl in front of the mirror and watch the full skirt spin out. Wow! The velvet looks vivid against my pale skin and gives me a cleavage that Jordan would envy, and my stomach is deceptively flat beneath the sash. Even with a head of crazy curls and a face splattered with freckles I look OK, if a bit Playboy Mansion meets milkmaid with a dash of Moll Flanders chucked in for good measure.

I could almost fancy myself!

I'm so busy twirling and posing in front of the mirror that I don't register the footsteps coming along the corridor or hear the door creaking open. The first I know that I am no longer alone is a clearing of the throat. I almost leap out of the dress, which would be unfortunate in the extreme because Alex is standing in the doorway. My face is the same colour as the velvet. Oh my God. How long has he been standing there?

"I'm sorry, I didn't mean to startle you," says Alex, slowly. "It's just I heard a noise. I didn't realise you were here."

Startle me? He's probably responsible for my first grey hairs.

Heart still pounding, I say, "I let myself in. Your mum gave me a key."

He nods. "Of course."

There's the weirdest pause. Alex is staring at me as though he's never seen me before, that intense jade gaze never straying from my face. Something odd has happened to my body and I can't move. Time seems to freeze. I'm aware of how still it is, the dust falling silently through the air and shards of sunlight spilling through the muslin curtains.

Alex breaks the spell. "You need lacing. Turn around."

Wordlessly, I do as he says. I feel his fingers brush against my ribs as he pulls the ribbons tighter, and his breath is warm at the nape of my neck as he concentrates. At least one of us can, because all I can think about is that his lips, that full, sensual mouth that is usually set in a sardonic line when I'm about, are inches from my neck, close enough to brush against the skin.

Whoa! I'm starting to sound like one of my pink books! Calm down, woman! This is grumpy Alex

Verney we're talking about here, not Mr Darcy. Heathcliff, remember.

But even bearing this thought in mind, goose bumps are Mexican-waving up and down my arms, especially when those strong hands stray to my waist (thank God I've lost weight) and slowly turn me around to face him. Alex is so tall I have to tilt my head right back to look up at him.

"Hello, Amber," he says softly.

"Hi," I breathe.

Oh God! Oh God! I've read this book! I know exactly what happens next! Any minute now he's going to lower his head and brush my lips with his in a kiss as soft as chamois leather. My pulse does a tango in anticipation.

"There's something I have to tell you. Show you, more to the point," Alex whispers. I'm so close to him now that I can see my reflection in his tar-dark pupils and smell the scent of his skin, a musky-sweet vanilla. Is he going to ask if he can kiss me? Oh Lord, I know I must be a bad girl, but don't ask! Just do!

I open my eyes wide. "What?" I murmur. Underneath the tightly laced dress my heart is trying to break through my ribcage.

Hands still on my waist, he steers me towards the window, where the gardens fall away beneath us. I'm pressed against the sill, and now I feel his hands on my bare shoulders. Every nerve ending I possess is fizzing like space dust. His full, sexy mouth is only inches from mine.

288

Then he ruins everything. Glancing over my shoulder, he makes a strangled sound and lets me go so speedily that my bum bounces on to the windowsill.

"I'll tell you *what*," he gasps. "Your bloody goat is in my lavender garden! That's what!"

CHAPTER
TWENTY

To say that I'm horrified is an understatement. Not only have I nearly made a total idiot of myself in front of Alex, but sure enough, below in the garden Mabel is trip-trapping along merrily with sprigs of lavender dangling from her mouth. That bloody goat! And my even bloodier mother!

"Please remove your goat from my garden," Alex says in a horribly clipped tone. "Now."

I gulp, remembering how Virginia told me that he'd planted the lavender walk for the mysterious Vanessa. I know how much it means to him, especially after seeing the bleak look on his face that one time. I cannot let that naughty goat wreck it.

"I'm so sorry —" I begin, but Alex just raises his hand.

"Never mind apologising. Let's just remove the goat," he suggests.

Bunching my skirts up in my fists, I fly down the stairs and through the hall, leap the steps leading into the courtyard and dash through the parterre and into the lavender walk. How I don't break my neck I'll never know, but such is my haste to grab the greedy goat and save the plants that I don't stop to think about my vintage dress or my platform boots. By the time I reach Mabel I'm beyond caring that I might trip or tear the frock. That would be nothing in comparison to the damage she's done.

Oh. My. God. It looks like a herd of elephants has stampeded through the lavender. Bushes are trampled and one clump is practically grazed bare. How can one naughty goat do so much damage? Alex is behind me, and I hear him give a strangled moan when he sees the state of the garden. He freezes, surveying the damage with that dark, glowering expression I've experienced before, while I grab Mabel's collar. Generally I detest cruelty to animals, but at this precise moment I could cheerfully throttle her.

"Bad goat!" I scold, dragging her through the trampled plants.

"Bad goat?" Alex echoes incredulously. "Have you seen what it's done?"

Indeed I have. This isn't a goat, it's a weapon of mass lavender destruction.

"I'm so sorry," I say uselessly. "I'm sure it looks worse than it is. The plants will spring back, won't they?"

He shakes his head. "I doubt it."

I brace myself for the tirade that will surely follow — Lord knows I deserve it with my out-of-control pets — but it never comes. Instead, Alex just sighs and rakes a hand through his curls.

"Maybe it's for the best," he says.

I glance at the flattened plants. "How do you mean?"

Alex shrugs his broad shoulders. "Nothing," he says, but the bleak expression on his face tells a different story. Oh God, he's sad. This is a million times worse than when he's angry. I feel terrible.

"I'm sure I can fix it," I insist. How hard can it be? Alan Titchmarsh does this stuff all the time *and* writes books and hosts a TV show. All I need to do is pop to a Wyevale, buy a few plants and stick them in. Simples!

"Forget it," says Alex wearily. "It's fine. Come on, keep a hold on that bloody goat and bring her round to the stables. Like I said earlier, there's something I need to show you. A bit more damage one of your animals has done."

"Whatever it is, it won't be Ken," I say with great confidence. "He's been under house arrest since he swallowed the smart key."

"Wait and see," says Alex grimly. "Come on."

He stomps off ahead of me, hands thrust into the pockets of his Levis, while Mabel and I scurry in his wake. Goodness, but he has a nice bum.

What! Get out of my head, unsuitable thoughts! What is it with me today? Note to self: dig out that potion Mum gave me and pop it in Ed's coffee, pronto. All this fresh air is doing stuff to my libido, and I need to nip any silly thoughts about Alex Verney in the bud ASAP. I can't believe I really thought he was going to kiss me earlier. How ridiculous was that?

Alex opens a stable door and we usher Mabel inside before securing the top and the bottom.

"Tether her," he orders me. "Get a long length of chain and make sure she doesn't escape again. Or

292

failing that, give her to Animal Land for their pets' corner."

Mabel bites and butts. She may look cute with her toffee-coloured coat and big eyes, but she is Attila the Hun in goat form. She'd probably savage some kiddie, and then I'd be sued and Ed would go mental. Mum might think tethering is cruel, but it's a lot less cruel than what I'll do to Mabel if she escapes again.

"Now," says Alex, opening the door of the furthest stable and ushering me inside, "tell me again that this is nothing to do with Ken."

The sunshine outside is so bright that for a moment I stand blinking in the gloom while my eyes struggle to recover. As my vision adjusts, I see that there's a wire run set up in the stable, and inside it is Sadie, the black Lab and object of Ken's affections. She's lying on her side, eyes closed and tongue lolling, and clustered against her are . . . are . . .

Oh bollocks. Surely not?

I look from the run to Alex and then back again.

"Puppies?" I whisper.

"Puppies," says Alex. He reaches in and rubs Sadie's glossy head. "I only realised a few weeks ago; I'd assumed the old girl was just on the plump side. I've been meaning to tell you but we never seem to bump into each other. I guess you're busy with Jinx."

I feel too terrible to reply, because this makes two things dear to Alex's memories of the mysterious Vanessa that animals of mine have wrecked. I'm amazed he's not hollering at me. Lost for words, I reach into the enclosure and touch one of the pups. Oh wow!

It's so soft and cute, a mixture of Sadie's inky fur and Ken's suede-like coat, and its little face is just so dear. I want one!

I look up at Alex, but the expression on his face is inscrutable. Is he cross?

Amber. Your dog has bred with his dead wife's pedigree Labrador. Of course he's cross. In fact, cross will be an understatement.

Oh. My. God. Is there a Puppy Support Agency?

Alex reaches into the run and scoops up a puppy. As he strokes the tiny dog, a dimple plays hide and seek in his cheek. Maybe he isn't angry after all.

"What was it you were just saying about this not being Ken's fault?" he asks.

There is no denying these puppies are Ken's.

I hang my head. "I'm so sorry about everything. I don't seem to do anything but cause you hassle. You must wish I'd never moved to Polmerryn."

"Life has certainly taken a more eventful turn since you arrived," Alex agrees with a half-smile.

"What shall we do about the child support?" I gulp. "I have to warn you, Ken isn't the most responsible male I've ever come across."

"You do surprise me," says Alex drily.

"I'll buy puppy food and clean them out," I offer, desperate to placate him before he flips. "I'll take a couple too, if it helps."

"You can have them all, with my blessing," says Alex. "But somehow I don't think your fiancé would be very happy. Anyway, don't worry about homing them. Your very good friend Jinx assures me he'll be able to find owners for them."

"But I want one!" I cry. I really do, too. I've always wanted a puppy.

Eventually Alex agrees that when they are bigger I can pick one of the puppies, and we come to an agreement that I will pay all Jinx's bills. I apologise over and over again for Ken's feckless behaviour and promise to get him neutered as soon as possible. In the meantime, I need to think of a way of breaking the news of our impending puppy parenthood to Ed. He's hardly Ken's biggest fan as it is, so bringing son or daughter of Ken home will go down like cold sick.

A mobile phone call diverts Alex's attention from the puppies.

"Charlie! Hi!" he says as he answers, a huge smile spreading across his face and making his eyes dance like sun-sparkled waves. "Great to hear from you!" To me he mouths, "I'm taking this call. See you later."

I nod, intrigued about the identity of the caller. Whoever the mysterious Charlie is, he's certainly cheered Alex up. His smile lifts his entire face and crinkles his eyes. He doesn't look like this very often when he's with me, which isn't surprising really, seeing as all I do is disrupt his life. No wonder he's normally so short-tempered and grumpy.

Leaving Alex deep in conversation, I glance at my watch and realise that it's now gone two in the afternoon. Ali is due to arrive any minute and I really need to get back home. I've so much to do: ring the local garden centre and order shedloads of lavender;

prepare a dinner party that will impress Ed's bosses and put Ed in such a good mood he'll say yes to a puppy; and turn myself into a goddess. I feel exhausted just thinking about it all. With one final pat of their silky coats, and a stern warning to Mabel to behave until I can return to collect her, I tear myself away from the puppies, change back into my own clothes and set back off for Hawkstone House.

I'm just at the bottom of the valley and dithering over whether to take the footpath over the fields or stick to the steeper but quicker lane route when the blast of a horn and a screech of brakes cause me to flatten myself against the hedge rather than end up as Amber jam. A bright red Lotus, hood down and driven by a female sporting a trendy spiky blonde hairdo, misses me by centimetres.

It's Ali, doing a great Mr Toad impression by turning the lanes of south-east Cornwall into Brands Hatch.

"Fuck me! That was close!" she says cheerfully as I dust myself down. "What are you doing in the middle of the road, you silly cow?"

"Believe it or not, I'm walking home," I say as I climb into the low-slung car. "Walking is something you do with your legs. You should try it."

"Bugger that!" scoffs Ali. "You've only been out of London for a few months but already your road sense has disappeared." She looks me up and down and raises her perfect eyebrows. "Hey, you've lost some weight. Looking sexy, babes! Country life is doing you some good."

"It's easy to lose weight when you're twenty miles from McDonald's, don't have a car and there's nowhere to buy lattes," I tell her. "Anyway, never mind me. What about you? Being a high-flying newspaper editor obviously agrees with you. You look fantastic!"

I'm not exaggerating. Ali is tanned, sports a head of glossy blonde hair and is dressed in a tight leather jacket, DVB jeans and tasselled pink Missoni scarf. With her immaculate make-up, designer clothes and French-manicured nails, she looks every inch the successful magazine editor, and I tuck my own hands under my thighs so that she doesn't catch sight of my short nails and ragged cuticles. I know I've let my grooming slide a bit, but there doesn't really seem much point when you're either covered in paint or digging the garden.

"I have a good Botox technician," Ali says bluntly. "He works fucking miracles, but even so it's nothing compared to whatever you're on. Your skin looks amazing. Is it that new Clarins fake tan?"

"It's called being out in the sunshine, Al, which certainly beats being stuck in the office."

But Ali shakes her head. "Don't give me that crap. That glow you've got is nothing to do with fresh air. Who are you shagging? Is it that hunky vet?"

I laugh. "I'm not shagging anyone, babes. Especially not Jinx. He's just a friend."

"Nobody?" Ali's eyes widen. "Not even Ed?"

My best friend has been in my company for approximately sixty seconds and already she's asking me about my sex life. Some things never change.

"Not even Ed," I confess.

"Fuck," says Ali. "Or maybe not."

I sigh. "I'm not sure what's going on between Ed and me. This move was supposed to be our new start, but it hasn't exactly worked out the way I'd hoped. He works harder than ever and I hardly see him. If it wasn't for working up at the manor house and having Ken to talk to, I think I'd have gone mental long ago."

My friend gives me a sideways look. "Do you think he's got someone else?"

"Ed! As if!" I splutter. "He's the least likely type to cheat."

"They're all the type," says Ali.

I recall my sister saying something similar a while back, but seriously, Ed? When would he find time to have an affair? And anyway, he loves me. Doesn't he?

"How's Liz?" I ask, to change the subject.

Ali shrugs. "No idea. I haven't heard from her since she quit. I emailed her a few times to offer her some freelance work, but she's never replied. Nobody seems to have a clue what she's up to or where she's gone."

"She always was a private person," I remind her.

Ali snorts. "Secretive, you mean. Anyway, to cut a long story short, I did pop round to her flat, but she's moved out and not left a forwarding address, so fuck knows where she is. Maybe she ran off with that mystery lover."

I'm just about to ask if she has any further thoughts on who this could be when Ali's mobile rings and her attention is diverted by Mike Elton wanting to talk circulation wars. As they discuss figures and targets, I look at the patchwork fields and rippling seas of wheat and feel suddenly very glad that I'm out of it all. My painting is going well, I love helping at the manor and even the column is a lot of fun. So I miss having Waitrose and Costa on tap, and I may have lost the plot a bit by hoping Alex Verney was about to kiss me, but generally life is good. If I can just sort out what the problem is with Ed, I think things would be, if not perfect, pretty darn close.

"Sorry about that," Ali says, swinging the car up the drive to my house. "No peace for the very wicked!"

"And are you very wicked with Mike?" I ask.

"You'd better believe it, baby!" grins Ali. "That man is filthy!"

This sets the tone, and we gossip and giggle for the rest of the afternoon.

While I unpack all the lovely M&S goodies and try to figure out how I can make them look home-cooked, Ali parks herself at the kitchen table, drinks copious amounts of coffee and strokes Ken, who, like most males, adores her on sight. She loves the house, is all agog about Alex's mystery wife, and when Jinx rocks up in the Aston, looking gorgeous in little more than shorts and deck shoes, her joy is complete.

"Darling, your column doesn't do him justice!" Ali declares as, bare-chested and looking like something out of an aftershave advert, Jinx waltzes into the kitchen. "He's fucking gorgeous."

"I don't know who you are, but you have excellent taste," says Jinx, kissing her soundly on both cheeks. "And you're pretty divine yourself."

"Jinx, this is Ali, my best friend and editor of the *Dagger*'s women's pages. Ali, this is Jinx. Vet, friend and often subject of my column," I say as I make vomit gestures.

"Vet and local stud, by all accounts," says Ali, going all throaty-voiced and batty-eyelashed. Oh no. She's got that look on her face, that look that says *I'm going to gobble you up*. Not that Jinx looks too bothered by it; in fact his own look says *Eat me!*

"It's a vicious rumour that I'm doing my best to prove," he says with a wink.

"I'm happy to help you look for evidence," purrs Ali, practically licking her lips. I roll my eyes. I won't get any sense out of her now. Or Jinx, for that matter, now that he's in full charm-offensive mode.

As Jinx and Ali continue to flirt and start to work their way through one of the bottles of the white Burgundy I'd been chilling for dinner, I heat up the vats of dauphinoise potatoes and creamy beef stroganoff and pray that the M&S boxes are buried deep enough in the bin to avoid my culinary deception ever being revealed. My friends are two peas in a very bad pod and I just hope they can keep their hands off one another sufficiently for us all to get through dinner. Old Mr Marchant and his wife will not approve if Jinx and Ali snog through the starters, and Ed will burst a blood vessel.

"Relax and have a drink, Amber." Jinx thrusts a glass of wine into my hand.

I eye it nervously. In spite of regular "business" meetings with Virginia in the Ship, I haven't really had a lot of alcohol lately. I daren't risk getting pissed when Ed's boss is coming over. That would probably be the final nail in my already nail-covered coffin.

"Go on," Ali says when I demur. "The food's already cooked, and there's nothing to do except have a bath. What can possibly go wrong?"

I'm not sure, but knowing my luck lately, something pretty horrific. Against my better judgement, I take the drink. I am so crap at resisting peer pressure.

Pretty soon the first bottle of wine is empty, the three of us are getting stuck in merrily to the second and before long-all my worries about the evening drift away. It's amazing with wine, isn't it? Suddenly nothing really matters.

It's just a dinner party for some friends and a couple of Ed's colleagues, I tell myself as I run a bath and leave the other two to chat in the sitting room. The food is warming on the top of the Aga, Ali's set the table and Jinx has lit the wood burner. The atmosphere is perfect and already my guests are in the party mood.

Tonight is going to be great!

I'm just blowing a few idle soap bubbles across the bathroom when there's a nervous rap of knuckles on the door and Ali's blonde head pokes round. Her lipstick is smudged and the neat blonde bob is no longer quite so smooth. Why do I feel like the parent of a teenager all of a sudden?

"Er, Ambs," she says awkwardly. "I've got something to tell you."

"If you're worried that I'll be upset about you snogging Jinx the minute my back's turned, don't be," I say.

Ali pulls a wry face. "That obvious?"

"'Fraid so, babes."

She looks in the mirror and wipes away the smudges. "Fuck, I look like something out of *Twilight*." She hands me my bathrobe. "Put this on and come downstairs a minute."

Bathrobe on, I follow her down the stairs and into the kitchen, where Jinx is on his hands and knees mopping the floor, the floor that is covered in pools of stroganoff, rich beef stock and creamy potatoes and dotted with islands of broken plates.

My dinner!

"I'm so sorry," Jinx says. "We totally forgot that the dog was in the kitchen."

Ken, looking very sheepish and full, thumps his tail and sprays gravy all over the walls.

My hand flies to my mouth, my gaze to the clock. The guests are due in just over an hour. What on earth am I going to do?

CHAPTER
TWENTY-ONE

So much for this being *just a dinner party* and *what can possibly go wrong?* Talk about famous last words.

I stare at the mess on the kitchen floor and my alarm bells don't so much ring as sound the nuclear attack signal. Ken has slurped up most of the food, and much as I'm tempted to scoop up the remainder, keep calm and carry on, I daren't risk giving anyone some hideous canine disease. Several of them are lawyers and would probably sue my ass off.

"Don't panic," says Ali, which is funny because panicking is *exactly* what I'm planning to do. "I'll just nip to Mark's and get us some more. Easy."

Jinx and I laugh out loud at this.

"Nice idea, Ali," I say. "Only flaw is that the nearest Mark's is at least thirty miles away."

"What about one of those ones in a petrol station?" Ali suggests, already jiggling her car keys.

"We don't have them here," Jinx explains. "We have a Spar, but that closes at six."

Ali looks shocked. "What sort of fucking place is this?"

"The countryside," I say wearily, sinking down at the kitchen table and placing my head in my hands. I am doomed. As if things weren't already rocky enough with Ed, they are now going to be a million times worse.

The three of us survey the carnage of my dinner party bleakly. Jinx is just wondering whether he could rustle up omelettes and Ali is contemplating putting a trip to Fifteen on expenses when there's a knock at the door and Alex bowls into the kitchen without so much as a by-your-leave.

I feel like dashing my brains out on the flagstones. Can things possibly get any worse? What does he want now? Another go about my out-of-control animals? Although bearing in mind what Ken has just done, I have a horrible feeling he might actually have a point . . .

"Sorry, I didn't realise you had company," Alex says when he sees Jinx and Ali. Stretching out a hand and smiling his crinkly green-eyed smile, he adds to Ali, "I'm Alex Verney, a friend of Amber's."

Friend? This is news to me. He didn't look very friendly earlier when Mabel was chewing up his lavender.

"Hi," breathes Ali, transfixed, and then giggles.

Hello? Did I just wander into a parallel universe? Did Ali, ball-breaking hard-nut fuck-'em-and-chuck-'em Ali, just giggle? Because of Alex Verney? I glance across at Jinx, who rolls his eyes at me and mouths *told you so*. Then I look back at Ali, who is totally transfixed. If she didn't have a razor-sharp power bob she'd be tossing her hair for sure, because it would go a treat with the simpering expression on her face. What has got into the woman? This is seriously scary. It's like watching Germaine Greer channel Doris Day.

Alex is dressed in his faded Levis, the soft moss-green sweater and battered tan Cat boots. With his tanned face, cinnamon sprinkling of freckles over his strong nose, and thick black hair held back with a strip of leather, he looks as though he's stepped straight out of a magazine advert for Henri Lloyd. Ali's eyes aren't saucers, they're dinner plates, and her chin in almost on the kitchen table.

And this is when the penny drops for me. Bloody hell! When he isn't stomping about and glowering at me about all my myriad wrongdoings, Alex is actually quite an attractive guy. OK, if I'm honest, he's a very attractive guy.

What a shame that most of the time I see him he's a miserable git.

"I thought you might want this. You left it behind earlier on, which was probably my fault." Nodding at Ali, Alex joins me at the table and hands me a carrier bag. Wishing that I wasn't modelling the drowned rat in tatty bathrobe and with no make-up look, I peep inside.

It's the red velvet dress.

He remembered that I wanted it. He's made a special effort and dropped it round. How kind is that?

Why is he being so nice?

"It was my fault you left it behind," he says, when I thank him. "My mother would probably strangle me if she knew you'd had to do without it because of me, so don't thank me, I'm being purely selfish. Besides, it suits you. You should keep it."

"Really?" Amazed, I look up at him. "Are you sure?"

Alex nods. "Absolutely. I insist. Anyway, I won't hold you up any longer. I know you have a dinner party to prepare for."

"You must join us!" Ali says quickly, digging me in the ribs with a bony elbow. "Mustn't he, Amber?"

Oh God. Can today get any worse? Not only do I have nothing except Winalot to feed my guests, but I'll also have to endure Alex's intense and glowering presence across the dinner table. Add to this guilt about puppies, wrecked gardens and newspaper columns, and it's just as well that there's no food, because I wouldn't be able to stomach a mouthful.

"Ali," I say slowly as I point to the remnants of the meal. "We can't have a dinner party, remember?"

Alex's dark brows shoot up into his hair when he notices my Jackson Pollock of a kitchen. "What happened here?"

"The dog ate the dinner," Jinx explains.

Alex nods slowly. "Ken. Of course. I should recognise his trademark trail of destruction."

"So, welcome as you are to join us, there won't actually be a dinner party now," I say sadly. "Go ahead. You can tell me my dog is out of control and that I'm a useless owner. I know all that."

He fixes me with a green-eyed stare. "I've never thought that. You've given Ken a home, and that bloody goat too, which is kind if a little misguided. And my mother has taken on a whole new lease of life since you started working with her. The house looks fantastic too. You are far from useless."

"Hear bloody hear," says Ali.

I laugh despairingly. "Tell that to Ed when he comes in and finds that I can't actually feed his guests."

"Ed's an idiot," says Alex bluntly.

"Amen to that," Ali agrees.

Alex places a hand on my shoulder. It's strong and comforting and for some reason makes me feel better. When he removes it, I feel a strange pang of loss.

"This is what we'll do," he says firmly. "Jinx, you pop down to the manor house, grab Mum and ask her to dig out the '69 claret and some cheeses from the pantry. Ali, you clear this lot up and pop some plates in the warming oven, and Amber, go upstairs and get yourself dressed up. I'll take care of the food."

I stare at him. Why is he being so helpful? "Really?"

"Really," he says firmly, fishing the keys to the Defender from his jeans pocket. "Now go and get ready."

I don't need telling twice. Ed will be home any minute now. While Alex and Jinx roar off in their cars, I race upstairs with the carrier bag and make a start on looking vaguely human. My hair has dried into mad corkscrews and straightening it will take far too long, so I just pin it up with a clip, drag some mascara on to my lashes and pull on the dress, teaming it with some glittery flip-flops. Then I tear downstairs again, where Ali has done an amazing job of clearing up. With the lamps lit, the floor spotless and candles flickering from the dining room, it looks like a scene from an aspirational lifestyle magazine, although quite who would aspire to my lifestyle is anyone's guess. Only a total masochist, I should imagine.

"Wow, you look amazing in that colour. And I'd kill for your tits! No wonder Alex is so keen to help out," says Ali when she sees me. "And talking of Alex, I have a bone to pick with you, young lady. You've never let on that Heathcliff is that gorgeous."

I laugh. "Because most of the time he's storming around with a face like thunder, that's why."

"He can storm around all he likes when he looks like that," says Ali, fanning her face. "He's fucking gorgeous! You lucky girl, having him running around after you!"

"He's hardly running around after me," I protest, but Ali shakes her head.

"He's just sped off to rescue your dinner party. Hmm, I wonder why he'd do that?"

I must admit I was wondering the same myself but have drawn a blank. Guilt for being so mean about Mabel? Or perhaps he wants a massive dollop of cash to pay for puppy care.

When I offer these ideas to Ali, she snorts and raises her eyes to heaven.

"If you can't figure it out then I'm not going to tell you. Christ. How the fuck did you ever work on a women's magazine? You are hopeless."

I'm just about to demand she does tell me or I will never write another word for her again and will cast her out into the Cornish M&S-less wasteland to fend for herself when Jinx returns with Virginia and a stunning redhead, all glorious Titian hair and legs up to her

308

armpits. Instantly I feel short and dumpy in comparison.

"Hello! I'm Charlotte Verney," she says, kissing me warmly and handing me a bottle of Moët. "Aunty V said it would be fine if I joined you. Alex should easily have enough food."

"You don't mind, do you, darling?" trills Virginia, waltzing into the kitchen with a bottle of claret in each hand. "It's just that Charlie's down for a few days and we don't want to leave her on her own."

Charlie? That rings a bell. Then I remember the call that Alex took. Charlie, short for Charlotte. Of course. No wonder he lit up like a searchlight when she phoned. Who wouldn't? I could never compete with that. She's like a virtual-reality Rossetti painting.

Not that I'd want to compete with her. Of course not. I meant hypothetically speaking, obviously.

"Of course I don't mind," I say. "Lovely to meet you, Charlie."

"You too!" she says. "I've heard so much about you."

"Really?" I'm rather alarmed to hear this. "What has Virginia been saying?"

"Not Auntie," giggles Charlie. "Alex! He's told me all about you."

"Fan-flipping-tastic," I mutter.

"Jinxy's told us all about your trauma! Too frightful!" carries on Lady V. To Ken she adds, "You are such a naughty doggy!"

"Naughty doggy doesn't come close," I say darkly. "I was almost ready to call Battersea and book him in."

"Darling! No! Not now he's a daddy! Besides, all is well now," Virginia insists, plonking down the wine while Jinx places a massive crate of cheese and biscuits on the table. "Look, here's Alex now with the food!"

Sure enough, Alex is outside unloading two gigantic tureens and gesturing for help. Jinx ignores him and turns his attention back to Ali, pouring her a glass of wine and whispering something in her ear.

"I'll give him a hand," offers Charlie, and I watch intrigued as she flings her arms around her cousin and kisses him warmly, while Alex, equally delighted, spins her around and hugs her back. Hmm. They're obviously very close. I've never seen Alex so relaxed around anybody before. He's usually so uptight.

Are they more than cousins?

And do I care if they are?

"She's gorgeous, isn't she?" I say nonchalantly to Jinx, who's joined me at the window.

"Charlie V?" He shrugs. "I guess so. Not my type, though."

"Really?" I'm taken aback. "But Jinx, she has a pulse!"

"Watch it, cheeky!" Jinx says. "Maybe I prefer blondes."

His naughty, twinkly smile makes me laugh and I'm just ruffling his blond hair affectionately when, unfortunately for me, Ed chooses this exact minute to storm in like a paratrooper. I know that seeing me clowning around with Jinx, whom he trusts as much as Tom trusts Jerry, will be enough to tip him over the edge, so we spring apart guiltily, which is only more fuel to the fire of Ed's bad mood.

"Amber! What the fuck is going on?" he demands. "Why have we got all these extra people here, and why are there caterers delivering food? I thought I told you that we're on a budget and that Mr Marchant only likes plain home-cooked fare?"

I'm poised to apologise, my default setting these days, when Alex's voice says smoothly from my open mouth, "Poor Amber had an Aga malfunction; you really should get it serviced. How anyone can cook while it's running so badly is a mystery."

Alex strides into the room and deposits the tureens, and Ed goggles at him.

"Who the hell are you?" he asks rudely.

"I'm Alex, Lord Verney," Alex says evenly, neatly playing his trump card and shaking the stunned Ed's hand. "I hope you don't mind me interfering, but a friend of mine knows Rick Stein, so I made a few calls and picked up some bouillabaisse. It's freshly made for tonight so I'm sure it will be fine for your colleague."

"Of course, of course! Apologies, my Lord!" Ed nearly faints with excitement when he realises that the lord of the manor is in his kitchen. If I know my fiancé, he'll be frantically hoping that he can win the estate business for his firm and earn a billion Brownie points. "It's my honour to have you join us."

My Lord? An honour? I nearly laugh out loud. Hello? Earth to Ed? This is still just grumpy Alex. But Ed doesn't seem to care; he's far too busy sucking up. Maybe he was a limpet in a previous life.

"We've got French sticks too," pipes up Charlie, bursting into the kitchen brandishing one like a light sabre. "And Auntie V has tones of booze. This is going to be a great party!"

Ed's eyes nearly fall out of his head when he clocks her. Now it's my turn to hope I score Brownie points for finding such good guests.

"I'm Charlotte Verney," Charlie says, dimpling up at him and widening those big green eyes in a winning manner. "I hope it's OK if I crash your party."

"Of course," says Ed, nodding frantically and beaming at her. "It's my pleasure. Delighted! May I get you a drink? Or some nibbles?"

Wow. This is amazing. I seem to have borrowed Harry Potter's invisibility cloak. And there was I thinking I almost looked good in my red dress. As Ali sorts the food and I pour drinks, I watch my fiancé flirt like crazy with Charlie and try not to feel jealous. This is actually quite easy, because I find I really don't mind a bit. Weird. Maybe it's because she's out of his league, and also because I suspect that she and Alex are an item. They were all over each other earlier, after all, and he was clearly thrilled when she phoned, which is pretty concrete evidence and means Ed is safe.

It's weird, but the thought of Alex and Charlie together *does* unsettle me. How odd. Maybe it's time I dropped that love potion into Ed's drink and reminded us both why we're together.

Ed changes into a clean suit, Ken is locked in the boot room in disgrace and soon the guests arrive. I meet and greet, make small talk and play the hostess.

Once everyone has a drink and has settled down, I breathe a sigh of relief. Jinx, now sporting a suit, is charming Ed's boss and his wife, Lady V is entertaining the two Rotarians and Ali and Charlie are ladling out the fish stew into ceramic bowls and buttering the crusty bread. I lean my head against the cool glass of the kitchen window and take a deep breath. Maybe this will all go according to plan after all . . .

"How are you doing?" His breath soft against the nape of my neck, Alex whispers the words into my ear. I don't turn around because I can see his reflection in the window. My skin ripples with goose bumps.

"Good, thanks to you," I say, smiling at him in the glass. "It's really kind of you to help out."

"It wasn't kind at all," Alex says softly. "I fully intend you to pay back the favour, make no mistake about that."

"I'll need to work a lot more hours up at the house to repay a Rick Stein dinner for eleven," I say, trying frantically to do the maths. Crikey. And sell a few pictures too. Maybe even my body, although I can't imagine anyone wanting that.

"I'm sure we can come to some arrangement," Alex murmurs. "Listen, Amber, about earlier, just before the goat interrupted us —"

"Alex! Amber! There you are!" Red curls flying, Charlie races into the kitchen, where she grabs another bottle of wine. "Come on, guys, I'm starving! We're waiting for you two."

"Interrupted for the second time," says Alex wryly. "I guess it'll keep." Putting his arm round Charlie he says, "Come on then, sweetheart. Let's eat!"

The bouillabaisse is to die for, conversation flows as easily as the gallons of wine that Virginia has provided and everyone seems to be having a good time. Once we are on to the cheese and port, I take the plunge and tip the love potion into Ed's cup. Or at least I think I do. I'm never much good at figuring which side you take your glass from at these kind of dos and I have a horrible feeling that I may have spiked Alex's drink by mistake.

Bollocks. I'm *sure* I've messed it up. That *is* the spiked glass Alex has picked up, and now Ed's saying that he's had enough to drink and wants a coffee. Alex has drunk my mother's concoction. I hope to goodness it's safe!

Get a grip! I tell myself as, leaving everyone scoffing cheese and chatting, I slip into the kitchen to make coffee. It's all utter nonsense. It's not as though I actually believe any of Mum's mumbo-jumbo, is it? If I'm honest, I know it'll take more than magic to help Ed and me.

I bury my face in my hands. Our relationship is on the rocks. Who am I trying to kid? Everything's falling apart. We've moved to a beautiful part of the world for a fresh start, but all we've done is bring our problems with us. Nothing's changed at all; if anything it's a thousand times worse. Whatever I do just seems to annoy Ed, be it the animals, the way I drive the Range Rover, my mother (although in fairness to Ed she really

314

is annoying), the clothes I wear, the television shows I like . . . the list is endless. Even though this dinner party is a huge success, I still know I'll be in his bad books for having to buy food in. Whatever happens, Ed seems bent on finding fault with me.

Our relationship is in its death throes. Maybe he's just looking for a way to end it.

Feeling choked at this thought, I step into the courtyard. Warm light spills from the windows and the chatter of my guests rises and falls in the warm breeze. A slice of moon drifts high above and pokes its face through a sky clotted with navy clouds. I trail my hands through the rosemary bushes that frame the path and breathe in the scent of Sunday roast and happier times. A tear, cold and solitary as a diamond, slips down my nose and splashes on to the ground. What has happened to my life? And what is going to happen? I can't carry on like this.

Something has to change. And change very soon.

"Amber?" From the shadows Alex steps forwards. Sparks fantail into the inky darkness. "I didn't mean to make you jump, I was just having a cigarette. Sorry, it's a bad habit of mine. I may be a reformed smoker but sometimes I can't resist."

I bite back my rising sobs. "Don't apologise. Everyone has to have one vice."

"Just one would be good," remarks Alex. "So what's your excuse for being out in the dark all alone? Secret assignation with Jinx?"

I laugh. "Hardly! No, I think he's got his hands full with my friend."

"Hmm, I wish him luck there." Alex looks thoughtful. "So what's up?"

I shrug. "I'm just feeling melancholy. Too much to drink, I expect."

Alex's eyes narrow thoughtfully. "You only had a couple of glasses. Hardly enough to knock yourself out."

He's right. I think I'm actually drinking myself sober. What a bummer. Suddenly I see my life stretching before me, years and years of stilted evenings spent talking to people drier than the Serengeti and pretending that everything in my life is fine and dandy. Ed will get old and fat and even more pompous and I'll just get sadder and lonelier.

This hideous thought makes me shiver.

"Are you cold?" Alex steps closer and brushes the back of his hand across my shoulder. "You are, you're all goose bumps."

If I wasn't before, I certainly am now, because just this slight touch from him makes delicious shivers Mexican-wave across my body.

"Here, put this on." He shrugs off his dinner jacket and drapes it across my shoulders. It's warm with his body heat and the spicy, heady scent of his aftershave, and my senses reel. As his hands skim over my collarbones, bits of me that I'd totally given up on suddenly come back to life. Hello, old friends!

"Better?" he asks. His face is very close to mine as he says this and his eyes are inky black in the darkness. Beneath my dress my heart is bouncing on a pogo stick.

316

I nod. Oh yes. You could say that I'm better. Better now on many levels.

"Then why are you still shivering?" whispers Alex.

That is a very good question indeed, because I am still a quivering mass of goose bumps. Every nerve ending in my body is on red alert and even beneath the warmth of the jacket I'm trembling. But not with cold. Oh no. I'm far from chilly; in fact my blood has turned into lava. What on earth is happening here?

I'm just trying to think of a plausible answer when Alex steps closer and winds his fingers into my hair, pulling my face to his and caressing my cheek with his thumb. Before I even have a second to think, he's kissing me. And to be honest, after this point I can't think at all, because the touch of his mouth on mine makes me forget everything else. The chatter of the dinner party fades away and I no longer care that I am in my garden, only feet away from my guests and my fiancé, kissing another man. Nothing else registers except for being right here, right now with Alex. The wider world evaporates like morning mist and I wind my arms around his neck, threading my fingers through those springy curls and pulling him closer. Alex's kiss deepens, his stubble rasping against my face. It's like a crazy chain reaction of desire, and when he finally and gently breaks away I'm dizzy and disorientated, surprised to find myself in the garden. For a few wonderful heart-stopping moments nothing else had mattered more than being close to Alex. I'd been lost in a world of sensation where time and space ceased to exist. As I gaze up at him, wide eyed, I feel my world spin on its axis as my heart drums beneath my ribcage.

Everything has changed.

We stare at one another. Although only seconds before we were closer than words, I suddenly feel shy.

"Hello, Amber," says Alex.

"Hello, Alex," I whisper.

His head dips and his lips brush the skin of my throat. Burying his face in my neck he murmurs, "I thought I knew how your skin would feel, but I never imagined just how soft."

And then he's kissing me again and this time his mouth is harder and more demanding. I'm losing track of everything, where he ends and I begin, when an irritated voice calls into the darkness,

"Amber? Where are you? Derek Marchant wants a word about you doing some voluntary art teaching. Amber? What are you doing out in the garden?"

Shit! Ed! I step back guiltily. For the past few wonderful moments I'd totally forgotten about him. What sort of person am I? Consumed with guilt, and only needing a scarlet letter to confirm it, I can hardly look at him when he joins us.

I certainly can't look at Alex.

"What on earth are you doing out here?" Ed demands. He's flushed from drinking and looks rather grumpy.

I open my mouth to reply but I can't find the words. Somehow I don't think that *snogging Alex Verney* will be quite what he wants to hear. Luckily Alex is possessed of quicker wits than me. That, or he's a practised seducer of attached women, a thought that really stings. Is this what he does for amusement? It's not as though he's ever been my greatest fan.

"Amber and I were just talking." Alex's eyes hold mine and I'm mesmerised. I couldn't look away if I tried.

If Ed has noticed my dishevelled hair and breathlessness then he isn't too bothered.

"Well, if I may borrow Amber back for a minute? My partner wants to talk to her," he says. "And you might want to go and rescue your cousin. That bloody Jinx is prowling. You don't want to leave her with him."

Ed takes my hand. His is hot and sweaty and feels all wrong. Oh God. Everything feels wrong all of a sudden, especially Alex leaving us so abruptly to find Charlie when I can still feel his kiss burning my lips. I stare after him and every cell in my body is screaming at me to follow.

But I can't, can I?

And more importantly, why do I want to? What is happening to me?

CHAPTER
TWENTY-TWO

I agonise over that kiss all night, and toss and turn so much that I make Macbeth look like a sound sleeper. What on earth was I thinking to let Alex Verney kiss me and, worse still, kiss him back? I can't blame it on the drink, at least not on my part, although of course I know that Alex's glass was spiked with my mother's love potion. That explains totally why he kissed me. What it doesn't explain is why I kissed him back, and why I wanted it to carry on.

And neither does it explain why that chamois-leather-soft kiss is haunting my every moment since.

To say I feel guilty is a total understatement. I know that things haven't been great between Ed and me for some time, but all relationships go through rocky patches. Getting distracted by somebody else, even somebody who makes my pulse race and my legs turn to water, is unacceptable and on a par with cheating. How could I do this to Ed? We've been together for such a long time, I should be focusing on how to repair our relationship, not daydreaming about another man. And Alex Verney of all people! Is this some kind of mid-life crisis come early?

In the last few hours, I've undergone some very dark moments of the soul. What sort of a person am I? I've always seen myself as loyal, not the type who would cheat or have an affair, but ever since Alex brushed his lips against mine and skimmed a trail of fire across my collarbone with his fingertips, I've been like a creature demented and can hardly focus on anything else. I feel as though my entire body has been plugged into the mains and I can hardly sit still for all the pent-up energy.

Aargh! It's killing me to feel this alive! What's happening to me?

"What the fuck is the matter with you?" Ali demands over brunch on Sunday as I stare sadly at my smoked salmon and scrambled eggs, unable to force down a mouthful. "You're agitated, you can't eat and you haven't listened to a word I've said either. Are you in love or something?"

I flush to the ends of my hair. "Of course I am. I'm with Ed, remember?"

Ali snorts and showers me with bits of masticated egg. "Oh yeah, Ed. Mr Love God. Is this the same Ed who couldn't come out for breakfast because he had to go to the office? The one who hasn't shagged you for months?"

I *knew* I'd regret telling her that!

"He's working hard, Ali!"

"On a Sunday? Get with it, Ambs! He's up to something." Her blue eyes narrow. "A bit like you are right now. Who is it?"

I sigh and push my plate away. We've strolled down to Polmerryn for breakfast and are sitting outside a small café overlooking the bay. Ed has raced off to work, some trauma with a will apparently, which means that I am fair game for Ali to interrogate.

"Is it Jinx?" She leans forward and scrapes my food on to her plate. "Yum. This is too fucking good to waste. I'll do two spinning classes this week, or shag Mike a bit more."

"Jinx? No way!" Dragging my thoughts away from Alex, I laugh at this idea. "Anyway, I thought you and he were an item?"

"Hardly! That was just a bit of flirting," says Ali dismissively. "I'm relieved. I'd hate to think of you eating your heart out over somebody as shallow as that. I mean, he's pretty, but there's not a lot going on between the ears, is there?"

Poor Jinx. I hope he hasn't made the mistake of falling for Ali. She's tough as old boots, that one. I fear he might have met his match.

"So if it isn't him, then who is it?"

I roll my eyes at her. "Nobody."

"Don't give me that," she says. "It's OK, Amber. You can tell me. What's said at the beach café stays at the beach café."

"Really?"

She punches the air. "I knew there was something! Yes, really! Now spill!"

"I kissed Alex."

Shit! I can't believe I just said that! Now that the words are out, it makes it real. Horrified, I clap my hand over my mouth, but Ali is looking far from shocked. In fact she hardly turns a hair.

"Well of course you did. Is that all? Just a kiss? Personally, I'd have shagged his brains out."

"That's where we're different," I say primly. "I would never cheat on someone."

"Well bully for you," Ali retorts, in between a mouthful of smoked salmon. "If only we were all so good." Putting down her fork, she fixes me with a hard stare. "But can you really, hand on heart, say the same for Ed?"

"Of course I can! Ed would never cheat on me." I'm insulted and rather tired by everyone questioning my fiancé. "What do you have against him?"

"Nothing, except that he's a crap partner," says Ali.

"He isn't!"

"Babe, he is." She reaches across the table and takes my hands. "He neglects you, he snaps at you, and he sure as hell doesn't understand you. I can't bear to see my beautiful, clever, vibrant friend so unvalued. Fuck me, he ought to be on his knees every day thanking God he's got somebody like you."

My vision blurs. "Thanks, Ali."

"Don't thank me. It's true! Babes, life is too short to be unhappy. If this gorgeous Alex does it for you, then my advice is to just go for it. Maybe things with Ed have come to their natural end?"

Maybe they have. I don't know. What I do know is that I owe it to Ed to talk about our problems rather than just dive headlong into another relationship. Not that I think for one minute a relationship is what I have with Alex. It was one silly kiss after too much to drink, that's all. And how horrified and sorry was he anyway? I still cringe at the thought of the look on his face afterwards.

"Alex only kissed me because I put a love potion in his drink," I confess. "It would never have happened otherwise."

Ali looks at me as though I'm mad, which given the circumstances is fair enough.

"Why the fuck did you do that? Are you turning into your mother?"

"Mum gave it to me. I thought I tipped it into Ed's port," I admit. "I thought it would help him fancy me again."

"Babe! You're gorgeous! If Ed doesn't want to shag you, then he's mad! If I was a bloke I'd bonk your brains out," Ali insists. "Christ! This isn't about anything you've done wrong, it's about him, one hundred per cent."

I trace a pattern in the grease on the tabletop. "Maybe. But it doesn't feel like that."

"It may not *feel* like it, but believe me it's true. And Alex wouldn't have needed some silly love potion to kiss you. From the way that man looks at you, it's obvious he's mad about you."

It is? I must have missed that then, because whenever I bump into Alex, he's either taciturn or silent. That's when he's not tearing a strip off me, obviously. Ali might claim to be an ardent feminist, but I have a feeling that working on women's magazines is starting

324

to affect her brain. She'll be off to Mills & Boon soon if she's not careful.

Tired of talking about relationships, I steer the conversation round to the topic of my column. Ali takes the hint and enthuses about my writing. Apparently my tales of demented car-key-eating dogs, escaping goats and hunky vets are so popular that a book deal is in the air too.

"Keep it under your hat," she warns. "Nothing's set in stone as yet, but the advance could be enough to buy you some space and time to sort things out."

My independence, I think excitedly. I earn some money from Virginia and from the column but it's hardly enough to run a house and pay for my animals. If I did secure a book deal it could allow me to make some changes if or when I have to.

But I still hope it won't come to that. Ed and I have history, and surely that's worth fighting for. And what about starting over in the country? This was supposed to be our new beginning.

Once Ali leaves on the Monday morning, I walk to the manor house. I make a mug of coffee in the kitchen and help myself to a handful of biscuits before attacking the nursery. With my sketches spread out before me, I sit back on my heels and plan where everything will go, from the dapple-grey rocking horse that we've had restored to the narrow cot bed and the huge Edwardian doll's house. I want the visitors to feel as though the children have just skipped out for a moment, with their games left exactly as they were the moment they stopped playing. Pretty soon three hours have passed, so, tummy rumbling, I return to the kitchen to make some toast.

And bump right into Alex.

Oh God, is there anything more excruciating than having to make conversation with someone who was snogging your face off the last time you met? How do teenagers cope? And do GCSEs? Respect to them, I say!

"Amber." Alex nods curtly.

"Alex," I say.

"Tea?" he asks.

"Please," I reply. "Toast?"

"Thank you," he says.

We circle one another warily, doing a strange dance around the kitchen in an attempt not to get too close as we make our lunch. While he fills the kettle, I load the toaster with fat slices of Mother's Pride and the elephant in the room does a tap dance and shouts "You kissed him! You kissed him!" I feel quite giddy, because I have never in my life been so aware of another person's physical presence. From the spicy scent of his aftershave to the sweep of his dark lashes to the corded sinews of his arms, my every cell is on red alert.

Who drank the love potion again?

"Look, Amber," Alex says awkwardly, while I try to be totally fascinated by my buttering of the toast. "About the other night . . ."

His voice tails off and he couldn't have looked more ill at ease if he was naked and walking down Oxford Street. Not that I am thinking about Alex being naked.

No way. Certainly not! The poor man is mortified at the thought of kissing me, horrified even. How awful is that? There's no way I can let on that I've thought of nothing else since.

"Oh that!" I say airily, whacking half a pound of Lurpak on to my toast and practically hearing my arteries weep. "Goodness, Alex, please don't worry about it! It was only a kiss. It didn't mean anything."

He leans on the kitchen table and I daren't look up. One glimpse of those intense green eyes and that sensual mouth and I'll be lost. I'll probably roll around on the floor begging for my tummy to be tickled like Ken.

"Right," he says flatly. "Only a kiss. I see."

"Nothing to stress about," I continue, which is ironic in the extreme, seeing as I've done nothing but stress since Friday. "We'd both had a bit to drink, hadn't we? These things happen."

Alex says nothing.

"Don't worry, I haven't read anything into it!" I trill, sounding like a budgie on speed. "We're grown-ups, we can put it behind us and keep working together, can't we? It's not as though it meant anything. I must stay off the wine, ha ha!"

"So do you always kiss other men when you drink?" Alex asks coolly.

Er, no, actually. Until Friday evening I hadn't kissed anyone but Ed for ten years, and I can't remember the last time I had a proper full-on snog even with him. I'd kind of resigned myself to the idea that kissing was something that got left behind after the early stages of a relationship, along with flowers and holding hands. It's such a shame. I love kissing.

And it terrifies me how much I love kissing Alex. If he can turn me on that much just with a kiss, then I can only imagine . . .

Whoa, Amber! Stop right there! You are *not* to have these thoughts!

"Are you all right?" Alex says. "You look flushed."

Flushed doesn't come close. I am a serious candidate for a cold shower. I have to stay away from this man or I am in real danger of making an idiot of myself.

"I'm fine, just really embarrassed about the other night," I improvise.

"Embarrassed," he repeats. "Fine. Well don't panic, Amber. It won't happen again. I'd hate you to be *embarrassed* on my account."

I look up from my toast. There's something in his tone that makes me think for a split second that he's offended, but his face is expressionless. Of course he isn't offended. He's probably relieved that I'm not about to declare my undying love or something.

"The silly thing is," I continue, "that it only happened by mistake."

Alex raises an eyebrow. "And how did you come to that conclusion?"

This is where I can really let him off the hook. Taking a deep breath, I explain all about how Ed and I have had a few issues and how I was daft enough to use my mother's love potion.

328

"So I slipped it into Ed's port but I think you picked his glass up by mistake," I say, forcing a laugh into my voice. Lord, I sound like a strangled chicken. "That's why you kissed me. So please don't worry."

Alex looks as though he's about to reply, but at this point Charlie breezes into the kitchen looking like something from *Britain's Next Top Model* in skinny jeans and a skimpy white vest. Within minutes she's draped all over Alex like a chest bandage and whispering into his ear. Whatever she says makes Alex smile, and he winds his arm around her waist. Suddenly my toast dripping with butter doesn't seem so appealing.

Goodness, but they look great together. How could I ever have thought he might have been interested in me? Thank heavens I just set the record straight and showed him how unbothered I am. Dignity, old friend, welcome back.

I make a big show of looking at my watch, a gesture only ruined by the fact that I've forgotten to put it on.

"I must get on," I say brightly. "I need to finish here and then meet Ed in Fowey. Have a lovely afternoon, you two."

Leaving them in the kitchen, I step into the coolness of the hallway. There's a horrible knot of anxiety twisting in my stomach and I'm aghast to discover that all I want to do is turn on my heel, race back in and hurl myself into Alex's arms. But his arms are full of gorgeous size-eight redhead, I am engaged to Ed, and anyway such behaviour would only lead to total humiliation. It was one kiss and it should be very easy to forget. It meant nothing to either of us. And it will never happen again.

So why then do I wish with all my heart that it could?

CHAPTER
TWENTY-THREE

Summer slips into autumn so gradually that I don't really notice it happening until the trees take on a gilded hue and the fields resemble cream and brown corduroy. In the mornings the air is as sharp as lemons, and when I fasten Ken's lead I notice that his coat has started to thicken. Swallows gather on the telephone lines, the beach café closes in the evenings and the roads are quiet, save for the odd rumble of a tractor or clip-clopping of hooves.

I can hardly believe that I've lived in Polmerryn for nearly six months. It seems impossible that time has flown by with such incredible speed. My old life in London feels like something that happened to somebody else, and it's almost hard to imagine an existence where I didn't drink tea by the Aga, walk Ken through lanes filled with fluttering leaves and spend my days rearranging antiques and long-forgotten treasures. Did I really used to wear suits and heels and fuss about designer handbags? Nowadays it's second nature to pull on my wellies, faded Levis and hoody and scoop my hair up into a ponytail. Rather than hanging out with Giorgio Armani my new best mate is George at Asda, and the strange thing is that actually I find I don't mind at all.

By the time October arrives in a burst of glorious golden-syrup sunshine and bright blue sky, I've managed to create my makeshift studio in the attic and have smothered the walls with my sketches and paintings. Pen-and-ink drawings of Ken jostle for pole position with watercolours of naughty Mabel, her mouth brimming with lavender, and pastels of the latest addition to the menagerie, Loopy, the love child of Ken and Sadie. A fuzzy black and tan bundle of energy, Loopy arrived at Hawkstone House with all the force of Hurricane Katrina hitting the US coast and a million times more destructive. She chews things, is still trying to master the art of house training and can teach Mabel a thing or two about escapology. The new sofa is now little more than a giant puppy chew, she insists on drinking out of the loo, and she buries everything from, gulp, Range Rover smart keys to cufflinks. She's about as popular with her master as a bout of diarrhoea, but nothing Ed could ever say would tempt me to part with her. When Loopy lays her head on my knee and looks up at me with her big brown eyes, my heart melts and there isn't anything I wouldn't do for her.

It's like being in love, but so much easier! Loopy doesn't want anything apart from my affection. She never huffs or sighs or snaps and she certainly doesn't spend every spare moment working or taking very important business calls. And most importantly she thinks I'm great, which is balm to my bruised pride.

If I'd thought things were tricky with Ed in the summer, it's nothing compared to how they are now. I've tried really hard to discuss our relationship with him, but I'd honestly get more sense out of talking to the wall, Shirley Valentine style. I've cooked meals, I've been tactful, I've been stroppy, I've even suggested we go to counselling, but all I get in return is Ed's insistence that he's working hard and I'm being difficult. Like Mabel, I'm at the end of my tether, and I'm really not sure what my next move is, but there is one thing I do know: I can't go on like this.

"If you'd only sit still, it would be so much easier to paint you," I tell Loopy, who is leaping about my studio and knocking paintbrushes and jam jars of water flying. I glance at my half-finished picture and sigh. The puppy just can't sit still and there's no way I'll manage to get any more done today. It seems that we can only work in ten-minute snatches. I could move on to the large oil of Sadie that Virginia has commissioned as a surprise present for Alex's birthday, but the sun is shining and it seems a waste to be cooped up inside. Deciding to abandon my work for a few hours, I pack away the paints, rinse my brushes and, opening the attic door, release Loopy, who tears down the stairs barking her head off.

"Noisy, isn't she?" I remark to Ken, who's in his favourite Aga corner. The dog lifts his head from his paws and gives his daughter a resigned look before returning to a happy doze while Loopy wreaks havoc. I open the back door and she tears outside, doing circuits at a full gallop and barking like a loony. Mabel, tied nowadays to a very sturdy metal post on the lawn, gives her a baleful stare before returning to munching the hedge. That metal post was a good investment. I couldn't afford to replace any more designer jeans.

Kettle on, I lean against the Aga and enjoy the warm sunshine as it floods in through the stable door and bathes me in a Ready Brek glow. Life isn't all bad, is it? Things with Ed can hopefully still be fixed, I have lovely friends, a beautiful house, wonderful animals and a job I enjoy. Sometimes I admit I find myself reliving that amazing kiss with Alex, and I've woken a few times with my heart racing and my nerve endings fizzing like sherbet only to be horribly disappointed when I realise I'm dreaming, but most of the time I'm able to put him out of my mind. At the house we manage to avoid one another pretty successfully, but when we do meet in the kitchen for coffee we are very polite to one another and seem to have called an uneasy truce. We've certainly not mentioned the kiss incident since, and to be honest, we've both been so flat out with work that there's hardly been time to dwell on it. It also hasn't escaped my notice that Charlie is down most weekends and spends an awful lot of time with Alex, closeted in his Defender or working on the estate. They're like Tweedledum and Tweedledee and they even have matching Sadie puppies.

"She was friends with Vanessa," Virginia explained when I brought up the subject of their closeness one afternoon. "In fact I'm sure it was Charlie who introduced them. She and Van were at Roedean together."

"Right," I said, pretending to be fascinated by a cobweb rather than the sight of Charlie and Alex chatting down in the courtyard, her Titian head so close to his dark one that they were almost touching. "How lovely for them to be together so much. They must have a lot in common."

Virginia looked puzzled. "Well of course they do. I practically raised Charlie. She grew up with Alex. She's like a sister to him."

"Maybe they're more than that?" I suggested lightly, but Virginia only laughed.

"Alex and Charlie! Oh darling! I don't think that could ever happen, do you?"

Actually, I did, but I decided to keep my opinions to myself. After all, it was hardly my business.

"And anyway, Charlie is just getting over a nasty break-up," Virginia added. "Sam was the love of her life and she was devastated when it finished. We didn't think she'd recover. It's good for her to spend time here."

I looked down into the garden, where Charlie was laughing at something Alex had just said, her face turned up to his like a flower seeking the sunshine. She didn't exactly look devastated. Seeing them together made my stomach do knitting, so I dug my nails into my palms and looked away. Since then I've done my best to avoid them both, which is easier said than done when working in the same place.

"Not for much longer, though," I say to Ken. "The launch is at Christmas and then it's all done."

Polmerryn Manor is almost finished; the rooms that are to be opened to the public are completed and, if I do say so myself, they look wonderful. The feeling I wanted to create was a sense that visitors are passing through a tunnel of time and that family members have only vacated the rooms moments before. I wanted the house to feel like a home and that the generations of Verneys who have flowed through it like a human tide have left a tangible sense of themselves behind. Books are left half open, reading glasses balance on the arms of chairs and even a bath is filled with bubbles. All that remains now is for English Heritage to give us the seal of approval, the tea room to be finished in the old Orangery and the guide book to come back from the printers. Alex has still refused to open the lavender walk, but the rest of the gardens are ready to be enjoyed during the dog days of summer.

Alex. My thoughts return to him with alarming regularity. It's like I've got Alex Tourette's! No matter what I do or how many times I tell myself not to dwell on him, my sneaky brain keeps retracing the conversations we've had and the times we've spent together. When I sketch, my fingers take on a life of their own and before I even realise what's happened his face glowers up at me from the cartridge paper.

I bury my face in my hands. Maybe I drank that flipping potion myself? I don't think I was even this obsessed with Robbie Williams when I was thirteen!

To distract myself I make some tea and then open the mail. Two are red bills, and I'm rather alarmed to see that they haven't been paid. The other is the credit card, with a balance so big it surely has to be wrong. How on earth can we owe Barclaycard this much money?

I spread the credit card statement on the table and sip my tea thoughtfully. That's a very scary amount of noughts. I know Ed has said that money is tight, but I really don't know quite how this has happened. He earns a great salary, I have my column money and my savings and last month the advance for *Sex and the Country* plumped up the joint account very nicely indeed. It wasn't huge, but enough to buy oil for the winter, pay off the (chewed) suite and get the fields rolled, harrowed and refenced. There's even a little bit left over for a car for me, with any luck. So why on earth has Ed been withdrawing large amounts of money from a credit card account? I'm hardly George Soros when it comes to finance, but even I know that's a stupid thing to do and that the interest rates are crucifying. Anyway, what's he spending it all on? The house is pretty much finished. The Range Rover is on finance. I haven't got a designer shoe habit. And, saddest of all, we don't even have Waitrose to indulge ourselves in.

So where's the sodding money going?

Oh God. Has Ed got a gambling habit I don't know about? You read about this kind of stuff all the time in *Take a Break*, don't you? The husband runs up a six-figure sum, maxes out his credit card, remortgages the house, and the first the wife hears about it is when the bailiffs rock up.

Alarmed, I shoot into the snug and fire up Ed's laptop but soon draw a blank when I discover that he's changed his password. I spend a fruitless thirty minutes trying everything I can, from the names of his nephews to the registration of the Range Rover, but all to no avail. Whatever is on that computer, Ed has no intention of letting anyone else see it.

It's work stuff, I tell myself sternly. Don't be paranoid, Amber. He's not hiding anything; he's just protecting his clients and their private legal business. He has to; there's probably some solicitor's rule about it.

But he never did anything like this in London. I was always using his laptop there, and his phone was often left on the side to charge, whereas now it's seldom out of his sight. As much as I try to reassure myself, somewhere a jigsaw piece slots into place. Something is very, very wrong. I know my mother is barking mad, but hasn't she always told me to trust my gut feeling and never deny my intuition? And right now my intuition is screaming at me, jumping up and down and bashing its head against the wall. I've ignored it for a while, but I have a horrible feeling that I won't be able to for much longer.

With trembling fingers I pull open the filing cabinet and pluck out our bank statements. Ed has dealt with the finances since we moved and, like an idiot, I've been happy to let him. Because I trust him, and trust is crucial in a relationship, isn't it? An hour later, though, I'm sitting on the floor of the snug surrounded by a sea of paper and my whole body is shaking. So much for trust. Our savings account is down to the last thousand, and there are several standing orders from the joint account that I cannot fathom for the life of me. It even looks as though he's remortgaged Hawkstone House, and there's a squiggle on the paperwork that may or may not be my genuine signature, because I have no recollection of anything like this at all. I'd surely remember if I'd remortgaged our home?

Of course I would. The payments are horrific enough as it is. There's no way I'd agree to this. What the hell has he been up to? What the fuck is going on? Am I living in a parallel universe?

Desperate now, I even look at Ed's mobile phone statements in case these can shed any light on the matter, but for some reason they no longer show any itemised calls, only the monthly amount that is taken by Orange. This is a figure so high that I need an oxygen tank just to read it.

My heart is racing and I feel sick.

This is such a cliché.

OK, Amber, breathe! Imagine that this is a magazine article you're writing. Let's call it "Ten Ways to Tell If He's Cheating" and let's have as an illustration you sitting on the floor surrounded by bank statements that make no sense what so-fucking-ever.

1. *Does he work odd hours?*
2. *Is he often out of contact?*
3. *Does he snap at you for no reason?*
4. *Has your sex life gone down the toilet?*

5. *Does he take his mobile phone with him at all times?*
6. *Has he changed his password on his computer?*
7. *Has he stopped having an itemised mobile bill?*
8. *Does the bank account have some strange gaps?*
9. *Does he go away for work weekends that partners cannot attend?*
10. *Does he shower the moment he comes home?*

Christ. Yes to all. This is like *CSI: Cornwall*. The evidence all points in one direction. All I need to do now is catch him.

I'm just wondering how I can prove anything — after all, I have no evidence except for lots of circumstantial bits and bobs — when the landline rings. It makes me jump, because it's not a sound that I hear very often. Now that Ed has joined a network that possesses a tiny bar of signal, all his calls come through to the iPhone, and I have always used my BlackBerry.

Uncurling my stiff and aching limbs, I locate the landline handset buried beneath a pile of ironing in the kitchen. I have good intentions about the ironing, I really do, but rather like my doing sit-ups and eating less chocolate intentions, it never seems to quite work out. And since I only go to the manor or the Ship these days, does it really matter if I look creased? Most of my clothes are covered in mud and dog hair anyway.

"Good morning," says a plummy voice on the end of the line. "It's Bob Bishop here, from Bishop's Property. Is it possible to speak to Ed White?"

I perch on the edge of the ironing pile. "Hi, Bob, it's Amber. I'm sorry, but Ed isn't in, he's at work."

"Is he?" Bob Bishop sounds surprised. "I tried his office when he didn't answer his mobile, but they seemed to think he was working from home today."

A cold hand squeezes my heart. "No, he's definitely at the office."

"Crossed wires then! Never mind," says Bob Bishop cheerfully. "Could you just give him a message? Tell him from me that the bank was able to accept him as guarantor for the rent of that cottage in Polperro. It wasn't easy seeing as he isn't the tenant but I managed to swing it. The deposit should have already come out of his account. That's the down payment of six hundred pounds and three months rent in advance as agreed. It's all gone through fine."

It's a good job I'm sitting down because my legs have turned to rubber.

"I'm sorry?" I say. I'm amazed that my voice sounds normal rather than all squeaky. "What cottage is this?"

Bob Bishop may be safely tucked up in his office in Fowey, but I can tell that he's rolling his eyes in irritation with the stupid woman who clearly never listens to her partner.

"The quayside cottage? Slipway? Pretty little place with steps right down to the harbour, opposite the Blue Peter? The one he's standing as guarantor for?"

341

"Oh, Slipway! Of course!" I exclaim, even though I haven't the foggiest what he's on about. "I totally forgot. I'm just so busy that it slipped my mind. Silly me!"

"It's business, you don't want to be bothered with that. Much better just to go shopping!" laughs Bob.

Chance would be a fine thing, especially if Ed is lending money out left, right and centre. What on earth is he thinking — risking our home by guaranteeing somebody else's rent? And why on earth hasn't he mentioned it? Our account is hemorrhaging cash and it seems that, as usual, I'm the last to know.

Once Bob Bishop has rung off, I wander into the kitchen like someone in a dream and pour myself an emergency brandy. Then another. And another. Only then does the warmth return to my limbs. The floor lists and rolls a bit, but I'll get used to that.

"Brandy rocks," I say to Ken, raising the glass to him. "Maybe I should get you to carry a flask."

Drink in hand, I curl up in the window seat. I cannot hide from the truth any longer. My fool's paradise is well and truly shot to pieces, because Ed's been up to all sorts behind my back. No wonder there are more holes in our bank account than in the local fishermen's trawls. I know he earns a good salary and that my advance was healthy, but even so we can't sustain the massive mortgage on Hawkstone House and pay the rent on another property if somebody defaults. Nor can we pay the huge payments on the Range Rover and the massive monthly lump to the credit card. Feeling faint with horror at the financial quicksand I've just discovered, I try calling Ed but the phone goes straight to voicemail, so I ring his office only to be told that he is working from home today.

He is? As what? The Invisible Man? When I get my hands on him he'll bloody well wish he was invisible. Fuming, I call his mobile again and leave a message in which I make it clear just how very annoyed I am. Then, tense and irritated, I start to pace the house, a frenetic Loopy bouncing at my heels while Ken pads behind at a more sedate pace. What should I do? Wait until Ed comes home? Call Ali and ask for advice? Or take some direct action? It's just as well he's not here right now. I have a full set of Sabatiers that are just gagging to be buried in his head.

"A dog is for life, a fiancé isn't," I tell Ken and Loopy grimly.

I'm pacing the kitchen for about the hundredth time when the Range Rover pulls up and the door slams. Ed never slams that door; in fact he nearly has kittens if I so much as tap it shut. He has obviously raced home to confront me.

Good. Bring it on.

Moments later he storms through the door looking agitated.

"What the hell are you playing at going through my private papers?" he demands, glaring at me. "How dare you read documents that belong to me?"

A-ha. The old attack-is-the-first-line-of-defence trick. Fired up by frustration and fuelled by brandy, I put my hands on my hips and square up to him. Easier said than done when you are only five-foot-three.

"And what are you playing at remortgaging the house without my permission? And forging my signature? And running up massive debts on the credit card?"

Ed steps backwards, shocked that I haven't backed down. Well, get used to it, mister! This worm isn't so much turning as doing a Zumba class. His mouth opens and shuts like a goldfish.

"Don't even think about denying it either," I say. "I know everything."

He drains of colour. "Everything?"

I nod. "Everything. From the credit card to the drained savings account to the remortgage to guaranteeing rent on a cottage in Polperro."

For a bizarre second, something like relief flickers across his face. "The money stuff," he says quietly.

"Yes, the money stuff! For God's sake, Ed! What have you been doing?"

"I was trying to release capital! I needed to realise the value of our asset so that I could take an investment opportunity," he blusters, his face turning red. "I've been buying shares. It's the perfect time to make a killing, while the markets are depressed and I can buy low. When things change we could make millions. There's no point trying to explain it to you because you don't understand how finance works, Amber. You have to speculate to accumulate."

"Don't give me that!" I hiss, riled beyond belief that he's dismissing me so quickly. I may have an arts degree, but I'm not stupid. I've never run up ten grand on Barclaycard, have I? "Who do you think you are?

Gordon bloody Gekko? I tell you what I do understand — you're risking our home and increasing our debt. This isn't just about your finances, Ed! This is about mine too. You had no right to do any of this without asking me."

Ed runs a hand through his hair. Goodness, but it's getting thin, not like Alex's thick springy curls.

He sighs. "You're right, Amber, of course you are. It's just that with the downturn, my pension and portfolio aren't worth a quarter of what they should be. I wanted to safeguard our future."

I stare at him. I may be paranoid, but something doesn't ring true here.

"Without running it by me? And forging my signature? For heaven's sake, Ed! What were you thinking? You're supposed to be a solicitor. That's fraud."

"I know it's unforgivable," Ed says quietly. "I just got caught up in it all. The sums will balance out. I know I can sort it all and make it work. I was only thinking of our future, babe."

I shake my head. "You weren't thinking about me at all. Still, maybe it could work out. We could sell this house, and downsize to something like the rental place in Polperro. We'll be able to recoup all the money and maybe even make some."

Ed looks horrified. "I'd never get the Range Rover through Polperro. And anyway, that cottage is rented for one of our clients not for me! I just used my personal account because the senior partner went away and didn't leave enough cash in the client account. I had to make up the shortfall. We could have lost their business if we cocked this up. Then I would have been seriously in the shit. You wouldn't have wanted that, would you?" His blue eyes hold mine. "Would you?" he repeats.

I swallow. Is he being truthful? How awful that I no longer know.

"So we'll get the rental money back?"

He nods. "Of course we will. When Marchant Senior gets back from St. Lucia he'll sort me out. Probably with a nice bonus, too. I told you, Amber, it's just business and nothing to concern yourself with. Just leave the finances to me in future, OK? I can't have you upsetting yourself like this."

Ed clasps my hands. His palms are slick with sweat and I slide mine away hastily. Something feels wrong.

"We just need to sit tight for a few months and everything will be fine," he continues. "We'll make money when the shares rise. I'll get a pay rise too for all this *and* your book will be a bestseller. Trust me, Amber."

"*Trust you?*" I echo incredulously. "After you did all this behind my back? Seriously, Ed, I don't even feel like I know you. How can I ever trust you again?"

"Please, Amber," Ed pleads. "I'm trying really hard to make everything all right for us. You have to believe me."

"Make what all right?"

My fiancé turns away and pours himself a triple whisky. When he adds ice, it rattles against the glass like the skeletons rattling in his cupboard.

346

"I can't tell you," he says quietly.

There's a strange whooshing in my ears and I feel as though I'm about to jump off a very high diving board. Once I leap, there'll be no turning back.

"Ed," I say slowly. "Are you having an affair?"

"What!" He looks so totally horrified at this notion that, in spite of it all, I almost laugh. "Of course not. Why ever would you think that? I love you, Amber!"

Wow. I think dodos are spotted more frequently than Ed utters these words, but since he's asking, I list my reasons for doubting his fidelity. I must admit they sound very women's-magazine-cliché and a touch paranoid even to my own ears. For my every suspicion he has a perfectly reasonable explanation, and even the mobile bill is explained away by the fact that the firm pay the balance and don't need to see the calls. After an hour of talking ourselves round in so many circles that I feel giddy, I'm starting to believe him. Ed has just made some very stupid decisions, that's all. He's been greedy and pig-headed and rash, but I think I understand why.

But he's lied to me, and I really don't know if I can forgive that.

He's broken my trust, too. Can that ever be repaired? If he can lie about something as huge as remortgaging the house to buy shares, then what else can he lie about?

So as Ed says he's sorry for the way things happened — explaining how he's been grumpy because he's worried sick about money, and asking me to give him a second chance — something inside me curls up and dies. And even as I kiss him and say that things will be all right, I have a horrible feeling that it might well be my love for him.

And if that's gone, then it really is over.

CHAPTER
TWENTY-FOUR

I know everyone says that you have to work at relationships, but what they never tell you is it isn't so much work as hard labour. In fact joining a chain gang, wearing a stripy suit and bashing at rocks for ten hours a day would be a breeze in comparison. Ed's so sorry for what he's done that he's in danger of wearing the word out, and if any more flowers arrive at Hawkstone House, people are going to start confusing us with the Lost Gardens of Heligan. When Ed starts being nice to Ken and Loopy I really feel unnerved and as though I'm living in a 1950s B-movie where aliens inhabit people who may look familiar and sound familiar but who behave very strangely. I know Ed loathes my dogs and hates my goat so he must really want to please me to try this hard. Which means I need to try hard back. So I press on, because I don't want to be like my parents and just give up on a relationship, and besides, if you want something to work, you have to put the time in, don't you? It's a bit like having to do violin practice when I was a kid. I never wanted to do that either. Come to think of it, I gave the violin up. Maybe not the *best* analogy.

Anyway, it's not that I don't want to be nice to Ed, but after six weeks of OTT gestures I'm starting to feel very worn out indeed. There's less to do at the manor so I don't have the excuse of being there for most of the day, and hanging out with Terry Tipple doesn't do my liver any favours. So I'm in the house a great deal, writing and painting, alongside Ed, who is genuinely working from home now. I'm awash with tea, am offered so many biscuits that I'm growing a pot belly, and, contrary as I am, I start to wish he was working long hours again.

"Who are you and what have you done with my fiancé?" I say when Ed relinquishes the TV control and allows me to replace CNN with *Girls of the Playboy Mansion*. Goodness, but their lives look like a doddle. All they have to do is be nice to Hef, show their cleavage and carry tiny dogs about. I'm sure I could easily do the first two, although I'd need a crane to lift Ken and arms like Arnie to carry him about. Still, nice work if you can get it! Maybe I should apply.

I'm even more freaked out when, a few days after confronting him, Ed takes me out for dinner and then makes love to me for hours. My girlie bits are traumatised — they thought they'd been retired — but it's quite pleasant, and if I can't help visualising Alex Verney at inappropriate moments, I'm sure it's nothing to worry about. After all, most women picture Brad Pitt or George Clooney when on the job, don't they?

"I bloody well hope not!" says Jinx fervently, when I repeat this train of thought, omitting the part about

Alex, obviously. It's early December and he's come over to accompany me to the Verneys' Christmas fancy dress party. It's a major event because it's Alex's birthday too, and also the official opening of the house.

"A bit of escapism is totally normal," I insist as I fasten on my fluffy angel wings. It's a good job we're inside tonight or I'd freeze.

"I'd want any woman I was with to be concentrating on nothing else but me," says Jinx.

I ruffle his hair affectionately. "Of course she would be."

"Hmmph," he says. "Your mate Ali didn't."

Aha. Houston, we have a problem. I fear that Jinxy, the Playboy of the South-western World, may have fallen for Ali. Not good at all.

"Don't take it personally. That's just Ali," I explain. "She doesn't do commitment."

"Neither do I," he insists. "Look at Julie."

Julie was Jinx's latest girlfriend. A statuesque brunette with a liking for all things equine, she was over the moon at pulling a vet and saving on bills, and even more delighted when Jinx let her have an ex-racehorse he'd been given in lieu of payment.

"She was lovely," I say. "Except for when she started texting non-stop and stalking you."

"Women tend to do that," sighs Jinx. "Thank God I don't own a rabbit. I should have kept the horse, though. At least I'd still have something to ride."

I bop him on the head with a roll of wrapping paper. "Stop it!"

Jinx gives me his Armitage Shanks-white grin. "All good column fodder. Feel free to quote me. And maybe in return you could give me Ali's number."

"More than my life's worth," I tell him. "Now, should I wrap that oil painting of Sadie, or just leave it? What would Alex prefer?"

Jinx's blue eyes narrow. "What do you care what Alex prefers?"

I feel my cheeks grow hot. "I don't, I just want to get things right for Virginia."

"You might have blown that by inviting your mother along."

I sigh wearily. Like the proverbial bad penny, Mum can't help herself and keeps turning up when she's "just passing" the house. Unfortunately for me, her obsession with all things Arthurian has yet to diminish and she's constantly paying visits to Cornwall. This time she's bumped into Virginia and wangled herself an invitation to the party, which makes me break into a hot sweat when I think of all the people she'll be able to shock and amaze. Virginia thinks she's wonderful, which she is — in small doses. Very small doses. Minuscule, in fact.

"At least Rain isn't here," I say. "And Great Running Wolf is invisible, thank God. How bad can it be?"

"How bad can what be?" my mother demands, swirling into the room in full Druid high priestess costume. Or rather, one that she's cobbled together out of duvets, pillowcases and a Cornflakes packet. With her mad badger hair and gnarled bit of twig ("It's a

352

hazel wand, darling, do listen!"), she looks like she's escaped from *Harry Potter*.

"Nothing," I say, while Jinx, dressed very appropriately as a devil in skintight red and black satin, kisses her hand and tells her she looks amazing. That's one word for it, I suppose. I'm an angel, in a short white dress, fluffy wings and glittery thigh boots rescued from a closing-down sale in Soho several years ago. I even have a halo, which is held firmly in place with wire, so no chance that it will slip. I wish I hadn't shrunk the dress in the wash, though. It barely covers my bottom. Hopefully everyone will be so busy looking at Mum they won't notice me.

"Ready?" asks Ed, doing up his cufflinks as he walks into the room. He's chosen to drive us over because he has to go to Fowey to meet his boss ("but only if you don't mind, Amber"). He's been very considerate about working late, but I haven't forgiven him yet for the financial debacle. My only comfort is that his boss is back now and apparently the rent issue is sorted. Ed says his boss told him he did the right thing so at least he's in somebody's good books.

Making sure that Ken and Loopy are secured in the boot room, we set off for Polmerryn Manor. It's dark by four now and the lanes are black as tar, just the sweep of the Range Rover headlights lighting the way ahead. A barn owl swoops before us and my mother goes into raptures.

"It's such a good omen!" she enthuses. "Wonderful things are coming!"

I hope she's right. I could do with some wonderful things, that's for sure.

The drive that leads to Polmerryn Manor is filled with cars as the great and good of south-east Cornwall arrive. Light spills from the mullioned windows and the fairy lights that Virginia and I strung through the trees dance and sway in the wind, throwing golden rays of light into the velvet blackness. Guests throng on the steps, where Virginia and Alex stand to greet them. I stash the portrait in the entrance and Virginia gives me the thumbs-up.

It's strange, but just one glance at Alex is enough to turn my legs to jelly. He's dressed in a simple DJ, the bow tie undone rakishly, and his thick dark hair falls across his high cheekbones as he shakes hands and makes small talk. Next to him is Virginia, resplendent in a purple ball gown and the glittery tiara she insisted on buying in Claire's the last time we visited Truro. His face is expressionless as always, but when he catches sight of us, his lips curve into a smile.

"Amber," he says, taking my hand in his before kissing my cheek. His lips graze the corner of my mouth and I'm so overwhelmed and tongue-tied that I feel about fifteen years old. Honestly, I could murder my mother; whatever she put in that love potion must be strong!

"Alex," I reply coolly. "The house looks wonderful."

He stares down at me. "So do you. It's a pretty dress. What there is of it."

I tug the dress down over my backside but only succeed in making the neckline just like something

Hugh Hefner would approve of. I don't think I've felt this self-conscious since my teens. Before I can make a real prat of myself, Mum charges forward.

"So you're Alex!" she says. "How wonderful! Amber's told me so much about you."

Alex looks down at me and gives me his crinkly smile. "Oh really? Not too much, I hope?"

"Hardly anything at all," I say hastily. "Just about the dogs and stuff."

"Right," Alex says slowly. "*Stuff.* Well, there's been a bit of that, I suppose."

Something glitters in his eyes and I feel my face flame. Luckily, at this point Virginia interrupts.

"I love your outfit!" she tells Mum. "You've come as a Druid priestess. How wonderful."

Mum looks perplexed. "It's not fancy dress. I *am* a Druid priestess."

She is? That's the first I've heard of it.

"I get messages from Spirit all the time," Mum continues. "It's my calling."

"Really?" says Virginia. "How lovely."

"Spirit is most insistent." Mum nods. "My guide, Great Running Wolf, is always very helpful. Actually, there's a spirit here now who wants a message passed on."

Virginia claps her hands. "How exciting! I do hope it's Daddy and not my husband; he was a bore even when he was alive so I hardly think death will have improved him."

"Mum! Please!" I tug at my mother's sleeve frantically. She is so not doing this to me at the social gathering of the year, and in front of all my friends! "Come on, let's go inside."

But Mum shakes me off impatiently. "Honestly, Amber! Have some respect for the dead. If you'd ever bothered to listen to them, maybe your own life would be a bit more sorted, hmm? You know how Great Running Wolf felt about your engagement."

Oh great. Never mind airing our dirty laundry in public; maybe we should just wash and tumble-dry it too? Great Running Wolf was adamant that Ed wasn't my soulmate and often voices the opinion that I could do better.

You know things are bad when even dead people think your fiancé's useless.

"Mum!" I hiss, but she's in full flow now and I have as much hope of stopping her as I do of winning Olympic gold for running.

"It's not a man, it's a woman." She cups her hand behind her ear and listens for a second. "Right, I understand. A young woman. Not very old when she passed on. She's here right now. She has long dark hair and she's tall too."

The smile has slipped from Virginia's face. Alex's lips have thinned into a tight line. I have a horrible sense of foreboding.

"She keeps trying to pass on a message," Mum ploughs on. "'Mossy be happy' is what it sounds like. Does that make sense?"

"Did you put her up to this?" Alex rounds on me with such fury that I shrink back. His eyes glitter with anger and his face is whiter than his dress shirt. "Is this your twisted idea of a joke?"

My heart is playing squash against my ribs. I've never seen Alex look so angry, which is really saying something.

"Of course not!" I tell him. "I don't have any control over what she says. Honestly, I don't."

"Do you know her?" Mum asks him. "She's insistent. She smells of lavender, if that helps."

"Is this your idea of a joke?" Alex grates.

"Of course not!" I'm horrified because he looks really upset. "Mum has these mad ideas —"

But Alex isn't waiting around to hear my explanation. He spins on his heel and stalks off through the hall and into the throng of guests. Moments later his tall, muscular frame is obscured by other partygoers, including Charlie, who sweeps towards him looking stunning in a green Tudor-style outfit. My throat tightens dangerously and I look away.

"What's the matter with him? I hadn't finished." Mum as usual has all the sensitivity of a house brick being lobbed into a greenhouse.

"You!" I say in despair.

"Don't blame me," huffs Mum, as I make our excuses to an ashen-faced Virginia before dragging her away. "I'm only the messenger. The dark lady's still here and she's very upset. She wants that young man to be happy. She's telling me that you need to talk to him."

"Will you stop it!" I snap. "Just for once in your life could you please behave like a normal human being? I want a mother, not an episode of *Most Haunted*. When will you get it into your head that people don't want to discuss all this death stuff? It freaks them out."

Mum opens her mouth to say something but, seeing the expression on my face, thinks better of it. Helping myself to two glasses of champagne, I swig one and then the other in rapid succession. The bubbles fizz and pop through my bloodstream but I don't feel any better, especially when I see Charlie drag Alex under the mistletoe and plant a huge kiss on his lips. He's hardly putting up a fight either.

Alarmed by the knife-edge of jealousy that slices through me, I look away. Alex means nothing to me anyway. I'm with Ed and working very hard to sort things out.

"What's the matter with you?" Jinx asks. He's been busy chatting to all and sundry and didn't witness the scene my mother caused. His devil horns are a bit wonky and he has a lipstick print on his cheek.

"My mother," I say through teeth gritted so hard they are probably stumps.

"Hello? I am here, you know," says Mum sulkily. "And so is the dark lady. She still wants me to tell your friend Alex that he needs to be happy. She says he needs to find love again and that it isn't far away at all. In fact it's in a very familiar place. She says it has been right under his nose all this time. She's getting most irate! I'd better go and tell him."

Mum truly looks as though she's about to go and harass Alex, which, judging by the clenched jaw and icy look of earlier, is a very bad idea indeed.

358

"Please don't," I say desperately, grabbing her sleeve. "You've really upset him."

But Mum is ignoring me, too busy cupping her hand to her ear and nodding as though listening to a conversation. "She says her name starts with a B. No! Sorry. V. Does that make sense?"

Jinx and I look at each other. His eyes are huge.

"Vanessa!" He gasps. "Alex's wife!"

I googled Vanessa following my chat with Jinx at the dinner party. She was tall, leggy and had a cloud of dark hair. In other words, not small and clompy like me.

Goose bumps ripple across my bare arms.

"You can't seriously tell me that you think Alex's dead wife is here?" I whisper.

Jinx shrugs. "It sounds mad, but how would your mum know about her? Maybe we should ask her if she knows what really happened to Vanessa."

I think of the light that burns every night in the turret. I'm sure it's Alex, awake and troubled. Whatever happened to his wife, it was something bad, but I'm sure he had no part in it. The hands that tenderly stroked my face and traced my collarbones weren't the hands of a murderer. They were too gentle and too kind.

"Whatever it means, she's certainly upset Alex. He looks even more of a miserable bastard than usual," Jinx adds.

I follow his gaze. Alex is talking to a group of local dignitaries and doing his best to be a good host, but the hand that grasps his drink is white at the knuckles. Mum has really done it this time.

"Don't doubt the spirits," Mum warns, crossing her arms. Her nose wrinkles. "Can you smell lavender?"

I've had enough. We've been at the party for ten minutes and already my mother has insulted the host, startled his mother and upset me. Goodness knows what Alex thinks now. He's probably convinced I've done nothing for weeks except gossip and speculate about him. He's an intensely private person and I know he hates the idea of anyone talking about him. The knowledge that I've upset him makes me feel quite sick. As though he senses my thoughts, Alex glances in my direction, but when he sees me he looks away. Moments later Charlie winds her slender arms around him and their heads rest together.

"They make a great couple," says Mum. "Maybe that's who the dark lady means."

"I don't feel well," I say, and I really don't. "I'm going to head home. I've got a terrible headache."

"You can't!" says Jinx. "What about showing off all your hard work on the rooms?"

I shrug. "Let Virginia and Charlie do it. It's their home."

Jinx and Mum both offer to walk home with me but I just want to be alone. I feel as though somebody has taken my emotions and poured them into a giant food mixer. My feelings for Ed slosh about uncomfortably, and for some reason I find I can't stop thinking about Alex. Sad, lonely, tragic Alex. Alex who is grumpy and difficult and brooding and whom I haven't been able to stop thinking about since he kissed me.

Why is everything so complicated? Moving here was supposed to be a new start for me and Ed, but the more I think about it, the more convinced I am that we don't have a future.

Feeling sad, I walk the mile home in the dark. When I first came to Cornwall, the stillness unnerved me and I would jump as though scalded whenever an owl hooted, but now I feel at ease and the route from the manor back home is as familiar as the Piccadilly Line used to be. The moon rides high over the fields and scatters silver glitter across the sea, and my breath rises like incense. It's cold and I can hardly wait to light the wood-burner and curl up with a hot drink. I'm just tired, that's all. Everything will look better in the morning.

I'm still a fair way from Hawkstone, hobbling in my stupid boots and feeling chilled to the marrow in my skimpy frock, when a blast from a car horn makes me jump.

It's Alex.

"Get in," he orders, as the passenger door swings open.

"I'm fine," I say.

"I said get in," he repeats. In the shadows his hawk-like profile is dangerous, and I shiver. "It's bloody cold and you'll get pneumonia."

The tone of voice tells me that he won't be argued with. Besides, it's freezing and my toes are throbbing, so I clamber in.

"Should you be driving after all that champagne?" I ask primly.

Alex shifts the Defender into gear. The hand on the gear stick is strong and I remember how it felt when it slipped to cup my cheek. Gulping, I look away.

"I don't drink," he says. "I gave up when Vanessa . . . when things happened. It would have been too easy to drink myself into oblivion."

"Oh." I stare down at my hands.

Really? Can I believe that?

"Charlie helped me through it all," Alex continues. "She was amazing."

Charlie. Oh great, almost forgot her. The stunning cousin he spends every waking minute with.

"She's very pretty," I say, which is about as sharp an observation as saying Everest is high.

"Yes." Alex turns in to my lane. He doesn't say anything else but he doesn't need to. Feeling a twist of disappointment, I look down at my hands.

"You're lucky to have her," I continue.

"I know," he agrees.

OK. Enough of Charlie. I think I have now ascertained that he has the hots for her. I am a pretty good reader of people, I think.

"Look, about earlier," I say awkwardly. "Please ignore my mother. She is quite insane and bonkers. She just says whatever comes into her head."

Alex waves his hand. "Forget it. I'm a little sensitive about certain things and I apologise if I overreacted. Which I know I did, because believe me my mother set me straight." He glances at me from beneath thick lashes. "The portrait of Sadie is wonderful, by the way."

"I'm glad you like it."

"I do," he says. "Very much. You're very talented, Amber."

In the dark I feel my cheeks colour. "Thank you."

There's silence for a moment. It grows and swells.

"Come back to the party," says Alex softly as he stops the car. "You deserve to be there after all your hard work."

I close my eyes, but all I can see is the image of him kissing Charlie under the mistletoe. It makes no sense, but this image makes me want to howl. No way am I putting myself through an evening of that. I'd rather pull my own teeth out with pliers or something similarly fun.

"I don't feel great," I say. "I need an early night. I'll pass on the party."

Alex sighs. "Fine. Catch you soon."

He leans over and kisses my cheek. The rasp of his unshaven skin makes my breath catch in my throat. I have to get out of the car now, before I lose the plot! Stuttering a goodbye, I open the door and launch myself into the darkness. Then the engine revs and Alex drives away, back to the party and back to beautiful Charlie. All that's left are the trails of his tail lights. I stare after these for a few minutes before pulling myself together sufficiently to walk down the drive to my home.

It's a big surprise to see the Range Rover parked outside Hawkstone House and the lights on. A plume of woodsmoke rises into the sky and I hear voices from the sitting room which must be the television. Ed's back! That was a short meeting. Maybe this is exactly what we need. A quiet night in together to relax and chat.

But when I open the door, I soon realise that Ed is not alone. The rise and fall of conversation ripples from the sitting room and the remains of supper are scattered on the kitchen table. A purple velvet coat is draped over the banisters and a lacy parasol is propped against the dresser, a feather boa piled on the floor like a dead ostrich. These things are very familiar yet very out of place here, and for some reason my stomach twists with unease. As I call out a greeting, abruptly the chatter stops.

"Amber?" I hear Ed say. "Is that you?"

I don't reply. Instead I push open the sitting room door and see Ed wearing a forced smile and looking strained.

Sitting on the sofa is none other than Liz.

"Hello, Amber," she says slowly. "It's been a while. I think we have some catching up to do."

CHAPTER
TWENTY-FIVE

"Liz! Oh my God!"

All thoughts of Alex vanish as I race across the room and hug my friend. For a minute Liz resists the embrace before she relaxes and hugs me back. My goodness, she's so thin, except for her stomach, which is . . .

"You're pregnant!" I gasp.

Liz nods, and the silk flower on her head, pink today to match her lacy gloves, bobs. Her eyes fill with tears.

"I'm so sorry, Amber, so sorry!" she says, and her shoulders shake in time with the words. "I didn't mean to."

"Oh babes, please don't cry. You've got nothing to be sorry about," I exclaim, aghast. To Ed I say, "Go and get us some kitchen roll. And put the kettle on, please. I think Liz is right. We really do need a good catch-up."

Ed hovers in the doorway. He looks reluctant to leave us so I shoo him away with my hand. Honestly, men! Sometimes they just don't get it, do they? Women need to be alone if they're going to talk properly.

Once he's safely out of earshot, I sit next to Liz on the sofa and take her hands in mine. The nails poking from the lacy gloves are bitten down to the quick.

365

Pregnancy doesn't suit my former colleague. Her pale skin is tinged almost blue and there are hollows beneath her eyes. She needs feeding up and looking after.

"Ali and I have been really worried about you," I say, reaching forward and brushing away her tears with my thumb. "When you left *Blush!* without a forwarding address, we couldn't trace what had happened to you. Ali wanted to offer you a job on the *Dagger* with her."

"She did?" Liz sniffs. Her dark eye make-up pools in the lines around her eyes, and I realise with surprise that she's a lot older than I've always thought. All the pale foundation and eyeliner masks who she really is. No wonder I've never been able to get close or to feel as though I know her. Liz has kept us all at arm's length.

"I would have invited you to come and stay here too," I tell her.

Liz laughs, but it's a joyless sound. "Thanks, but I don't think Ed would have liked that very much."

I have never understood the animosity between Liz and Ed. It doesn't make any sense.

"He'd be fine," I say firmly. "And you are definitely staying the night, no arguments!"

"Thanks." She glances down at her bump. "This one takes all my energy."

"I'm sure it does!" I squeeze her hand. "Do you want to tell me how it happened?"

She shrugs. "The usual way."

Ed is hovering in the doorway again, and I glare at him and mouth *go away!* "So what are you doing here, anyway?" I ask. "I'm over the moon to see you, but it's hardly near to Putney."

"I don't live in Putney any more. The flat was too expensive when I gave up work," Liz tells me. "I'm in Cornwall now, not far from here really. I just thought I'd pop in."

There was no car on the drive, which means she's come by taxi or braved public transport. In Cornwall, nobody pops anywhere. We only have one bus a month. When I say nothing, Liz adds, "I took a chance you'd be in."

I squeeze her hand. "I'm very glad you did. But how weird that you live in Cornwall too. What's the likelihood of that happening?"

Liz shrugs. "The baby's father lives here, so it made sense to move down."

I'm intrigued. "So is the father the secret guy you were seeing just before I left? The one you'd never tell us all about? You used to drive Ali nuts."

She smiles. "Yeah, that's him. He's moved down recently so I came as well. That's why I gave up my job. I'm hoping that we'll be together soon."

There's an almighty crash from the kitchen. Ah, the dulcet tones of Crown Derby hitting stone. Well done, Ed!

"If you want something done, do it yourself, eh?" I say to Liz. "You stay there and I'll make the tea before Ed wrecks the place."

"That woman puts me on edge," Ed hisses when I join him in the kitchen. Shards of china are strewn across the tiles and tea pools in the crevasses. Fetching a cloth, I begin to soak up the liquid while Ed sweeps up the china.

"She's having a hard time," I say. "Give her a break."

"What did she say?"

I squeeze the cloth into the sink and wet it. "Not much. She never gives a lot away."

A frown digs itself in between Ed's brows. "Who's the father? Has she said?"

"No, and I'm not going to push for the details," I say firmly.

Ed nods slowly and exhales. "Right. Well, shall I drive her home? It isn't far."

I'm just filling the kettle, but something about the way he says this just doesn't sound quite right. Ed can't stand Liz, for one thing, and secondly, how does he know that her home isn't far away?

"Where does she live then?" I ask slowly.

A flush starts to build up on Ed's neck. "I think she said Polperro, but I could be wrong because I wasn't really listening."

Liz lives in Polperro. Where Ed just happened to loan a client money to secure rental on a house? Is it me, or are there too many coincidences here? I feel as though I'm playing a giant game of Sudoku and the numbers are just starting to make sense.

I snap the kettle lid shut. "Weren't you supposed to be in Fowey?"

Ed nods. "Elliot cancelled. I probably should have joined you at the party but I was tired. I was looking forward to slumping in front of the telly."

368

"You still can," I say. "If she doesn't want to stay the night, I'll drive her home."

He looks horrified at this idea. "No, no. It's late and you've had a drink. I'll do it."

He stomps back into the sitting room. I make the tea but my whirling thoughts are far from hot water, milk and tea bags. The strangest thoughts and connections are whizzing around my mind, but I daren't voice them out loud because it will just sound so crazy. I need to take a deep breath, because I'm being ridiculous. Ed and Liz are not having an affair. They can't bear the sight of one another.

In the sitting room, Liz stares into the fire and Ed scowls at CNN. The atmosphere is delightful. I try to engage them both in conversation, but once the topic of *Blush!* is exhausted, Liz has very little to say. It's a relief when she asks if she could have a lift home and the pair of them leave. I feel sad that a friendship I once valued has dwindled to almost nothing now that we have so little common ground. For a minute I contemplate calling Ali for her input, but resist because she'll be demanding showdowns and strops. That so isn't my style.

Besides, it isn't the thought of Ed and Liz having an affair that keeps me awake for the rest of the night, my eyes heavy and gritty as I toss and turn beneath the duvet.

No. It's the thought of Alex and Charlie together that tortures me. And there's nothing I can do to make myself feel better.

I feel so bad about my mother's lunatic behaviour —
which culminates in her arriving home at four a.m. and
waking everyone up with her loud chanting to the
moon — that in spite of only having had about three
hours' sleep, I get up really early, liberate the dogs from
the boot room and set off for the manor house. I'm not
sure quite what I'm going to say to Alex, but I do know
that he deserves more of an explanation than I gave
him yesterday. I also want to tell him how sorry I am
for being less than sympathetic and understanding in
the past. The poor man lost his wife. No wonder he's
short-tempered and unapproachable at times. My own
life may be a mess right now, but at least I can sort
things out with my friends. And Alex, difficult and
brooding as he is, has been a friend.

"You're early!" says Virginia when, Loopy and Ken in
tow, I arrive in the kitchen. She has her head in her
hands and a pint glass brimful of an evil concoction, on
the top of which floats a raw egg spotted with Tabasco.

"Hangover cure," she explains when I back away
nervously. "Mine is from Satan! Far too many
champagne cocktails. Still, this was my pa's own
remedy and it never failed him. He always managed to
drink all night and hunt all day. Chin-chin!"

She lifts the glass and downs the brew. I nearly gag
just watching. Even the dogs cower.

"That's better," says Lady V, wiping her mouth with
the back of her hand and smacking her lips. "Super!
Now, whatever happened to you last night? I sent Alex
to get you back and he said you weren't feeling well."

She looks at me thoughtfully. "Darling, you're very pale. You're not up the spout, are you?"

The irony of this makes me laugh. "No, you've nothing to worry about there. I just felt a little under the weather. I didn't sleep very well last night."

"Nothing to do with feeling a bit embarrassed by your ma?" Virginia asks. "Because you really oughtn't to. She's a character, that's all. We enjoyed her company hugely."

"She really upset Alex, going on like that about his wife," I say. "I felt terrible. She is a total liability."

"Darling, don't be too hard on her. Your mother has a gift!"

Yeah. A gift for putting her socking great feet in it nonstop.

"Besides," Lady V continues, "I thought it was lovely if that was Vanessa she was channelling. Alex *should* move on and find somebody else; he's young and handsome, and no matter how much things hurt sometimes, life does go on. It has to. I'd like nothing more than to see my son happy again. It breaks my heart to know how sad he is. He thinks he can hide it from me, but I know he doesn't always sleep well at night because I hear him pacing."

So it *is* Alex who has the light on until the small hours. What a pair of insomniacs we are.

"He adored Vanessa," Virginia continues sadly. "It broke his heart when he lost her . . ." Her voice tails off and she gazes sadly out of the window. "Towards the end, he would carry her down to the lavender garden he'd planted for her. I don't know how much she could

371

see by then, poor darling, but she enjoyed the scents so much that he would just wrap her in a blanket, sit with her on the seat and hold her for hours while she slept. He still wears his wedding ring."

My eyes fill. In my memory I see Alex wandering through the lavender garden, trailing his hand desolately through the flowers, and picture again the stricken look on his face when Mabel was rampaging through the plants. Oh God. I have really messed up.

"Virginia," I say slowly. "I know it's a big secret and something that you never talk about, but what happened to Vanessa?"

Her bright Mrs Tiggywinkle eyes meet mine. "You've been wondering, haven't you? I expect you've heard the rumours. That Alex and Vanessa went away and she never returned. That maybe he murdered her in a jealous rage."

I feel about as low as the worms. Of course I've heard all this, and even speculated at length with Ali and Jinx as to what happened. All of a sudden I feel really bad that I've allowed Alex's personal life to become a topic of conversation.

"I have heard that," I confess. "I didn't believe it, though."

"Not even when Alex was so rude to you, and so angry?" Virginia sighs. "Don't look so worried, Amber, he's my son and I know how he can be. He's volatile, but he feels things deeply. Especially when he's uncertain and confused."

"Uncertain and confused?" That sums up how I feel right now. But Alex? "Why does he feel like that?"

She smiles at me. "I'm not going to explain, darling. That's one I'll leave you to work out in your own good time. And my son too, come to think of it."

I sit down next to her and lean my elbows on the table. "So can I ask what really happened? Or has Alex specifically asked you not to discuss it?"

"Alex only never speaks about what happened because that's what Vanessa wanted," Virginia says, a faraway look on her face. "He followed her wishes right to the end, even though it meant sacrificing his own good name and leaving himself open to gossip and vicious rumours." As though sensing her sadness, Ken pads over and lays his head on her knee, and she strokes his head thoughtfully. "Vanessa had ovarian cancer, darling. It was brutal and she was so brave and fought it for as long as she could, but in the end there was nothing they could do. She was only twenty-seven when she passed away."

Twenty-seven. I close my eyes. It's no age, no age at all.

"She was a beautiful girl. She'd been a model, after all, and she found it so hard when the chemotherapy robbed her of her hair. She'd had beautiful hair too, long and dark and thick, and it was heartbreaking to see her lose it. One morning she came to see me and asked if I would shave it all off because she couldn't bear to see it fall out any more." A tear rolls down her cheek and splashes on to the table. "I begged her not to but she insisted it was the only way she could cope. Alex was devastated for her and went to London and brought back the best wig money could buy. He told

373

her she still looked gorgeous, but she became very reclusive and refused to go out and see anyone outside of the family. She said she couldn't bear the looks on their faces when they saw her. By the last few months the steroids had bloated her and she was so jaundiced that she looked like a different girl. She told Alex that she didn't want anyone to see her looking that way. She wouldn't even see Charlie or me."

Virginia buries her face in her hands and weeps. I fetch some kitchen towel, tear off a few squares and hand it to her. She blows her nose noisily. "Thanks, Amber. Gracious, I'm so sorry! I know it was three years ago, but it still breaks my heart, especially when I think about Alex. He was so kind to her and nursed her so patiently, and even though I know it must have been killing him, he never showed any self-pity. Not once. He loved Vanessa every second of every day, planted the lavender for her, and towards the end he'd just sit and hold her and now and then drop a kiss on the top of her head."

I blink away the tears that fill my eyes. How did I get Alex so very wrong? He isn't a bad man, just a heartbroken one. And it's no surprise to learn that he's kind too. Just look at how he rescued the dinner party and took the trouble to bring the dress over for me. He's always been kind, even when I've behaved appallingly. How could I have been so stupid?

"So what happened?" I whisper.

"When it was clear that nothing more could be done, Vanessa made Alex promise not to let anyone see her looking the way she did. She just wanted her privacy and to spend her last days with him. They went away to a private hospice, and when Alex returned after four weeks, he was alone. And he's stayed that way ever since."

"And nobody knew?"

"Nobody. It was family business and Vanessa's parents live in Paris; they weren't terribly close. Alex scattered her ashes in the lavender garden. That's why it's special to him and he doesn't want it opened to the public."

I wince. Oh God. I have been drifting through my days with my eyes shut, refusing to notice what's really happening all around me.

What else have I chosen to ignore?

Virginia blows her nose noisily. "Sorry, Amber. So much for the stiff upper lip. You didn't need to know all that."

I give her a hug. "I think I did. I wish I'd known earlier. It would have helped me to understand Alex."

"Oh no! He'd have hated that. Alex can't bear pity."

"It's not pity I feel for him," I say slowly. "It's admiration."

Admiration, and something else I don't dare even think about.

"Why don't you see if you can find him?" Lady V suggests, dabbing her eyes with the scrunched-up kitchen roll. "It'll cheer him up to see you. There's so much clearing up to do from the party that he's bound to be about somewhere. If you can't find him in the hall, he's probably in his room in the tower. Just bang on the door."

"Charlie won't be in there, will she?" I can't think of anything worse than bowling in and disturbing the two of them.

"Charlie? Don't be silly, darling. She has her own room here." Virginia's brow wrinkles as a thought occurs. "Come to think of it, I didn't see much of her last night. I wonder where she went."

Oh God. I really hope she didn't spend the night with Alex. I know it's none of my business, but I really, really can't bear the thought of it.

Leaving the dogs with Virginia, whom they totally adore because she stuffs them silly with treats, I search the house for Alex. The caterers we hired for the party are hard at work clearing the detritus, and the stables and kennels are clean, which suggests he's already been there. Even the lavender garden, iced with frost on this chilly December morning, is empty. My boots crunch on the frozen grass and my breath clouds the air as I search for him, and I shiver, burying my hands in my pockets. Crossing the courtyard, I see that the Defender is parked up and Sadie is lazing in a patch of sunshine outside the back door. Alex can't be far away. Now I know the truth about him, I want to apologise more than ever; not just for my mother, but for everything.

I have never ventured into the tower wing of Polmerryn Manor before. According to the guide book we put together, it's the oldest part of the house, dating right back to Norman times. As I duck my head to enter the twisting staircase that leads to the tower, I can well imagine ladies in sweeping velvet gowns meeting their lovers for trysts in the shadows. It's even colder here, and although the ancient radiators are cranked up, their feeble puffs of heat hardly touch the chill. It's dark too, and I have no idea where the light switch is, so I fumble my way and feel glad that I'm wearing my trusty wellies and not last night's glittery thigh boots.

Up and up I climb until I start to feel puffed. Finally, just when my lungs are thinking about calling their union, I reach a wooden door. For a moment I pause. This is the room I've gazed across at for months, wondering what's inside. For a split second I wonder if there is a madwoman in the attic about to fly out at me, before I laugh at my own vivid imagination. Get a grip, Amber Scott! The only madwoman around here is you!

I rap my knuckles on the door.

"Hello? Alex? It's Amber. Can I come in?"

There's no reply, so I knock a little harder, and this time the door swings open. Thinking that Alex must have opened it, I step inside, but quickly realise that there's no one here.

For a moment I stand transfixed. The room is pretty minimal, with bare wooden floorboards, a plain sink, a large sleigh-style bed and a big oak wardrobe. A flat-screen TV hangs above the enormous fireplace and there are long red curtains at the window, the rich colour echoed in the crimson throw on the bed and the thick rug on the floor. As though in a dream, I cross the room to the window and stare out across the valley to Hawkstone House. That white dot is Mabel! There's the Range Rover, windows glinting in the sunshine, and that's my bedroom right under the eaves.

377

Like Goldilocks, I find I just can't help myself. Before I even have a second to rationalise it, I'm looking at the picture on the bedside table of a beautiful couple, arms entwined and so wrapped up in one another that they're not even looking at the camera. The woman is beautiful. Slender and willowy, with skin like thick cream and a cloud of hair the same hue as a blackbird's wing. The man is equally as heart-stoppingly beautiful, but what really makes me gasp is just how happy he looks, his full mouth curled into a smile and his eyes filled with love.

It's Alex, and he looks like a different man.

As though in a dream, I pick up another picture, this time of Alex and Vanessa on their wedding day. They're on a tropical beach, drawing hearts in the sand, her simple dress flowing into the blue sea while Alex looks proudly at her. *The happiest day of my life. I love you Mossy* is scrawled across the bottom of the photo, but the writing is blurred, as though perhaps the ink has got wet. From tears maybe? A lump rises in my throat. I can't bear to think of Alex looking at this picture, his heart breaking. How terrible to find real, true love only to have it snatched away so cruelly. Is that worse than never finding it in the first place? And then to have to listen to people gossiping about what happened to your wife. I know Alex now; he's a proud and private man, and a kind one too. This couple really loved each other, and it makes me realise that I have to end things with Ed. What we have isn't love, it's habit.

And then there's Liz. Some things are starting to add up, and though I'm not much good at maths, even I can figure out this simple equation.

On the chair by the bed is the tatty moss-green sweater that Alex often wears when he's working on the estate. As though in a dream, I find that I am picking it up and burying my face in the soft worn wool and inhaling his scent as though my life depends on it. The sharp, spicy smell makes my senses reel and suddenly I feel giddy with longing.

Oh. My. God.

I am in love with Alex Verney. How the hell has that happened?

Horrified, I drop the jumper on to the chair and back away from it as though it's alive. What on earth am I doing, snooping around in Alex's bedroom and touching his personal belongings? I've got absolutely no right whatsoever to be in here. I am seriously losing the plot.

I've been buried down in the countryside for far too long. I need to get back to reality, because I am not functioning like a normal human being.

Shaky with adrenalin, and with my heart beating at a crazy rate, I tear out of the bedroom and shut the door behind me firmly. Then I flee down the stairs, though whether I am fleeing from the room or from myself I'm not quite certain. But the steps are narrow and twisty and I'm in a panic, which does not make a happy mix. As I turn the first corner, I catch the toe of my welly on the edge of a step and reach out for a handrail only to discover that there isn't one, and then I'm pitching forward into the darkness.

Downwards I fall, over and over, the cruel stone steps digging into my arms and my legs and bashing against my head. It hurts! It hurts more than the last spinning class Ali dragged me to, which is saying something.

And then I land with a thud and a yelp and there's nothing. No thoughts of Alex, no fears about Ed and no horrible lurching guilt that I've got things so wrong.

Just a world of blissful emptiness.

CHAPTER
TWENTY-SIX

"It's just a nasty bump on the head and a sprained ankle. With a few days' rest you'll be as right as rain. Isn't that great news?"

The doctor, who must be all of about fifteen, scribbles something on to a chart and then beams at me. I don't beam back. To be quite frank, I'm about as far from beaming as it's possible for a girl to be. My head throbs, I feel as though I've just woken up after a night on the tiles and my right ankle has trebled in size. I don't feel as though this is great news at all.

"Are you quite sure it isn't broken?" I peer down at my ankle in alarm. It looks broken to me. Surely it shouldn't be this swollen and sitting at such a weird angle. I'm no expert, but my years of being an avid *Casualty* watcher have taught me something, I should imagine. And this doctor doesn't look as though he should be out without his mum. What does he know?

More than me, apparently.

"I'm one hundred per cent certain that it isn't broken," he reassures me. "You can even have another look at the X-ray if you want."

There's a snigger from one of the nurses. OK, I get it. I'm a rubbish patient and I've looked at my X-rays far too many times, but so would you if your foot hurt this much. And what about the bump on my head? They haven't done a brain scan.

Mind you, given my recent behaviour, I don't suppose they'd find much.

"It's OK," I say. "I believe you."

"Good." Looking relieved, the doctor shines a torch into my eyes. "That all looks pretty normal too, Miss Scott, but we'd like to keep you in overnight for observation, just to be on the safe side. The stitches will dissolve in a few days' time and there will hardly be a scar, so no need to panic."

Fibber. I felt every single stitch. I probably look like the Bride of Frankenstein.

"I can't stay, I don't have anything with me," I say. I'm a patient: get me out of here! Sadly for me, though, the doctor is wise to such avoidance tactics.

"Don't panic, we have a shop, or maybe you can ask your husband to fetch you some bits from home?"

"My husband?" For a moment I start to think that I really have damaged myself, then I realise that they mean Alex! After I tumbled down the stairs, Virginia had a hysterical fit, blamed herself for sending me up into the tower, and then summoned Alex. Although I protested, he insisted on picking me up and carrying me to the car (he'll probably need Minor Injuries himself after that), cleaning my cuts with an equine first-aid kit and then driving me all the way down to Truro so that I could see a doctor. Much as I insisted it was just a twisted ankle and a bump on the head, he was adamant that I saw a medic and wouldn't take no for an answer. Once in the car, a dog-hair-covered blanket was tucked around my legs and a packet of frozen peas clamped to my temple to ease the swelling. He even found a pillow for me to lean my aching head on and didn't so much as wince when I bled all over it. Even in my injured state I couldn't help thinking that Ed would have been having a fit about the damage I was doing to it; anything, quite frankly, would have been more important than the damage done to me. In contrast Alex couldn't have been kinder or more sympathetic, and not once did he ask me what I was doing in his room.

If he had done, I'm not sure I could have answered, and not just because I'm a bit dazed. Just what was I thinking, picking up Alex's jumper like that? And as for burying my face in the soft wool and inhaling his scent . . . Have I totally lost the plot? And all this *before* I bumped my head too.

"He's not my husband," I tell the doctor. "He's just a friend."

The doctor smiles a *yeah, right* smile. "Then that's a very good *friend* you have. I'd hang on to him if I were you."

If only, I think as I gulp back the two painkillers offered. As if someone like me could ever be with someone like Alex — if I were free and unengaged, of course. No, the only person hanging on there is Charlie.

I groan aloud at this thought and have to pretend that it's my head hurting me. I wish it was. I don't think they've invented pills that can make this ache get better.

"That's Alex Verney, isn't it?" asks the nurse as she lassos me with the blood pressure monitor and cranks it up so high that my eyeballs nearly pop out. "I remember him when he was here with his wife. I worked in Oncology back then."

"Really?" I squeak. Ouch, I think my arm's about to be severed. Shouldn't she be looking at the monitor rather than gazing dreamily out of the cubicle into the corridor where Alex is sitting thumbing through a dog-eared *Reader's Digest*?

"He was so devoted," she sighs while the armband tightens alarmingly and I try not to squeal. "He was at her side every day; nothing was too much trouble for him. His wife was a lovely girl too. She had a funny name for him." Her brow ploughs upwards as she tries to remember it. "Now what was it again? Grassy? Greeny? No, Mossy! That was it. She called him Mossy."

Goose bumps crawl over my skin, which is quite something seeing as it's subtropical in this ward. Didn't my mum mention that name? The name that was on the picture in Alex's room? But how could she have known? There's no *way* she could have known.

Unless her imaginary friends aren't quite so imaginary after all.

"Mossy?" I repeat. "Are you sure?"

"Absolutely. I remember thinking how funny it was. There's nothing old or mossy about Alex Verney, is there?"

I think of Alex's tall body, arms corded with muscle, and the presence that fills a room without a word being spoken, and I close my eyes. "No."

"Such a kind man, too. Even when things were at their worst I never heard him snap or be impatient. Kindness is so important, isn't it?"

"Hmm," I agree. I rack my brains to think of the last time Ed was kind to me and I'm stumped. Oh dear. Things aren't looking very good on that front, are they? What on earth am I going to do?

"Oh! Your blood pressure's shot up!" Looking alarmed, she whips the cuff from my arm. "We'll need to put you on half-hourly obs. I'll let you tell Lord Verney you're staying, shall I? I'm all done here — he can come in."

Before I can even protest — much as I like Alex, I'm not sure I want him to see me in a hospital gown with my bum hanging out — she's whizzing back the curtain and beckoning him over. No! I haven't got any make-up left on either. And my stitches give me a distinct resemblance to Chucky. Not a good look.

"How are you doing?" Alex bends over my bed and kisses my forehead. "You poor thing, you really are in the wars. They've told me you have to stay the night. I'm going to pop to the shops in a minute and get you some overnight things. What do you need? And what size are you?"

As if I'm going to tell Alex Verney what size I am! (12–14 on a good day, in granny pants and with the wind behind me). No woman ever divulges that kind of information to a handsome man. No. Much better to let him believe I'm sylph-like.

"Eight to ten," I say, and it's miraculous my nose doesn't grow. "Maybe just a nightie, some knickers and some wash stuff? If it's not too much trouble."

"Too much trouble?" Alex echoes incredulously. "You could have killed yourself falling down my stairs and you're worried about causing me trouble? I think this is the least I can do. What Ma was thinking letting you go up there to look for me I'll never know. Those steps are lethal. I only use that room because it's too steep for her to follow me and tell me she's worried about me or that I'm not eating properly." He grins at me and pulls a face. "I'm thirty-one! I need some space from my mother!"

I laugh. "Tell me about it. You've met mine."

"Indeed," nods Alex. For a moment there's a pause. Oh shit. I haven't bumped my head so hard that I've forgotten what happened last night.

"Look," I say, awkwardly, "I'm really sorry about what she said. I know she upset you and that's unforgivable. But in her defence, Mum always does things with good intentions.

Alex sighs and sits down on my bed. One long, lean thigh rests against mine, and when he takes my hands in his, all I can think is that it's a good job I'm not wearing the blood pressure monitor. It'd probably explode.

"Amber, I've been doing a lot of thinking lately," he says slowly. "And maybe what your mother said wasn't quite so crazy after all."

"I doubt that very much —" I begin, but Alex places a finger over my lips.

"No, listen to me! This is going to sound crazy but in a weird way it did make sense. There is a lady with dark hair and she did tell me once that she wanted me to be happy, not to shut myself away but to be open to people." He pauses and squeezes my hands. "Or maybe not people in general quite so much as one person."

"One person?" I repeat. Ooo! My heart just did a funny jumping about kind of a thing. Is that a side effect of the fall or of something else?

He nods, his green eyes dark with emotion. "One special person, somebody I've seen a lot of recently. Somebody like —"

"Amber! There you are! This bloody hospital! The staff don't know their arse from their elbow. I've been sent just about to Land's End and back!"

Charging into my bay like a red-faced sandy-haired rhino is none other than Ed. Shocked by how disappointed I am to see him, I slap a rictus grin on to my face and try not to stiffen when he drops a kiss on my lips. What a bloody stroke of bad luck that he's appeared just when Alex was about to say . . . well I don't know what exactly, but it sounded hopeful. In pink-book land it would have been that the special person was me. Imagine that!

My heart rises like a helium balloon at the very thought, and that's when it finally really strikes me: I don't love Ed any more. If I'm honest, I haven't done for a while, and I don't think he loves me either. Something needs to change, and soon. I can't go on any longer pretending to myself that everything's going to be OK in the end, because it isn't. It really isn't.

"What happened? Did you fall somewhere? We can sue," Ed says, his eyes lighting up at the thought of litigation. I see a look of distaste flit across Alex's mobile features before he composes himself hastily, and I feel embarrassed.

"I'll leave you two to be together," he says politely. To me he adds, "I'll call later to find out how you are, Amber."

I feel ridiculously bereft as he walks away. My eyes seem to be glued to the top of his dark head as it weaves its way through the ward until I can't see him any longer. My hands still tingle from where he was holding them, and I wish he'd stayed to hold the rest of me.

Oh God. I wish he'd never go.

How hard was that bump on my head?

"Are you listening to me? Where did you fall? Were the surfaces wet? Was it signposted?" Ed is saying impatiently.

I blink. Alex has gone and my fiancé, far from holding me and soothing me, has whipped out his iPad and is poised to make notes about how I got injured. Not because he cares, but because he wants to make some money. And that's when I have it, my blinding flash of clarity: Ed is with me for financial reasons. On paper we work well. We have joint savings, credit cards and mortgages, and we are tied together by the bottomless pit that goes by the name of Hawkstone

House. To split with me would cost Ed money, and what does he love?

Money.

I stare at my fiancé and it's like looking at a stranger. The funny, sweet and ambitious boy I met at university has long since left and I hardly recognise the plump man with the petulant expression and floppy blond fringe. I've been in love with a dream and a person who hasn't existed for a very long time.

And it took a smack on the head to see it.

"Amber!" Ed barks. "What happened?"

"It was my own fault entirely," I say.

"Where there's a claim there's blame," Ed chants. "Tell me what you did."

"I said I fell and it's my fault. There's nothing more to say." Why does he never listen to me? "I'm staying the night, Ed, for observation, and I need some bits and pieces. Will you pop into Truro and get them for me?"

Ed looks as pained as someone who's been asked to repaint the Sistine Chapel in his tea break. He glances at his watch and sighs. "It's three o'clock on a Sunday, Amber. I'll never find anywhere to park. And the rugby's on at five. Can't you make do until tomorrow?"

I am in a blue gown with my bum hanging out, my mouth feels like the bottom of a budgie's cage from all the tablets and I'm frantic for a wash. Yet my fiancé, the man who is supposed to love me above all others, is more worried about getting home to watch the rugby.

It's over.

I've known it for a long time deep down, but now, in a narrow hospital bed on the top floor of Treliske

Hospital, I finally admit it to myself. Our relationship has run its course. Like all the other things that began in the early noughties, it's now little more than a museum piece, a snatch of music heard on the radio that brings back memories, a faded snapshot of a sunny day, a note from a long-forgotten friend. I loved the boy Ed was, the man he could have been, and the impatient, rather materialistic man who is scowling down at me now bears absolutely no relation to that person.

The question is: what do I do about it?

So much for our new life and starting over.

Right then and there in the hospital I make a decision. As soon as my ankle and my head are better, I'm telling Ed it's over. I'll move out, maybe find a little cottage to rent, or perhaps ask Virginia if I can stay at the manor for a few weeks while I get myself together. But whatever way I choose, I know one thing for sure. I owe it to myself and to Ed to be honest. Maybe there are different ways to start over.

And perhaps now I'm about to find mine.

"Darling, I really think you should eat something," my mother says to me. "You haven't had anything since yesterday, and if you will insist on taking all that dreadful medicine the doctor gave you, then you must line your stomach."

I'm lying on the kitchen sofa with a duvet over me, the dogs snoozing contentedly at my feet, while my mother stirs a concoction that spits and bubbles on the Aga. With her wild grey and white hair, flowing purple dress and the frothing pan of green goo, she looks a dead ringer for somebody out of *Macbeth*. Every now and then she throws something else into the saucepan and I find myself wondering whether it's eye of newt or tongue of bat. She's so nuts I wouldn't put it past her.

Still, nuts or not, my mother is very kind and is looking after me in her own way, and if that involves long conversations about me to Great Running Wolf or brewing up soups that she alleges will make me stronger, then at least she means well. The trouble is that nothing she can cook will solve my problems.

"I'm fine," I say firmly. "Honestly. I'm not hungry."

Mum looks disbelieving, and so she should, seeing as I am the girl who once ate an entire frozen Sara Lee gateau because she was still hungry after Sunday lunch. The thing is, in those days, back when Mum was normal, we ate roast beef and Yorkshire pud, not sludge that smells like old pants.

I'm not fibbing, though; I really have lost my appetite. And not because my ankle hurts or because I'm higher than a kite on codeine phosphate, but because all I can think of is Alex.

Not good, Amber! You are a twenty-nine-year-old woman, not a twelve-year-old in love with JLS! Get a grip. Alex is not interested in you. He is a billion times out of your league, and even if he wasn't, there is nothing you can do about it until things are sorted with Ed. On this score I am adamant. Of all the things I hate most in the world, cheating on your partner has to come pretty close to topping the list. I saw first hand how devastated Dad was when Mum did it to him, and, love her as I do, it's something that I find hard to forgive. In my book people should be honest about their feelings. What's the point of lying? If you find somebody else then just come clean about it; don't lie and deceive and make an idiot out of somebody you once said you loved.

It's beyond me how people can cheat anyway. Alex and I only had one kiss, albeit it one mind-blowing, bone-melting blood-fizzing kiss, and I feel terrible. I even feel bad just thinking about him. Last night I lay awake in hospital tortured by guilt for even contemplating betraying Ed. Maybe Mum has a point about reincarnation. I must have been a Catholic in my past life.

"That's a big sigh, Amber." Mum ladles soup into two thick earthenware bowls, slams the lid down on the Aga and carries a bowl across to me. "Here, nettle and potato. Hot and soothing."

I eye the soup warily. It's spitting and bubbling like a geyser. "Maybe in a minute, when it's cooled down."

Now it's Mum's turn to sigh. "You have to eat."

Even if the soup was remotely edible, which I don't think it is, I couldn't stomach it. Guilt has snatched my appetite, and if I don't talk to Ed soon, I'll be a size zero by next week.

"Well, I'm tucking in," says Mum huffily. "Even if you don't want any." She scoops up a huge mouthful and slurps enthusiastically for a while, smacking her lips and murmuring "mmm" at regular intervals. I could be wrong, but it sounds to me as though she's trying to convince herself.

"Anybody home? My, something smells good!"

Virginia bowls into the kitchen, bearing a wicker basket piled with bread, cheese and honey. The kitchen smells like a chemistry lab to me, but each to their own, I suppose.

"You must have some!" Delighted that somebody is eating her soup, Mum fetches Virginia a bowl. I watch with interest to see if Lady V gags, but she soldiers through bravely. It must be all those inedible public-school meals, or else she actually likes it, because she's mopping her bowl with bread and fetching seconds. Mum looks at me. *See!* says the expression on her face.

"I'm sorry I haven't been up earlier," Virginia says apologetically, once she's polished off another bowl of slime, aka soup. "It's been a busy morning. Terry Tipple phoned to say that there appear to be travellers in our meadow."

"How wonderful!" My mother claps her hands. "Just like on that wedding programme! Were they all wearing pink frocks?"

If I hadn't already walloped my head yesterday, I'd feel like hitting it now. She is mad. It's official.

"Er, no," says Virginia. "There was only one van, a yellow VW. You know how Terry can be with his counting. After a few drinks he often sees double. Anyway, I popped down there but nobody was in. I would have sent Alex but he's gone away."

I stare at her. "Gone away? But it's Christmas in a few days."

"I know, it's terribly inconvenient, especially since you're out of action too and Charlie's gone with him. I don't see how I can possibly open the house now."

There's a horrible twisty feeling in my tummy and I don't think it's the drugs. Alex has gone away with Charlie?

"He'll be back soon," Virginia says bravely. "He won't let us down. And if the house can't open until the spring then it's not the end of the world. It's more important that you get better, Amber. How are you feeling today?"

"Fine," I say, swallowing the lump in my throat. "A bit sore, but I'll be fine. Please don't worry,"

"Well I can't help that. I blame myself. The steps to Alex's room are worn thin; they've always been dangerous. Going up there is always —"

My mother's head swivels to look at me, so fast it's like a scene from *The Exorcist*.

"Amber! What were you doing in Alex's bedroom?"

What am I? Thirteen? "I was looking for him. I felt the need to apologise for *someone's* ridiculous behaviour."

Mum sniffs. "It's not ridiculous. I'm just the messenger. You can huff and puff and pull faces all you like, my girl, but I am only doing what they ask. And FYI, that lavender lady is still with me. And she still wants to get a message to Mossy, whoever that is."

Virginia stares. "What did you say?"

Mum flaps a hennaed hand. "The spirit who's with me now is insisting that I give a message to Mossy. She's the one who smells of lavender. She wants Mossy to know that he should move on. He's found his true love and it's right he's with her."

"Oh my!" Eyes wide, Lady V stares at us both. "Mossy was Vanessa's nickname for Alex."

Of course! That was the name scrawled on the wedding photo and the name the nurse mentioned.

My eyes widen. "Mum! How did you know that?"

"I didn't, darling, Spirit told me. I do wish you'd listen," she says airily. "I know you think I'm mad, but really I'm not."

"When Alex met Vanessa he was wearing a moss-green sweater," Virginia explains, her hand over her mouth. "It became a bit of a joke between them. She called him Mossy and every anniversary she bought him a new moss-green sweater. You may have seen him wearing the last one, Amber. It's a bit tatty now."

I recall how I picked the sweater up and buried my face in it, drinking in the delicious scent of his skin. It was soft with repeated washing, holey in parts and threadbare in others. Much loved and much worn and all that's left of his adored wife.

My throat clotting with tears, I turn my face to the wall and try hard to ignore the excited conversation.

Alex loved Vanessa with all his heart, and now, crazy as it seems, it sounds as though she's giving him her blessing from beyond the grave to make a new life with her best friend. The beautiful, young and unattached Charlie.

Did I really think, even in my wildest dreams, that I could ever compete with that?

CHAPTER
TWENTY-SEVEN

"I'm all for people living a free lifestyle," Virginia says
to me the next day, "but it's a rather rum do when they
camp on one's land and don't so much as ask."

It's a bright and sunny December morning. The
ground is white with a thick hoar frost that glitters like
diamonds, and iced spider's webs lace the naked tree
limbs as though Mother Nature has Gok-Wanned them
and asked them to parade about in their smalls. Not
me, though. It's bitterly cold, and I'm dressed up in my
thickest jumpers and an ancient duffle coat that I found
in the Verneys' porch. I may look like the Michelin Man
but at least I'm warm. In Cornwall nobody bothers too
much about style anyway, thank goodness.

Virginia parks the Defender in the gateway, cracking
the ice on the puddles, and then hops around to the
passenger side to help me out. With my swollen ankle
I'm hobbling about like Long John Silver. Not that
such a minor detail will deter Virginia from dragging
me across the rutted meadow. Honestly, who's the
pensioner here? As I lurch along clinging to the arm of
a sixty-eight-year-old woman, it's clear which one of us
is the sprightlier. God, I wish I was at home on the
sofa, eating Rich Teas and swigging coffee.

"Aren't you glad you came out?" Virginia says happily, while I nearly fall flat on my face as a frozen rut does its very best to sprain my other ankle. "What a glorious day! I love December, don't you? With any luck we'll collect loads of holly for the hall, too. Maybe even some more mistletoe!"

"Hmmph," I say. Can't imagine I'll have much use for *that* this Christmas. Ed and I are hardly talking. I waited up for him last night, determined to have a real heart-to-heart, but he didn't get home until really late, and then he snoozed on the sofa until the small hours. By the time he came to bed I'd been overcome by a mixture of misery at the lack of light in Alex's tower, total exhaustion and a cocktail of prescription drugs. When I next awoke he was dressing for work and looking as though he was in a hurry.

"Ed," I said, clicking on the bedside lamp and raising myself on one elbow so that I could see him properly, "we need to talk."

Ed was busy fastening his cufflinks, new ones I noticed, and in the shape of hearts. He sighed heavily.

"What do you want to talk about now, Amber? The size of our Christmas tree? The state of the global economy? Maybe the fucking mess your dogs have made of the three-piece suite. Or how about this for size. The latest big scratch on the Range Rover."

I knew I shouldn't have borrowed the car to buy milk the other day. And I'm sure the gateposts have got narrower anyway. Switching off the parking monitors had nothing to do with it.

"None of that actually," I said calmly. "I want to talk about us."

He stared at me as though I'd said I wanted him to hop on a broomstick and play a game of Quidditch before breakfast. "Us?"

"Yes, us! Our relationship." I took a deep breath. Oh God. Once I said this, the genie was out of the bottle for good. "Ed, things aren't working any more, are they?"

"Christ, Amber, you certainly pick your moments." Ed sat down heavily on the edge of the bed. "I'm trying my best to wind things down before Christmas, I have a breakfast meeting and a hideous trust fund to decipher by eleven, not to mention your lunatic mother drifting around my house like Morticia fucking Addams, and now you want to talk about our relationship? Are you deliberately trying to stress me out?"

"No!" I protested, hurt. "Of course not! It's just that things haven't been great, have they? And we need to talk. We can't go on like this."

"Maybe," Ed agreed. "But not right now, for Christ's sake. Bear in mind that some of us have more important things to do than navel-gazing. Now I have to get to work."

And there endeth the conversation. I bashed my head against the pillows and howled in frustration so loudly that Loopy and Ken joined in from their boot room prison, really sending Ed over the edge. Moments later the Range Rover roared into life and sped off down the lane, a screech of brakes echoing up the road when Ed took the bend too fast as always.

I was in despair. How was I supposed to do the right thing and sort things out if my fiancé wouldn't talk to me? It was impossible. Thank God Mum had pushed off for a couple of days to celebrate the winter sabbat at some stone circle in the middle of Bodmin Moor, otherwise she'd have heard every word of the whole exchange and would by now be swinging crystals to heal the energy flow or some other such bollocks.

It would take more than a crystal to sort out my relationship with Ed. Even a miracle would be hard pushed to do it.

I limped downstairs, fed the dogs and let them out, and was just seriously contemplating spending the day in bed with a bottle of pink wine when Virginia arrived on a mission to drag me out into the fresh air. No matter how hard I protested that I didn't feel up to it and could hardly walk, she refused to take no for an answer.

Which is why, rather than being curled up in my cosy bed feeling sorry for myself, I am limping across a frozen field towards a cat-sick-yellow camper van.

"In the spirit of Christmas I'll let them stay," decides Virginia, holding me up as me and my poorly foot stagger drunkenly across the frozen grass. "Besides, I voted ten times for that lovely traveller man who won *Celebrity Big Brother*, and one wouldn't want to be a hypocrite."

We approach the camper van. The awning is up and the curtains are closed.

"Maybe we should let them sleep in?" I say.

"Sleep in?" Virginia echoes. "It's ten o'clock! Practically the middle of the day!" Undeterred by my lack of enthusiasm, she bashes on the door with her fist. "Morning! Wake up! You're on my land!"

I gulp. "What if whoever is in there isn't very pleased to be disturbed?"

Just a thought. I mean, I wasn't exactly delighted myself.

But Virginia has no such worries and continues to thump on the door.

"Hello? Is anybody home?"

"All right! All right!" calls a voice, and the van rocks a little as a body hauls itself out of bed. "I'm coming! Can't a man sleep in peace?"

Wait a minute. I know that voice. Surely not? It can't be . . .

"Dad!" I squeal as the door opens and my father's head pops out, remaining hair standing up like a surprised baby bird. "Daddy!"

And suddenly I'm five again. Sprained ankle forgotten, I hurl myself into his arms and hug him tight, breathing in the familiar scent of Old Spice and coal tar soap. Suddenly nothing feels quite so bad any more because my dad is here. And my dad can fix anything.

My father hugs me back and drops a kiss on the top of my head. "I thought this was the right neck of the woods for you, but I couldn't remember where you lived. I was going to trot down to the village after breakfast and put some feelers out."

"But what on earth are you doing here in a camper van?" I ask. "Where's the boat?"

"Come on, Ambs, you know I'm not really much of a sailor," admits my father. "I got tired of drifting up and down the Solent, so I sold her and bought Daisy — that's my camper — instead. Now I can travel anywhere! It makes perfect sense, especially in the winter. I'm more of a landlubber really, aren't I?"

"I understand totally," I say, standing on tiptoe and kissing his cheek. Saddle-brown and flecked with grey stubble, it's so dear and familiar that my eyes fill. I can't believe just how happy I am to see him.

"And who's your friend?" Dad asks me, one arm pulling me close as he smiles at Virginia, who's hovering beside me, all agog. Bright blue eyes twinkle beneath his white eyebrows as he holds out his hand. "I'm Chris, Amber's father."

"I'm so sorry!" I say. "Dad, this is my friend Lady Virginia Verney. It's her land you're actually trespassing on."

"Delighted to meet you, Mr Scott." Instantly Virginia snaps into lady of the manor mode, shaking my father's hand as though they've just met at a village fete rather than in the midst of her field where he has absolutely no right to be. "Your daughter is a credit to you."

"Chris, please," says Dad, and believe it or not, Virginia giggles.

"Chris," she says.

"As for being on your land, well, I do apologise. It was late when I arrived, and by the time I realised I was in the wrong place, Daisy's battery had gone flat and I was stuck in the mud. I'll move her as soon as I can."

"I won't hear of it!" Virginia shakes her head, the pompoms on today's knitted hat boinging like Zebedee. "You're Amber's father and our guest. Please, stay as long as you like. In fact, stay for Christmas. I insist!"

Dad rubs his chin thoughtfully. "I don't know. I'm like that rolling stone; I keep moving and gather no moss."

In his slacks, deck shoes and Sebago coat, it's hard to imagine anyone less like a Rolling Stone than my father. Unless he's Mick Jagger's much squarer older brother.

"We'd love to have you," Virginia insists. "In fact you must come to the house and eat with us. Amber, you and Ed too, and your mother if she's here. Alex and Charlie will be there too, of course! We can use the dining room and light all the candles. How wonderful! I can't think of anything more fun."

The thought of trying to eat Christmas dinner with Ed glowering, Mum insisting on setting a place for Great Running Wolf and Alex and Charlie being all romantic together makes me feel quite faint. I don't think I could manage a mouthful. Never mind the fact that I spent three weeks designing the dining room and setting it out to look perfect. I'm just on the verge of telling Virginia that I can't make it and that she needs to keep the rooms in pristine condition when Dad says, "Well, that's very generous indeed. Thank you. We'll look forward to it, won't we, Amber?"

"Of course," I say obediently, and then feel like kicking myself with my welly.

"Come in for a cuppa," says Dad, and so Virginia and I traipse in. The camper, filled to busting with all Dad's clothes and assorted belongings, looks like a jumble sale and smells of ripe old bachelor. I perch gingerly on the edge of his unmade bunk while Virginia goes into raptures over the tiny cooker and fridge. While they talk and Dad brews tea, I put my head in my hands and try to figure out just how it all came to this. I'm in a relationship that's dissolving like mist in the sunshine, my dad is living in a clapped-out VW camper at the age of sixty-two while my barking mother is off finding herself. Shouldn't we all be settled down? I should have popped out a couple of grandchildren for them to dote on, Dad should be enjoying his allotment and Mum's idea of the height of excitement should be a trip to a National Trust property.

"Your father is splendid!" Virginia tells me when, tea over and eviction long forgotten, we trudge back to the Defender. "Such an interesting man. And so attractive, too!"

"Mmm," I say, wincing.

Believe me, there is nothing worse than the sight of old folks, one of whom is your parent, flirting. It put me right off my chocolate biscuit, let me tell you. I know Dad and Mum aren't together any more, but a part of me, the part that's probably about six, lives in hope that they'll get back together. Surely it's only a matter of time? Mum's crazy menopausal behaviour can't continue for ever, can it?

After drinking so many cups of tea that I could double for a mug of PG Tips, I decide to pop into Fowey to do some last-minute Christmas shopping. Virginia drops me into town and unusually decides not to stay for moules in Sam's, insisting that she's needed back at the manor. It's a lovely morning: the sky is the dazzling blue of a child's painting, the river is sparkling in the sunshine and a flotilla of little boats chug merrily up and down. I treat myself to a coffee and a pastry, which I eat on Town Quay, enjoying feeling fatly warm in all my layers. Then I limp slowly round the shops, spending far too much money on bits for Emma, and enjoying the festive atmosphere, as holidaymakers down for Christmas flock through the streets like colourful gulls. After this I decide to hobble down to Ed's office to apologise to him for the scrape on the wing of the Range Rover and to give him the spare key, which I know he loves to keep in the office safely out of Ken's way. I know that to me it's just a Discovery in a party frock, but he truly, madly, deeply loves that car and I feel terrible for inflicting yet more damage on it. As if chewed seats, swallowed smart keys and dog hair on the sexy leather seats wasn't enough, now I've scratched the paint again. At this rate he'll be programming the memory seat to eject me through the sun roof the second my bum touches the leather.

I check my bank balance at the cashpoint and resolve that I'll use the surplus to get the wing resprayed. Then maybe we'll have a happy Christmas. Feeling slightly better, I limp down the high street, ignoring the siren calls of Fat Face and all the other boutiques. I will save my money, sort Ed's car out and then, in the New Year, sit him down for a full and frank discussion about our relationship. I have to. If I'm starting to even dream about Alex, then my subconscious is telling me something, isn't it? Even if I can't be with Alex, I know deep down in my heart that things with Ed are over. We don't talk, we don't have common ground, we don't even seem to spend any time together. Hard as it will be, I know that I have to find the strength to do the right thing. Otherwise I might wake up in my sixties never having known anything else. And I would rather be on my own for the rest of my life than risk never feeling again the way I felt when Alex kissed me.

I smile at the receptionist as I hobble into Ed's office. "Hello, I'm Ed White's fiancée. I saw his car outside. Is he about?"

A blonde with a face so covered in make-up they should hang it in the Tate Modern stares blankly at me. *Trudy Pucky* reads her badge.

"Trudy, is Mr White here?" I say patiently.

Honestly. It's only a simple question. *Yes* or *no* will suffice. It's not as though I've asked her to outline the fiscal policies that will define the future of the euro. But she's staring at me as though I'm speaking another language.

"I thought he was with you," she says. "I called a taxi to take him to Polperro — you know how he hates trying to squeeze the Range Rover down those narrow streets, and he likes to keep his parking space here."

I do, but I have no idea why Ed would need to go to Polperro. Anyway, I thought he said he had a lot on today. Wasn't that his reason for not being able to talk about our relationship?

Trudy sighs. "I'm so sorry. He specifically told me to remind him that his girlfriend was having her six-month scan today, which I did! I promise! He missed it, didn't he?"

There's a loud rushing sound in my ears and suddenly Trudy's voice sounds as though it's coming from very far away.

"You poor thing. Did you have to go to the hospital alone? Men! They're so useless, aren't they?"

I can't speak, but I am pretty much in agreement, though *useless* is not quite how I'd put it at this exact moment. How about a total fucking disappointment to all of womankind?

"My Adam fainted when our Kyle was born. It's not the same for them, but I'm sure it'll be all right when the little one arrives," says Trudy blithely. "And Mr White is really excited; he's always talking about the baby. And just think of all that lovely stuff he bought last week for the nursery!"

I clutch the reception desk. Am I still concussed, or is the floor really moving? Scan? Baby? Nursery?

"He's worked so hard getting the nursery together, hasn't he? It can't have been easy carrying all that lot through Polperro to a cottage with no parking. So he's not all bad! You'll forgive him for being such a scatterbrain, won't you?"

I still can't speak. My brain couldn't process the words anyway because it's far too busy. Oh my God. For months I've been looking at the wrong side of a tapestry, haven't I? The colours were sort of right but rather tangled, and nothing made any sense at all. But Trudy, with her lack of guile and her genuine interest in her boss's life, has flipped the tapestry over and now everything looks crystal clear. The patterns, the colours and the design are very plain to see.

Ed has been living a double life. No wonder things have been so odd.

"Are you all right? You've gone ever such a funny colour," I hear Trudy say. There's the sound of a chair being pulled across, and moments later I find myself sitting down with my head between my legs and a glass of water in my hand.

"It's your blood pressure," Trudy decides authoritatively. "I think it must be really high."

Too right it bloody well is. Any higher and I'll be exploding all over the office. I sit still and let the blood rush into my head as I have more murderous thoughts than both of the Macbeths put together. Upside down is good. The blood needs to be there to oxygenate my brain, because, let's face it, that hasn't been doing much work recently, has it?

How could I have been so stupid?

"You're flushed. Let's get you out of your coat," Trudy says, slipping it from my shoulders. This is followed by her unwinding my big woolly scarf, before tugging off the giant thick jumper until I am wearing just my black vest top. She gasps. Sitting up slowly, the room dipping and rolling, I see her staring at me, eyes wide with horror as the dreadful realisation dawns.

"Oh shit! You're not pregnant, are you?"

I shake my head. "No, we can safely say that I'm not."

"But you are Mr White's fiancée?"

I glance down at my engagement ring. All of a sudden it feels tight, far too tight, on my finger. I can't have it there for another second. I tug it off and hand it to her.

"I was," I say.

Then I stand up and walk slowly out of the office, back down Fore Street and out of my old life for ever.

CHAPTER
TWENTY-EIGHT

They do say that shock does strange things to people. What I've never heard before is that it gives you a sudden urge to go joyriding in your (ex)-fiancé's beloved Range Rover Sport. Almost without knowing what I'm doing, I find myself clambering into the car, pressing the memory button to get my driving position sorted (bet the car has tried really hard to forget that one), and pretty soon I'm roaring out of the town as though Fowey is a new racing circuit.

Wow! This thing can shift. Brrm brrm! While the hedges are whizzing by in a blur of greens and browns and for as long as the lanes twist and turn like tangled liquorice bootlaces, I find I don't have to think. With my foot clamped down on the gas and the wheel balanced at my fingertips I head out of town as fast as I can, desperate to put as much distance between myself and Ed's office as possible. My blood is tearing through my veins every bit as fast as the car is tearing round the lanes, because I am so fucking furious that it's a miracle I don't combust right there on the leather seat. Tears blur my vision and my breath comes in short sharp gasps. I feel like howling.

Liz and Ed. How could I not have realised? Why didn't I see it? No wonder they couldn't bear to be in the same room and went to such lengths to avoid one another, in public anyway. And of course Liz couldn't tell Ali and me about her mysterious new man — he was engaged to me! And she was supposed to be my friend.

Bastards! Both of them.

I thump the steering wheel in fury. After all I did for Liz, taking her under my wing, guiding her and putting her forward for promotion when I left, and all the time she was sneaking about with my fiancé! That really hurts. She was supposed to be a friend, a colleague, and I was never anything but nice to her, and this is what I get.

And as for Ed . . . what the hell has he been thinking? Did he really believe I'd never find out? Or did he hope that it would all go away? No wonder he was so keen to move to Cornwall and keep his two women apart. Maybe he hoped Liz would lose interest if he wasn't around. Or maybe he thought I would be so miserable here that I'd leave and then he could move Liz in. Or maybe he just wasn't thinking at all. All the late nights, they make sense now, as do the business meetings at peculiar times and the alleged company meals and weekends away that I was told partners weren't allowed to attend. His bad moods, the money draining from the account, his constant irritation with me — it was all because Ed was having an affair. He was angry and stressed, but none of it was my fault!

410

The fact that our relationship is on the rocks isn't because I didn't try hard enough, get thin enough, make him happy or any of the crap that I've worried about. Nor has it failed because I find my thoughts turning to Alex Verney as naturally as a sunflower turns its face to the sun's warmth, and neither is it because I am like my mother and don't try hard enough or take commitment seriously.

No! My relationship with Ed has failed because he is a lying, cheating lowlife!

With a very small dick!

Oops. Not sure where that came from. It just popped into my head. As have all the hundred and one other things that have annoyed me about Ed for a very long time. Like the way he hogs the car, for example. This car rocks! I press the gas harder and the Range Rover surges forward, racing up the hill and overtaking everybody. God! I'm channelling Lewis Hamilton. Or how about the way he always decides what we watch on television, or where we eat? And then there's how he's totally stingy and uses feminism as an excuse to make me pay for at least half of everything. And how about the sexless presents? The food mixers? Or the way he hates dogs and moans about their hair being everywhere when he should look at his own pillow every morning? And what about the way he always insists on having meat with every meal? Or, on the rare occasions we did have sex, always making love in the same position? Talk about needing to look at the log in your own eye!

What shall I do first? I know! I'm going to watch non-stop *Location, Location, Location* and eat pasta for every bloody meal. In fact, sod pasta! I'll eat toast and Marmite in bed and the dogs can sleep up there too and get hair everywhere. I'll eat whatever I want, whenever I want, cash in the ISA and spend it on knickers and find myself a hot new man who can't keep his hands off me and who works his way through the *Kama Sutra* in an afternoon.

So there!

And then it hits me. I am not upset that Ed has been having an affair. Neither am I distressed that he's having a child with another woman or distraught that our engagement is over. No, far from it actually. I am fine.

No. I'm not fine. I'm more than fine. I'm happy. No, more than happy. I'm ecstatic.

Oh. My. God. I've just discovered that my partner has been having a long-term affair, has lied and cheated about pretty much everything for the past eight months, has deceived me and in effect left me, and I'm driving down the road singing.

What kind of person does that make me?

As I drive towards Polmerryn, I test my feelings a bit like the way you probe the place where the dentist has extracted a tooth. It feels weird; a bit sore perhaps, and different too, but not altogether unpleasant. It's good to know that I'm not mad; all the strange things that haven't added up weren't in my imagination after all. They really were happening. I'm not demanding, or paranoid, or fat, or any of the things that Ed sometimes implied. No! I was right!

So I kissed Alex. One kiss. All right, so it was one mind-blowing, knees-to-water kiss, but I didn't ever do anything more, much as I might have wanted to. The bottom line is that I am not a bad person. And this mess is not my fault.

It's not nice to be cheated on and lied to. It does hurt, and I am angry, but more so about being deceived than because Ed has been living a whole double life. But am I sad that I know the truth and that our relationship is over?

Er, was Peter Andre sad to divorce Jordan?

Somehow, without actually being conscious of it, I find that I've driven miles along the twisty B roads that wind through the Cornish countryside from Fowey to Polperro. Talk about the subconscious taking over. The Range Rover glides down a steeply wooded valley, the road clinging for dear life to the side of a hill before looping around into a huge car park. In the summer it's busier than Oxford Street on Christmas Eve, but on a weekday in December it's empty, save a few lonely-looking vehicles and a deserted ice-cream kiosk. I park up, kill the engine and rest my head on the steering wheel.

Well, for stressful days this one has to take some beating. First of all my father turns up unannounced in a tatty old camper van, looking like something out of *Waiting for Godot*, and then I discover that my fiancé has been having an affair with somebody I once counted as a friend, and has got her pregnant to boot. What next?

Actually, I don't think it could get much worse. I already know that our finances are shot to pieces and that Ed has used up all our savings; in addition, my mother is a lunatic, and worst of all, Alex is in love with Charlie.

Have I deliberately turned a blind eye to Ed's shenanigans? This is a question that's been on repeat all the way from Fowey to Polperro, and try as I might, I just can't answer it. I don't think I have. I know that there were lots of things that haven't made me very happy, and that recently I've thought a great deal about breaking off our engagement. My growing feelings for Alex have been a massive barometer, but I don't think I was deliberately deceiving myself. Emma and Ali both hinted that Ed could be having an affair, but the bottom line is that I trusted him and believed that he was committed to us; believed him when he said that he was working hard or was late because he had to entertain a client. But now the truth is so clear that I could bash my brains out on the walnut dashboard. All the signs were there: the restaurant that had been long closed, the meetings at odd times, the strange gaps in the bank account, the weird third setting on the Range Rover, the way the mobile phone was always glued to his hand. I could go on and on if I could only be arsed.

I sigh. The bottom line is that I didn't want to turn into my parents. OK, I didn't want to turn into my mother; didn't want to have a long-term failed relationship behind me. Didn't want to be responsible

414

for hurting another person by telling them that it was over and I no longer wanted to be with them. After all, hadn't I seen first hand what that could do to a person? It's not as if my father is a well-adjusted example of a human being. So it was easier to sacrifice my own happiness and tell myself everything would be all right rather than hurt Ed. I left London, my job, my friends, did without a car, tolerated his moods, sat alone, felt guilty about my growing feelings for another man, just because I didn't want to hurt Ed. Ed who as it turns out was busy shagging another woman and wouldn't have given a toss anyway.

Aargh! Just paint me green and call me Kermit!

"They fuck you up, your mum and dad/They may not mean to, but they do," I groan. Blimey, good old Philip Larkin. He knew what he was talking about all right. I have lived most of my adult life trying very hard *not* to be anything like my parents, and look what's happened. I've been a total idiot.

Well, it's high time I got my self-respect back. From now on I'm going to grow some balls, metaphorically speaking of course, and take control again. Mrs Nice Person has left the building.

Needing to share these revelations with the relevant parties, I flip on the Bluetooth and dial my mother, but there's no answer. Bloody typical. The one and only time I want to talk to her, she's not there. It's all right for her to bug me non-stop with her chanting and her toy boys and her psychotic goats, but when I need a mother-and-daughter chat she's about as easy to find as Lord Lucan. OK, well I'll try my sister then. She'll understand where I'm coming from, won't she? Her set-up with Jeff is about as antithetical to Mum and Dad's disastrous marriage as anyone could possibly get. Feeling all fired up for a sisterly heart-to-heart I dial her number.

"Hi, Ems! It's Amber!" I say when she answers. "How are you?"

"Shit," says Emma bluntly. "And bloody stressed! *I said leave your brother alone!* Never have kids, sis, that's all I can say. School holidays should be outlawed. *Harry! I said do not climb on the dog!* Jesus! They are driving me mad. You don't know how lucky you are, living in kid-free bliss. All I want to do is cook lunch and have a nice peaceful afternoon to wrap the presents. But do I get one? Of course not. Then I'll have to fight my way round Waitrose for sodding goose fat and spend ages customising some of their mince pies so the mums at Brownies think I made them. Can I call you back? This is a bad time."

"You're telling me," I mutter as she hangs up without a cheerio. So much for family support. Thanks goodness Dad's about now. He'll know what to say. If I actually bought in to all Mum's dippy-hippy bollocks, I'd say that the universe has sent him.

Feeling calmer, I decide firmly against charging through Polperro like a storm trooper (not easily done with a sprained ankle anyway) and resolve instead to drive slowly back to Polmerryn. I'll seek Dad out, take him down to the Ship for a drink with Terry Tipple and then tell him my woes. Dad will make it better. He always used to back when I was a child. There wasn't much that a hug from him and a biscuit couldn't cure.

God. I wish I was five. Life was so much easier then. Why does nobody ever tell you that? Being a grown-up sucks.

I'm on the verge of starting the car and heading back when a small red Nissan Micra turns into the car park and stops by one of the spaces reserved for residents. The passenger's door opens and to my surprise Ed jumps out and unhooks the chain while the driver parks up.

You know what I was saying about how things couldn't get any worse? Well, I was wrong. Apart from the fact that Ed is in a Micra, which to him is Satan's car, he is also with Liz.

I know in my heart that I don't love Ed any more, haven't for a long while if I'm really honest, but seeing him with another woman is still like a sucker punch to the guts. They are together in broad daylight, and quite clearly this isn't a first.

Bastard!

The blood seems to freeze in my veins as I watch this simple scene: a couple parking their car, unloading the boot and chatting. He's anonymous, wearing a plain suit and with his thinning blond hair blowing in the breeze, while she looks startling in a floor-length crimson velvet coat with a big sunflower pinned up on top of her hair, teamed with a feather boa and black fingerless gloves. The swell of her belly is clear when she senses my gaze and turns to see me watching. Seconds later Ed swivels round too, and it's hard to say who looks more horrified.

Hmm. Actually, I'd say that it's Ed. After all, I'm behind the wheel of his beloved Range Rover, aren't I?

Abandoning Liz and their shopping, Ed strides towards me. I flick the lock button and unwind the window. A tsunami of adrenalin surges through my nervous system. Oh God. I have a feeling that I am about to be very bad.

"Well, well, Ed," I say sweetly, when he draws up alongside. "Be sure your sins will find you out."

"What are you doing in my car?" demands Ed. Typical. Never mind that his fiancée and his mistress may be about to come to blows, or that his double life is collapsing like the proverbial house of cards; all he's worried about is his flipping Range Rover. Maybe if I'd had a bonnet and climate control he'd have been faithful to me?

"Apparently we have a hospital appointment," I say sweetly. "I couldn't quite think where to meet you, and then I had a flash of inspiration. Hi, Liz!" I wave jauntily out of the window and Liz looks away, her eyes sliding from me like grease off a Big Mac.

Ed swallows. His Adam's apple bobs nervously. Goodness, how come I've never noticed before what a scrawny little neck he has? Not like Alex, whose throat is strong and tanned and just crying out to be nibbled.

Er. Amber? Can you stop thinking about Alex for ten seconds and get back to the job in hand? Namely your cheating fiancé.

"Babes," says Ed, running his hand through his sparse hair. "It isn't what you think."

Wonderful! You couldn't make this up. Here he is, with his pregnant other woman, in the village where there's a property she co-incidentally rents, and it isn't what I think?

"Ed," I say patiently, as though talking to a rather dim four-year-old, "it is *exactly* what I think. How long have you been shagging her?"

"You won't believe this, babes," he continues, "but it's not what it looks like. Nothing's ever happened."

I look at Ed, at that familiar round freckled face that I've seen every day, and realise that actually I don't know him at all. Oh, of course I know what cereal he eats, that he cleans his toothbrush under the hot tap and has a horror of bad smells, but as for what goes on in his mind? I can honestly say I haven't a blooming clue. Then slowly I turn my head to look at Liz, my eyes dropping to her abdomen, before I look back at him.

"You're right, Ed," I agree calmly. "I don't believe it. And I'm not going to waste another nanosecond of my life listening to your lies. You've got the rest of the day to go home and pack your things. After that, anything you've left behind will be in bin bags at the gates."

His mouth is swinging open so wide that I could drive the Range Rover in without even needing the parking sensors (although as usual I've turned the annoying things off). Enough said, I think.

Feeling curiously elated and very proud that I didn't run him over, I press the start button and whack the car

419

into drive. It bounds forward like Skippy on speed. Oops. Maybe release the handbrake, Amber? Still, it's worth it just to see the expression of agony on Ed's face in the rear-view mirror as I zoom away in his beloved car.

Hope he enjoys the Micra. I'll swallow the smart key myself before I give this one back. I may even take Ken and Loopy for a very muddy walk and let them roll all over the cream leather seats, just because I can.

As I tear up the hill out of Polperro, I laugh and laugh and laugh. It's partly hysteria, and partly relief that I wasn't really going mad. If I thought I was starting over when I moved to Cornwall, it's nothing compared to what's going to happen now. My life is really going to begin!

CHAPTER
TWENTY-NINE

I'm not sure quite how I get back to Polmerryn, because I'm so busy laughing one minute and fuming the next that I barely notice where I'm going. At one point I'm at a traffic lights and recalling how Ed told me that *it isn't what you think*, which makes me laugh so hard I totally miss the green and get hooted at and various hand gestures from the other drivers. I just smile and wave jauntily at them, because I am almost drunk with relief at not being insane.

The rest of the journey passes with a long Bluetoothed conversation to Ali, who is suitably gobsmacked. We say *bastard* and *fucker* and *fucking bastard* a lot while the news sinks in, and then we abandon the profanities for a good gossip. Or at least I do. Ali can't manage this.

"Fuck me!" she breathes over and over again. "Ed and Liz? I never saw that coming."

"So it isn't just me, then?" I think I need to get this clear. If everyone else had known about Ed's affair and didn't dare say, then I think I'd want to die. There's nothing worse than being the clichéd cheated-on partner who everyone pities.

"Christ, no! She's the last person I'd ever imagine he'd go for. I mean, Ed is so Mr Corporate, isn't he? He's the kind of man who wants an adoring little woman at home to look pretty on his arm and generally think he's wonderful. I was always surprised that he could bear to be with someone as successful as you."

"Successful? Me?" I'm taken aback at this thought. "Hardly."

But Ali isn't having this. "Yes, you, and that prick couldn't bear it. You're creative and artistic and if you'd been allowed to stay in London and take that promotion, I bloody well know you'd have been running *Senora* in a few years' time. Then there's your column, which is bloody genius." She pauses. "I hate to sound like a selfish cow at such a shit time, but you're not going to give it up, are you?"

I laugh. "Apart from the fact that I'm going to seriously need the money now, no way! I've got the best column fodder ever. Just wait for Sunday's offering!"

"Glad to hear it. I can hardly wait," says Ali. "I know it's early days, hon, but what do you think you want to do? Stay in Cornwall? If you come back to London, I want you working with me. I can talk to Mike this evening if you like."

I'm approaching Polmerryn, just cresting the hill before dropping down into the valley. The days are so short now that already the light's fading and long, lazy shadows are starting to spill across the lane. The windows of the cottages in the village glow with cosy light, and woodsmoke rises in purple plumes from the fires. The sea is gunmetal grey and crested with white horses that gallop in to the beach as though racing home for a feed, and a small smile of moon dances just above the horizon. To my right is Polmerryn Manor, and in spite of all my resolutions I can't help but look towards the tower. This place is beautiful, and even though I had my reservations about moving here, I've found that it suits me. I love the frosty mornings, the long walks along the cliffs with my dogs and warming up in front of the fire with a drink. I even love bloody Mabel and, amazing as it is, I'm quite fond of my Aga too. And then there's Virginia and Jinx and Terry Tipple and all the other friends I've made here, human and animal. I'm not sure if I could be happy going back to life as a tube rat.

And if I did, would I ever see Alex again?

"That's really kind, but I think I need some time," I say.

"Course you do. That's just me being a selfish bitch," agrees Ali cheerfully. "Look, I'll do my best to get you as much freelance stuff as I can, OK? That'll buy you some time and bring in some dough as well."

"Brilliant." Amazingly, I'm at the manor already. Up the hill a little further and then left to the field where my dad has parked his wheels. There's a very narrow-looking gate as I recall from this morning, complete with massive concrete post and nasty-looking spike. I've no intention of walking across the field, so I need all my powers of concentration to make it through in one piece. Telling Ali I'll call her later, I stop in the gateway and flex my fingers over the wheel.

"Right, car," I say to the Range Rover. "How do you fancy being a proper four-by-four and doing a bit of off-roading?"

Ed has never, ever taken the car off-roading. He used to mutter something about motorway tyres, whatever that means. But a four-by-four is a four-by-four, right?

Taking a deep breath, I creep the car very slowly through the gate. Goodness, it's tight, barely a few inches either side, but I do it, and pretty well too if I say so myself. I should be on *Top Gear*.

"Eat your heart out, Jeremy Clarkson," I say.

Then across the field I go, fairly cautiously at first because I've never driven anywhere before that doesn't come with tarmac. But this is fun! The Range Rover thinks so too, because it's bouncing about like crazy and slithering a bit, which I guess is what it's meant to do. Mud sprays the bodywork and splatters the windscreen, and a grin stretches across my face. If Ed could see me now, his pee would boil!

Revenge is sweeter than an eat-all-you-like pass at Cadbury World!

The camper is still there, a bright yellow pimple on the grass. Although it's only mid-afternoon, the curtains are drawn and a finger of light spills out into the afternoon. Dad's home.

This thought makes me feel so much better. I park the car, not locking it as another two-fingered salute to Ed, and limp across. Just think, in a few minutes' time I'll be drinking treacly tea, eating Rich Teas and telling Dad all about my bad day. He'll give me a hug, say that Ed's an idiot and then everything will feel much better.

Maybe he'll even come home with me and help me pack up Ed's stuff. I know Ed won't be difficult — he's a typical bully and won't dare stand up to me if I really lose the plot — but it will be so nice just to have my father with me, somebody who's on my side totally. Maybe we can even cook some dinner together and have a good old catch-up.

Feeling heartened by this thought, I haul myself up the steps to the van, rap my knuckles on the door and burst in.

"Dad! It's me! You'll not believe what's happened —" I begin, but the words shrivel on my lips as I catch sight of my father, my father who is in the middle of making love to a woman. And not any old random woman either.

No. To my total mortification and embarrassment, my father is in bed, his small VW camper bed, with none other than Virginia Verney.

"Amber!" gasps Dad, pulling the covers up to his chin. "You can't just come in here without knocking!"

"Sorry!" I clap my hands over my eyes and back away hastily. "I'm so sorry! I never thought . . ."

I trip over dad's Sebagos, abandoned by the door in a fit of geriatric passion maybe, and nearly break my neck in my haste to get out of there. I hear him and Virginia calling to me to come back, but I can't, because this really is one shock too many and I can't even reply. In fact I don't know if I will ever speak again. I may even need serious therapy to overcome this. Dad and Virginia? But they only met this morning! What is the matter with everyone here? From Ken to

425

Ed to Jinx to my parents to Ali, they are all obsessed with sex.

In the car I put my foot down and hurtle across the field. Oh God. I have just interrupted my father and my friend in the middle of IT. My heart is banging and my face is hotter than the latest *X Factor* boy band. I don't think I have ever been so embarrassed in my life! All I want to do is get away from here as fast as I can, go home, dive under the duvet and stay there for about a thousand years.

Actually, even that's not long enough.

There's also a small, childish part of me that's really put out that Dad is busy just when I really need him. Never mind Virginia, says my nasty, selfish side, I'm your daughter! What about me? I've just found out that my fiancé has been cheating on me for months, has set his mistress up in a love nest and been planning to deceive me in every way a man possibly can, and you're too busy with your own love life to give a hoot.

I didn't ask to be born!

Thank the Lord for supercharged Range Rovers, because right now I feel the need, the need for speed. Channelling my inner *Top Gun*, I put my foot down and the car leaps forward, tearing down the field in a shower of mud and grass. It can't move quick enough for me — I just want to leave that embarrassing scene behind. Honestly, don't they realise that free love ended with the sixties? Or is this the lady of the manor's alternative to rent? Eugh! Either way, I don't want to think about it. And besides, it's pretty depressing to have to admit that even my parents have better love lives than me.

Anyway, enough of dwelling on thoughts like that, because that heinous gate is coming up fast and I need to apply all my powers of concentration to squeezing the car through it. I touch my foot to the brake but nothing happens. That's odd. Maybe I haven't pressed hard enough? I stomp my foot down, but the Range Rover may as well have its fingers in its ears and be singing *la la la* for all the notice it takes. The tyres continue to spin in the mud, which propels the car forwards at a crazy pace.

Oh shit. I'm skidding. Instantly my brain goes blank. What am I supposed to do again? Brake hard? Turn the wheel? Right or left? Frozen with indecision, all I can do is keep the car on a straight route and hope that even at such a silly speed I manage to clear the gateposts — especially the one with the rusty metal spike. Clutching the wheel so hard that my hands go numb and praying to whatever deity might take mercy on me, I hold my breath as the gates rush towards me. Seconds later the Range Rover goes sailing merrily through, accompanied by the hideous screeching of metal against metal.

I've hit the spike! Oh God! Oh God! I think I close my eyes at this point because there's no point in looking now, is there? Just like that bit in *Titanic* when the ship hits the iceberg and punctures umpteen holes in the hull, so the Range Rover impales itself on the spike, the metal peeling back and opening up like a can of sardines. How to wreck sixty grand's worth of car in five seconds flat. It surely is some kind of a record.

Once free of the gate, I'm hoping that I can just limp home and call the AA, but this little dream is soon shattered when the car makes a groaning sound and grinds to a halt. Instantly everything electronic shuts down, leaving me sitting in the middle of the road without even Radio 4 to cheer me up.

I'm no mechanic, but this doesn't look good.

I lower myself out of the car and brace myself to inspect the damage. Sure enough, the passenger side looks like something from *Scrapheap Challenge*, with its peeled-back metal and flaking paint. But worst of all is the back rear panel. Never mind dents and scratches. The bodywork looks as though it's had a close encounter with a car crusher, and a tangle of wires and electrical cables is hanging out like entrails.

I gulp. Not good, Amber. Not good at all.

In a burst of hope over the reality in front of my eyes, I heave myself back into the driver's seat and press the start button. Nothing. I take a deep breath, count to ten and try again, but still nothing. The car is dead.

I burst into tears. I know it's pathetic and girlie but I can't help myself. Everything suddenly feels huge and overwhelming and just so bloody difficult. Why do these things always happen to me? All I wanted was a cup of tea and a hug and someone to tell me that everything will be fine, and instead what happens? I write off a brand-new car and end up stranded miles from home. I must really have done something bad in my past life.

It's at this point that the euphoria of confronting Ed and realising that I'll never again have to pander to his moods or blame myself for anything starts to ebb. At the same time I become very aware of the pain in my ankle as the painkillers and the adrenalin rush wear off. In a perfect example of pathetic fallacy, the sky decides that now is the perfect time to turn pewter grey and tip down the kind of deluge last seen by Noah. So I am marooned in the middle of nowhere and a very long walk from home, which will take me hours to manage with my gammy leg, and will hurt too. Still, what's my other option? Shuffle back to Dad's camper and disturb him and Virginia for a second time? I don't think so.

Long walk it is.

I set off for Hawkstone House with the hood of my duffle coat pulled up and my head bowed against the driving rain that blows in straight off the Channel. There's sleet in it now, and after only a few minutes I'm soaked through to my knickers and shivering so hard my teeth could double for castanets. My ankle is throbbing painfully and I have to stop and rest every few steps. At this rate I'll be lucky to make it home for Christmas, if I don't die of hypothermia first, that is.

Thirty minutes later I'm still limping forward, my cheeks raw from a mixture of rain and tears, when the bold sweep of headlights turns the wet road to diamonds and a battered blue Defender rounds the corner. My heart sinks, because this is who I want to see the most, but also who I dread seeing the most, especially when I'm rocking the drowned rat look. Horrified at the thought of Alex seeing me like this, I

429

flatten myself against the hedge, shrink back into my hood and hope he doesn't spot me.

But as usual, Fate flips me the bird.

The Defender slows down and the driver leans across to lower the window.

"Amber? Are you OK?" Alex says. "I saw the Range Rover in the road — I pushed it out of the way, actually — and you probably don't need me to tell you that the electrics are dead. Whatever happened?"

Where to start? With Ed? The baby? Or maybe the fact that Alex and I may very soon be step-siblings?

"You really don't want to know," I say wearily, or rather I try to say this in between my teeth chattering.

Alex looks at me consideringly. "Actually, I think I do. But maybe not right now, because I don't really like that blue tinge you've got going on. And why on earth are you out and about on that ankle?"

Oh Lord, not this, the old concerned and pitying number. I bite my lip. "I had some last-minute Christmas shopping to do. Then I stopped off and . . . and . . ."

"Did some off-roading?" There's a ghost of a smile on his lips as he hops out and helps me into the passenger seat. Moments later, warm air is blasting out of the ancient heater and he's handing me that soft moss-green jumper, still warm from his body. That wonderful strong body that's haunting my every waking moment.

"No, put it on," Alex insists when I protest, knowing of course what it means to him. "You need to get warm."

430

He isn't wrong; even my goose bumps have goose bumps.

"In future," he continues, passing me a mug of coffee poured from a battered flask, "you call me if there's a problem and Ed isn't about. Don't struggle on your own."

I stare sadly into my coffee. If Alex only knew that he was the only person I wanted to call. How on earth am I supposed to get him out of my system and be happy for him and Charlie when he says things like this? He's seeped into my every cell, as much a part of me as I am.

"I'm fine," I say. Which is clearly a blatant fib.

Alex raises a disbelieving eyebrow.

"Anyway," I add, "I thought you'd gone away with Charlie."

"Charlie? I had to drop her off but she was meeting a friend so there was no point me hanging about. Anyway, I'm not very good company right now, so she's better off without me."

I glance at him from beneath my lashes. Alex is a very sexy, intense and thoughtful man. How anyone could be better off without him is beyond me.

"I doubt that very much," I say.

Alex shrugs. "Doubt it all you like. This is never a great time for me."

It's on the tip of my tongue to ask him why, but there's such a bleak expression on his face that I quail. His face is paler than usual, the dark stubble stark against his skin, and he's lost weight too. Even his deep emerald eyes have lost their sparkle and are underscored with purple shadows. I suddenly know that I want to get to know this man and understand him, crawl right under his skin and share every thought and emotion. It's such a new feeling for me that my breath catches in my throat. With Ed I was always happy to do my own thing and live independently, but when I'm with Alex all I want is to be close to him. Nothing else matters. The silly fast cars (that I tend to trash), the big houses, the good looks, none of these things matter so much as just wanting to see him smile again and know that he is happy. The thought of him feeling sad and lonely breaks my heart.

I am head over heels in love with Alex Verney. It's crept up on me over the months; like the most tenacious ivy, he's wound himself into my every thought and even coiled deep into my heart. All the stuff with Ed fades away when I'm with Alex, every nerve ending is crackling with excitement and terror, and I can't think of anyone else but him. Want nothing more than to be near him.

OK, Heathcliff and Cathy. I totally *get* it now.

All these thoughts are racing through my mind as Alex drives me home. The lights are off in Hawkstone House, which means that Ed has either been and packed a bag or can't be bothered. It doesn't really matter; either way he's leaving.

"Are you warmer now?" Alex asks as he parks. He reaches forward and cups my cheek with his hand. "You're still icy cold. You need someone to run you a hot bath."

432

For a split second I imagine the big claw-footed bath inside brimming with bubbles and Alex and me all warm and soapy beneath the water. He's wrapping his arms around me, pulling me back against his strong chest and then . . .

In a moment of what I can only describe as pure madness, I turn my head and press a kiss into the palm of Alex's hand. For a second he doesn't move, then he slowly takes my hand and kisses the inside of my wrist, the light touch of his lips sending shivers through my body that have absolutely nothing to do with the cold and everything to do with the heat that is now gathering in my body. My wrist is an erogenous zone? Wow. Whoever knew.

"That sounds nice," I whisper.

Alex exhales slowly. "Yes, yes it does."

And then he pulls me into his arms and kisses me, a deep and searching kiss that makes my heart race. I love the way his mouth feels on mine and how his fingertips skim across my face wonderingly as though I'm something rare and wonderful and amazing. My poorly foot, chilled body and topsy-turvy life are all forgotten as I kiss him back and slip my fingers inside the neck of his T-shirt, just wanting to touch his skin.

But as soon as I do this, Alex tenses and pulls away.

"What the hell am I thinking?" he breathes, to himself rather than to me. "Christ, today of all days too." He runs a hand through his thick black curls and shakes his head. "I'm so sorry. That should never have happened. As if you haven't got enough to deal with."

He looks so horrified that I'm stricken. Is kissing me really so awful? I reach out to touch his arm and he flinches.

"Don't. I can't." Those green eyes meet mine, and now they are bright with pain. "I'm sorry, Amber."

He's *sorry*? He kisses me like that, as though he meant it, as though he was melting into me, and now he's sorry? What the hell is happening here?

"It's fine," I say brightly, slapping a smile on to my face. "Forget it. We're both adults."

"Yes, yes, we are," he agrees. "But there's something you should know."

Oh God, here we go. This is the bit where he tells me that I'm a great girl and he likes me as a friend but he's in love with Charlie and wants to be with her. I don't think I can bear it. I think I was happier when I was miserable with Ed, back before I knew there was an Alex in the world. I was happier in my ignorance than I will be knowing it's possible to feel this way but that it's so out of reach. I have to bail out now before I really make a prat of myself.

"Alex, we both have partners," I say quickly. "I'm with Ed, so of course we can forget this. Probably best if we do. I can't imagine Charlie would be too chuffed either."

"Charlie?" Alex looks perplexed, but I'm really not sticking around to hear any more. With a heart that feels as though barbed wire's being dragged through it, I push open the car door, thank him and make my escape. Only when the front door is shut behind me do I give in and cry. The events of the past few days catch up with me in earnest and hot tears make the kitchen dance and blur. I hear Alex's engine start up, but I don't go to the window and wave him off. Instead I fetch a box of tissues and work my way through them. I have never felt more humiliated or less desirable in my life. Rejected by two men in one day. That has to be a record.

Blowing my nose, I wander round the house. There are gaps in the CD collection, the wardrobe and the wine rack to prove that Ed's been here on a flying visit. But apart from this, nothing feels any different. Except for me, that is, because I find I'm more upset about Alex's rejection than Ed's moving out.

How on earth has this happened?

CHAPTER
THIRTY

"You have to get a grip!" Ali storms over breakfast, brandishing her fork for dramatic emphasis. "Ed is a wank-bucket of the first order and you cannot waste another second of your life on him. There should be a law against pricks like him. I swear to God, if I ever get my hands on him he'll be wearing his balls as earrings."

"I am getting a grip," I say. "I've cleared all his stuff, haven't I?"

"You have indeed." Ali nods. "And I was bloody proud of you that you gave it to the binmen. A nice touch, I thought."

I thought so too. Rather than playing the abandoned-fiancée card, I find it far more satisfying to play the feisty-liberated-chick card. So when the binmen rocked up the day after Edgate, they found me in the courtyard surrounded by more sacks than Santa and with mugs of tea and HobNobs. Soon the story of Ed and Liz had been told, the binmen were suitably horrified and all the stuff Ed had failed to collect was filed under T for trash. All in all it had been a great morning's work.

"It's a shame about the Range Rover, though," Ali continues thoughtfully. Her back to me, she is stirring porridge on the Aga, a job she's taken to like a duck to water since coming to stay for Christmas. "Did you really have to do such a complete job on it?"

"That really was an accident," I protest. "I'm annoyed with Ed, but not sixty grand's worth annoyed."

This is true too. If I wake up in the night with wet cheeks or find myself drifting into a melancholy reverie as I curl up alone by the wood-burner listening to carol singers, it's not because of Ed. To be honest, apart from the hassle of having to sort out our finances, I haven't really thought much about him at all. Instead it's Alex who haunts my thoughts, and I relive that last kiss over and over again until it's like self-harm for my self-esteem. How could he kiss me like that and not mean it? Am I really so repulsive, or so totally crap at reading male signals? I'd always thought it was quite obvious. If a guy kisses you and spends time with you then it means he likes you.

Guess that's where I've been going wrong.

"Amber? Earth to Amber?" Ali waves an oven-gloved hand under my nose. "Are you thinking about it again? I was sure we'd agreed that not another thought is to be wasted on Dick-Ed. Or is something else bothering you? Or someone, hmm?"

It's not by accident that Ali has become one of the most respected hacks in London. She has a nose for a story and not much gets past her. When she arrived on Christmas Eve and found me huddled over a bucket of pink wine at the table and in the same pyjamas I'd been wearing for three days, she soon twigged that there was more to it than met the eye. Pretty soon my clothes were in the wash, I was in the bath, the tree was decorated and Jinx had been ordered to walk the dogs. I hadn't seen him for a while — he always seems to be busy lately and nipping off at unusual times, and I'd assumed he'd been tearing up and down the M5/M4 in the Aston to see Ali. Anyway, while he stomped across the cliffs with the hounds, I told Ali all about Ed, in the kind of full and glorious detail that you just can't indulge in over the phone.

It didn't take long for the ugly details to come spilling out. Ali did some digging too — or in other words scared the shit out of the juniors at *Blush!* until they spilled the beans — and discovered that Ed and Liz had bumped into one another at a Law Society do where she'd been accompanying her father. They'd got chatting, met up for lunch soon after, and it doesn't take the brain of Stephen Hawking to figure out what happened next. Anyway, to cut a long and very sordid story short, the affair had been going on for at least six months before Ed got cold feet and tried to call it off, which was when he decided he had to move to Cornwall. He'd been worried that if everything came crashing down, he'd lose a lot of money.

Well he's not wrong. Starting with those ridiculous Armani jeans that got chewed up by the goat, Ed *is* going to lose a lot of money. I intend to sell everything. As of next week, Hawkstone House goes on the market, we sell the shares too, and anything we make we'll divide between us. So what if the markets have crashed?

438

I just want to untangle myself from Ed as quickly as I can.

Read my lips. *I don't care!* I just want to be free of everything and everyone.

All except one person, who has made it abundantly clear he doesn't want to be with me.

"I'm fine about Ed leaving," I tell Ali, deliberately avoiding her questions. I'm not fibbing either; I am fine about being on my own. The bills are a bit scary, of course, but I can live on toast, and the royalties from *Sex and the Country* will help too until the house sells.

"I know that." She dollops porridge into a bowl and trickles condensed milk over the top. "Get that inside you, you're far too skinny."

"I wish," I say. My clothes are looser, but it's hard to eat when all I can think about is Alex pushing me away. Last night I swear to God I felt a hip bone emerging. The misery plan has some good side effects.

"Your dad was worried on Christmas Day," Ali says, sitting beside me and tucking into her breakfast with gusto. "He was really sad you didn't go up to the house and eat with the Verneys. He told me that he thinks you don't approve of him and Virginia." She gives me an arch look over her bowl. "Is he right? After all, whatever other reason could there be for choosing to eat tofu and nut roast with your mother?"

"I'm fine with Dad and Virginia being together," I say, making holes in my porridge and watching them fill with gooey condensed milk. "I admit that catching them at it was a bit of a shock, but at least they're happy."

She grins. "They're at it like rabbits! Of course they're happy!"

I put my spoon down with a clatter. "A bit like you and Jinx?"

"Me and Jinx? Fuck, no!" Ali's next spoonful hovers precariously between her lips and the bowl. "Where did you get that?"

"So you're not seeing him?"

Ali shakes her head. "Nope. I mean, he's sexy and cute, but he's not really my type. And anyway, what do you think it'd do for my career if I gave Mike Elton the runaround?"

Hmm. Interesting. So where has Jinx been going in his sporty little car? He's definitely seeing someone, and unusually for him, he's been very cagey about who it might be, which is why I'd assumed it was Ali. The plot thickens.

Porridge finished, Ali turns her attention back to quizzing me. "So, if you're cool about things being over with Ed and you're delighted that your dad is getting his oats, then what is it that's giving you a face like a slapped arse?"

I know that Ali's trying to make me feel better, but actually she's making me feel worse. Here I am getting tea and sympathy from just about everyone I know, from Terry Tipple to Annie in the village shop, because they all think my heart is broken, when in actual fact I'm pining for Alex Verney. I feel such a hypocrite. I'm also in danger of becoming a stalker, because all my walks seem to lead me past the gates of the manor and my bedtime routine consists of staring out across the valley at his tower. Sometimes I wonder if he senses my gaze and looks back in my direction. The light hasn't been on for the last three days, so maybe he's changed rooms to avoid seeing my light, or perhaps he's moved into Charlie's room. This thought makes a massive lump fill my throat and I push the porridge away because there's no way I can eat now.

I haven't seen or heard from Alex since the day I wrecked the car, which doesn't bode well. He's obviously horrified at what happened and is doing his best to avoid me. He must have heard about Ed and me by now, from Virginia and Dad if nobody else, but he hasn't come over to see if I'm all right. Maybe he's terrified that now I'm single I'll try and jump his bones again. Or maybe he's just happy all snuggled up with gorgeous Charlie.

"Well?" demands Ali.

I sigh. There's no point talking about Alex. Most of what happened between us was probably in my head and, let's be honest, there are many reasons why I shouldn't be his favourite person on the planet. Besides, when I say it all out loud — as I often do to Ken and Loopy — it sounds totally bonkers. My fiancé's run off with somebody I thought was a friend, has been deceiving me for months and left me broke and humiliated, but actually all I can think about is kissing Alex Verney. Not that this is really a new development. If I'm honest, I've been thinking about this for ages. While Ed was cheating in reality, I was cheating in my head, wasn't I?

Wasn't I?

"Just everything," I hedge. "I've got Bob Bishop coming over later to put the house on the market, the bank need to talk about the overdraft and Ed's wanting to come and take a few more bits."

"Well Ed can fuck off," says Ali, crossing her arms over her chest and brandishing her spoon like a porridge-eating Boudicca. "He'll have to get past me first, the little pipsqueak. And if that mealy-mouthed Liz comes anywhere near, I'll shove one of her silk flowers so far up her arse it'll be sprouting through her nostrils."

I laugh. Liz is not Ali's favouite person. Nor mine really. I have lain awake wondering what it was about her that Ed preferred to me, but to be honest, after about ten minutes I'm sitting in the window again and staring out at Polmerryn Manor wondering what Alex is doing. I'm still hurt that Liz betrayed me, and I do wonder what sort of person could pretend to be friendly to my face while deceiving me in the worst way that another woman can, but I guess the answer is not a very nice person. And the same goes for Ed. When I think of Liz now, having to put up with Ed's sulks and idiosyncrasies, I actually feel as though she's done me a big favour.

Ali starts to stack the dishwasher, clattering plates noisily as though slamming them into Ed's head as per the anger management therapy she's been telling me about. Ouch. That Le Creuset she's bashed into the frying pan could have been lethal.

"Today I'll deal with the estate agent and the car repair people," she decides. "You need to get out and have some fresh air. You've been cooped up for days."

"I like being cooped up," I protest, but Ali's having none of this, and before I know it, I'm bundled up in a hat and coat, my feet are shoved into my wellies and the dogs are bounding around excitedly with their leads wound around my wrist.

"Now have you got your mobile?" fusses Ali, tying a scarf around my neck and tugging it tight. All I need are mittens on strings and I really will feel like a toddler.

"It's still in the Range Rover," I remind her. It's actually been lovely not having a phone for a while. Maybe now that I've gone cold turkey from all the texts, calls and Facebooking I'll stay that way.

"Well, that should be back later so we'll dig it out then. You'll have loads of catching up to do." Hand in the small of my back, she propels me to the door. "Have a lovely walk and get some inspiration for that warts-and-all cheating-bastard piece you're going to write for me. It's much better for you than rotting away on the sofa."

I've actually enjoyed rotting away on the sofa feeling sorry for myself but I know better than to argue with Ali, so outside I go, towed by the dogs down the path and past Mabel, who gives us a baleful look. It's a cold January morning and my breath rises in clouds and the tip of my nose tingles with cold. Frost sparkles on the grass and the sea glitters like pewter in the dip of the valley. Horses in fields are wrapped up fatly in New

Zealand rugs and stand in muddy gateways hoping that somebody might bring them in for some hay. I pause and stroke their velvety noses and catch my breath, which the icy air keeps snatching away. Then the dogs are pulling on the leads again and I practically ski down the icy lane to the village. I think about popping into the manor house but I still feel a bit awkward about Virginia and Dad, and also the work on the rooms has finished now so there's no real reason for me to be there.

I'm just dithering at the side of the road, trying to talk myself out of wandering past the house in case Alex is about, when an Aston Martin zooms out of the lane to the manor like a bolt of blue lightning. I glimpse a flash of blond hair and the gleam of perfect teeth, and as the driver pauses for a millisecond at the junction, a woman in dark glasses and headscarf waves at me. The sun is in my eyes and I can't make her out, but I wave back anyway. Yet another of Jinx's conquests I suppose. Then they roar away, leaving me flattened against the hedge and breathing in their dust. Pretty much sums up my life, really.

Ignoring every instinct, which are all screaming at me to go to the manor house, I continue straight on and head into Polmerryn. The village is surprisingly busy for such an early January day, or maybe it's because as the newly abandoned partner of the local solicitor I'm a cheap alternative to a visitor attraction. Either way everyone comes up to say hello and to ask me how I am. By the time I reach the beach and let the dogs off the lead for a run, I'm shattered and have used the words *I'm fine* so many times I'm in serious danger of wearing them out. I stomp along the tide line for a while to get myself together, throw clumps of thick seaweed for Ken to fetch and groan when Loopy decides to swim. Then, chilled even through my layers by the shrill wind, I head back along the high street. Ali's right about exercise doing me good and my stomach is growling, so I tie the dogs up outside the village shop and pop in for a pasty.

At least that's my intention, but I can't even see the pasty display because there's such a gaggle of bodies crowded around the counter and excited female voices are chattering like magpies. A woman in a green woollen hat with her back to me stands with her hand out while the village matriarchs admire an engagement ring the size of a cream egg

"Oh! It's beautiful, my love!" I hear Annie coo. "How many carats is it?"

"Have you set a date?" says another voice.

The woman laughs. "I only popped in to get some ciggies! But yes, we want to get married by Easter. There's no point waiting, is there? Not when you've known each other for years."

In spite of my aversion to all things engagement right now, I can't help but be drawn forwards to have a look. Don't ask me why. It must be some ancient atavistic female bonding thing, like all getting your periods at the same time.

"You make such a gorgeous couple!" gushes Annie. "I've always thought so. What took you so long?"

The girl laughs. "Let's just say he had some issues to address. But yes, you're right. We are good together and I always thought we would be."

Hang on a minute. I know that voice . . .

Pushing my way to the front of the group, I am able to see the smiling face of the young woman wearing the massive engagement ring. Beneath the woolly hat are thick tresses of rich hair the colour of autumn leaves, and eyes that are achingly green and familiar. My poor heart, which is just about held together with Elastoplast, goes into free-fall.

Oh my God. It's Charlie Verney.

"Amber!" squeals Charlie when she sees me. "I'm so glad I've bumped into you! I haven't seen you for ages."

Yep. That'll be because I'm avoiding you.

"I've been busy," I hedge. "I've had quite a lot on."

The village matriarchs tut and nod understandingly and lean forward ears flapping just in case a juicy morsel of gossip falls in their direction. They're already scrutinising me for the telltale signs of despair.

"Of course. God, sorry, I am so bloody tactless," says Charlie. "I can't believe what a shit Ed turned out to be."

"Well that makes two of us," I agree.

"But don't hide away. Come up to the house. Auntie V is really missing you, and your dad is such a hoot! They are brilliant, you have to see it. Don't be angry that they're together."

I grit my teeth. It's not Dad and Virginia I'm avoiding. "I'm not. I've just had a lot on."

"Sorry, sorry. Ignore me. I'm just so excited that I can't think straight! I've got tons going on too!" Charlie rolls her eyes and then stretches out her hand for me to admire. "We got engaged on Christmas Eve! Can you believe it?"

My mouth is as dry as Gandhi's flip-flops. Alex and Charlie got engaged on Christmas Eve? That means that when I kissed him he must have been planning it all. No wonder he was horrified! How could I have got things so wrong? How could I have thought he wanted to kiss me too?

"Congratulations," I say, leaning forward to peck her on the cheek.

"Thanks! I know it's been fast, but sometimes you just know when it's right, don't you?"

The irony of my being asked this is supreme, but Charlie is so excited she doesn't stop to think. Still chattering away about how wonderful her fiancé is, she holds up the ring to catch the light and all the women in the shop ooh and aah accordingly. Wow. It's certainly huge and flashy, which surprises me. From what I know of Alex, I'd have thought he'd have chosen something understated and classy. But then again, I clearly don't know Alex at all.

And, as has become very apparent in recent weeks, I am useless at analysing men.

"You don't mind, do you, Amber?" Charlie says quietly.

OK, time for Oscar-winning acting skills.

"Of course I don't!" I smile brightly. "Just because Ed and I have split up doesn't mean I can't be happy for other people."

She stares at me. "I didn't mean Ed. I mean you don't mind about who *I'm* engaged to? I know you guys have been really good friends and have spent a lot of time together . . ."

Her voice tails off awkwardly. I feel hot all over. Is it really that obvious how I feel about Alex? And there was I thinking I'd hidden it so well.

No Oscars for me, then. I'd better stick to the day job, whatever that's going to be.

"I'm thrilled for you both," I say firmly.

"Phew!" Charlie beams. "I thought you would be but he wasn't so sure. He said you'd been a bit funny about him seeing other women."

I'm astonished. Have Alex and I *ever* talked about that? Men. Honestly.

"We're having an engagement party. You must come!" she enthuses while I buy my pasty — which is now destined for the dogs, because I don't think I'll ever eat again. The idea of attending a party where Alex and Charlie celebrate being together is like a knife through my heart. I really don't think I could bear it.

"I'll let you know," I say, as I untie the dogs and create an explosion of canine joy. At least my faithful hounds love me. "But I don't think I'll be around much longer."

Charlie's pretty face falls. "That's a shame. We'll miss you. Where are you going?"

Now that's the million-dollar question. The answer is I have absolutely no idea, and I make vague and non-committal sounds in reply. But as I walk home, with tears turning my cheeks raw in the bitter wind, there's one thing I do know, and that is I need to be as far away from Alex Verney as possible. Even if it breaks my heart in the process.

CHAPTER
THIRTY-ONE

Ten days later I'm stunned to receive an offer on Hawkstone House for the full asking price. I'm just in the middle of sorting out my bedroom when Bob Bishop pulls up to break the good news. As we sit in the kitchen drinking tea made on the Aga, I can't help but think how much things have changed in the months since I first saw the house. There's no more burned toast, dogs lie sprawled on the flagstones and the Range Rover has a few more war wounds. I'm also one fiancé lighter. Life is certainly stranger than fiction.

"Mr White is very keen to accept," Bob Bishop informs me, tucking into his third Rich Tea. Biscuit crumbs dust his moustache liberally before plopping into his mug.

I look out of the stable door and my heart twists. It's a beautiful bright blue winter's morning. Mabel is chewing contentedly in the paddock, brave little snowdrops are pushing up through the lawn and the sea is glittering between the hills. A horse clops by behind the Cornish bank and gulls call busily. I'm going to miss it all so much, but what choice do I have? I can't afford to stay on my freelance salary, and anyway, what is there to stay for?

I sigh. "I'm sure he is."

Bob Bishop says gently, "He's the joint owner, Amber. He can force a sale if he chooses."

Of course he can. Ed, being Ed, isn't one to sit around navel-gazing, as he once accused me of doing. No, he's an onwards-and-upwards person. In the past few weeks he's flexed the muscles of the law to sort out our affairs and has very clearly stepped into his new life. All that remains to sort out now is the house. If we sell at the asking price, it should clear any remaining debts and give me a lump sum to make life easier for a few months. I should be jumping at this opportunity.

I sigh. "I know. And you're right. It is a good offer."

We sip our tea in silence for a minute. Ken stretches out in a patch of sunshine on the floor and yawns contentedly. He and Loopy have already had a long walk over the cliffs before breakfast — we no longer take the route past the manor house — and later on I'm going to drive them to the moors. The thought of going back to London, even with a lump sum, makes me feel very sad, and the thought of never seeing Alex again even sadder, but it seems this is what I must do.

"OK," I say slowly. "Tell them I accept too."

Bob drains his tea and nods approvingly. "It's the right decision, maid. This is a big house just for you. A fresh start is what you need."

I bet nobody ever tells the Queen that Buckingham Palace is a big house just for her. Still, he means well, and once he's zoomed away to close the deal, I try to tell myself that it's all for the best. Everyone is starting over. Ed and Liz. Alex and Charlie. Myself and . . . well

451

the dogs I suppose and a grumpy goat, although God knows what I'll do with her in London. As I unload the dishwasher and tidy the kitchen I worry about the animals and where I'll be able to keep them. I can't imagine that any landlord would want two massive dogs and a goat moving in. But I can't part with my pets. I just can't!

"Maybe we can stay here?" I say aloud, but as soon as the words are out of my mouth I know it's impossible. Since I saw Charlie in the village shop I have been a virtual recluse in Hawkstone House. If I want milk or essentials I drive to St Austell rather than braving the village, where I may have to hear more about her and Alex. I've left my mobile phone flat, ignore my landline and avoid humanity in general, but I can't carry on like this for ever. Dad keeps knocking on the door and he knows I'm hiding. If I don't email copy, Ali will be zooming back down the M5, and if I'm really unlucky, Mum will pop up for another visit. No, a move miles away from Alex and my memories is what I need. A fresh start.

"Morning, Amber!" calls Pete the Postman, leaning over the stable door and making me jump. He brandishes a handful of letters at me. "All yours. None for twat-face. I reckons he's had all of his redirected."

"I did that for him," I say. "We don't have to talk now."

I don't have much contact with Ed. He did pop in to pick up some files and he looked dreadful, overweight and even thinner on top. Having worked with Liz for several years I know how highly strung she is and can

452

imagine that this combined with pregnancy hormones does not a happy combination make. I made him tea and was civil, and I was pleased that actually, apart from mild irritation, I felt nothing for him at all. It's hard to really when all my waking moments are haunted by springy curls and heart-stopping green eyes.

"Best way," says Pete cheerfully. "You're a hot babe, Amber. You'll find somebody. I'd offer myself but I think my Maureen would be a bit put out."

"That's very kind of you," I say. "But I'll probably survive alone."

One of the things about being single is that instantly you're a target. From Pete the Postman to Bob Bishop to Terry Tipple, all the men, single or otherwise, have made a beeline for me. Another reason to be a hermit. I don't mean to sound ungrateful, and I know I'm not exactly Angelina Jolie, but I think I can do slightly better . . .

And of course the only man I would like to see hasn't been anywhere near, which is typical. Typical and unsurprising, seeing as he's engaged. What else did I expect? That he'd realise he'd made a big mistake with Charlie and that really he loved me deep down? The ordinary girl who loved him best?

Get a grip, Amber Scott! That kind of stuff only happens in the movies.

"Is that parcel for me too?" I ask as Pete makes to leave still clutching a brown paper package. Closer inspection reveals my mother's handwriting in lurid purple ink, and my heart sinks as I wonder what bright idea she's had now. Pete waits hopefully in case I open the parcel or offer him tea, but when neither is forthcoming he says a sulky goodbye and pedals off on his bike, back to the post office and his formidable wife.

I make more tea, leaning against the warmth of the Aga, and then sit at the table and open my parcel. Out falls a wodge of tissue paper, which I unravel for what seems like years until a tiny china cat, glittery star confetti and a note scrawled on lumpy handmade paper fall out. Great. Another useless present from my mother.

> *Darling!*
> *Rain and I are in Japan! I never realised until Great Running Wolf told me, but I am also a reincarnation of the Emperor Kamuyamato Iwarebiko! Isn't that amazing? Sorry you are still having a hard time, but believe me, the universe is full of abundance; you just need to be open to receive it. Here is a lucky Japanese mini cat. He comes with one wish, so use him wisely!*
> *Blessings! Mum x*

You seriously couldn't make her up. Here am I, in the middle of a total life crisis, and my mother is swanning round the globe. Most parents would send a cheque, and what do I get? A china cat the size of my fingernail. I kid you not, the woman is barking mad.

"So," I say to the china cat, because I may as well embrace the family madness and chat to an inanimate

454

object, "what should I wish for? A normal mother? A million wishes? Ed's cock to wither and drop off?"

The china cat looks back at me with wise painted eyes.

"How about this?" I hold it close to my mouth so that I can whisper into its minute china ear. "I wish that things between Alex and me could be made right. How about that?"

The cat, of course, says nothing and I feel even more stupid than normal. Has it really come to this? That I am talking to a piece of china? Bob Bishop is right. Selling up and starting again is definitely the best thing to do.

I take my tea upstairs to my bedroom. I've been busy sorting out piles of clothes and belongings and now there are lots of gaps and blank spaces. I may as well just carry on and start to clear the lot. Maybe I can drop a load of my old clothes that are now too big in to Oxfam. That would be very cathartic. Or perhaps I should do some housework first and start with the washing pile.

I have been in such a state that I can't remember the last time I actually picked up an iron or sorted the laundry. This lot all neatly folded and ironed must have been done by Ali when she stayed over Christmas. Goodness, I think as I start to put it away, I can hardly remember Christmas dinner. I think we heated up some nut roast in the Aga, and didn't Dad pop in at some point with a sheepish Virginia? I was too busy polishing off my third bottle of pink wine to notice much at all. Ali has been such a good friend to me. I really must get my act together and write some kick-ass articles for her. It's high time I stopped moping about and got my life together again.

Deep in thought about how I can turn my life around, I reach the bottom of the washing basket and my fingers brush against something warm and soft. Leaning in, I pull out Alex's moss-green jumper and hold it against my face, breathing in the scent of Comfort and closing my eyes at the softness of the fabric. For a brief second it's the dinner party again and he's holding me close against his chest out in the blues and purples of the twilit garden.

This is the last jumper that Vanessa gave Alex. I remember how Virginia told me about their joke and how she'd nicknamed him Mossy; I've seen the wedding pictures and glimpsed the aching loss in his eyes. I know he's in love with Charlie now and is ready to move on, but even so I'm certain that he would still want to have this jumper returned, even if it is just to pack it away in a box of treasured memories. He was kind enough to lend it to me when I needed it, so the least I can do is be kind enough to return it. Maybe this will be what the Americans call closure?

See, all those days sitting on the sofa watching reruns of *Oprah* haven't been entirely wasted.

Before I can chicken out, I drag a brush through my curls, which, unattended for months now, reach halfway down my back, and pull on a chunky sweater and my scuffed Timberlands. Then I dig the smart key out from its hiding place in the teapot and hop into the Range Rover. The poor car probably trembles when it sees me coming these days, so I pat the dashboard and promise that I'll be careful. No more extreme off-roading for me. It was nearly a write off and I can't afford to do that twice.

"If you play your cards right, you'll soon be a Chelsea tractor," I tell it.

Ten minutes later, having successfully navigated the lanes, gates and cattle grids, I park outside the manor. Although it's only been a few weeks since I last visited, already I can see signs of change. New gravel has been laid and raked neatly, signs direct visitors to the tearoom and the gardens and the window frames have been freshly painted and the glass polished until it gleams. The house looks like a grand old dame who's come out in her diamonds after years of living in rags. To think that I have helped to play a part in this makes me feel very proud indeed.

I park the car at the front of the house, figuring that it may be tempting fate to try and negotiate the narrow gateway that leads to the rear. Key in hand, I dither, shy suddenly, and nervous. Before, I would have just let myself in around the back, called out a hello and stuck the kettle on. Then Alex, Virginia and I would have spent an hour or so drinking tea and chatting before the morning's work began. It was all so easy and familiar and comfortable then.

"Amber!" Dad is strolling across the front lawn, hand in hand with Virginia. Letting her go, he runs towards me and folds me in an enormous bear hug. "Sweetheart, it's so good to see you!"

"It's good to see you too, Dad," I mumble into his chest. And it is too. As I hug my dad and breathe in his familiar scent, I could kick myself for staying away. So Alex doesn't want to be with me? Deal with it, Amber. Other people still love you.

"You've lost weight." He steps back and eyes me critically. "You're not eating properly. We'll have to do something about that."

I laugh, because my dad burns water. Baked beans on toast have been the height of his culinary success.

"I cook now," he says proudly. Pulling Virginia against him, he drops a kiss on her head and adds, "I'm not bad, am I, love?"

Virginia smiles up at him adoringly. They look so loved up that I can't help smiling. At least my parents are happy, even if it isn't with one another. I guess there's more than one way to have a romantic ending.

"You're getting there, Chris," Virginia says kindly. To me she adds, "Although we nearly had to call the fire brigade out after he made chilli. Alex thought his mouth was melting."

Alex. The name makes my nerve endings fizz, and like a junkie I have to get my fix.

"How is Alex?" I ask casually. "I found this jumper that he lent me. I thought I'd better return it before I go back to London."

Virginia's eyes widen when she sees the moss-green sweater. "Alex lent you *that*?"

I nod. "It's a long story. I was wet and cold."

She swallows. "Amber, I told you before, that sweater means an awful lot to him. He must really think highly

458

of you to have lent it." Then she laughs. "What do I mean, he must think highly of you? I know he does. You've been a breath of fresh air to him and he's missed seeing you about the place."

There are some things that mothers don't need to hear about their sons, so I keep quiet. I don't want Virginia to know that Alex has avoided me and rejected me in the worst way that a man can a woman.

"I'm sure he's been far too busy with the engagement to miss me," I say lightly. There. That tells them that I know and that I'm fine about it all. I'm so good at this.

But Virginia is looking confused. "What engagement?"

My God, she is loved up with Dad if she's forgotten that her own son is engaged.

"The engagement to Charlie?" I say patiently. "I saw the ring when I was in Polmerryn a few weeks ago. You must be thrilled."

"Well of course! We were all delighted when Charlie got engaged," says Virginia. "But I've no idea why you think it's to Alex. Whatever makes you think that? Darling, she's engaged to Jinx."

What! I stare at Virginia and everything seems to spin around me. Alex and Charlie aren't together? Charlie's engaged to Jinx? I clutch the Range Rover bonnet for support. How is this possible? Everything seemed to add up.

"Have you been drinking?" Dad says suspiciously, because now laughter is building up inside me and I'm starting to giggle hysterically. His brow furrows. "When

459

Tish left me I'm afraid I hit the bottle. It could be genetic."

I certainly feel drunk. Drunk with relief. All the signs that I'd interpreted were totally wrong! It was Jinx all along. No wonder Charlie asked if I minded; he'd been my bosom buddy for a while and the subject of my column. And the flashy ring makes perfect sense when purchased by a man who loves silly flashy cars. Of course it's Jinx!

"Alex has been really low lately," Virginia says once I've recovered my wits sufficiently. "We've been very worried about him. You do know that Vanessa died just before Christmas, don't you? It's always a hard time for him and he tends to keep himself to himself."

My breath catches in my throat. I'm horrified. No wonder he pulled away from me.

"It's four years now, though, and he needs to move on." Virginia looks stern. "I'm sure he's coming to the same conclusion too, in his own way. He's been staying with Vanessa's parents for a few days, working things out. You know Alex. He doesn't wear his heart on his sleeve, but he feels things deeply." She looks me straight in the eye, and I have the feeling she's gazing into my soul. "Some things very deeply indeed. He could certainly see how cut up you've been about Ed leaving."

I shake my head. "He was wrong. It wasn't that at all."

"I know," says Virginia kindly. "I've known for a long time, Amber, but it isn't my place to interfere. Maybe you should tell Alex yourself when you give the jumper back. I'm sure he'd much rather you returned it in person."

My heart is racing. The jumper hangs in my hands.

"He's in the lavender garden," says Virginia, giving me a gentle nudge. "You know where that is; go and find him, and leave us old folks to put the kettle on."

As though in a dream, I turn and follow the neat clipped pathway that leads across the parterre and the formal gardens. The trees and hedges are bare, but there's still a bleak beauty to it all that breaks my heart. A robin shouts at me and a chilly rabbit scampers away as I follow the pathway. Then I skirt the rose garden and duck through the archway into the private lavender walk that the kindest man in the world made for his dying wife.

The kindest man in the world who is sitting all alone on the wrought-iron bench with a sprig of lavender held loosely in his hand. Sadie and two of her half-grown puppies doze at his feet, but on my approach they leap up and greet me joyfully with licky tongues and waggy tails.

"Amber?" Alex looks taken aback. There are dark purple bruises beneath his eyes, and he's so pale in the winter sunshine that he could be straight out of *Twilight*. "What are you doing here?"

I sit down next to him. "I came to return this."

Alex's fingers curl around the soft wool. Then he closes his eyes and exhales slowly. "Vanessa loved this place," he says quietly. "Towards the end, when she was really sick, it was the only place where she could get any rest. She'd sleep here with her head in my lap, and

461

sometimes I had to place my hand on her heart, just to be sure she hadn't slipped away."

I don't speak, but I put my hand on his. Like a drowning man, Alex clutches my fingers tightly.

"It was special to me," he continues, still looking ahead, "because it was special for her. But do you know something? She'd have wanted everyone to enjoy it. The last thing she would have wanted would be for it to be locked up. She'd have loved to think of other people getting pleasure from it."

"Alex," I say awkwardly. "When I had a go at you about opening the garden up to visitors, I had no idea what it meant to you."

He turns and places a finger on my lips. "It's OK. I know that. But you were right, right about so many things." He glances at the jumper and smiles. "I don't need to wear this any more. Vanessa will always be a part of me, but in the same way that the garden has recovered from Mabel's snacking and taken on a new shape, I think it's time I did the same."

"Me too," I whisper. "Oh me too. Alex, about Ed? It was over with him a long time ago. I just never had the courage to admit it."

He cups my cheek in his hand. "Sometimes it's easier to live with something that's dead than to be brave and face the future. It feels safer to stick with what's familiar than risk being open and hurt by something new."

I turn my head and brush the palm of his hand with my lips. Alex gets it. He really gets it.

"The other day? In the car?" Alex's lips are inches from the corner of my mouth. My entire body is fizzing like sherbet. "I wanted to kiss you, Amber, so much, but it didn't seem right. There were things I had to do first. I needed to tell Vanessa's family that I was ready to move on. That I had met someone."

"Met someone?" I echo.

"Met someone," he agrees. "Someone infuriating and annoying and chaotic and incredibly sexy when she wears nothing but a coating of green slime. Someone who I haven't been able to stop thinking about ever since she nearly ran me over in a muddy lane."

I gulp. His mouth is now very close to mine indeed.

"Someone a bit like me?" I whisper.

"Someone exactly like you," says Alex with a smile. "I think we've got some unfinished business? Don't you?"

And then he's kissing me, properly kissing me this time, and there's no holding back and no doubts and no misunderstandings. I wind my fingers into those soft springy curls and pull him closer and closer, forgetting about everything else. Nothing matters any more except being close to Alex Verney.

We break apart, eyes wide and mouths curling into delighted smiles. When Alex takes my hand in his, I feel that the wedding band has gone.

"I don't need to wear it any more," he says, following my gaze.

I look at him and my heart constricts with love. Difficult, tortured, complex Alex. Sad Alex. Lonely Alex. Why has it taken me so long to really see the man underneath? Slowly and tenderly I drape the green sweater over his broad shoulders, loving the warmth of his skin beneath my fingertips as they brush the nape of his neck.

"When you love someone you don't have to let them go," I say.

Alex nods and reaches up to cup my face in his hands.

"Exactly! And I don't want to let you go, crazy dog and goat girl. Don't go back to London, Amber. Stay here."

My eyes widen. "Stay here?"

He nods. "With me." He pauses, and then shrugs as though there's nothing to lose. "I love you, Amber Scott."

It's amazing, but my lips and tongue and vocal cords all have a life of their own. "I love you too," I whisper. "I have done for so long."

"Well," says Alex, brushing a curl from my face, "that's just as well then!"

And he kisses me again, holding me close until I am giddy with happiness. Then a horrible thought occurs and I pull away sharply.

"Wait, though! My mother made me put a love potion in Ed's port that night at the dinner party. I told you about it remember?"

Alex raises his eyes to Heaven and laughs. "Yes, I hadn't forgotten!

My heart plummets. "I think you drank it by mistake! What if none of this is real?"

But Alex isn't looking concerned. In fact he's laughing so hard there are tears in his eyes.

"You are totally crazy, Amber Scott! And that is one of the things I love about you. Apart from the fact that I don't drink, if there was a love spell then you cast it the day you yelled at me for being on your land. There you were, all flowing golden curls and crosspatch face, and I didn't think I'd ever seen anything sexier in my life. And as for that day when you came into the kitchen naked . . ." He gives me a slow stare that makes the blood race to every surface of my body, "Let's just say it's been hard to put that image out of my mind. You're the only magic I need."

I bury my face in my hands. Maybe I won't mention the lucky Japanese mini cat.

"Anyway," continues Alex thoughtfully, peeling my fingers away from my face and tilting my chin up with his forefinger. "I think good old Jinxy was minesweeping that evening; he certainly helped himself to my drinks. And come to think of it, didn't he meet Charlie that night? So there was certainly some kind of magic in the air."

And then he kisses me again, and I don't know about that evening at the dinner party, but there is certainly something magical happening right now. The winter sun smiles down on us, and fanciful as it sounds, I'm sure I smell the faintest scent of lavender, even though there's not a bloom in sight. Somebody somewhere approves, I just know it.

Then, hand in hand, with the dogs bounding ahead, Alex and I walk back to the house, where Dad and Virginia will be waiting with tea and cake and smiles.

We pause by the back door. Alex puts his arm around me and pulls me close. "Ready to tell them?" he says softly. "Ready for the start of something new?"

I nod, then rise to my tiptoes and kiss him. "So ready."

I know I have never been so happy in my life to start over as I am with Alex. Amazingly, all my wishes are coming true.

Maybe there is something in Mum's magic after all.

Also available in ISIS Large Print:

Chocolate Shoes and Wedding Blues

Trisha Ashley

Tansy Poole dreams of weddings, shoes . . . and chocolate. And when she inherits a run-down shoe shop tucked away in the village of Sticklepond, Cinderella's Slippers is born — providing footwear gorgeous enough to make any fairytale wedding come true. She'll even sell shoe-shaped chocolates as wedding favours! But soon Tansy feels like she's starring in her very own Cinderella tale. With two awful stepsisters causing no end of trouble, a long list of chores, and the tall, dark and handsome actor Ivo Hawksley on her doorstep — though sadly he's more of a Prince Brooding than a Prince Charming. Ivo has come to the village to nurse a broken heart, but could a happy ever after be closer than he thinks?

ISBN 978-0-7531-9152-1 (hb)
ISBN 978-0-7531-9153-8 (pb)

What I Did on My Holidays

Chrissie Manby

Sophie Sturgeon can't wait for her annual summer holiday. Not only will it be a week away from work, it will be a chance to reconnect with her boyfriend Callum.

So this upcoming trip to Majorca is a big deal. Sophie's spent a lot of time getting ready. She's bought a new wardrobe. She's determined she and Callum will have the best time ever.

Then Callum dumps her, the night before they're due to leave. In a show of bravery and independence, Sophie says she'll go to Majorca alone — but in fact, she hides in her London flat. But when her friends, family, and even Callum seem so surprised and delighted at her single girl courage, Sophie decides to go all out and recreate the ultimate "fake break" . . . with hilarious results.

ISBN 978-0-7531-9094-4 (hb)
ISBN 978-0-7531-9095-1 (pb)

Girl on the Run

Jane Costello

Abby Rogers has been on health kicks before — they involve eating one blueberry muffin for breakfast instead of two. But since starting her own business, after watching one too many episodes of The Apprentice, the 28-year-old's waistline has taken even more of a back seat than her long-neglected love life.

When Abby is encouraged to join her sporty best friend's running club — by none other than its gorgeous new captain — she finds a mysterious compulsion to exercise. Sadly, her first session doesn't go to plan. Between the obscenely unflattering pink leggings, and the fact that her lungs feel as though they've been set on fire, Abby vows never to return. Then her colleague Heidi turns up at work and makes a devastating announcement, one that will change her life — and Abby's — forever.

ISBN 978-0-7531-9038-8 (hb)
ISBN 978-0-7531-9039-5 (pb)

Breakfast in Bed

Eleanor Moran

Take one newly single woman: At 31, Amber is being bombarded with wedding invitations just as she's collecting her divorce papers — and her bossy best friend has gone one step further and made her chief bridesmaid. It's high time Amber regained control of her life and career.

Add a passionate and fiery celebrity cook: Amber's joy at landing herself a coveted role in Oscar Retford's kitchen soon fades as she discovers Oscar is as famous for his furious temper and addiction to firing people as he is for the legendary meals he creates.

Turn up the heat: As passions start to run high, and her past catches up with her, it looks like Amber's cooked up a recipe for disaster . . .

ISBN 978-0-7531-9032-6 (hb)
ISBN 978-0-7531-9033-3 (pb)

Monday to Friday Man

Alice Peterson

He proposed, she accepted. He changed his mind, she was heartbroken

Gilly Brown now finds herself alone in London with only her little dog Ruskin for company. It's time to move on. On a friend's advice, she looks for a lodger, a Monday to Friday one, and eventually finds just the right man — Jack Baker, a handsome reality television producer. The extra cash is great, but she'd be lying if she said she didn't enjoy his company too. Friends and family see Jack as the perfect tonic for Gilly, except for Guy, the newest recruit in her dog-walking group. What does he see and why does he feel it so strongly? And what exactly does Jack get up to at the weekends?

ISBN 978-0-7531-8936-8 (hb)
ISBN 978-0-7531-8937-5 (pb)

ISIS publish a wide range of books in large print, from fiction to biography. Any suggestions for books you would like to see in large print or audio are always welcome. Please send to the Editorial Department at:

ISIS Publishing Limited
7 Centremead
Osney Mead
Oxford OX2 0ES

A full list of titles is available free of charge from:

Ulverscroft Large Print Books Limited

(UK)
The Green
Bradgate Road, Anstey
Leicester LE7 7FU
Tel: (0116) 236 4325

(Australia)
P.O. Box 314
St Leonards
NSW 1590
Tel: (02) 9436 2622

(USA)
P.O. Box 1230
West Seneca
N.Y. 14224-1230
Tel: (716) 674 4270

(Canada)
P.O. Box 80038
Burlington
Ontario L7L 6B1
Tel: (905) 637 8734

(New Zealand)
P.O. Box 456
Feilding
Tel: (06) 323 6828

Details of **ISIS** complete and unabridged audio books are also available from these offices. Alternatively, contact your local library for details of their collection of **ISIS** large print and unabridged audio books.